it in one of these books. *A Power Unbound* is a deeply satisfying conclusion to this series." —*Polygon*

"I squealed with delight. Marske delivers a prickly love story while adeptly tying up all the loose ends of her series, involving a long-ago bargain between human magicians and ancient fae, and how the magic that resulted has been twisted by mortal greed." —*Literary Hub*

"A spectacular and satisfying series conclusion . . . If you love historical fantasy, complex magic systems (maybe based on ancient contract law?), begrudging groups of friends (dare I say . . . families of choice), or enemies learning they have more in common than they thought (and falling in love about it!), then this is the series for you!" —Powell's Books (Best Books of 2023: Science Fiction and Fantasy)

Praise for the Last Binding trilogy

"Stunning, sensual . . . A thrilling mystery and a lush historical fantasy that will leave readers breathless—both from its exciting plot twists and its captivating romance." —*BookPage* (starred review)

"Fans of C. L. Polk's *Witchmark,* period queer novels, and creative fantasy will all clamor for more." —*Publishers Weekly* (starred review)

"A delightful blend of Edwardian fantasy and romance, with enough twists and questions to have readers clamoring for the next." —*Library Journal* (starred review)

"The prose is sublime, the world-building top-notch, and the magic system is fascinating and unique." —TJ Klune, *New York Times* bestselling author of *The House in the Cerulean Sea*

TOR

TOR PUBLISHING GROUP
NEW YORK

A
POWER
UNBOUND

FREYA MARSKE

This is a work of fiction. All of the characters, organizations, and events portrayed in this novel are either products of the author's imagination or are used fictitiously.

A Tor Book
Published by Tom Doherty Associates / Tor Publishing Group
120 Broadway
New York, NY 10271

www.torpublishinggroup.com

Tor® is a registered trademark of Macmillan Publishing Group, LLC.

The Library of Congress has cataloged the hardcover edition as follows:

Names: Marske, Freya, author.
Title: A power unbound / Freya Marske.
Description: First edition. | New York : Tor Publishing Group, 2023. | Series:
   The Last Binding ; 3
Identifiers: LCCN 2023045857 (print) | LCCN 2023045858 (ebook) |
   ISBN 9781250788955 (hardcover) | ISBN 9781250788962 (ebook)
Subjects: LCGFT: Fantasy fiction. | Queer fiction. | Novels.
Classification: LCC PR9619.4.M367 P69 2023 (print) | LCC PR9619.4.M367
   (ebook) | DDC 823/.92—dc23/eng/20231003
LC record available at https://lccn.loc.gov/2023045857
LC ebook record available at https://lccn.loc.gov/2023045858

ISBN 978-1-250-83190-3 (trade paperback)

Our books may be purchased in bulk for promotional, educational, or
business use. Please contact your local bookseller or the Macmillan Corporate
and Premium Sales Department at 1-800-221-7945, extension 5442,
or by email at MacmillanSpecialMarkets@macmillan.com.

First Tor Paperback Edition: 2024

Printed in the United States of America

0 9 8 7 6 5 4 3 2 1

For my family
& for everyone who's built their own

CHEETHAM HALL, 1893

Elsie Alston's running feet hit the grass like pale secrets. During daylight hours she could usually be persuaded to wear shoes, but the day was fading and Elsie had unfastened everything of herself that could be unfastened. Shoes, stockings. Corset strings. The locks of her dark hair, which fell to the small of her back and bounced as she ran. She enjoyed the sensation of it tugging against her scalp, and Cheetham Hall enjoyed her enjoyment where it sang through the soles of her feet.

"I'll leave you behind," Elsie called, "see if I don't."

"Oh, will you now?"

Jack's footfalls were stronger, firmer. Not to mention: more shod. He'd followed his sister into the world, and he'd been following her ever since.

Now he stopped dead in the last line of beech trees before the grove opened out to the slope of lawn. The distance between the twins widened, then faltered, as Elsie slowed. She looked over her shoulder. Her brother grinned, teeth white as the tree trunks in the purpling light, and threw cradlespeak: negation, with a private illusion-clause tweak that meant *you're bluffing.* He didn't believe she'd ever leave him behind, no matter what she threatened.

Elsie laughed and cradled a lash of a spell to trip Jack to the ground. The grass caught him soft and held him fond as he cursed, laughed in answer, and pushed back to his feet. And then they were running again, strides nearly matched with the length of their eighteen-year-old legs, up towards the Lady's Oak. The

Hall's awareness spooled out to follow, hooked burrlike into the magic that surged within its young heirs.

Of the generations of magicians who had called Cheetham Hall home, there had never been anyone like Jack and Elsie Alston.

Their parents, the Earl and Countess of Cheetham, had been properly raised in the oldest traditions. The twins were only a few hours old when they were carried around the Hall and shown to every mirror in every room. Then taken outside into the grey brightness of a winter morning and introduced to the bees. Some of their own blood, pricked from tender heels, went into the soil at once. Not many families would have bothered. The Hall was glad.

This is Elsie Leonora Mary Alston, and she is first of our line.

This is John Frederick Charles Alston, and he will inherit you, one day.

Years passed and no further heirs were forthcoming, but Cheetham Hall and the Alstons were more than content with those they had. The twins were indulged in wildness. They spent their early years roaming and claiming their land, seldom leaving its boundaries. Riding, walking, clambering up trees, swimming in the lake.

Jack was trained in the use of his gifts and taught most of it to Elsie, if only to have someone to share with, play with. When he went away to school, as boys did, Elsie stayed rooted.

Elsie Alston had magic to bring down the wind. She had everything her brother had passed on to her—and more than that, an instinct for wielding the power that dwelled beneath her often-bare feet. She was a girl of dusk and dawn and everything in between.

And tonight she was alight with mischief. Her parents were away in London and her twin was home between terms before Oxford dragged him away again, and they had a secret.

The Lady's Oak crowned a low hill. Older and taller than anything else on the grounds, it muttered creaks in blustery autumns when it threw acorns to be faithfully gathered by undergardeners. Now, in summer, it stickied the air and spread its towering leaves beneath the sun.

From the hillcrest gnarled with the oak's roots, Cheetham Hall's lands stretched out in every direction. To the south, the Hall itself and the formal gardens were hidden by the birch grove. To the west, human eyes might catch the top of the distant gatehouse, its blocky corners and regular arch standing stark against the dusk-stained sky.

The two men tucked within the shade of the tree didn't seem interested in Cheetham's views. They leaned against the oak's lowest branch—as thick as a normal tree all on its own, it bent at the waist and came down moss-furred to touch the ground before curving up again—and conferred until the noise of Elsie's arrival had their attention.

"Cousin," said Elsie primly, and dropped a curtsey. Dirt clung between her toes. "Uncle John."

Both men nodded welcome to her and to Jack, who arrived panting in Elsie's wake. "Uncle," he said. "George. Lovely night for it."

"Lord Hawthorn," said George.

Only Elsie recognised the way their cousin George Bastoke spoke the title: with so much respect it was a kind of mockery. The Hall hummed its ready sympathy to her annoyance but did nothing else. These men had guest-right: not part of the household, but family nonetheless. George in particular was rich in the gifts of the dawn, his magic orderly and strong within him, with a brassy-cold and sweetly ravenous edge that the Hall did not trust.

The Alston twins sat on the looping branch. It was a favoured spot for slow summer afternoons bickering in the shade. Of all the places on the estate, this one was the most theirs.

"*Now* will you say what this experiment is?" said Elsie. "If you'd told us more, we could have practiced."

"I don't want you two practicing this where someone with more skill can't step in if it goes wrong," said their uncle John. His body beneath the dark overcoat was held stiff, as if fighting a pain somewhere. "There's a good chance it will be dangerous."

The twins exchanged a glance of pleasure. Broken bones,

countless sprained ankles, and at least one scar on Elsie that not even the best potions could fade were all testament to the fact that danger had never stopped them before. Being careful, the Alstons had agreed almost as soon as they could speak, was for dullards.

"So that's why we're doing this when Mother and Father are off to town," said Jack. "Do you think they'd disapprove?"

"Almost certainly." John smiled. "I'd have your mother in my ear for months. But I think the two of you are old enough to make your own decisions, don't you agree? And if it works, it can be a grand surprise when they return."

"If *what* works?" Elsie bounced on the branch.

"Transfer." George, a few years older than the twins, had nearly his father's height and more ease to his carriage. He spoke as if words were stepping-stones leading him across a brook: steady, deliberate, refusing to be rushed. "We think we've found a way for a magician to draw on another's magic and wield it as their own."

"That's impossible," said Jack. "Everyone knows that. Can't be done."

"What if it could?" said George.

Jack, marginally more prone to forethought than his sister, listened hardest to the explanation that followed. Their uncle already knew that the twins had a knack for simultaneous spell-work. He'd asked them, on previous visits, to demonstrate how they could wield their individual magics towards a single end, until it was almost as if a single pair of hands were doing the cradling and a single will directing it.

Almost.

They were doing this on the grounds of Cheetham Hall because, like most magicians with blood-oath binding them to a particular place, the Alstons found magic easiest there. The Hall stirred uneasily when George used a spell to split the finger-skin of each twin in turn, adding a clause against clotting so that their blood flowed to mingle in a small copper bowl. But there was no threat. The twins gave their blood willingly to the spell—and Alston blood spilled in ritual in this place was normal, natural.

Elsie flicked her fingers and a light grew, tinted the blue of robins' eggs, just above the bowl, which George had set on the ground a yard from her white toes. Jack's light was the colour of apricots. It brushed against his sister's as if to tease.

"Now," said John. "Try to make it one light. One spell. Think of the lights as *being* your magic, and see how closely you can mingle them. From what I can determine, you must make an oath on it."

The oath that bound Elsie and Jack to this land had been made on their behalf, by their parents. Neither of them had ever tethered their magic with words. They obligingly echoed their uncle: "As our blood is the same, so let our power be one and the same."

The two lights wavered, then began to merge, to occupy the same space above the bowl of blood.

Elsie made a face. "Jack, your magic tickles. It's all bristly."

"Yours tastes like bad milk."

They bumped shoulders, briefly much younger and sillier children; their first instinct, as always, to make a game of it. Their magic thickened and darkened and began to take up more space. Soon it was a glowing mist nearly the height and arm span of a man, its colours mingling as if stirred with a spoon.

"Is it working?" John asked sharply.

"I don't know," said Jack. "Elsie?"

The light, as if in answer, pulsed. And then pulsed again. The orange-pink and the blue set up a rhythm, one shade threatening to swamp the other entirely—and then the other, at the last moment, becoming overwhelming in turn, like a war of tides on the shore. Like a heartbeat.

And it was a heartbeat. The Hall felt the moment when Jack and Elsie's own pulses fell into harmony, two young hearts contracting as one. Colour drained from the mist until only the glow remained, near-white, bright as a star.

John's face lit up with hunger. "At last."

"Is it . . . ?" said George.

The twins, hands outstretched, were still engaged in making

faces at each other. The light put out an occasional tendril to wrap around Elsie's bare forearm or Jack's shirtsleeve, but otherwise it seemed to have reached an equilibrium.

"They haven't the maturity to tell," said John. He cradled a new sharpness, which he applied to the side of his own finger, and knelt awkwardly, one stiff knee at a time. He shook off George's hand when his son offered assistance. The bowl of blood was inky in the dying daylight, reflecting Jack and Elsie's spell with a deep scarlet undertone.

John's blood made new ripples when it dripped into the bowl.

He reached out, moved through a cradle, and spoke, harsh and fast—"By the echo of my blood in the blood of these magicians, I call this power to me, to me, to me—"

And *pulled.*

The magic writhed at once. Bolts of miniature lightning flashed through the mist; all four magicians flinched their eyes shut. John still had his hands out, fingers clawed with desperation, unmoving even when the smell of burned flesh spilled into the air and every nail on his hands split down the middle with a black line and a curl of smoke. He made a guttural sound and bent at the waist.

"*Father—*" said George, but he was drowned out when Elsie screamed.

A red hue now curled awfully up from the bowl of blood and saturated the light of the twins' magic. The cloud of it shook and boiled and shook some more.

Cheetham Hall recoiled. Its own wordless horror grabbed at the roots of its trees and the stone of its walls. Blood they had given, oaths of commingling they had given, but its heirs had not consented to *this.* Not this agonising, violating drag on their magic, as if by lips clamped greedily on the end of a tobacco pipe.

With a sudden wrench the magic tore itself in half and vanished back into the skins of the magicians who made it. Still red. Still raw, and wrong, and shredding them from the inside.

Jack toppled from the branch to the ground. His back arched and he let out a cry of pain.

Elsie lifted her head at the sound. She too slipped down from the branch and grasped for her brother's wrist. Now *she* pulled, and the twisted sharp-edged magic came at her call. All of it. It fled through the contact and scraped itself wholly into the vast potential that was Elsie Alston, the strongest magician that England had seen in centuries.

The Hall threw *Danger!* unspoken, the warning crashing through the land and reverberating between its walls. But the master and mistress were nowhere where they might feel it. The only people whose blood sang to this soil were right here. One gasping, bereft and dizzy with his gift ripped away from his control; the other burning, eyes bright coals of pain as she said, *"Help me."*

She wasn't speaking to her relatives. She spoke to the Hall, and it answered her.

It didn't want to; it knew the harm she was doing to herself. But her will was inexorable. Between them, the girl and the land built a fence at her skin, to keep the awful roil of magic from escaping and doing any further damage to Jack.

George swore fervently under his breath. "Father," he said. "What now?"

John teetered, on his feet now, staring down at the twins. The bowl had tipped sideways in Jack's initial writhing. Fresher blood flowed from Elsie's nose, thickened her cough, and brightened her lips as she tried to take hold of the soil for strength. Her eyes had lost focus. Still, the blue of them burned for another few seconds before she crumpled in a dead faint.

Danger! shrieked Cheetham Hall, and Jack gave a jerk.

"No," John mumbled. "No, *no*. We were so close. It was going to work—it should have worked—"

"We can't leave them like this," said George. And, after a moment, calmly, "You're more practiced with secret-binds than I am, sir."

Jack, now shaking his sister's shoulder and rasping her name, tried to strike out when George took hold of his arms. But he was still weak and dizzy, and George was strong enough to pin him even with no magic at all. John built the bind precisely, drenched in power, even with his spell-burned fingers.

You will speak of tonight to no one.

The red light of the bind slid from the cradle and between Jack's uselessly tightened lips.

Jack didn't cry out again as the bind seared itself like a cattle brand onto his tongue. His face formed a dark grimace.

He nearly erupted out of George's grip with a hoarse cry, however, when John knelt down to slither a matching secret-bind into Elsie's bloodstained mouth. She didn't wake.

Deep beneath the foundations of Cheetham Hall itself, tangled with the solid roots of the oldest trees, the ley line was a river swollen with poison rain. It spat the danger down its own channels, reaching in futile hope, but there was no one to feel. No one to witness.

In another year's time the danger would overboil its banks entirely, lashing out in response to fresh tragedy—or rather, to the inevitable endpoint of the tragedy set in motion today. But that was yet to come.

Jack was released. He glared in hatred at his uncle and cousin.

"I—I re—" he gasped, but the bind was too fresh, and his meaning too close to what it was designed to suppress. The Hall couldn't revoke guest-right on its own.

It didn't need to. George took his father's arm and helped him to hurry away, across the grounds, towards the boundary road where their man waited with the carriage. He cast only one glance over his shoulder as they went.

"Elsie," Jack said, scrambling to pull her into his lap. "*Elsie,*" as her breathing shallowed and her pulse, already rapid, became a whisper. The Hall could feel her slipping. Jack reached frantically for his magic and bent at the waist to retch when he found only the jagged edges of where it had been. "Take whatever you need from me," he snarled. "Save her. *Do it.*"

The Hall tried. This, too, it hadn't done for centuries. It found the hooks of its own power, the land's power, buried deep inside its heir; and it pulled. And pulled again.

This magic was not meant for fine work on human bodies, beyond worm-chewing them gratefully to enrich the soil. It had never tried to mend. But it held Elsie Alston steady. Held her living. And Jack Alston sat beneath the Lady's Oak with his arms a cage of agony around his sister, his mouth swollen with secrets, and endured.

Away past the birch grove, all of Cheetham Hall's front windows shattered at once.

Finally, the alarm was raised. People spilled from the Hall like ants from a nest, exchanging cries, growing rapidly aware of those who were missing.

Those who were found, before long, bloodlessly pale and shivering in sleep, curled into each other like dead leaves: but alive, alive, for now.

SPINET HOUSE, 1909

Jack awoke in the small hours of the morning with his tongue hot in his mouth, a savage twist of a dream fading from his mind, and music in his ears.

The dream was nothing new. The music meant that someone was trying to break into Spinet House. Again.

He muttered a curse and threw back the covers. The music was growing steadily louder—not that it could be described as music, really. It was a single note, unbroken, as if played by a bow drawn ceaselessly back and forth across the world's largest violin.

Jack tapped the brass guidekeeper on the nightstand without thinking, then slapped the wood with annoyance. He almost never had slips like that. He hadn't for years. He'd shed the mannerisms of his past, all those actions that came unthinkingly to magicians. He'd burned them out of himself. It had taken time and bloody-minded effort.

And then three months ago an unmagical girl had accosted him on a ship, inserted herself inconveniently into his life, and forced him back into magical society and magical conspiracy. Back into contact with his family and his past.

The point was: Jack Alston had no magic, and Spinet House owed him no allegiance. The guidelight didn't move according to his unspoken will. It stayed where it was, a softly wavering yellow light like a long-wicked candle. Jack donned slippers and dressing gown, took the pistol from the nightstand, checked it, and slipped it into the gown pocket. His right calf cramped in sharp protest. He stretched and shook it until only a dull ache remained.

His walking stick leaned against the wall by the door, waiting for him, and not because of the pain in his leg. That pain was unpredictable. *This*—the attempted incursion into Spinet House by anonymous enemies—was, depressingly, less so. They'd all begun keeping weapons to hand.

Only as Jack opened the door and crossed the threshold of the room did his guidelight detach from its keeper and come to hover above his shoulder. The corridor was empty, but he could hear approaching footsteps. His grip on the stick loosened when the stairs disgorged Maud and Violet into view.

"Violet," called Jack. "Where should we be?"

"Oh, for—shush, Hawthorn, I almost had it!" Violet called back. Jack walked down the hall to join them. Both girls were clad in dressing gowns with their hair plaited back for sleep. Their guidelights illuminated the smooth yellow of Violet's tresses and the longer, thicker, more mussed brown of Maud's.

"Ground floor." Violet held a tuning fork in her hand. "It's low enough that—oh, Dorothy, there you are. What do you think?"

Spinet House's senior parlour maid, hurrying toward them down the corridor leading to the servants' stair, sang in a choir on her evenings off. Aside from Violet, she had the best ear in the house.

"Kitchen entrance, miss," she said.

Violet struck the fork on her own forearm, held it to her ear, and nodded. "That was my guess. Shall we?"

Maud, being Maud, went to lead the way. She held a small pearl-handled revolver. In a world full of magicians laying siege to their abode and trying to steal something from them, Maud had pointed out, unmagical people could do worse than to carry unmagical weapons.

Her brother Robin had bought her the gun. Jack had taught her to use it.

Now Jack blocked Maud with his stick and raised his eyebrows.

"Hawthorn, *really*," said Maud.

"I have your word, and I will make it an oath if you don't behave," said Jack.

"He will too," said Violet. "Stay in the middle, darling, or I'll have Dorothy shut you in a cupboard."

"Traitor," said Maud, with a peek of dimple, but she fell behind Jack and let him lead the cautious way down.

The ache in Jack's leg was no more than a soft throb by now, though it seemed to pulse along with the persistent note in his ears. It flared tightly when the stairs, with no warning, tilted beneath their feet and turned from flat, carpeted wood to an outright slope. Jack swallowed an unpleasant leap of acid in his throat as Maud—and her pistol—collided with his back. Maud gave a muffed squawk.

"Grab hold!" said Violet.

The entire party took grim hold of the banister with their free hands. Jack concentrated on not slipping any farther down what was now something like a fairground slide, and also bracing himself for any of the women behind him to lose their balance and create an unfortunate human landslide. The soles of his bloody house slippers weren't exactly designed for grip.

"Violet," he said through his teeth.

"The poor thing's skittish. Little wonder. Give me a moment."

Jack risked a glance back over his shoulder. Violet had her free hand on a wood panel of the wall and her forehead on her hand. She might have been singing, or whispering. Jack couldn't hear above the music, which was starting to feel unpleasantly as though it were emanating from the centre of Jack's own skull.

Slowly, the floor beneath their feet tilted back into stairs. Jack got them moving and down to the ground floor before Spinet House's capricious carpentry could interfere further.

The kitchen was at the back of the house. The floor creaked musically as they made their way through the largest dining room, through the butler's pantry, and down a short service corridor to the top of two flagstone steps. The dark expanse of the kitchen was still warmed by the ashes of the main cooking fire, which was still used despite the large modern stoves that lined one wall of the kitchen. Hints of moonlight sang off the copper of hanging saucepans.

Jack lifted a hand and paused before stepping down through the doorway. Hair prickled along his arms. The external kitchen door appeared to be closed, and the high windows showed nothing but the dark of night. He should have left his guidelight behind. Nothing to announce your entrance and ruin a reconnoitre like a gleam of yellow light.

Was that a hint of movement in the shadows? And—

Jack jerked back into the shelter of the passageway, treading on someone's foot. A supple line of red light lashed across the room, bright enough to carve aftereffects in his sight and leave him blinking. It snapped to nothing against the doorframe.

"Violet, shield!" he said sharply.

The golden shimmer appeared like a fishing net flung forward over the whole party. A rather ragged net, unfortunately. Violet was at her best with illusion magic; she was still struggling to improve in other areas. Jack had no way to cram his own dusty education wholesale into her head, and most magic was a hell of a lot more complicated to teach and learn than firing a gun. Jack steeled himself to ignore the darting gaps in the spell. Nothing to be done. You worked with the arsenal you had.

He was about to retrieve his own pistol when a gangly figure darted into full view, both hands raised. Jack leapt down the steps and lashed out with his stick, aiming at one of those hands before it could begin a cradle, and landed a glancing blow.

A youthful yelp emerged. Familiar. Jack hesitated, pulling his second blow—which would have smashed a kneecap—even before the figure said, "Wait! My lord!"

"Oliver," Jack barked. "*What* are you doing?"

"Oliver?" said Violet, behind him. The shield blinked out.

Maud and Violet and Dorothy came down into the kitchen. The insistent musical note decreased considerably in volume, presumably because Spinet's mistress had arrived at the site of trouble.

Jack's valet, now rubbing his wrist, looked shamefaced. "Mrs. Smith said she'd leave me a morsel of something, my lord. For when I got hungry in the night."

When, not *if*. Freddy Oliver was seventeen and not done growing, and Violet's food bill had probably doubled when he and Jack came to stay in Spinet House.

"Where's your guidelight?"

"Snuffed it, when I heard—"

A rattle came as the kitchen door shook against its hinges. Leftover sparks of magic flared nervously in Oliver's hands as if someone had blown a glow from dying embers. So this wasn't a false alarm created by Oliver's midnight hunger pangs, then.

"Someone's trying to break in!"

"Thank you, Oliver. A formidable grasp of the obvious."

"Pack up your temper, Hawthorn, this is hardly the time. The warding's holding for now," said Violet. "I can try something if it falls, but . . ."

"Good. Do that. Maud, Oliver." Jack jerked his head and pushed his way back into the house. The other two followed him at a run up the servants' stairs. Apologies tumbled from the boy's mouth, and Jack shushed him with a wave.

"You're lucky I didn't break your fingers. Or shoot you. And you'll owe Miss Debenham a new guidelight. What in the damned—does this stair go from ground to attic without pause?" The staircase had thankfully remained stairs, but they'd passed two boxed-in landings that should have led out into the house itself. "I want a window overlooking the kitchen entrance."

"The house must still be skittish," said Maud. "I suppose we can't exactly *complain* that James Taverner was a fiend for security spells, all things considered."

"These stairs respond best to staff, miss," said Oliver. He cradled a light spell and let it brighten as he returned to the previous landing, where he rapped his knuckles politely on the wall. After a moment, a panel slid aside, and Oliver beckoned them into a sparsely furnished sitting room.

At Jack's direction, Oliver cast a curtain-spell that would muffle sound as well as hide them from view, and they cracked open first physical curtains and then the window. Jack peered out and down.

A thinly veiled gibbous moon illuminated the scene below. Two figures, both with their faces obscured by the fog-masks that George's conspirators seemed to favour. One stood a few feet from the kitchen door, methodically sending bolt after pale bolt of magic against it.

The other man was tucked in against the wall of the house, a spell hovering uncast between his hands. Protection and backup. Neither of them seemed to be making any effort to experiment, or do anything fiddly to unravel the warding, even though they must have realised how sophisticated it was. Blunt power only.

Jack described the scene, mostly to prevent Maud from shoving her own head out.

"Oliver, can you manage a location-fix clause on a fire spell? Or anything that will distract them? Hell, *itching* would do. You want it to arise in a specific spot, not come in a line from your hands. You'll need to define the precise distance."

Oliver gulped. Even at the best of times the boy looked like a cricket stump wobbling in the aftermath of a ball, and his reddish hair had gone hedgelike in the excitement. "Never tried one, my lord."

"But you know—yes, that's the clause." Not quite, but Oliver was strong enough that he could afford some sloppiness in his cradles. "Give it a try, see if you can scare them off. But keeping the curtain up comes *first*. Miss Blyth can get off a few shots as long as they can't see her."

Maud nodded, looking just as excited. Jack felt old and tired. Giving combat orders to young people while heavy with fatigue was like reaching for a guidekeeper: another habit he'd fallen easily back into. He didn't like it any more than the other.

"If—" Oliver started, but was interrupted by a redoubling of Spinet House's alarm note.

No. Now it was *two* notes, an uneven chord.

Jack cursed. "Signal if they break through the door," he said, and left them to it.

He hadn't a complete tin ear. The new, prominent note was higher than the first. He found his way to the main staircase and heard footfalls ascending at a run. Violet looked angry and out of breath.

"So," she panted. "The kitchen's a diversion, do you think?"

Jack nodded. Violet pointed upwards and Jack let her lead the way. His leg had begun to hurt again. The second note softened to match the first when Violet stopped outside a room on the uppermost floor before the attic level. She hesitated with her fingertips on the door, which had neither lock nor handle.

"We haven't fully puzzled this one out yet," she admitted. "It's one of the queerer ones."

Many of Spinet's queerer rooms were those hosting secret passageways to elsewhere in the house, so this didn't make Jack feel any better about the prospect of a break-in. He had an unpleasant vision of fog-masked attackers creeping out of the wall in the sitting room where Maud and Oliver had all their attention on the window.

Jack leaned his stick against the wall and drew his gun instead. "Stay out of sight until we know what's happening."

Violet didn't argue. Unlike Maud, she didn't need to be browbeaten into letting Jack take the lead when they were in danger. Jack didn't know if it was her history of taking direction on the stage or simply a matter of personality.

She said, "Don't go too far into the room if you can help it. And—move like a knight."

Before she could explain further, there was a click as the door catch released. Jack shoved it open and stepped through, gun raised in the other hand.

The room was small. It had no wallpaper, no rugs, not even any cushions or upholstery on the chair at the writing desk. It was all wood. The floor was an unsettling chessboard of dark and light, the same pattern running up the walls all the way to the ceiling. The floor, however, was decorated with shards of broken glass from the main window, and they winked in the light of a small lantern set down near the frame.

A man stood among those shards. He had whirled around when the door opened; his clothes were dark, and a fog-mask obscured his face. There was a soft crunch and skitter as his movement shifted glass underfoot.

"Hands—" Jack started to say, but then his muscles went rigid— he couldn't even twitch a finger against the trigger—and he almost toppled over. *Damn.* Easy enough for an intruder to anchor an immobility charm in front of the doorframe, wasn't it?

"Where's the cup and the knife? We know you have 'em both. *Where are they?*"

It wasn't Morris's voice. Jack had been half expecting his cousin's loyal agent to be the one dirtying his hands with his work. A bland, tense city accent. Perhaps somewhere south of the river. Jack also couldn't *speak* at the moment to answer the bloody question, so the masked man wasn't as bright as Morris.

The crackle of a spell washed over Jack. A negation. Violet.

All his muscles relaxed at once. Unfortunately, this meant that he both stumbled a little and dropped the gun.

Jack cursed and bent for it. The masked man dived for the nearest thing resembling cover, which was a tall standing wardrobe. He wrenched the door open as if to use it as a shield, and Jack straightened with the gun in hand, and—

Afterwards, he struggled to remember exactly what he'd seen. Violet would say that the intruder climbed into the wardrobe. To Jack's eyes, it looked as though something had snagged the man's sleeve and pulled him in, like a piece of factory machinery. And what happened after that—the way the wardrobe seemed abruptly half its own height, then seemed to become a standing cabinet with elegant gaps and drawers, then back to a wardrobe again—happened so fast, in a dim room, that it could have been one of those bizarre visions the mind threw out when it was trudging up the shorelines of sleep.

The sound was distinct, at least. A bloodcurdling shout, cut off even more alarmingly by a wet noise. And then silence.

Real silence. That musical chord was gone as well.

Violet and Jack looked at each other. Dawn had begun to trickle in through the window. Violet looked bloodless in the soft grey light.

"I'm not touching it after that," said Jack. "You're the mistress here, not me."

Violet swallowed hard and eased her way across the room, following an uneven pattern on the floor. Forward, across—ah. Moving like a knight.

"Maud worked this one out," she said. She paused again in front of the wardrobe and settled her shoulders, visibly pulling on a persona, then yanked the door open.

And slammed it shut again almost as fast.

"Oh, *no*. No thank you. Oh fuck buggery hell." New York shoved into Violet's vowels when she was being unladylike. She put the back of her hand to her mouth and retched, twice. Jack began calculating a knight-path in case she outright swooned, but Violet straightened with a determined and paper-white expression.

"That can be dealt with later," Jack said. "Let's check on the kitchen."

It didn't sound as though the man—or what remained of him—was in danger of going anywhere. Nor was the glass on the floor. Jack would send some of the stronger-stomached servants to clean up later.

The kitchen was no longer under siege, and Maud and Oliver had made their way there. Oliver was worriedly clutching a tin of biscuits. Dorothy had vanished, but a kitchen maid was busy scooping coal into the largest stove. Given the hour of the day, the house's guests were crowding out what would very shortly be a working kitchen. Jack announced that they were moving into one of the parlours, where at least arses could be parked on comfortable chairs.

"Bring the biscuits," he added to Oliver.

"They didn't like being shot at," said Maud to Jack once they'd relocated. "Or having a fire set at their feet. They took off in short order."

Jack nodded to Oliver, who turned pink at the implied praise.

"What happened upstairs?" Maud asked.

"Someone got in. The house . . . dealt with it." Violet went to sit next to Maud, who responded to some invisible signal and wrapped an arm around Violet's waist. Violet dropped a kiss on her hair.

"He must have come down from the roof, to access that window," said Jack. "You'll have to strengthen the wards up there, Violet."

Violet stifled a yawn. Everyone's guidelights blinked out as the hall clock began to chime six o'clock. The sky was properly lightening now. Jack might be able to snatch a few more hours in bed.

The last strike of the clock melded into yet more music, though at least this time it was a melody instead of a held note. It announced that someone or someones recognised as friendly by the house wards had entered through the Bayswater tunnel.

"Early for a visit," said Violet. "I hope nothing's gone wrong on their end."

"Oliver, bring them through here and then go and dress," said Jack, giving up on the prospect of sleep. "I'll be up to wash shortly."

Soon afterwards, Oliver ushered three people into the parlour. Or rather, he scurried in the wake of Sir Robin Blyth, who was moving with urgent strides towards his sister, and managed to actually do some ushering on behalf of Edwin Courcey and— Jack blinked—Adelaide Morrissey. All three were in full evening wear, including a cloak over a deep red gown and white gloves on Adelaide, and they had the tight-eyed, radiant dishevelment of people who hadn't touched their beds.

"Don't you look splendid, Addy," said Maud. "Oh, it was the Home Office ball, wasn't it?"

"Yes, and one of the undersecretaries hosted a *truly* lethal party-after-the-party," said Adelaide. "When Robin dragged us away there were people asleep in the ornamental fountain."

"I had a vision. One of the urgent ones. You're unhurt? All of you?" Robin peered with concern at Maud, who said hastily, "Yes, yes."

"I see our assistance is unnecessary after all," said Edwin. He looked particularly pinched. The idea of Edwin Courcey, of all people, attending an all-night social affair that left guests draped over fountainry was bizarre.

Jack settled himself further into his armchair. "You may inspect us for holes, though there might be complaints were I to disrobe. Or perhaps you wish to see if memory holds up."

He let his gaze catch on Edwin's. The man's jaw set and annoyed colour filled his cheeks, but the only motion of his eyes was pointedly down to Jack's bad leg and up again. An interesting showing of claws. This particular mouse of a magician had changed since taking up with Robin Blyth. He was becoming more fun to tease.

"Shut up, Hawthorn, there are ladies present," said Robin without much rancour.

"His lordship is more than welcome to make a spectacle of himself. I doubt anyone here is interested enough to comment." Adelaide's dark brown eyes did a good line in a skeweringly superior stare. There was a giggle from Maud.

Violet let out a sigh and stretched her arms above her head. "Well," she said, "I'd better tell Mrs. Smith there'll be six for breakfast."

"Only one battle wound this morning, Hawthorn," said Violet, when Jack arrived in the breakfast room. "Oliver's improving."

The nick on Jack's jaw itched all over again. He forced himself not to touch it and went to investigate the food instead. Violet's cook had never met a vegetable she couldn't over-boil, but she was a genius with anything that had once been part of an animal. Jack was prepared to accept the necessity of living in Spinet House as glorified bodyguard to Maud and Violet as long as the supply of ham was kept up.

"The boy resists the urge to cut Hawthorn's throat despite being daily presented with the opportunity," said Edwin. "There should be an award."

Oliver was in fact a prodigiously skilled valet for his age and took fierce pride in his work. He was still just terrified enough of *accidentally* cutting Jack's throat that it made him shaky. He'd settle down to it in another few weeks.

Jack's old valet Lovett had served him well for years, but Jack was living in a magical household for the moment. He'd sent Lovett with a glowing reference to a man at his club and had engaged Oliver instead.

Or rather: Oliver had been, like greatness, thrust upon him.

"We're all here now," said Maud. "Tell us about the vision, Robin."

There wasn't a great deal to tell. Robin had been on the verge of nodding off in a corner of the undersecretary's house when one of his unsummoned visions of the future burst into his consciousness: Jack himself, stick in hand, recoiling from a magical attack.

"It was very quick and crisp, and left me feeling like someone had been at my temples with a pickaxe. That usually means it's one of the imminent ones. Just didn't know *how* imminent."

"I can only imagine what the cabbie must have thought of us, bundling in in a tearing rush at dawn and demanding to be driven to an Underground station halfway across the city," said Adelaide.

"Addy used her maharajah's-daughter voice on the poor man," said Robin. "He was quite overwhelmed."

Adelaide grinned and stopped tapping her ring on the table in order to pile the last of her scrambled eggs onto a fresh piece of toast, then piled a large amount of chutney on top of that.

"This is the fourth vision in a fortnight," said Edwin. "Always when he's falling asleep, and they always leave him feeling ghastly. I don't like it." He and Robin exchanged a conversation of a glance.

"Edwin's trying to find a way to suppress them for me," said Robin.

"Is that wise?" Violet set down her fork. "I hate to be a bully, if they're getting as bad as all that, but . . . Robin, you're one of the few things we have that the other side doesn't."

"The other side *does* have me." The sleepless night was suddenly visible in the weight of Robin's jaw. "I'm still under oath of truthful report to the Assembly, and the more the visions intrude on their own, the fewer spare ones I can manage to bring on at will so that I have something harmless to recite for them."

"I'll find something," said Edwin, grim.

Robin gave him a small smile. "I know you will. Buck up."

Edwin muttered something into his cup of tea, but his free hand turned over when Robin's own slid against it, and he laced their fingers together. Edwin had never been comfortable with casual touch when Jack knew him. He gave off a miasma that discouraged it—and when *intimate* touch was involved, he submitted to it with an intensity that set Jack's teeth on edge. Jack liked his bed partners to push back, and to laugh. Not every tumble had to be approached like the end of the world.

"Speaking of the fourth time in a fortnight," said Violet, "I'll have to start giving Dorothy hazard pay, or whatever it is they gave medieval armies. None of my household staff signed up for a siege."

"Spinet seems to be holding up well," said Edwin.

"Yes. Though we're being credited with either more skill or more luck than we've had. The man who got in upstairs asked Hawthorn where the knife *and* the cup were."

A vaguely depressed silence reigned over the breakfast table. The Last Contract, physical symbol of the fae bargain that centuries ago left magic in the hands of humans, existed as three disguised silver objects. The coin, which had last been seen in the hands of Edwin's brother, Walter Courcey. The cup, which Violet and Maud had successfully bluffed their way into keeping, on board the *Lyric*. Since then their enemies had obviously worked out that they'd been left holding a fake.

And the knife. Which quite possibly looked nothing like a knife at present. And which had belonged to Spinet's previous mistress, Lady Enid; and had therefore been inherited by Violet herself.

Which would be all very well if they could *find* the damned thing. Spinet was a more difficult house than the average to search from top to bottom. Not least because top and bottom, as well as the points of the compass and many other aspects of spatial geometry, seemed in several parts of the house to be treated more as guidelines than rules.

Jack had grown up on an old magical estate that adhered to old traditions. Spinet House was a young thing, built by a master carpenter-thaumoluthier and his energetically creative wife.

It was a fortress. It was a musical, magical puzzle box.

It was a fucking headache.

And it was partly Jack's headache, at least until the business of the Last Contract was over. Every day was one day closer to Jack being allowed to escape back to his own townhouse and his old life, where he could once again pretend that magic didn't exist.

"We should do some more work on the ley lines," Edwin said to Violet, breaking the silence.

"I thought there weren't any near here," said Violet. "Or have you dug out an even older and dustier map to bore me with?"

"Violet," said Maud.

Violet's head turned in an irritated motion, as if she were on the verge of snapping at Maud, too, but she caught herself. "Sorry, Edwin. It's been a busy morning."

Edwin accepted the apology with as much grace as it had been offered with: not a great deal on either side. The Blyth siblings had the stubbornness of two people who had each adopted a stray cat with a terrible personality and were determined to have them cohabit. They'd made progress. But nobody could yet describe the reserved Edwin and the deliberately extravagant Violet as *friendly*.

"There aren't any ley lines that cross Spinet, no, but we know that the knife will be exerting an effect on those close by," said

Edwin. "And I've been experimenting with the major London nodes of the line that runs longitudinally through Sutton—I really do think there's something there, some trick we're missing that will allow us to stretch the problem of distance—"

And he was off, his own sleepless night apparently not making a whit of difference now that he'd sunk his teeth into an intellectual problem. Both Blyths were listening to him—one with the same green-eyed interest that she swept over the entire world, and the other with the comfortably besotted gaze that said Edwin could be speaking Chinese, or Old French, or the forgotten language of the fae, and Robin would be just as happy to bask in the simple sound of his beloved's voice.

Jack was bored to tears by the time words like *remote cata-lyst* started marching alarmingly through Edwin's sentences. He met Adelaide's eye, and she quirked her mouth at him, but was either too loyal or too involved in demolishing her pile of eggs to show him any more sympathy.

Violet, the supposed target of Edwin's monologue, was the one who cast Jack a speaking glance. She set down her teacup and cradlespoke *help needed* at him.

Edwin broke off from one sentence to the next. His hand slipped out of Robin's. His eyes were on the door, behind Jack's shoulder.

Jack turned in time to see Mr. Price enter the room with more speed and less calm than usual. Spinet House's butler had a fussy elegance to him, like an orchestra conductor eternally on the verge of lifting his baton and frowning at the brass section.

"You've a visitor, miss," he said to Violet. "A journalist, from the papers. I told him to stay in the hall, but he didn't, and he somehow pushed right through—"

Right through the private wards, one assumed. Not something you could blurt out in front of the average unmagical person. The butler let the words die in his throat as this person— probably not even average, certainly much shorter than Price— slipped through the doorway behind him and took a few steps into the room before stopping, gaze dragged to the covered salvers on the sideboard, as if business had been momentarily post-poned by the smell of bacon.

Disapproval wafted from every inch of Mr. Price, who cra-dled a spell before anyone could speak. Jack couldn't see what it was—perhaps something designed to subdue the intruder for long enough that he could be escorted firmly back to the door.

Belatedly Violet said, "It's all right, Price, he's—"

The green spell had already left the butler's hands like a hand-ful of hornets. The short young man gave a shake of his black hair and a twitch of one shoulder as if he really had been stung, and frowned.

Two green sparks flew back towards Price's hands. The butler shook his fingers and made an affronted sound of surprise.

In the ensuing pause, Edwin stood, eyes narrowed. Trans-parently on the verge of saying *Do that again, where I can see it properly.*

"Unbusheled," finished Violet with a sort of laugh. "Thank you, Price. We know him."

"Do we?" said Robin.

The young man in question looked around the breakfast room. He hadn't changed. He still looked like a graven angel that had stepped down from the entrance to a church, shaken off the greyness of stone, and decided to go about the world clad in restless flesh and dark, dark eyes.

Those eyes slid over Jack in their tour of the room, and the back of Jack's neck tensed in preparation for an argument.

"How d'you do. So, do you welcome all your morning vis-itors by hurling magic at them, Miss Debenham," said Alanzo Rossi, "or only members of the press?"

3

If he tried to list every question he had about the more baffling aspects of upper-class life, Alan would run out of fingers, toes, and probably pubic hairs and stars in the sky as well.

Fairly high on the list, however, was: *Why breakfast?*

If you lived the sort of life where a small army of people was responsible for fetching your food, setting it in front of you, and then hovering near the wall to replenish or replace as needed, what was the point of abandoning that habit for one single meal of the day? Alan could only assume it was a daily exercise in which the rich and lofty entertained delusions that they'd be any use at all if thrown into a world where they had to fend for themselves.

See! one could imagine them saying over the blackcurrant jam and kippers and eggs done three ways. *We do retain the ability to transfer food onto our own plates, and carry those plates to the table, and even refill our own coffee cups!*

Where does the food come from? Why, it just appears, of course. Like all food. What a silly question.

The spot between Alan's shoulder blades was still smarting from the zap of pain that the butler had magicked him with. He was standing among magicians. Perhaps their food *did* just appear.

"Members of the press?" said Miss Debenham. "No. Standard procedure for thieves, though. Oh—no, Price, I'm just making fun. Thank you."

The butler exited, leaving Alan alone with three people he knew and three he didn't.

When Alan had written up his fawning, gossipy article about the first-class crossing on the *Lyric,* he'd described Miss Debenham as a well-born eccentric heiress with a scandalous past and a fair beauty. All of which was more or less true, even if Alan was the least qualified man in London to pass judgement on feminine beauty. Didn't matter. Anyone well-born or well-moneyed enough was beautiful on paper.

Given the truthful run of his pen, he'd have called Violet Debenham a cautious minx of an actress.

Right now, she looked relaxed. Mistress of the manor and all. Alan managed not to glance at the breakfast dishes again. His stomach gave a gurgle that he hoped went unheard.

"We probably shouldn't be making jokes about thieves, given everything," said Miss Blyth. "How d'you do, Mr. Ross. How good to see you again!"

"Miss B." A more genuine smile for her. Maud Blyth was composed mostly of dimples and idealism. As aristocrats went, at least she made rooms feel warmer instead of colder. It *was* good to see her again.

It might have been the one and only good thing about the grim situation that Alan currently found himself in.

"How did you do that?"

The question came from one of the unfamiliar men. Tallish, slimmish, looked like he had possibly made the acquaintance of a single sunbeam back before the turn of the century.

"Do what?"

"Whatever you did when Price—" A practiced flick of the hand.

"I didn't *do* anything." He'd assumed it was meant as a warning. Something to put him in his place. It had felt like he'd jerked his neck at the wrong angle and needed to wriggle his nerves back into comfort.

"But it went *back* to him."

Alan didn't speak magic. He shrugged.

"It was the same on the ship," said Miss Debenham. "I couldn't get an illusion to stick to him properly."

"And Price said he got through the entrance wards without being invited," said the pale one, looking more excited than displeased at this apparent gap in their security. "This shouldn't be—wait a moment, I think I *did* read something . . ."

"You'd be Mr. Courcey, then," said Alan, as several mental notes from the voyage on the *Lyric* clicked themselves together.

"Pardon? Yes." Courcey met the gaze of the brown-haired man who looked a lot like Miss Blyth and even more like an advertisement for an athletic nutritional tonic, and muttered *pleasedtomeetyou* as if it were a word in another language. "Front door or back? Where did you enter?"

From anyone else that would have been a dig about the tradesman's entrance, but Courcey hadn't a whiff of snobbery about him: just urgent curiosity.

"Front."

"Really? Don't you feel uncomfortable? Like you shouldn't be here and are desperate to leave?"

Alan had a lot of experience keeping his expression neutral in the face of idiotic questions from his social superiors. He couldn't quite suppress his tongue, though.

"Now that you mention it, perhaps I do. Why d'you think *that* would be?"

"Mr. . . . Ross?" said the brown-haired man firmly. "I apologise for everyone's manners. Why don't you sit down and join us, if you're staying. Violet can do the introductions properly." This would be Miss Blyth's older brother. The baronet. His posture said he was used to being the highest-born person in a room.

Which wasn't actually the case right now, was it?

Alan took a seat and finally lost the battle he'd been having with himself since he walked through the door. He allowed himself to glance again at Baron Hawthorn.

The man sat as still as a predator and twice as keen-eyed in one of the gorgeously carved wooden seats at the table. Alan had known Lord Hawthorn would be here. He'd prepared himself, he thought.

He'd been wrong. He'd forgotten the speed with which this hatred rose simmering within him. He'd forgotten that the edges of it crossed boundaries where it stopped feeling like hatred and became something wilder and more dangerous.

Miss Debenham introduced Alan to Sir Robert Blyth, Mr. Edwin Courcey, and the last unfamiliar face: a young Indian woman with humour around her mouth and eyes as dark as Alan's own. None of these watercolour British looks for Miss Adelaide Morrissey, whom Miss Debenham introduced as Robin's . . . awkward pause.

"Colleague," said Sir Robert.

"Typist," said Miss Morrissey cheerfully. She eyed Alan for a second longer and then pushed the toast rack across the table: the only foodstuff not miles of etiquette away under silver covers. "Do have something to eat, so I'm not the only one still working on my breakfast. Make yourself useful, Hawthorn, pour the man some tea. How do you take it, Mr. Ross?"

Alan was torn between choking on his breath and swearing eternal friendship. She'd shoved Lord Hawthorn into the role of tea lady through sheer aggressive good manners.

"Black, three sugars."

Hawthorn wielded sugar tongs like he was thinking of using them to pull Alan's fingernails. Alan helped himself to toast and butter, *real butter,* huge yellow pats of it just lying around on the table.

Courcey interrogated the others about the specific ways in which Alan was, apparently, an oddity. Alan demolished his toast and his tea. So far nobody had asked him *why* he'd come to breakfast and walked through some invisible set of Keep Out signs. As far as Courcey was concerned, Alan might as well be a gift from Saint Catherine.

Miss Morrissey caught whatever expression was on Alan's face and laughed. "Don't take it personally. Edwin does this with everyone. Magicians. Foreseer. Medium. Whatever you are."

"And you?" Alan asked.

"I'm ever so dull. No magic at all." Still cheerful. But she was sitting beside a baronet and stealing toast and mushrooms from his plate, and despite her dark skin she had an accent you could see your reflection in. Alan wanted to fight how much he liked her. He wanted to ask how many servants her family had.

"So he's not completely resistant to magic—I've never heard of *that* being possible, anyhow—just sends it askew," said Courcey, once he'd finished grilling Misses Blyth and Debenham. "And are you sure you haven't seen him in any visions, Robin?"

"If so, it was one of the ones I don't remember well."

Courcey snapped his fingers. "Perturbator. That's what Guignol called it. There are some case studies in one of his collections. But *never* in someone unmagical. It's always arisen in a magician, or at least in a magical family."

"We're not magic," said Alan. "We're Catholic."

"Sends it askew," said Sir Robert. "Sounds like this house of yours, Violet."

"It's like foresight. Not much known and even less written down. If I could do some experiments . . ."

Alan was used to being looked at like he wasn't there. Being looked at like a butterfly pinned to a board was a new one.

"Edwin," said Miss Blyth, laughing. "Leave the poor man alone."

The word *experiments* sounded moderately hideous. But it was a way to be useful to them, wasn't it? Alan sat up straighter and returned Courcey's look.

"I'd consider it. What's the hourly rate?"

Lord Hawthorn laughed. The sound climbed Alan's spine with thoughtful fingers. "Careful, Edwin. This one haggles like a Whitechapel fishmonger."

Alan turned to glare at him. The cool amusement in Hawthorn's eyes made him wish he hadn't.

Alan was dressed in one of his two good work suits: trousers and waistcoat of tough brown material that he'd bought in the hope they'd look sober and smart for a long time and hide the dirt enough not to need washing too often, so the fabric would last. And it had lasted, for a while. Now he badly needed new ones. He needed a new pair of shoes, just like everyone else in his household. Like half of London. Needing new shoes might as well be a permanent state of being, like being Catholic, or having eyes so blue they made goose bumps appear on the arms.

He could always feel the wafting disapproval of his shabby appearance from the editors and senior writers at the *Post*. And that was nothing to the way he felt here, in this beautiful room in a huge Bayswater townhouse, with an earl's son looking at Alan as though he were counting every shiny patch and every place where Bella's neat darning showed.

Lord Hawthorn's waistcoat had a subtle play of purple thread down the grey panels, and small silver buttons in the shape of knots. His shirtsleeves were blindingly white, his collar crisp. He probably had two pairs of shoes for every day of the week and employed a different bootblack for each pair.

Alan wanted to tear off every single one of those buttons and grind his worn-down heel into the top of his lordship's foot until he felt the bones crunch. He exhaled.

Hawthorn said, "I'll wager you'd never heard the word *perturbator* before any of the rest of us. So which of your many talents are you here to sell, Mr. Ross?"

Shame and anger tangled within Alan. Sainted Mary, he hated being here, having to do this. Guilt tried to send out a black squirming arm to join the fray. He squashed it. He didn't have a choice.

"You never called on me for help with your silver-seeking quest, Miss B. Thought I'd drop by and make the offer again, if you needed it."

"What," said Hawthorn, "is there nothing left to steal in London?"

"Someone told me to stick to peddling pornography." It was out before Alan could remember that this wasn't the *Lyric*. Miss Morrissey was a gentlewoman who hadn't been party to that heady, ludicrous evening where Alan's stash of erotica-for-sale had been the entertainment. And Sir Robert—oh, Christ, Sir Robert was the older brother of the girl he'd sold the stuff to.

Miss Debenham gave a delighted cackle. "Going door-to-door with the business now, are you? That's very enterprising. I hope you brought more samples."

"Shut up, Violet," said Miss Blyth amiably. She directed her dimples at Alan. "You're right, we haven't needed your services yet, but I'm sure we could find something. How did you know where to find me?"

"I know a bloke writing for *Tatler*. Got a nose for gossip like a bloodhound." Alan managed a smile through his tension. "The young and unmarried Maud Blyth is staying practically unchaperoned in the same house as Lord Hawthorn, their debauchery encouraged by the wildly scandalous Violet Debenham. Nobody thinks much of her brother for letting it happen, sir," he added to Sir Robert, fishing for anything below that affable smile.

It didn't work. "Nobody ever thought much of me anyway," said Sir Robert. "But it's true. People keep telling me that nobody's going to entrust their daughter's hand in marriage to someone with so little care for his own sister's virtue."

Miss Morrissey hid a spurt of laughter behind a napkin.

"My virtue is in daily peril." Miss Blyth flicked a crust of toast at her brother. "Robin. I demand you do something."

Laughter between the two of them. Alan glanced from one Blyth to another and made a rapid decision.

"I'm around and about the city a lot for the *Post*; they don't expect me to stay in the office all day. If you have a use for me, Miss B—anything at all—I'd appreciate it. I won't ask for charity, just work. But my own sister's husband was injured last month, and he can't bring in a wage for a while, so things are tough for their little ones."

Miss Blyth's face melted at once into concern. "Of course we can find something."

"I wasn't joking," said Courcey abruptly. "We *could* use a perturbator, and not just for studying. Violet—if he isn't affected as much by magic, then some of the difficult doors . . ."

"Like a canary in a mine?" Miss Debenham raised her eyebrows at Alan. "You don't have to agree, Mr. Ross. The thing is, we haven't found Lady Enid's knife yet, and this particular house is making the search . . . interesting. It's not safe or easy work, even before you consider that our enemies are constantly trying to break in at night."

Alan hesitated. If something happened to him, then what would become of Carolina and Dick and their family—Bella, who had no prospects in her condition—his mother—?

And if he *didn't* agree, what would happen to them then?

"No less safe than running around a great ship with a pack of murderers," he said. "If you think I can help with the hunt, you've got me."

"Well, you can name what you want in return," said Miss Debenham. "If Dorothy deserves hazard pay, then you certainly would."

Alan had been turning this one over. Asking baldly for money seemed grubbier and more obvious, here in someone's fancy dining room, than it had on the *Lyric*. Not to mention that he felt like a bloody blackmailer, coming back to dip his hands greedily into the same pot.

Besides: no matter how deep the pot, you couldn't keep coming back to it forever. He wanted something that would sustain him and his for longer than a single payment. What was the saying? Give a man a fish . . .

He forced his voice into its mildest talking-to-superiors form—the one he used on his editors—and turned to Lord Hawthorn. The largest fish here, if Alan could land him.

"Quid pro quo," he said. "I want a favour."

4

The cab to Westminster wasn't the most awkward enclosed space Jack had ever been in, but it was muscling its way towards the top spot. Summer had squeezed a muggy morning over the city. Jack's hairline prickled with sweat, and the heat was already battling Oliver's best efforts at starching his collar. Ross sat across from him and stared fixedly out the window with discomfort written in the clench of his hands on his knees. Those hands were ink-stained at the edges of the nails and were a shade darker than the olive complexion of Ross's face. Turned to the side, his sharp profile was shown to good advantage.

Not that he seemed to have any *unattractive* angles.

Jack could hold a silence with the best of them. And Alanzo Rossi, Alan Ross, was in Jack's five-day experience of him a pitch-dark room scattered with mousetraps. Almost any topic of conversation could become a fight.

It had been an age since Jack had been in a proper fight. Not many people argued with the Earl of Cheetham's heir; most of those who did had been at breakfast in Spinet House. He was not yet reduced to the indignity of turning up on his own doorstep and picking a fight with Makepeace, if only because his butler knew him far too well. Makepeace would have the argument, but it would be a kindness, and they'd both know it.

Jack stretched his leg out across the carriage. It wasn't hurting any longer, but knocking his knee against Ross's gained him a suspicious dart of the eyes.

If anything was going to be a fight, then Jack could pick his poison, couldn't he?

"Why the *Morning Post*?"

"The *Post*'s readers have been closely following the debate in the Lords over Mr. Lloyd George's bill," said Ross.

"That's not what I meant."

"Forgive me, my lord. I'm used to spending my time with people who pay attention to the clarity of their words."

Snap went the trap. Jack almost wanted to snatch back his toes.

"How did *you* come to work *there*?"

"How and why are different questions. And I think the words you're looking for are *educated above my station*."

"And here I was going to call you a workhouse brat with delusions of vocabulary."

That hit something, somewhere. It flashed like a distant lighthouse in Ross's expression and then vanished. When he spoke again, his accent had dropped some polish and found some geography. There were probably linguists who'd be able to place his origins precisely within one of London's neighbourhoods.

"I write for the *Post* because the *Post* had an opening. I read a month of back editions in an afternoon and wrote the editor a stuffy, bloody-minded column about how hardship is good for the soul and government charity only encourages laziness and breeds sin." A smile with no humour. "He started me the next day."

Jack did not take the *Post,* merely glanced over its front page at newspaper stands, but that was certainly in keeping with their philosophy. They'd probably been delighted to condescend to a working man who fit their ideal pattern of gratitude.

"Writing advertising copy on the side was a step *up* on the ladder of truth," added Ross dryly. "And . . ." He looked out the window again. There was a rearranging sort of pause. "And one day I'll either choke to death on it or get booted aside in favour of someone's nephew. I need the security of a better position."

"And for that you need connections." Thus the quid pro quo. Thus Ross in Spinet's breakfast room, saying *I want Lord Hawthorn's escort to the House of Lords, and the promise of his help.*

Jack steadied himself as the cab took a corner at speed. Ross's mouth was a thin, unhappy line. On the *Lyric* he'd tried to hurl every generous gesture of Jack's back in his face and been forced into acceptance by circumstance. Being here, asking this of Jack, was clearly solidifying his personal dislike into crystal.

"Mr. Shorter liked the society piece I did about the voyage, but I'll never be invited to the right sort of parties to write for *Tatler*. He'd take me for the *Sphere* if I could get a sub-editor position at the *Post*. Or at least some more prominent stories."

"Prominent meaning political."

"Right. The People's Budget is out of the Commons, now— it's all about the fight in the Lords. And I can be educated up to the bloody rooftops and talk like it too, but as soon as someone asks about my *people*, I have to admit that my dear papa was a Clerkenwell ice-cream seller and *his* parents were farmers who came over from Italy when the alternative was starve to death in the famine. You," he said, shimmering with loathing, "probably rubbed mud into rugs belonging to half the peers in the House when you were a tiny lordling. I don't need to be invited to tea, but I want introductions. Contacts. I want a few peers who'll recognise my name and let me flatter a juicy statement out of them. There."

Jack faked a yawn. "Tedious. Are you sure you won't take jewels instead?"

"Oh fuck *off*, you overbred streak of goat's piss," Ross snapped.

The silence was tight as cradling string. Ross's hand made a motion to cover his mouth before he shoved it back down and kept glaring.

After an enjoyable moment, Jack drawled, "I can't imagine why you've had such trouble making connections in civilised society, Mr. Ross."

"Let me rephrase." All the polish came back, cloyingly mocking. "I *strongly dislike* you."

"And do you think I enjoy the company of an unrelentingly hostile East End criminal?"

That lighthouse expression flashed again. Jack pulled air over a catch in his own breath. But Ross, out of mousetraps for the moment, didn't step on Jack's. Didn't say: *Yes, it's terribly obvi-*

ous that you do. Didn't say anything else for the rest of the trip to Westminster.

The palace and its grounds were crawling with robes and suits, briefcases and bowler hats, as the work of Parliament began for another day. Jack took them through the main public entrance into St. Stephen's Hall.

Ross seemed determined to be unimpressed by the marble politicians who bracketed their progress down the hall, as well as the robed and wigged flesh-and-blood versions of the present day. His eyes roamed sharply, a faint crease between them, and he gripped his hat to his chest.

By the time they reached the Central Lobby, Jack had already exchanged nods with several people, none of whom had paid any attention to the shorter man at his elbow.

"I can find you some *Post*-friendly voices, if you think you can resist the urge to erect a guillotine beneath the mosaic of Saint George."

"I've managed not to bite you yet," muttered Ross. "Can't hardly get any worse."

The Viscount Austin, who was nearing eighty and wheezed when he spoke, was in discussion nearby with two equally ancient peers. Jack was on the verge of directing them across to join that group when—

"Hawthorn!"

He turned. Pete Manning had a hand upraised, the other arm full of papers. Only half a head taller than Ross, broad-chested and with a neat, dense beard, Manning made his way across the lobby like a bulldog parting pigeons.

"Damned refurbishments, forcing me halfway round the palace to get to my own office," he puffed. "You owe me a chat and a pint, Hawthorn. What's this? Found yourself a proper secretary, have you? How d'you do, boy. Don't let his lordship bully you, he's mostly bark, y'know."

Jack had no idea how that would go down, but a glance showed him that all of Ross's animosity had been packed away beneath the sharp features.

"This is a journalist friend of mine—unbusheled, Pete—Mr. Alan Ross. He's interested in the fuss over the budget. Ross, this is the Honourable Peter Manning, Member for some insignificant hedgerow or other."

Manning's look of surprise at the word *unbusheled* gave way to a throaty chuckle. He extended a hand. After a moment, Ross shook.

"How d'you do, sir. Should I congratulate or commiserate with you on the budget passing the Commons?"

"Cheeky sod, isn't he?" Manning grinned approvingly. His own accent had the Somerset burr rubbed smooth by education. "I'm of Asquith's party, boy. I'll take the congratulations. Someone needs to hammer the words *public good* into those peers of the realm who are screaming like foxes in traps at the prospect of their precious lands being taxed."

Ross's hand went instantly to his pocket and emerged with a notepad and pencil. Jack could already see the next day's fox-based caricature if Ross had worked for a more progressive paper.

"And I heard the Irish Party's not pleased about the proposed import duties either?"

"Hah. Yes. Glad it's not my fight any longer. It'll be a messy business. But I suppose you know that, given how hard Lord Hawthorn here is working to haul it past the screamers and through the Lords." Manning's head rose at the sound of the bell for the Commons. "It's going to be a devilish long day. Best to your family, Hawthorn."

"And yours. Did I hear Arthur's doing some work at the Barrel now?"

Manning gave Jack a sharp look from beneath his heavy brows. Their friendship over the past several years, like most connections that Jack had maintained with magicians, had been based in pretending that both of them were as unmagical as the next man.

"That's right. My son," he explained, for Ross's benefit. "Barrister. Trained up in magical law as well, so he stands as dicentis in the Library when he's called upon. Just got himself engaged to be married too." He brightened with pride. "Now, if only the wife and I could drag Abigail's head out of her books and get *her* to show some interest in the prospect. Ah, well. Time enough. Better be off."

Jack beckoned Ross towards the Peers' Corridor. "As he said, it's out of that House's voting power now. We'll try the Peers' Lobby. That's where the properly screaming ones congregate."

Ross, however, showed no sign of moving. He stepped aside to allow for the northward migration of MPs towards the exit to the Commons, and drew Jack, by an impatient tug on the sleeve, to stand in one of the small alcoves beneath a monarch's statue. The glare was back.

"What did he mean, you're working for it to *pass*?"

"Are you criticising the clarity of his words?"

A frustrated hiss emerged from Ross. Jack smothered a smile and leaned against the smooth, ancient wall. Power drenched this place as surely as it did Spinet House, even if it was of a different sort.

"You'll inherit an earldom!"

"There are several Liberal-affiliated peers in the House. I believe this is how government works."

"And the supertax clauses—you're rich as bloody Midas."

"Well," said Jack, "I have been trying to give some of it away to the ungrateful poor, but I've only had limited success." He adjusted his cufflinks. Ross followed the action with his eyes, and spots of colour appeared in his flawless cheeks. "Taxation has the appeal of efficiency."

"You're—no. I don't believe it."

Jack could have pointed out that not once, during the frequent displays of Ross's anti-aristocratic principles aboard the *Lyric,* had Jack ever given any indication that he disagreed with them. Instead he shrugged and turned away, striding to the southern exit and down the corridor quickly enough that Ross would have to scurry to catch up. The light of the man's indignation made Jack feel alive. He could have stood there all day, stirring the embers of it whenever they threatened to dim.

There were certainly enough Conservative-affiliated peers in
the lobby that it was easy to steer Ross at a cluster of them, once
he'd spent a few seconds transferring his glare from Jack to the
gilt decoration above the Brass Gates.

"Not a word about magic to anyone here, or I'll cut your tongue
out," Jack murmured. "How d'you do, Hunterbury. Morton."

He introduced Ross in this company as the son of an enlisted
man he'd served with—"Good, solid fellow, saved my life in the
Boer. I promised to look out for his son, and only just found
him. Writes for the *Post*," he added, which would be far better
currency here than with Manning.

A gleam of grudging approval came through the Earl of
Hunterbury's glasses. Little prompting was needed; the People's
Budget wasn't far from anyone's mind at the moment. Ross's
notepad came out to receive a stream of complaint about that
frothing socialist Lloyd George and his grasping, unreasonable
piece of legislation.

"I'm sure Hawthorn would have you believe Lloyd George
cares about the welfare of the British people," Hunterbury finished sourly. "Stuff and nonsense. He wants to gut us."

"Do you think the Lords will vote to reject, my lord?" asked
Ross. "As you haven't the power to amend it."

"Be a piece of damned foolishness not to," said Hunterbury.

"In which case Asquith has all but promised to take aim at the
Lords' legislative power, if he wins re-election, and *that* gutting
would be done with a rusty fork," said Jack. "Better to swallow
a few taxes now, surely?"

Hunterbury harrumphed. Lord Morton roused himself to
say, rather meanly, "No need to spill your sour grapes here,
Hawthorn, just because you haven't a seat yourself and you
don't like the way your father's voting." He looked at Ross. "I
hope you plan to speak to Cheetham. We've a committee meeting later this morning. I'm sure he's in the building."

The pause was like missing a step: short, but jarring to the
stomach.

"What a good suggestion, my lord," said Ross.

"Indeed," said Jack.

Eyebrows rose when he took Ross by the arm and marched him to the other side of the lobby, but nobody expected good manners from Baron Hawthorn.

"Oi," snapped Ross. He pulled his arm away more showily than he needed to. No doubt Jack could soon add the charge of *manhandling the press* to his reputation. "Why didn't you suggest this in the first place? A direct statement from the Earl of Cheetham. Just what I need."

Jack unclenched his jaw. "No."

"Quid pro quo."

"I did not agree to a personal tour of my family tree."

"Not much of a tree. Barely a branch." Ross's smile appeared like a tiger from behind grass. "Any good journalist knows that when someone's up in arms like this, it's time to keep pushing for the story. What is it? More than political disagreement. Bad blood? Perhaps he's not your father at all?"

Jack's mixture of invigorating irritation and amusement tipped over into real anger. He wanted to put his hand at Ross's jaw and force up his chin, wanted to dig his fingers in and cause a bruise, and be damned to the fact that they were in public.

"A century ago I'd have called you out for that."

"We're a civilised society now." Ross set his shoulders. "I'm not haggling, my lord. There's my price. One more introduction and I'll leave you alone."

"I agreed to burden myself with you for the day, not to inflict you upon my relations," Jack snapped, but forestalled the next comment with an impatient wave of his hand. "Very well."

Ross was right about one thing. Arguing further would only convince him that there was a story to be sniffed out.

Jack had never visited his father's office in Westminster. He had to collar a House messenger to ask directions, which did nothing to erase the growing curiosity on Ross's face as they made their way to the fourth floor of the palace.

"Less gold twiddle up here," Ross murmured, when they were in the right corridor and Jack was counting numbers on doors. "Is it for show, when Lloyd George comes to visit? Pretend that the peerage is crippled by taxation already, and can't even afford one tiny little tapestry for their office wall?"

Jack's enjoyment of this hostile East End criminal's company was certainly coming to an end. He rapped on the door before his urge to hesitate could win out.

"*Now* what?" came an impatient call from inside.

"Ah," said Ross. "This would be this *good breeding* I hear so much about. Can definitely see where you get it from."

The sooner this happened the sooner it would be over. Jack opened the door and stepped right into the path of the Earl of Cheetham's glower. Having it delivered from behind a desk was like being hurled back in time. An eight-year-old version of Jack quailed and longed to sidle behind Elsie, whose fault it probably was that they'd deserved the look in the first place.

The thirty-four-year-old version simply cleared his throat. "Sir."

"Hawthorn." Cheetham was standing. His hand, holding a sheaf of papers, fell to his side. "Thought you were—never mind. Has something happened?" The lines of his face deepened in worry. "Your mother?"

"No, no. Nothing of the sort," Jack assured him. He felt too large for this tiny, overwarm office. His father, not a small man either, looked even broader in shirtsleeves. A wig and robe hung on a stand in the corner.

The last time Jack had seen his father had been three weeks ago at the house in Belgravia. The atmosphere had been one of a door gingerly cracked open, through which two men—both of whom no longer knew what manner of person the other was—might begin an awkward conversation.

The time before *that* had been nearly seven years ago, when the Earl of Cheetham went to his knees at his son's hospital bedside and outright pleaded with him not to return to the war and risk depriving the countess of her one remaining child.

"Who's this, then?" His father nodded at Ross, who'd closed the office door behind him.

This time Jack told the truth: that he owed Ross a favour. His father would understand that overcoming both Jack's personal feelings and his politics.

The introductions hooked a *how-d'you-do* out of Cheetham, and a *my lord* from Ross that was twice as sincere as any he'd slid in Jack's direction. Cheetham checked the clock on his desk and agreed he had time to sit down with the *Post*.

"I'll go for a walk," said Jack. "I'm hoping to have a word with some people myself."

If he stayed in the room while his father explained in fervent Tory detail the reasons why the People's Budget was an outrage, then he would argue back. And no matter how much help Alan Ross the perturbator might yet prove to be in the hunt for Lady Enid's knife, he had *not* earned a front-row seat to a debate between Jack and the father he'd only just started talking to again.

"People you'll try to convince to vote against their own interests, no doubt." Cheetham snorted. "Come back and collect your journalist in"—another glance at the clock—"a quarter of an hour."

Ross shot a look at Jack that might have had alarm in it somewhere. Jack resisted the urge to inform Ross that his father only slaughtered peasants on Tuesdays.

"Ah. Hawthorn."

Jack turned.

"Polly's at the Hall for the rest of the summer. I know she'd appreciate a visit from her only son."

Trapping him in front of company. His father was a politician, after all.

"I'll keep that in mind, sir," Jack said, and escaped.

The Earl of Cheetham's politics were exactly what Alan would have expected. He could have written the quotes himself.

Though he would have attributed them just as readily to Baron Hawthorn, and he'd have been completely wrong about

that. The fact kept trying to sidle to the front of his mind and
wave for attention. He had to keep kicking it back.

After ten minutes, someone else in that ridiculous wig-and-
robe combination rapped on the door, asking Lord Cheetham to
come and discuss an upcoming vote. Ross closed his notebook
and rose, assuming he'd be hustled out the door, but his lordship waved him impatiently back into his seat. "Stay here. No
point you and Hawthorn playing a parlour game trying to find
each other if you're both roaming the halls."

"Thank you for your time, my lord."

"Hm. I'll have a stern word with Lady Bathurst if you mis-
quote me," Cheetham said, but by now Alan had begun to feel
out what sort of man this was. What had Manning said about
Hawthorn? *Mostly bark.* Cheetham was gruff and brusque, and
yes, indignant as the next aristocrat at the idea that someone
might remove the smallest stone from his vast monument of
power, but one sensed that the fuse of his temper was longer
than his impatient manner would suggest.

Alone in the office, Alan flipped to a new page and began an
outline for the article. But the novelty of where he was, on top
of the fact that *Lord Hawthorn was claiming to be a fucking
Liberal*, drummed in his mind. His focus fell apart.

The window was small and didn't look out over the Thames,
to Alan's disappointment, though it did provide a new angle
on the pale spires of Westminster Abbey. He paced back and
forth, resisted the urge to go digging in the solid wooden filing
cabinets—he wasn't *that* sort of journalist, and to his deep annoyance he found himself wanting to live up to Cheetham's gesture of
trust—and realised quickly that he was in search of magic.

Cheetham hadn't been told Alan was unbusheled. The topic
of magic had not come up during an interview on the People's
Budget. But the Earl of Cheetham was, one assumed, as magical
as his son. More so. Alan had only the haziest idea of what had
happened to Hawthorn—had been a magician, and now wasn't?
Through choice? Through accident? Something relating to his

sister, for which a char of a secret-bind had been laid on his tongue?

Horror spidered between Alan's shoulder blades as he remembered seeing the bind flare to life. The most disturbing thing had been the sudden and brutal crack in the infuriatingly unflappable Lord Hawthorn's composure.

Lord Hawthorn. Fighting for the People's Budget. Alan kept coming back to it, tripping over it: an inexplicable gap in the floorboards of the universe.

Usually it took until mid-afternoon for Alan to feel this abrasive with swallowing his feelings. Despite the *Morning Post*'s interests, his lowly status there meant that he interacted with mercifully few titles. Now he was surrounded by them. And it had been his own bloody idea.

"When you complained about the lack of gold, I didn't realise it was because you'd been hoping to steal it. Art's a little harder to slip into your pockets."

Alan turned from where he'd been gazing unseeing at a dull pastoral painting. He gave his sweetest and least sincere smile, the one that used to pluck pennies from the purses of softhearted women on the street and direct them onto his mother's spread-out shawl.

"I'll settle for the inkstand, that looks worth a few pounds."

Hawthorn's mouth didn't twitch. He'd found that composure again in his brief period out of Alan's sight. Alan waited to be ordered peremptorily out of the office, and readied himself to make some kind of provocative demand to see the rest of Westminster Palace. He didn't *want* to see it. But a fight might at least purge the miasma of aristocracy from his lungs.

Like Cheetham, Hawthorn didn't hurry Alan anywhere. He closed the door to the office and, rather bewilderingly, did some pacing and gazing of his own. It wasn't the kind of room a man of Hawthorn's size could pace comfortably. His stride ate the rug in two gulps. Alan found himself nearly perched on the edge of the desk to give him space.

Fuck it. There was only one weak spot he was sure of.

"So that's what your pa's like," he said. "What about your ma? *Polly*, was it? Why don't you visit her more often?"

Hawthorn gave him a look that blazed right through that composure and went for Alan next, like flames leaping from house to house, greedily searching for fuel to consume and hurt. It was even better than Alan had expected.

"My family are magicians. I am not. This fact is equally as distasteful to them as the reminder is to me."

Alan touched the inkstand. It *did* look expensive. His fingers left smudged prints against the gold. "Do they know anything about this Last Contract business?"

"No." Then, reluctantly: "Not so far as I know."

It had been telling, that instant denial. There was a faith in it. Who was to say that Hawthorn's parents weren't involved with the wrong side of this magical conspiracy, given they all knew that his cousin George was likely the ringleader?

A new spider of fear tried to attack Alan's shoulders. He distracted himself with the next unwise question, managing to make it come out in the same tone of journalistic inquiry.

"Do they know you fuck men?"

Hawthorn took a single step forward. It was a motion in the realm of crowding Alan further back against the desk, and it sent another jerk of hot sensation through him.

He should be more careful with this. He'd been so careful, for so many years. He looked up into Hawthorn's blue, implacable eyes and felt like hurling stones at the sun.

"Are you trying to blackmail me, Master Cesare?" said Hawthorn. "On what grounds?"

"Reading material."

"I don't believe I've admitted to even a passing familiarity with whatever filth you peddle."

Alan's fine-tuned nerves told him that there was no real threat in this conversation. They were tossing a grenade back and forth, each of them pretending that it was primed to explode, but it wasn't.

"Then I suppose it'd be hypocritical trying to explain how I knew, wouldn't it?"

"How *did* you know?"

"On the ship? I was defending the right of the literate working man to his little pleasures. And I said something about the man who cleans a lord's windows, and you said"—Alan altered his voice—"that he could *thereby experience being fucked by the aristocracy in more ways than one.*"

A pause.

"You've a good memory," said Hawthorn.

And that particular sentence, delivered in that deadly drawl, certainly hadn't played itself over and over in Alan's mind ever since. No. He shrugged. "I was forced to memorise chunks of Scripture and poetry at school. Weren't you? Suppose half of yours was in Latin too."

Hawthorn didn't take the bait. "Hm. I do remember saying that. You'd made me think of . . . I can't recall the name."

"*Bootblacks and Groundskeepers.*" No power could have stopped Alan's unwise tongue from filling that in. "There's a story in that one about the man employed to clean all the windows of a huge country manor. He looks through the study window and sees the master of the house bringing himself off, and . . ."

And is spotted in return, and holds eye contact all through the lord's leisurely release, and the scene kicks off a series of voyeuristic exchanges culminating in the cleaner being fucked up against one of the largest windows.

Alan found his fingers curled around the edge of the desk, and made them uncurl.

Hawthorn's eyebrows rose. "There's that memory again. That was an early one, I believe. Must be nearly a decade ago. Are you a collector as well as a purveyor? Or were you a startlingly precocious boy?"

In a conversation that began with the mention of blackmail, it would be radiantly stupid of Alan to tell him. But his nerves still refused to shout danger. And powerful men were always more comfortable dealing with you if they had something to hold over your head.

That wasn't the reason, though. Alan wanted to knock that superior look clean off his lordship's face.

He reached out and touched his fingertips to the crook of Hawthorn's elbow. The man's pupils twitched. How had Alan *known*? For fuck's sake. This man had wanted for nothing in his life, and had never had to hide how much he wanted a thing when he looked at it. Alan had known from the first time they spoke, even if he had been held at the business end of a pistol at the time.

"Why, m'lord Hawthorn," he said, as obnoxiously common as possible. "I wrote 'em."

Hawthorn jerked his arm back, then looked equal parts furious and surprised. The expression melted almost at once into one of flat, dubious uncaring; too late. Alan was back under this lord's skin.

"*You're* the Roman?"

"My pa's parents came from nearer Naples, actually, but why split hairs?"

Another delicious moment of silence. Hawthorn's right hand formed a fist. Opened again.

"Nice try, but I don't believe you. You're too young. The Roman's been putting out work for ten years."

"Nine. You never thought it might be a group of people? Or an inherited pen name, passed on from man to man? Woman to woman?"

That got a blink. "Woman?"

"You'd be surprised," said Alan. "But no. All me, I'm afraid. The first one was published when I was eighteen. And now I'm twenty-seven. Do you need an abacus, my lord, or did you manage to fit in some arithmetic around all the Latin?"

Alan was going to become greedy for these off-balance silences. Finally Lord Hawthorn rubbed his forehead and said, sounding plaintive enough that he was almost a real person: "Twenty-*seven*."

"Why, what was your guess?"

A short bark of a laugh. "Very well, Ross. I believe you."

"If it helps, I was a sallow, weedy thing when I was *actually* twenty."

"And you're such a vigorous specimen of manhood now." Hawthorn's eyes flicked down to Alan's feet and back up. All five and a half feet of him.

"Not as vigorous as the boys I write about, but I *do* try."

He'd overshot that one, perhaps. He couldn't help it. The longed-for fight was refusing to manifest properly. Instead, there was this game of catch and thorns, and Alan was enjoying it too much. He needed Hawthorn to do something to put a firm end to his enjoyment. To push too hard; to take advantage, as powerful men always did.

To prove that Alan had been right about him after all.

But Hawthorn stepped back, not forward. Looked amused, instead of angry. More air and more sound began to trickle in around them.

"Very well. You're the Roman and I'm a Liberal. Are we square?"

"Not even close," said Alan. "But I suppose it's a start."

5

There were probably many working men in London who made their way home, at the end of the day, thinking about the oasis of relative peace that would be their own house. Perhaps some chatter of children, or the crackle of fire. But in general: a respite from the noise of the workplace and the city streets.

Alan let himself into the small Clerkenwell house and smiled when the first shouts hit his ears. It was suppertime. Food in the Rossi household waited for no man.

"Who'll guess where I went today?" he shouted, stepping into the kitchen's warmth. He reached up to absently touch the doorframe as he did so, an adopted habit of his mother's that travelled from house to house and created a shiny-smooth patch in any place that the Rossi family inhabited for long enough. For the first time he was aware of the fact that a tall man would have to duck to pass under that frame. Houses here weren't built for men of Lord Hawthorn's proportions.

The noise dipped for a mere half a moment at his question, then redoubled.

"Paris!" called Bella, and "Circus!" came from Tom, who had lived and breathed circuses since he saw a poster for one the previous week. The suggestions escalated in volume and absurdity until—*The moon!*" screeched Emily, who then fell to cackling breathlessly around a mouthful of bread.

"All wrong! I live in a house of ignorant fools!"

"Speak English, Alanzo," said his ma reprovingly. She swept an illustrative hand at the children and then—an afterthought—at Carolina's husband, Dick, who came from pure Spitalfields stock.

Alan grinned and sat down in the narrow space formed by Carolina ordering her two eldest to squash together on the bench. He and his siblings—the two sisters in this room, and precious oldest son Emilio—had grown up hearing and speaking both tongues. His ma had insisted that they sound as English as possible so they'd have more choices than working within the tiny Italian-London communities like those of Clerkenwell.

And it had only taken one overheard comment about *lazy dago brats,* when Alan was fifteen and first trying to get work, for him to change his name. Alan Ross was a sharp, careful Londoner with an employable accent, who just happened to turn a nice burnished colour in the sun. Alanzo Rossi now existed only under this roof, with these people.

So yes: Alanzo Rossi slipped into Italian when he could, if only to savour the feel of it in his mouth.

"Al'right, mate," said Dick. He pushed a bowl of cold potatoes in Alan's direction. Alan began to fill his plate.

"Haven't chopped it off yet?" He nodded to Dick's leg, wrapped and propped up on a stool.

"Nah. Waiting for pork chops to pass a shilling the pound. Caro will hack it off herself, then, out of thrift, and serve it up for supper."

Alan laughed; the children went into spasms of gleeful disgust at the prospect of eating their father's leg; Caro said, "*Oi,*" and tossed a crust at her husband's face. Maria Rossi broke into overlapping complaint about how pork chops had been *ten pence* at the markets last Friday, and shocking quality for the price, according to Tatiana—

Alan smiled to himself and ate. At least Emilio and his wife, Eva, who'd been dubiously blessed with two sets of twins, had their own place. They only added the extra noise of their six children to the household on Sundays when they all piled in for dinner after morning Mass.

"Where did you go today, then?" asked Bella. "You never said."

"The Houses of Parliament."

Bella rolled her eyes. She'd have preferred the moon too.

Nobody in Alan's family had energy to spare for politics, though Dick had started to pay attention when Alan read him some pamphlets on workers' rights. He'd been away from his construction job longer than expected after breaking his leg, and then laid off entirely; he had the makings of a staunch unionist.

Alan got down his potatoes and chickpea stew and bread with margarine—no perfect plush pats of butter *here*—and drank his tea with no sugar at all. He'd just polished off the last crust when there was a banging at the front door.

"That'll be Berto," he said, rising. "He's picking up some papers."

His cousin Berto was indeed coughing on the doorstep. The light had gone dusk-purple, the heat of the day starting to dissipate. Alan let Berto into the dim entryway and handed over the small pile of paper that was his latest manuscript, handwritten pages carefully wrapped and tied.

"Don't read it."

"Fuck off," said the illiterate Berto amiably. "Nothing else? My man keeps asking if there's any more coming, after those choice bits you gave me."

Berto was far more of an East End criminal than Alan had ever been. His many connections, both professional and romantic, ran deep into the underbelly of the city. Alan did tell him he'd turn up strangled in the Thames if he kept fucking men with names like Bloody Joe, but Berto was useful. He knew a lot of fences—including the one who'd taken care of Lord Hawthorn's pocket watch and cufflinks—and was a trustworthy and discreet middleman between the anonymous pornographer known as the Roman and the underground printer who produced his purple pamphlets.

Besides, they were the two invert cousins in the Catholic horde of their family, and that gave them a bond.

Alan lowered his voice. "I'm not stealing any more. I promised Mamma."

"Maria don't need to know—oi, all right." Berto lifted the

parcel in surrender. "Got it. I'll be round with the payment for this next week."

Carolina and Dick took their family to bed soon after supper. The house had a small downstairs room that served as a parlour, warm enough in summer to sit there in the evenings without a fire. Bella sat in a chair with a huge basket of the darning she took in for a small fee, balancing one garment at a time on the bulge of her belly. Her brow furrowed as she squinted at her rapidly moving needle.

"Do you want to wreck your eyes like Mamma?" Alan said sharply. "Light another candle, or put some pennies in the gas meter. We can afford it."

Bella made a face at him, but did so. The light played on the glowing curve of her cheek and her glossy black hair. Emilio and Carolina were nothing to sneeze at, but all the best looks of Alan's family had been saved for his little sister, as if to let her grow into the promise of her name. And pregnancy suited her, not that she'd have appreciated hearing it.

A long sigh from his ma. "You're a good boy, Alanzo."

Alan pulled up a stool and sat next to her chair, which was threadbare but cushioned. Maria had found work as a fur puller after Alan's father died, and like most women in that profession had lost the best part of her eyesight to it. Alan's writing had meant she could stop before she lost her lungs as well.

The prospect of this conversation had been poking Alan in the side all day. At least she was in a soft mood now. He took her hand in his own and patted it shamelessly.

Perturbator.

"Mamma," he said. "When I was a boy, was there . . . I mean, did I . . ." Damn it. "Mamma, I need to know. Are there magicians in our family? Witches, sorcerers?"

"*Witches?* What are you on about?" asked Bella.

Their mother sat more upright in her chair. Her hand slid out of Alan's so that she could cross herself.

"Don't say such things! We're good people. The Lord knows

that. He gave us the strength to turn away the devil when he tried to do his evil work through my little ones. No witches. No."

"What evil work?"

Maria crossed herself twice more and glared at him. So much for Alan being the good boy. He'd never been suited to that role anyway.

"It is nothing. We prayed, we used the rosary with you just as my nonna taught me, and see? The devil passed on. No evil in you. Even if you break your mamma's heart by never coming to Mass," she added pointedly.

"The devil— Madonna santa, Mamma!"

"*Alanzo!*"

The argument over his taking the Holy Virgin's name in vain took another two minutes, while Bella—sinfully pregnant and unmarried Bella, who wasn't *allowed* to go to Mass or indeed leave the house, in case anyone caught sight of her—fairly shook with smugness. Eventually, Alan managed to make his ma realise that he wasn't going to drop the subject, and she threw up her hands and sent him upstairs to the tiny bedroom she shared with Bella, to fetch Nonna Sofia's rosary from where it was curled up on the scratched old dresser.

Alan ran the beads through his fingers, an instinctive habit, as he took it back into the parlour. The skin of his hand warmed and tingled. The smaller beads were pale wood, the decade beads and the cross a deeper brown. All smooth and glossy with generations of prayer.

"I used to play with this," he said. "When I was a boy."

The feel of the wood had summoned it from the borderlands of memory. How young must he have been? Five years old, six? Living in a house like this one, his mother still sprightly and full of laughter, his father a beloved, black-whiskered presence who always smelled of sweet old milk. Being handed the rosary and taught how to say the prayers—being bored of that quickly and just enjoying the sensation of the beads running between his small fingers. His ma's sharp voice if he stopped.

He'd completely forgotten. He'd tucked it away with all the

other small pieces of painful happiness, during the bad years, and never brought it out again when life eased back from desperate to merely exhausting.

"*I* was never allowed to touch Nonna Sofia's rosary," said Bella to her darning.

No. Because only Alan, apparently, had thrown a tantrum that shattered two plates on the other side of the room. Maria had taken it as a sign that the family devil had reared its head, and the rosary had been shoved into Alan's chubby hands the same day.

Now Alan sat with an odd clenching in his chest. He wanted to pick this up and run with it somewhere, as if it were a scandalous broadsheet wet from the printer. He wanted to—to wave it at Lord Hawthorn, who would say something puncturing so that Alan could lash back.

"Why do you ask about this now?" His ma's eyes fastened on him as keenly as if her sight were perfect. "*What happened?*"

He had, damn it, sworn to Miss Blyth that he would keep what he knew about magicians secret. Alan produced a weak story about a crack in the cobbles spreading from beneath his foot when he was excited, knowing as he did that it would produce another flurry of exclamations and an exhortation that he must start using the rosary again, *at once*. His ma gripped the arms of her chair as if on the verge of scurrying out into the night to find a priest.

Alan hurriedly said a Hail Mary to pacify her and exchanged a final set of insults with Bella before retiring to his own room on the excuse that he had to write. Perhaps he even would. He wasn't too tired. That strangeness still coursed beneath his skin, on top of the crackling irritation that had followed him away from Westminster, away from Lord Hawthorn's aggravating largeness and deep voice, and through the rest of the day.

Alan drew the small stool up to his writing desk and lit his own candle. He rested his chin on folded forearms and watched the flame flicker. A few insects danced shadows onto the wall.

Everyone else in the family shared. Alan, unmarried and

currently the sole source of household income beyond Bella's darning pennies, had the luxury of a bed and a room to himself, even if it was this poky slice of attic space. It was a far, far cry from living on the streets, or those two basement rooms in Shadwell where they'd been constantly fighting the damp of the docks.

Still, it was a step down from the neat bachelor's boarding-house room Alan had rented until four months ago.

Four months ago was when Bella had been dismissed from the lady's-maid position that she'd worked so hard for. Well— Alan's forged references had got her the place in the house, but her own quick wits had done the rest. She'd been trusted and valued by the young lady she attended, earning a good wage, secure in her prospects.

And then that fucking rat's arsehole of a boy who called him-self the son of the house had grown tired of her placating smiles and sidestepping, had stopped heeding when she said *No, sir,* and had done what all men raised in the cesspit of wealth and power did: took what he wanted, because he believed he had a right to it.

And then three months ago, a piece of timber had fallen on Dick's leg.

And so Alan had quit his lodgings, stared grimly down the barrel of his finances, and moved the whole lot of them into this house. He'd pulled every meagre string he had to get the copywriting job for the White Star Line and the society article. He'd arranged through Berto to sell dirty books on behalf of the Charing Cross establishment that usually sold his own; he had Berto give him, in addition, some tutorials in lock-picking.

Thanks to Lord Hawthorn, he'd walked away from the voyage on the *Lyric* with even more wealth than he expected, and had promptly packed his family off to the seaside for three weeks, because his ma's cough had thickened and Caro's kids were looking dangerously hollow-eyed.

Paying for housing and fuel and food was one thing, but a seaside holiday . . . it had been obvious, then, that he couldn't have come by the money honestly. His ma had been incandes-cent with anger. Alan hadn't cared, seeing how much colour her cheeks had regained with the fresh air. But none of her children had ever out-stubborned Maria Rossi, and eventually she'd made him promise. No more theft.

There was enough of Hawthorn's money left now to keep them afloat a fair while. Provided Dick's leg healed eventually and he found work. Provided Bella's delivery was easy and the children stayed well, and they didn't need the expense of a doctor. Provided Alan kept his position at the *Post,* or found a better one. Provided he was never found out and thrown in prison for writing the Roman books. Provided his clothes didn't wear out too fast.

Alan would manage. Tom and Emily and baby Lizzie would never know what it was to live without the safety of a roof and four walls. *Never.* If Alan had to drag his principles through the mud, if he had to go begging for help from people he resented— well, you begged, if you had no other choice. Everyone knew that.

Alan shook his head and took out pen, ink, blotter, and drafting paper. Lord Hawthorn was the last person in London he'd wanted to beg for anything. When he made the request, he'd thought that at least forcing himself to spend time with the man would be a useful reminder of what an unbearable, arrogant arse-wipe he was.

But today had been . . . bearable. His lordship could have taken that grenade of danger and made Alan swallow it. Alan was still reeling uncomfortably with the knowledge that instead, Hawthorn had laughed. Had taken all of Alan's hostility and treated him not quite as an equal, but with abrasive respect.

The candle flickered again. Alan glanced up at the broken windowpane that had been patched with paper, and through which a small draft insisted on leaking. *This* was what he needed to remember. The reality of his life, to be held up in ruthless comparison with the wooden grandeur of Violet's house and the over-gilded halls of Westminster.

He had nothing in common with those people. He wasn't on their *side.* To anyone of that station, someone like Alan was only a tool to be used.

Surely Hawthorn's show of respect was an illusion. Bella's situation represented the truth of the world. Some toffs might claim to like it when people stood up to them, but it was a lie. Oh, they might enjoy a bit of token banter, but they'd always exert their superiority pretty damn fast if actually challenged. If the natural order of things was threatened.

Or else they wanted to be humiliated, wanted the excitement of feeling themselves degraded by associating—sexually, *not* socially—with the lower classes.

Alan wasn't interested in being used as a filthy rag to add grime to someone else's soul. And he preferred the illusion of degradation the other way around.

A workhouse brat with delusions of vocabulary.

A hot breath escaped Alan's lips as if it had been jolted loose. Fuck, *fuck*. It was even worse than before.

Fortunately, he'd built into his life a way of dealing with the desires he could neither indulge nor ignore. He looked at the candle's flickering flame for a few moments more, letting the first sentence arrange itself. Then he dipped pen to ink and wrote:

The owner of this remote and ramshackle manor had hair dark and thick as the night in which I found myself stranded. His eyes, lit by the lantern uplifted in his hand, could have been two sapphires set there by a master jeweller. Despite the chill of my wet clothes, despite my entire wretched situation, a thrill of heated excitement seized my body as it was subjected to his cruel regard. His expression, turned as it was upon the no doubt unfortunate figure that I presented, was that of a patient creature who had finally worn its prey to exhaustion and now had the leisure of choosing when to strike: ravenous, intent, and with not a speck of mercy to be found.

6

Jack slipped his much-thumbed copy of *Bootblacks and Groundskeepers* into an inner pocket of his jacket to read on the train. He also bought a newspaper to disguise it in, on the slim chance that any of the other denizens of his first-class compartment on a midweek train heading to the southeastern corner of Essex were also readers of the Roman.

The paper was the *Morning Post*. He couldn't justify that, really, except that it arose from the same prickle of prurient interest that had made him burn to reread some of Ross's erotic work in full knowledge of the author.

The elderly man sitting across from him from London to Wickford looked liable to remain asleep even if a full brass band marched through the carriage. Unlikely to crack an eye to pass judgement on Jack's reading material. Jack found himself reading the newspaper anyway. Like Ross himself, the *Post* made him enjoyably angry—just in the other direction. He kept a mental list of political causes he would donate to out of petty spite because the *Post* frothed over them.

He had the compartment to himself after changing to the older, pokier car of the local line. It was a fine day, and the South was showing off its summer wardrobe: lush patchworks of grazing green and golden crops sailed past, the vivid pastoral colour all but giving off a harmonious hum that Spinet House would have envied. Morning sunshine warmed the side of Jack's body through the train window and shone merrily onto the pages of the Roman booklet.

Those pages had never seen this much sunlight before. Bedside

candlelight and furtive lamplight were the more usual illumination of—well.

> *"No more, please," I gasped. My legs were loose jellies, too*
> *weak to hold me up, and what had been a delicious ache*
> *in my backside two rooms ago was now on the horizon of*
> *pain. "I can't—and surely you are spent, after so long—"*
> *"I find myself inspired," my tormenter said, in that low*
> *growl that by now was a signal of exquisite anticipation to*
> *my nerves. I groaned in surrender; his strong hand gripped*
> *the back of my neck and pushed me down until my cheek*
> *was against the polished wood of that immense dining ta-*
> *ble. An audience of cold-eyed oil portraits stared down at*
> *us from the walls. "I will have you again at least twice be-*
> *fore the sun sets, insolent thing, and you will writhe just as*
> *sweetly around my prick as you did the first time."*

It was impossible not to speculate.

Could a man write that and not reveal something of the channels down which his own desires ran? Yes, if he were a cha-
meleon as skilled and shameless as the socialist who aped the
ideology of the *Post* for a wage.

But the Roman had been consistent from the very beginning.
It was why Jack had become an instant and avid collector. Always
there was power on one side and little on the other. Always something was *taken,* some barrier stepped over or broken through.
Only on the other side of the barrier would shame and protesta-
tion be stripped away so that the narrator's helpless enjoyment
could soak the text.

Jack closed the booklet firmly and, to punctuate, slapped it
rather too hard against his own palm. Hm. There was at least
one Roman collection about naughty schoolboys and strict masters, wasn't there? And—

And this was a pointless line of thought.

Even with Jack's favour discharged, Ross wasn't about to
vanish from his orbit entirely. Jack could only imagine how

uncomfortable it would be, living in Spinet House while a magical knife-hunt was conducted by *two* men whom Jack had fucked. Fielding Robin's protective glares around Edwin was quite bad enough.

And no matter how much spice a bit of antagonism might add to a fuck, Jack's tastes didn't run to people who didn't actually *want* it. Ross's provocation was mere prodding. It was only hope driven by furious lust that had Jack reading anything more into it.

He banished the booklet back into his jacket, reopened the *Post* to the Letters section, and diverted himself with some healthy rage instead.

The man he paid for a cart ride to the estate either didn't recognise him or was doing an excellent job of pretending not to. Cheetham tenant farmland began at the edge of the town and stretched for a good two miles before they hit the road leading to the estate proper. Jack shaded his eyes and looked about. Were those *his* cornfields? His dairy herds? Hawthorn land was a large chunk of this; the ancient earldom had been created by merging a modest barony with the adjacent land, on which Cheetham Hall had been built.

Jack managed it, as he did most things, at a distance. For years he and his father had communicated about agriculture and rents and land management via stewards, as he imagined some married couples communicated via the household staff.

The Hall looked the same. High, pale grey stone frontage, dark roof and eaves, comfortable with age. The glass of the front windows was comparatively young: only sixteen years old. It had all been replaced at once, after it shattered.

A figure moved at one of those windows. Jack turned his face from the house and did not climb the stairs to the terrace and the imposing front doors. Instead, he walked around—around, *around,* he'd nearly forgotten the sheer size of the old pile—until he could follow the hedge of fragrant rosemary that bordered the kitchen garden. Dimly he heard voices in the kitchens. And above that, louder and louder as Jack turned away from the rosemary and walked across a patch of summer-lush lawn, was another sound like a thumb run ceaselessly over the tines of a comb.

And there, beneath a handful of trees, were the hives.

Jack stood for a time, looking at them. There were ritual words for blood-oath; there were words for all sorts of contracts. And there were words for this, awkward as it was.

"Hives and queens of Cheetham Hall. It's been a long time," he said. "I'm sorry for that. I'm . . . doing well." How to expand on that? Healthy? He was. Secure, prosperous? Certainly. Exerting his wealth and his power in a manner that satisfied his conscience? Yes.

Happy?

No, but it probably said something that it was the last emotion he considered. Real happiness had been replaced, when it shattered, with things more complicated and opaque.

Bees danced busily in the air. A handful wove near Jack, investigating, but didn't consider his dark jacket worth landing on.

Having neither wedding nor childbirth nor recent bereavement to report, Jack bowed once in the direction of the hives. The heels of his feet prickled in his shoes as he straightened. A sensation of cold ants climbed his legs and his vision went dim at the sides, dark clouds dotted with sparks, for a few over-loud heartbeats.

He breathed until it all settled, then went back to the front door of the Hall. The bees were one duty and this was another. The long-absent heir to Cheetham set his knuckles to the door and knocked, and did not enter without invitation.

Mr. Blake was too experienced a butler to exclaim in surprise, but a violent twitch of his brows suggested it was a narrow escape. Jack handed over his hat and jacket as Blake— now recovered enough to behave as though Jack sprang visits on his childhood home every other week—informed him that her ladyship had a guest, and they were taking tea in the conservatory.

"Thank you," said Jack.

Every spot in the house was a memory. This rug was faded

and threadbare at the centre from running feet. This picture had been knocked down in a game of flung spells and had to be re-framed. This parlour's wallpaper might have absorbed Elsie's wild, smug laughter as she coaxed the curtains to wrap around Jack's leg and hold him in place while she stole a book from his hands.

The past had a heavy fist around his heart. What he was waiting for was for it to *physically* hurt.

The year of limbo between the loss of Jack's magic and the loss of his twin had been like walking with a large, sharp pebble embedded between sock and shoe, and afterwards—even worse. The Hall's magic had taken Elsie's death as a stain, and rebelled. Part of Jack wished his parents had given up gracefully and sold it; but they hadn't.

And he'd turned his back on magic, on Cheetham Hall, and—by necessity—on them.

The conservatory was cheerful with sunlight, tucked into a northern-facing corner of the ground floor, the glass walls giving a view out towards the birch grove and the hill of the Lady's Oak beyond that. Jack had intended only to peek in and then withdraw until the guest left, but his mother's chair was angled towards the doorway. He felt her eyes landing on him like a falcon alighting on the wrist.

Those eyes widened very slightly. The teacup in her hand arrested midway to her mouth. For Lady Cheetham, this was a vivid physical betrayal of surprise.

"—reaction would show a human *soul*. It's *unfeeling,* it is," the other woman in the room was saying. Not a voice Jack recognised. A village accent, climbing with annoyance.

"I quite understand," said Jack's mother, soothing.

"*How* can you . . ." The woman stood abruptly. Now Jack could see her better: a woman perhaps a handful of years older than himself, slim and pretty and fair, dressed plainly. "I—oh, *curse you with rot.*"

To Jack's astonishment, she cradled a spell—faint, murky green—and flung it onto the table, where a tea service was laid.

A dainty cake stand held a profusion of sandwiches, every one of which went an unpleasant blue-white as the spell coated the food with mould.

A surprised silence hung in the air. Into it the fair woman made a choked, aghast noise. "Your ladyship—" she said, and burst right into tears.

Jack contemplated sidling back out of the room.

His mother stood as well. She said, quite kindly, "Let's try again next week, shall we, Margaret?"

Margaret hiccuped and gave a lurching nod-curtsy, then fled for the door where Jack stood. Her red, tearstained face was covered with her hands. She didn't seem to register his existence as she exited.

Lady Cheetham sighed and turned the cake stand to inspect it. She cradled a general reversal. Food was a beast to manipulate with magic beyond heat and cold; Jack wasn't surprised when half of the mould clung stubbornly despite the spell, along with a general unappetising shrivelling of everything. His mother sighed again, cradled a Server's Bell, and touched her fingertips to the nearest pane of glass. The peal of a real bell sounded deep in the house.

Only then did she look her son frankly in the face.

"Well, Jack, my dear," she said, "you do have impeccable timing."

Jack crossed the room and kissed her cheek. It trembled only a little. "Polly."

Her hair had greyed young and was now, in her sixties, almost entirely white. Her well-lined face was illuminated with pure emotion as she held his gaze. Mary Bastoke, now Mary Alston, Countess of Cheetham, known to her loved ones as Polly. Never beautiful, but always vibrant, as if born with an invisible guidelight burning inside.

"Who was that?" asked Jack.

"That was Margaret Oliver. The poor thing does have a temper. I wanted to ask how her Freddy is getting on in London—he writes to her, you know. Ah, Millie. Do have someone gather this up for the pigs—it's not fit for the downstairs table, I'm afraid. And Lord Hawthorn will be accompanying me on my morning walk."

The maid's wide eyes fixed on Jack. He resisted the urge to bare his teeth and growl.

"Yes, my lady."

Braced at every moment for questions, Jack followed his mother through a side door of the conservatory and to the stone-floored hallway that led out to the old gamekeeper's pantry. A line of wooden pegs held a floppy, wide-brimmed hat and a sturdy apron, which his mother donned in silence. She swapped her house shoes for a pair of Wellington-style rubber boots.

Jack lost the battle with his own question.

"He writes to her, does he?"

His mother looked at him. A smile played around the corner of her mouth, though no guilt at all. "One letter, Jack. *One letter,* after all this time. You hadn't let me do anything for you for years, and I suddenly had the chance to do you a favour with my reply."

"Send me a valet who'd report back to you?"

She unlatched the heavy wooden door. Sunlight spilled across the stones. Jack raised a hand to shade his eyes.

"Write me more letters yourself, and I won't have to rely on Freddy Oliver's to *his* mother for news of you."

"I'm not angry you sent me a spy." Jack waited until they were halfway across the ivy-wreathed courtyard, which even in this heat smelled of the pond tucked in the corner, before he added: "I am a little angry you decided to send me a brother."

In front of him, his mother's back halted. She took a moment before turning.

"Ah." She sounded close to laughter. "Is that why you're here?"

Jack nodded. He didn't mention the pointed prod from Lord Cheetham during the visit to Westminster. It had tipped the balance, but he'd been considering it before then.

The blue eyes he'd inherited regarded him thoughtfully, hungrily, from within his mother's face. Other long-absent sons might have returned to angry shouts, or hysterical tears and embraces, or cold, punishing courtesy.

"How did you know?"

"He's the spit of Father's old portrait in the ballroom," said Jack. "And that red hair. Just like Aunt Hetty and Christopher. He's seventeen? It must have been—before."

Before the secret-bind. Before Elsie died and the Hall's land turned.

"Leo told me just before the boy was born." Polly tucked her skirt higher as they stepped off the courtyard's paving stones and onto a trodden-flat dirt path that began to slope down. They were doing the *proper* walk, then. Her voice was fond. "He's always had a robust conscience."

"Oliver himself doesn't know."

It wasn't a question. Either Freddy Oliver had no clue he'd been fathered by Frederick Leonard Charles Alston, Earl of Cheetham, or he was wasted as a valet and should be on the stage.

"No, he doesn't. Margaret changed her mind about telling him, once he was happy in service. She's still waiting for the other shoe to drop, I believe—always thinking I'll whisk her off to some dungeon out of jealous pique. She's a nice girl, despite the temper. Superb nurse, Dr. Jenkins says."

"Powerful, too." Jack stepped around a series of puddles that muddied the path in a shadowy, insect-dense little wilderness; his mother, in her boots, tromped straight through. "That spell of rot. No wonder Oliver's as strong as he is."

"Too strong for the education he had," said his mother bluntly. "I'd have stepped in sooner, if I'd realised. He needs someone to teach him control."

"Yes," Jack said dryly. "I have realised that." He remembered being that age, brimming with magic freshly come to its full strength, taking all his lessons and practice to keep it leashed to his will. Again he felt compelled to point out: "I hired a magical valet, Polly. I didn't take on responsibility for *teaching* magic to a half brother."

That got him an unimpressed look over her shoulder. Jack's heart, like an unoiled piece of clockwork, gave a grudging tick of love for his astoundingly pragmatic mother. She hadn't kept on trying to change Jack's mind when he abandoned magical society. She knew it would only push him further away. She'd simply left the door open.

In his more cynical moments over the years, Jack had tried to convince himself that he'd burned all the responsibility out of himself along with the instinctual actions of magic. That the ashes of it had been dumped somewhere in the dry veldt of the Boer, in that chill morning before he was transported back to England.

It wasn't true. Even at the time, he'd known it. Jack had hated everything about the war except for the men who surrounded him, and you couldn't shed responsibility in a place like that. It clung. It found the chambers of the heart and made a gritty home, which had been left vacant for years and then been all too willing—apparently—to welcome Maud Blyth and Violet Debenham.

And his mother had enough faith in him, after all this time, that she'd responded to his first step back through that door by immediately sending him someone else to look after. He didn't know how to feel about that.

The walk took over an hour. It took them to various corners of the estate, where Lady Cheetham murmured about things that she must get the gardeners to keep an eye on, and pointed out recent changes as if giving a tour. Jack had to steel himself for the climb to the Lady's Oak. But when they stood shielded from the high sun by branches, breathing in a gust of grass-smelling air, he felt . . . looser. When he touched the tree's bark he remembered Elsie screaming, yes, but also the years before that.

He didn't speak until they descended the other side of the hill. Then he said, "What's happening here?"

Laid out below and to the right was the lake. There was an enormous new hump of earth on the northern edge of the water, a slope leading up to a flat terrace with an edge of white balustrade and white pots. You could stand there and look down to the water. Beneath it, a sort of stone grotto was being shaped out, with the lake's edge lapping at its base.

"We're hosting the equinox gala."

"That's this year?"

"Yes—next month."

The triennial gathering marked the close of a term of the Magical Assembly, before the election to determine its members heading into the next three years. Traditionally it was a time for last-minute discussions of who would be seconding whose nomination, and handshakes over the punch bowl. It was also the grandest and oldest event in magical society's calendar. Cheetham Hall had last hosted it when Jack's great-grandfather was alive.

Jack looked at the white pots. Empty, but one almost expected orange trees. "Very Mediterranean."

Lady Cheetham smiled, tipping back the brim of her hat to follow his gaze. "It seemed a good excuse to do something special, and we can't fit everyone in the ballroom. So we're landscaping. Leo asked George if he'd—"

"*No.*" It came out before Jack could stop it, and the bind on his tongue sensed the edges of its secret. Pain flooded his mouth and he coughed into the back of his hand.

"Jack? Is everything all right?"

Jack pressed his lips shut until he could be sure that the bind wouldn't show when he talked.

"Fine," he said then. "Leo asked George . . . ?"

"To help," she said slowly. "As it was his suggestion for us to host in the first place. But there's some sort of brewing trouble at the Barrel, so he sent his apologies and a handful of junior Coopers that Reeves—he's head gardener now—could bully for a few days until the main work of the earth-shifting was done. Our own men will take care of the rest."

The Coopers were a kind of police force, a tool which magical society could turn upon itself, and George Bastoke had taken firm control of them several years ago. He'd shown no compunction in using them to advance his own ends in pursuit of the Last Contract. Violet had killed one of them, the ambitious and unpleasant Arthur Chapman, aboard the *Lyric*.

So Cheetham hosting the gala had been George's suggestion. Jack stared at the sprawl of inviting lawn and imagined it full. Hundreds of magicians all in one place. Perfect for ceremony.

And very tempting, if you intended to use the Last Contract to draw on the magic of every British magician and knew that proximity could make a difference. George might be working to a deadline. Was it making his hunt more urgent, explaining the attempted break-ins at Spinet House? Or was there some reason he felt confident in his ability to get his hands on the contract pieces by that date?

Next month.

"Jack, are you sure you're—"

"I'm fine." He began to walk back to the house. He was not fine. A rope of anger held him upright. How *dare* George come back to this place. Jack would tear him to pieces. He would hurl him into the lake and drown him.

He would—do nothing, because George Bastoke was a magician. And he was not.

If he talked in careful circles around the bind's constraints, his parents *might* agree to cancel the gala. Even at this damningly short notice. Even with the damage it would do their standing in society. Even on no satisfactory explanation at all.

And then what? A new location for the gala, one where Jack could exert no control? This place wasn't George's to exploit and gloat over. It had been Jack's home once, and he was sworn to it. That might be enough.

They finished the walk at the side of the house. The path they were treading ended at a latched gate set within a new stone wall.

Jack stopped entirely. He was a solid root-knot of denial, with that creeping feeling writhing over his legs again. It would have taken the magic of three magicians to force him through that gate.

His mother drew up beside him. For a hot moment he wanted to strike her simply for being there. Then he wanted to bury his face in her shoulder. She reached out, touched his cheek, and then took her iron self-possession back within herself.

"It's still part of the land, Jack. We owe it recognition. But I'll understand if you wish to go straight on inside. Are you—will you stay for lunch?"

Jack nodded. He looked past her at the wall that enclosed—not a large scrap of land, really, tucked beneath the sheer drop from the Hall's highest rooftop. His tongue cramped in his mouth. He felt young and desolate, ripped in half, even here on the threshold.

He said, "Doesn't it hurt?"

"Yes," said Elsie Alston's mother.

She went through the gate and closed it behind her.

7

Alan presented himself at Spinet House at the directed hour. He was ushered into a room that contained a lot of books, plush furniture, and three large musical instruments set on stands, all of them shaped like a violin but varying wildly in size. The fairy tale about the three bears and the little trespassing girl sprang instantly to mind.

Lord Hawthorn was not present. The room contained Edwin Courcey—who was frowning at the nearest bookshelf as if finding it wanting—and Misses Debenham and Blyth. The latter was pinning a pink hat atop her head.

"Come, you're one of us now," she said to Alan after his greeting. "No more of this Miss B nonsense. Call me Maud."

Alan didn't want to lean into intimacy with these people. Neither did he want to offend them. This was an easy way to please her.

"Alan."

"Good! Now you and Violet and Edwin can be friendly and get on with things, and tell me all about it over lunch."

"You're not staying?"

"No, I'm off to see Helen—Bernard, you remember? Her father had the menagerie? The family's in town. And I'd only be in the way with whatever experiments you're doing. We've already established there are no ghosts anywhere in this place."

"You are abandoning me," said Miss Debenham. Violet. "With Edwin and his books."

"Your books," said Maud and Courcey in unison, and exchanged an amused look. "Besides," added Maud, "now you have Alan to protect you, if you insist on being a delicate maiden about it."

Violet made an outraged face and swatted at Maud's arm; Maud dodged and came up close, clearly going in for a kiss. Now it was Violet's turn to dodge. She kept Maud at arm's length and looked at Alan.

The urge danced into Alan's mouth to ask her whether he emitted the aura of someone who was likely to disapprove, and if so, could he blame the Catholicism? And also, did she and Maud really think they'd managed to behave on that ship like two people who *weren't* fucking?

Maud saved him before either question leapt free.

"Oh, fiddle," she said with warmth, and pulled Violet's hand to her mouth to drop a pointed kiss on it. "He was such a good sport on the *Lyric*, and we've already trusted him with the secret of magic *and* the Last Contract. I think we can trust him with this."

That easy assertion slid between Alan's ribs.

"If you say so, O General," said Violet. A delighted shriek came from Maud as Violet grabbed Maud by the waist and dipped her, then leaned down for a closemouthed kiss that belonged more to the theatre than real life. Maud laughed into it, and kept laughing when she was set back onto her feet.

Alan smiled. He felt at home among couples like this, who had nothing quiet or sedate about the way they loved.

Speaking of which.

"If you were wondering," Alan said, looking at a point just past Edwin Courcey's shoulder, "you and Sir Robert don't have to be subtle around me either."

It was a pause filled with the wariness of half-wild creatures. Alan had to move his gaze in the end simply to know if Courcey was looking at him or not.

"I don't think anyone's ever described Robin as subtle before," Courcey said. "He'll enjoy the novelty."

Maud departed, and Violet perched herself on the arm of an

overstuffed chair. "Sorry," she said. "I love Maud, but she does rather bully you into intimacy once she's decided you're *hers*. You don't have to be on first-name terms with us if you don't wish it."

Alan hesitated, considering the retreat thus offered, but it was too late now. He would just have to hold it firmly in his *own* mind that he was not their friend, merely the hired help. At least it would be easier to remember that in the absence of Maud, whose irrepressible likability slid under one's guard.

"After the *Lyric*, there's no point standing on ceremony," he said. "I'm fine with it if you are."

Violet gave a small smile and nodded. After a moment, Courcey—Edwin—did as well.

"So," said Alan. Nonna Sofia's rosary was in his pocket, but he liked to gather information before he revealed any. "I'm here. Talk me through the business."

Edwin, clearly one of nature's explainers, did so.

Of the three items that comprised the Last Contract, they had the cup—yes, Alan vividly remembered a lot of haring around an ocean liner after a parrot's water bowl—and the other side had the coin. It was at least theoretically possible to triangulate the position of one of these items through magic, as that was how the coin had been located in the first place, although Edwin didn't know how to do that. (His narrow face pulled into an expression that conveyed his dislike of *not knowing*.) His hope was that having two of the three would make things simpler.

"Things want to be complete," he said. "It's a law, of sorts, in magic. Broken items want to be whole. Sets want to be together. And the coin, cup, and knife were stored together for most of their existence. They were only separated by the Forsythia Club a handful of decades ago."

Alan nodded. He'd been present when the ghost of Mrs. Navenby, the third member of the Forsythia Club to die, had told the story of how she and her friends first discovered and then re-hid the three items.

"So, what's your plan?" he asked. "The other side wants to use it for power, and you don't, but—what *do* you want? Can you melt the things down, at least?"

"We can't *destroy* the Last Contract," said Edwin, looking aghast. "It'd take a vast amount of magic, and in any case—it'd be breaking the contract itself. No magic for anyone."

"We want a better hiding place," said Violet. "Ideally somewhere that nobody can ever get at again, not even us."

"Oh? Found one of those, have you?"

"No," said Edwin. "I have hopes of making them unusable, somehow. Preserving the contract itself, which is vital for the continuation of magic, but making it—less tangible. Perhaps it can be transferred. Or perhaps the need for anchoring silver was part of the working. I don't know enough. And I'll work on it for as long as it takes, but a new hiding place would at least keep the contract from being exploited out of greed in the meantime."

"Seems like the knife is well hidden already," Alan pointed out. "Can't it stay there, wherever it is?"

"That'd work if Bastoke and his friends didn't *know* that Lady Enid had it," said Violet. "If someone's going to pull Spinet apart in the search, it should be me." She smoothed a hand over a chair. "At least I care enough to do it gently."

"Right," said Alan. "That's why I'm here."

Edwin beckoned him over to the desk, which was a sturdy masterpiece of carpentry. The edges undulated and swept into curlicues at the corners, with engraved ferny leaves bordering the dark leather surface. The wood's warm, glossy polish made it look barely used. Something to be looked at. Something that sang of wealth.

Spread out atop it were sheets of drafting paper covered in lines and figures.

"Plans of the house?" asked Alan.

"Of a sort," said Edwin. "I'm no architect. We'd hoped the original designs might be in James Taverner's files, but we can't find them. I made these with a sympathy spell."

"Like how Maud found the silver on the *Lyric*," said Violet.

Bright lines cast on the wall; Alan remembered that too. "But Spinet's fussier than an ocean liner."

"That's one word for it," muttered Edwin. "The plans make even less sense than the house. The sympathy did the best it could, but . . . there are no passageways drawn where we know there are some. Two rooms overlaid on the same spot. Rooms that seem to be missing entirely." He tapped the nearest piece of paper. "The missing bits are the most promising, if we're looking for hiding places for the knife."

"Most of the house's magic has to do with *access*," said Violet. "A lot of doors and rooms won't open, or show you their full contents, unless you meet the right conditions. Or sing the right tune." Rueful. "The staff know a lot, they've helped us fill things in, but much of Spinet was built expressly for Mr. and Mrs. Taverner. The last time I was here myself, I was sixteen. It seemed so different when Lady Enid lived here. And she knew all the tricks. There was a room you could stand in and whisper, and another room where someone could hear everything you said, clear as day."

"And for all we know they might be different rooms, by now," Edwin said. "Violet, I still think the orrery—"

Alan cleared his throat. He didn't have all day, even if they did; he had a deadline to meet this afternoon and would already have to write faster than usual. But all the throat-clearing accomplished was to invite himself into what was clearly a well-worn dynamic. Violet turned a look of playful exasperation onto him.

"Edwin here hates anything that doesn't make logical sense."

"I own a magical house, Violet," snapped Edwin. "I *know* their magic works by different rules. Sometimes no rules at all. By emotions."

"Emotions! The enemy," stage-whispered Violet.

Edwin had his hands splayed over the diagrams. His nail beds were pale, as if even this non-argument was the equivalent of someone throwing furniture around and raging. But he looked at Alan and said, in a level, tutorly voice, "The magic of

those old estates and lands—it's like a different language. But the
Taverners *made* this house, only half a century ago, and they
put all the magic in themselves. Most of what we've unearthed
so far does have a logic to it. Not that it helps, necessarily."

Violet said, "It's like being invited to play cards at a table
where everyone else knows the rules and you have to work
them out as you go. But *you* . . . if magic really has less effect on
you . . ."

"You want me to be a cheat's mirror," said Alan. "Let you see
some of the cards, so you aren't fleeced while you're learning the
rules."

"Exactly," said Violet.

It made sense. Alan had been trying to let all this detail glide
over him, alert only for anything that he needed to tuck away
for later, but he was interested despite himself. And wary all
over again. He wondered what a magical house thought of a perturbator who was about to be used to pry into its secrets.

"And the stakes aren't low," said Violet, as if following his wor-
ries. She nodded to a wall of the parlour that backed onto the garden. "We tried to fold that wall out into a balcony, because there's
a painting in the master bedroom which shows it. Edwin did an
opening-spell and it slid half the floorboards apart instead. He
nearly broke his neck when it dumped him in the cellar."

"I'm almost certain the cello and the double bass are key,"
said Edwin. "I don't suppose you play anything that comes with
a bow?"

"Sorry," said Alan. "Didn't have time for music lessons, what
with all the fencing and elocution and watercolour painting."

Edwin blinked.

Violet grinned. "Maud and I are both respectable on the piano, but there's not a fiddler amongst us. I know musicians and
Edwin knows magicians, but we don't want to drag anyone into
this business who isn't involved already."

And here Alan was. Involved. He pulled the rosary from his
pocket and told them what his ma had said about the family dev-

ils and the use of the rosary to banish them. Edwin's eyes went wide, then narrowed in furious thought, and he pulled out a pen that began taking notes on its own while he fired questions at Alan about his childhood, any magic he might have accidentally used, and how it felt to handle the rosary. The answer to most of which was "I don't remember."

Edwin paused awkwardly, halfway to taking the rosary from Alan's hands, as if hearing a voice reminding him to be polite. "May I?"

"What?" Alan was staring at the moving pen. Perhaps he could ask for one of those as part of his fee. But it was only taking dictation; the act of forming words with his hand was part of how Alan slowed his thoughts enough to arrange them into meaningful sentences. A neat thing, though. "Oh. Here."

Edwin put the rosary on the desk, then gave Alan a hopeful look that was almost a smile.

"Now, *this*," he said, "is a beautiful bit of magic."

He pulled from his pocket a loop of twine and a solid beeswax disc the size of an egg, with the honeycomb pattern intact, set in a circular frame of pale wood.

"Violet, do you know where I put Mrs. Sutton's wood monograph?"

"I never know where you put anything," said Violet, but she began to sort through a stack of books.

Edwin cradled the string about his fingers until all his fingertips glowed dark blue. Ink-stained like Alan's own. He touched first the wax and then his hovering pen, and the blue magic disappeared at once. Dropping the string, he touched the cross of the rosary to the centre of the wax for a few seconds. Then he carefully isolated two of the smaller beads and touched those to the wax in turn.

Alan waited for something dramatic to happen to his family heirloom. Nothing did.

Edwin gave an impatient twitch and picked up the paper on which the pen had, Alan realised, been writing. The words

BEECH and *ROWAN* were there in a thick hand with Germanic flourishes to the letters.

"It . . . knows the wood?" Alan said. "How?"

It seemed a pointless question the moment it left his mouth—how did *any* of this work? Surely the answer was just going to be *magic.* But Edwin gave an approving nod that reminded Alan of Mr. Voight at the charity school, who would load Alan up with books every week and only wince a little when they came back smudged with ashes or with the pages torn.

"It's a Holzprobierer. A wood-taster. It's German-made, so Taverner must have found someone to layer a specific translation-spell over it." Edwin set it on the desk and the pen wrote *WALNUT.*

"Here's your monograph," said Violet, handing over a small booklet not much larger than Alan's Roman pamphlets.

"Rowan. Rowan. I don't think we've seen it anywhere in Spinet." Edwin flipped to the back of the book, and then began to leaf through more slowly.

"Flora Sutton exchanged a lot of letters with the Taverners," said Violet to Alan. "She specialised in living plants; they specialised in what you could do with the wood. They learned a lot from each other. And Mrs. Sutton organised it and wrote it down."

"Here," said Edwin. "Only one entry for rowan wood. *A warding against magic. See: all the old tales.* Hm. Usually she gives more detail than that."

"So it's turned Alan here into a sort of walking ward?" said Violet.

"Beech is a common magical concentrator. This frame is beech." He touched the wood-taster, then ran the rosary through his fingers. "More magic and less magic. It seems rather pointless to use the two of them together. I'll have to do some reading."

A sudden hot sting of sensation struck Alan's upper arm. He flinched and slapped at it as if a wasp might have snuck into the room.

"Ow," said Violet mildly. She sucked the tip of her thumb.

"It's not just a ward, if it can turn magic back around on the caster like that."

"And you keep telling *me* not to treat people as experimental apparatus," said Edwin. But he was so obviously itching to give it a go himself that Alan, with a show of long suffering, stretched his arms out palm-forward. Edwin said, "Tell me *exactly* what it feels like," and picked up his string. This one was a pale green spell that sent a sensation of icy water flooding over Alan's body, which came out in immediate goose bumps. He shook himself, feeling unpleasantly like a dog emerging from a winter pond.

"Bloody *cold*. Is what that feels like."

"That didn't rebound on me." Edwin frowned. "What did you do differently?"

"I'm not *doing* anything," said Alan through his teeth. "How is this helping to find hiding places in the house?"

Edwin sighed and looked at Violet. "Let's try him on something where we know the effect already."

To Alan's relief, this involved neither cold nor stinging. They took him to a corridor on the third floor of the house, via a staircase with further elaborate carving adorning its railing. The corridor held three pairs of closed doors along the lengths of its walls and ended in a window.

Violet nodded down the corridor. "What do you see through the window?"

"Sky," said Alan blankly. "Clouds—wait. Is it . . ." Something about that window made him queasy, as if it were suspended on a string and swinging slowly towards him and away. The longer he looked at it, the more the corridor seemed indecisive about its own length.

He squinted one eye shut, then the other. He took a few steps down the corridor. The cloud-fractured sky began to take on brownish hues, and the window frame itself blurred.

Three more steps and the window was a ghostly mirage. Beyond it Alan could clearly see several more feet of floorboards, ending in a panelled wall with a framed portrait and a low wooden plinth, atop which stood a curious carved contraption like a globe made of rings. Tucked at the corridor's end was a side opening to a poky narrow staircase, leading down.

"The picture frame is maple wood, projecting an illusion," said Edwin. He and Violet strode through the illusion too, though Edwin shut his eyes in order to do so.

Alan dutifully described the way the illusion had fallen apart as he neared it—"But I still didn't *feel* anything. What's it meant to hide? The staircase, or this?" He knelt to look more closely at the ringed globe. It was the size of a football, made of intricate wooden rings all set at angles to one another, marked with notches and small symbols, set on a solid round base. Around the base were engraved lines of writing.

"Both," said Violet.

She moved a lever and the interlocking rings began to rotate. A simple tune rose into the air, as if somewhere at the centre was an unseen instrument with a hollow voice.

"I like that," said Alan. A stab of unfairness hit him. If things had been different, would magic have been his birthright, *his* world? Instead he was a walking ward. Something that couldn't help but turn magic away. Make it lesser.

Unfairness was part of the world's fabric. Alan was used to it. It still made him angry every time.

"It's an orrery," said Edwin. "The music-box portion was broken, but we had Hettie Carroll around to look at it, and it was only that the gears needed cleaning."

The melody swelled louder. Violet sang along. Her voice, strong and tuneful, seemed to fill the hollow at the heart of the orrery's sound. And what she was singing, Alan realised, were the words written around the base.

"*—nature burning bright as stars, to pay the dusk its due.*"

Through the music came the sound of wood sliding against itself in a smooth groove. Alan stood and looked at the narrow, illusion-hidden staircase, which was now more inviting, somehow. Wider. Better lit.

"Come on," said Violet, breaking off her song. "Now we know you work, we can start trying you out on things."

"One canary, ready for service."

The orrery kept playing behind them as they walked down the staircase. The song had the hummable simplicity of nursery rhymes. Alan would probably wake up tomorrow with it repeating in his skull.

He was tensed for any sort of magical nonsense—nobody ever *told* the canary what was going to happen in the mine—but the staircase was well behaved. It led down in a spiral, lit along the way by balls of glowing light set in the wall like lamps. After a few turns it unwound itself and they walked along an enclosed corridor that ended in yet another door. This one had no handle.

Violet cradled a spell, which came alive as visible lines of gold string in her hand. She rolled the spell into a brassy ball and then reached out to the door. The spell slid free and became a doorknob, and Violet twisted it and led them into what she called the spinet room.

It was a room of more doors.

It was small, octagonal, and with no windows; only five more knobless doors in addition to the one they'd passed through, all of different-coloured woods. The room was lit by several standing lamps of plain glass giving off the same too-clean glow as the magic in the staircase.

In the centre of the whole stood the spinet. Or so Alan assumed. It looked like a glossy brown piano that had met with an accident of geometry and turned into an off-centre triangle. The open lid gave it the unfortunate silhouette of a coffin. The keys were black, the panel just above them done in a pretty mosaic of paler and darker woods.

Edwin looked with barely contained eagerness from the spinet to Alan, to the doors, and then back to Alan, who swallowed a laugh.

"Go on then. If you don't tell me everything about the wood, I suppose you'll explode."

A pause. Perhaps he'd misstepped. In his household that would barely count as a friendly hello, let alone a proper dig at someone, but Edwin Courcey was . . . touchy.

But Edwin's face creased in something that was close to a smile. "You're right, there's no point going into detail. This is mostly a way station, in any case. It's the only way we've found down into a double set of bedrooms that we're having trouble with. But all of the woods here do have a magical property." He pointed at one of the doors, a beautiful reddish shade. "That one's jarrah. It's so hard and durable they use it for paving roads, but it also *sustains* the effect of a spell." He pointed out the other doors briefly: the one they'd walked through was mahogany, and the others were cedar, fir, ebony, and Brazilian rosewood.

"And that one?" Alan nodded at the dull brown door on the other side of the room, which Edwin hadn't bothered to introduce.

"The spinet? It's mostly cherry, but the sounding board is spruce—"

"No, the seventh door."

"There isn't a seventh door," said Violet, but Edwin's face was already transforming. This time his hand got all the way to grabbing Alan's arm before he remembered his manners and snatched it back.

"You can see another one?"

Alan gazed steadily at the door. It didn't waver or shift like the illusion had. It was inarguably there. And inarguably a door. "Yes?"

Edwin stared just as hard. His head twitched in surprise. "I had it for a moment. Violet?"

Violet pulled out the stool before the spinet and sat. She trailed her fingers down the span of the keys without pressing down. "That's it," she said, to nobody in particular, and then looked right at the same place. She winced. "Oh. Yes. It's like trying to look at a light that's too bright, but I've got it now I know it's there."

"Keep the house calm. I'm going to try to stabilise it."

Out came his string. Edwin tried two or three quick spells, none of which made much difference to Violet's squinting or his own frustrated head-jerks. Finally he built a slow, complicated pattern of string that pushed blue light around his hands like eddying water. He walked carefully towards the troublesome door and Alan went too, curious to see what he'd do.

They were within two yards of it when deep dread began to collect in Alan's body. He remembered Violet at the first breakfast saying *it's not safe work,* and now he *believed* it. Only the acute awareness that he needed to remain useful to these magicians stopped him from bolting right back through the mahogany door. But Edwin had stopped as well.

"And there's a warding on it," Edwin said acerbically. "Wonderful."

He took a deep breath and blew across his cradle, and the blue magic danced out like mist under a wind, spreading over the door and then vanishing.

The door looked no different to Alan. The dread was still there. But Edwin made a sound of satisfaction and his gaze sharpened. "I'll need to look at the charts, but I'd swear there isn't *space* behind there," he said. "A door to nowhere."

"That's where I'd hide things," agreed Violet. She left the spinet and came up next to Alan, then grimaced as the dread-feeling—the warding—clearly got her as well.

First Edwin and then Violet tried some more spells to see if they could get rid of the warding. Alan retreated to sit at the spinet and let them do it.

"This is getting us nowhere. Give Alan the wax thing," said Violet after a while. "Knowing the wood always helps, and he might have a chance of getting close."

"*Holzprobierer,*" muttered Edwin, but he pulled it from his pocket and handed it over to Alan without hesitation. He also had the charmed pen and a small notebook. "All you need is to get the wax in contact with the wood. I don't know how you're doing whatever you do, but . . . visualisation helps most magic.

Try to picture a shield in front of you, perhaps? Something to keep the wrongness at bay."

A shield. Alan's free hand made a fist as he approached the door.

He'd pushed through bad feelings before. Gnawing, exhausting worry. Hunger that wore away at him like the story about the bird sharpening its beak on a mountaintop. Today alone he had healthy doses of fear, anger, and guilt all on the boil, bubbling away beneath the curiosity.

He could live through this too. It was only a feeling. Only magic playing a trick.

Thinking of a shield doubled the effort it took to keep moving in the direction of the door, like trying to walk into a gale with an umbrella held out in front. Alan gritted his teeth and managed another meagre foot. Push, *push*.

The eddying blue of Edwin's spell came into his mind, and the green ice-water spell from earlier. Water in gutters built up behind a blockage, but you could release it in trickles and rob it of its force.

Feeling an absolute fool, Alan closed the imaginary umbrella. He stopped imagining a blunt protective surface and instead let things—*flow*. The wrongness surged closer, trying to drive him back, but Alan refused to be forced into anything. He was stubborn and a thief and he *would* go where he wasn't wanted.

He took two staggering steps forward, arm outstretched, and the Holzprobierer touched wood.

Edwin might have said something. Alan couldn't make out the words. A surge of energy came down his arm and he couldn't direct it, couldn't manage the flow, couldn't do anything. His skull screamed pressure like a painfully overstuffed cushion. His next breath was a terrible warning that there wasn't enough room in him for air as well.

He fell back hard onto the ground, whacking his elbow against the floorboards. His hand fizzed. His vision was dim and dull. Jesus *Christ*, his head hurt.

The blue-clad blur of Violet reached him first and touched his shoulder. Some of the pressure lessened at once, with a sense of blissful relief, as if she were siphoning it off.

She gasped and snatched her hand back. Alan wanted to grab for her again, siphon off *more,* but couldn't persuade his limbs to cooperate.

"What is it?" said Edwin.

"I don't know. He's giving off something. It's like magic, but I can't use it."

Alan could breathe and see now. He was not surprised when Edwin approached with a set frown and reached out a determined hand to Alan's cheek. Edwin Courcey would probably emerge from an exploding building with the desire to see if he could make it happen again.

Sure enough: another gasp. Edwin's fingers shook with effort, and he held it longer than Violet, then he too withdrew.

"How do you feel?" he asked Alan.

Scientific concern was better than none at all. Alan managed to sit up. "It's . . . settling down," he said. "Ugh. I don't think this house is impressed with me." Not that he could blame it.

Edwin held up his notebook to show him the new-written word *OAK.*

"That explains why the warding's so powerful," Edwin said, even though no it fucking didn't.

"Do you have anything for a headache?" Alan asked.

Violet swept into hostess mode and told Edwin that they were done experimenting, at least until after some food. She offered Alan her arm for support, in a faintly hilarious display of chivalry, but he waved her off. There was only a lingering throb behind his eyes now. He could handle it.

The mundane magic of domestic service caused tea and muffins and cakes to appear in one of the parlours. The maid who brought it exchanged a few friendly words with Violet and met Alan's eyes curiously. Alan caught himself in an odd pang of disappointment, as if he'd wanted to catch Violet in the act of mistreating her staff.

He was looking for another reason to keep these people at

arm's length. Another *reminder*. He heard his accent shift toward Clerkenwell as he thanked the maid—another bloody inconvenience of spending time with toffs. He always had the urge to set himself apart, make it obvious he was part of the downstairs team, even though he wasn't. Not here. He was on no team but his own.

Alan had three heavily buttered muffins and a cup of sugared tea, into which Violet put a dash of something she claimed would help his head, while Edwin read about oak in Mrs. Sutton's monograph and theorised on what they could do next. Alan saw more unpleasant umbrella-shoving in his future. That oak door was certainly keeping *something* hidden.

"Could I take some of these for my sister's kids?" he asked Violet, of some golden cakes that smelled of lemon. "They never get sweets this good."

"Of course!" Violet even called the maid back to put together a *basket*, which made Alan's skin itch with the violent familiarity of receiving charity. Well, he'd already shoved his pride and his shame down enough to be here in the first place. Spinet House had bruised him for prying. He'd take today's hazard pay in the form of sweets for Emily and Tom.

Edwin's rambling, which had taken on the absent tones of someone working things out on his own with no need for external contribution, was interrupted by melodically chiming bells, followed by the arrival of Sir Robert and Miss Morrissey. This time Alan knew where they were coming from; Violet had explained that when Spinet was being built, the nearby Underground station of Bayswater was also under construction. Magicians could make all sorts of things happen in secret. Including a tunnel running between a side corridor of the station and Spinet's cellar, with both ends magically disguised and warded.

"Oh, *cake*," said Miss Morrissey, descending upon the tray. She lit up at the first taste of lemon cake in much the same way that Edwin had when Sir Robert entered the room.

"Robin," Edwin said. "Have I forgotten a meeting?"

"No, no. But the Office received a letter that we want your eyes on, sooner rather than later, and—I had a vision."

Edwin's mouth went worried, which seemed odd. Having visions was what Sir Robert *did*, as far as Alan knew.

"When?"

"Perhaps two hours ago, before the briefing with Knox." Sir Robert settled himself next to Edwin and reached for a muffin. To Alan he said, "I don't know if anyone's told you this part, but I'm under blood-oath to report my visions to the Assembly, in exchange for Walter Courcey leaving myself and my household alone. When I'm having plenty of them, I can be selective. But I hadn't had one for a while, so when this one hit, it was the only one I *could* tell them about."

"What was it?" asked Edwin.

Hesitation didn't sit well on Sir Robert's affable face. He glanced around the room. "I was hoping Maudie would be here. It was her. She was standing in a graveyard, looking down at a grave."

Edwin made a small movement as if stopping himself from reaching out. He and Sir Robert exchanged a look dense with uneasy emotion. Alan felt uncomfortable all over again. He was an interloper in whatever was happening here.

Violet set her teacup in her saucer with a deliberate noise. "What was Maud wearing?"

"Pardon?" Sir Robert tore his eyes away from Edwin. "Er—a coat. The pale blue one. And her blue-and-white hat."

"Not in mourning, then," said Violet.

Sir Robert's posture relaxed and he remembered the muffin in his hand. Now it was Violet and Miss Morrissey's turn to exchange a look.

Miss Morrissey said, "And I assume Knox didn't think to question you about something as frivolous as her clothes either, did he? Good. Let them assume the worst from it if they wish."

"You mentioned a letter," said Edwin. Sir Robert wiped butter from his fingers before opening his briefcase and pulling out a stamped and opened envelope, which he handed to Edwin.

At first glance of the handwriting Edwin made a fastidious face. "The Grimm?"

"I know. Read it," said Miss Morrissey.

"Aloud," said Violet pointedly.

Edwin did so.

You know really if you're given a gift the least you could do is Not be careless of it

More than half a century of peace since that last little snarl in the tapestry and now everything's MOVING again the paths are lying full like floods weak like drought You were supposed to be the Leaders and you're letting it all go to waste

But that's the least of it the dawn's borrowed gifts won't help past dusk you need your own stars for that and indeed all you can get with the Midnight that's coming I told you and the Song Told You and I'm telling you again

Years on years you've been losing sight of the stars in favour of looking down at your own hands well there's no point in a cradle with Nothing to put in it is there

                          yours the Grimm of Gloucester

P.S.

look I took My Own self My Own bones to that church in the North and if YOU don't know where the silver is now YOU have a problem we ALL have a problem or soon will

Edwin's voice changed on the word *church,* and his eyes were wide as he finished.

"Yes," said Sir Robert grimly. "Makes you think we should be paying attention to the rest of the nonsense, doesn't it? And you know I've no hope of deciphering it, but . . ."

Something of importance was happening and Alan had no bloody idea what. He *did* remember that the Forsythia Club had hidden the silver of the Last Contract in a church in North

Yorkshire—so, someone else knew about that? And was writing to say that they knew?

And—"Stars?" Alan said, looking at Violet.

"What?" said Edwin.

"You were singing something like that," said Alan. "Stars and dusk. The orrery."

Violet's eyes widened. "Yes. It's something like a nursery rhyme—any English magician knows it."

"Man's marvellous light," said Sir Robert. "Edwin, you said it was by—Dumas? Something?"

"Dufay," said Edwin in his teaching voice. "Alfred Dufay. *The song told you.* Blast, I hate riddles."

"No, you don't," murmured Sir Robert.

Edwin reached out without breaking his hungry perusal of the letter and flicked the back of Sir Robert's hand, winning himself a smile that he didn't notice.

"That postscript is the most sense the Grimm's ever made," Miss Morrissey said.

Edwin nodded. "And the timing . . . how . . . I can't believe I'm asking this, but has anyone in the Office ever tried to write *back*? Adelaide?"

"There's a return address, if we want to try."

"Or *visit*." Edwin looked almost as shaken as when Alan had revealed the seventh door. "How did we miss this? I should have been reading these letters all along."

"Sorry, but before we go down that rabbit hole—there's something else." Sir Robert had a second envelope in his hands, this one sealed with a round of purple wax, and he held it out to Violet. "It was in the liaison pigeonhole at the Barrel. Addy's been checking it daily. But it's addressed to you."

"Well, that's . . . making a statement," said Violet.

"Yes. I don't think there's any point pretending they don't know we're all equally involved in this," said Sir Robert.

Violet slid her finger beneath the sealed edge to open it. She made a startled sound as the purple wax melted abruptly, forming a dark trickle that wrapped up her finger like a vine and wriggled its way to the back of her hand. And then there was no wax at all, just an intricate bracelet that encircled Violet's wrist like a woven strand of purple leather. When she touched it, her fingers slid over her own skin. Not woven. Written. Inked, magically.

"Hell," said Violet. "More bloody runes."

The room was quiet and tense as her eyes flicked down the single typed page. Violet's face was set in one of her theatrical masks now, but her fingers tightened on the paper. She looked at the marks on her wrist, then up at Edwin, when she was done.

"It's a summons," she said. "To a hearing at the Barrel, to-morrow, about the details of Lady Enid's will. I assume the runes will provide a painful reminder if I fail to turn up."

"Let me see." Edwin took the letter and gave a sharp, empty laugh. "And it's signed by my brother Walt. Of course it is."

Miss Morrissey and Sir Robert both peered over Edwin's shoulder as he read. Miss Morrissey was the first to look up, worry creasing her brow.

"It's not just a hearing, Violet. We've been waiting for their next move in regards to getting inside Spinet, and this is it. It's a direct legal challenge to your inheritance."

There was a loud, splintering *crack* from the floor. Alan jerked. One of the floorboards had torn itself free and snapped in half.

"*No,*" snarled Violet, and her voice had splinters in it too.

8

Spinet House might agree with Jack that he was no longer a magician, but the Barrel seemed to be siding with Cheetham Hall on the matter. He walked over the threshold without feeling the warding or needing a pass-token for the unmagical like Robin did.

Jack hadn't been to the seat of the Magical Assembly since he was a boy. It hadn't altered from his memory. The lead-and-glass ceiling of the main foyer, over which people walked. The standing oak doors set in their frames, scattered across the marble floor, which could take you anywhere in the building.

It was coming up on noon. The foyer wasn't busy. Their small group—Robin, Edwin, Violet, and Jack himself—garnered curious looks from the attendants in the Barrel's blue livery.

Perhaps it was mostly Violet. Edwin had tried to encourage her to dress soberly, but Violet Debenham wasn't the sort of person to treat formality as armour. Quite the opposite. She was in full eccentric-heiress mode: her boots and skirt were both bright bottle-green, the skirt crawling with gold thread embroidery, and at least two ostriches were feeling colder in service of her ridiculous hat. She stood with her gloves clutched in her hand and an expression on her face that was obviously stolen from some character or other.

"Where's this fellow you've hired for me?" she asked Jack, who looked up at the clock on the far wall. The season-clock was a boxy thing of stained glass and ebony wood, with a little balcony halfway up the face. There were charmed wooden figures inside which would emerge and act out various scenes from magical history: a different one for every hour.

When Lord Cheetham had taken his twins to the Barrel to deliver the hair after their lock ceremony, a delighted Elsie had dashed across the floor and floated herself up the wall to investigate the clock before anyone could stop her. Jack remembered the minor uproar, his father's angry apologies, and the smugness on Elsie's face later that day as she triumphantly pulled a carved fox from her pocket to show him. Away from the clock, it never danced again, but she didn't care.

"I told him a quarter to the hour," Jack said. Violet nodded tightly and began unpinning her hat. Jack looked at Robin and Edwin, who were sitting close together on one of the benches. "You two come here all the time. Stop looking as though you're expecting snipers. Nothing will happen to you in the Barrel. It's neutral ground."

That was a truism hammered into the bones of British magicians. The Barrel was an absolute.

Robin, who was not a magician, gave Jack one of his stubborn Blyth looks. "I suppose *nothing* happened to Reggie Gatling. I suppose *nothing's* ever happened to anyone that these Coopers of yours take against."

"They're not—" Jack started, and noticed the trap too late.

"No," said Robin. "They're your cousin George's."

Jack didn't have grounds to argue. He'd tripped over a pothole and caught himself on an assumption. Lord Hawthorn, son of the Alston line, never felt unsafe anywhere in England; the Barrel least of all. But he did know how far the powers of the Coopers stretched. And he knew what had happened to Reggie Gatling, and knew how dangerous George and Morris and the rest of them could be, with or without the Assembly's support.

And when he let his thoughts rest properly against George Bastoke for more than the customary few seconds, instead of whipping them away again as if burned, he *did* feel something close to fear. It tasted like blood and char in his mouth.

It wasn't real. A secret-bind couldn't respond to thought alone. But bodies didn't always play by the rules.

A nearby door glowed bright around the bronze knob and opened to emit a broad-shouldered, freckled young man with limply curling fair hair. He wore the dark suit of most office workers, carried a briefcase in one hand and two thick books in the other, and looked apologetic as he extended a finger to pull the door shut behind him and then hurried over to them.

"Sorry, sorry, I'm late—are you Miss Debenham? And— *Robin?*"

Robin acquired a plank-whacked expression. He glanced at Edwin, then back at the new arrival. "Arthur?"

"How—what—" Arthur Manning, son of the Honourable Pete Manning, turned a telling shade of pink. "How the *devil* didn't I know you're a magician?"

"I'm not," said Robin. "Er. Long story." This time his glance to Edwin was rather desperate. "Edwin, Manning and I were at Cambridge together."

"Yes. Ah—how d'you do." It was addressed to Edwin, but Manning continued to stare at Robin as if the sun were rising and setting in his face. Jack had never in his life felt the slightest urge to fuck Robin Blyth, but it was enough to make him briefly wonder if he was missing out on something.

Edwin did not return Manning's greeting. His eyes narrowed.

"Your name is Arthur Manning? A. Manning? Did you write a thesis on visual illusions, a few years back?"

"Er . . ." Manning didn't seem confident in his eventual answer of: "Yes?"

The next few sentences began sensibly enough but soon spiralled off into a level of judgemental detail about cradling minutiae that was extreme even for Edwin. Robin began to open his mouth, then closed it again.

Manning was clutching his books to his chest as if they'd save him. Finally he managed to interrupt—"Stop! I—look, I *didn't* write it. It was my sister. Abigail. But you can't tell anyone. Our parents don't approve of her fiddling around with spells."

"Well," said Edwin sniffily, "you can tell her it's sloppily argued and lacking breadth."

"I'm sure it's a damn sight better than anything I'd be able to do!" Manning flared. "And it's not as if anyone gave her proper training!"

"Edwin," said Jack, "you're wasting time. Apologise."

This was the most amusing thing to happen in weeks: a jealous Edwin Courcey trying to wield secondhand academic cattiness against someone who'd fucked his partner. Normally Jack would have enjoyed the show and mocked Edwin about it afterwards. But they needed Manning. Antagonising him wouldn't help.

Edwin glared at Jack, but delivered a halfhearted apology that Manning accepted with relief.

"Lord Hawthorn. Pa sends his regards."

"How d'you do, Manning," said Jack. "Congratulations on your engagement are in order, I hear. This is Miss Violet Debenham. Violet, Manning here will be your dicentis."

"I'll do what I can. I don't want you to think I'm stuffed full of experience."

"As long as you don't tell me this is your very first day on the job, I'll take whatever help I can get," said Violet.

"Er. Third?"

"Third day?" said Edwin, who'd unwound a tad at the word *engagement*.

"Third time standing dicentis for anyone. So . . . yes?"

"He's not attached to the Assembly," said Jack. "There's no telling who they'd saddle Violet with otherwise, or even if they'd grant her a dicentis at all. I'm sure you'll do very well," he added to Manning, leaning pointedly into the words.

Manning swept another uncertain look around the group, but nodded. "We can use one of the preparatory offices. Follow me."

He set his briefcase and books down to cradle and then sketch a silver rune on the nearest door.

"Oak," murmured Edwin to Violet.

"*Runes*," she said in return.

Translatable enough. Jack was going to be called on to help with the next part of their Spinet investigation.

The rune glowed, and Manning opened the door and ushered them all into a modestly sized office on one of the building's highest floors, going by the view from the small window. They settled around a table.

Violet didn't have a copy of Lady Enid's will. She pulled out a letter from Lady Enid to herself, confirming the inheritance and telling her to do whatever she wished with it. It gave a sense of great personality in few lines.

"She signed it with her married name," said Manning. "Mrs. James Taverner. Was that usual for her? Do you have any of her other correspondence?"

"No," said Violet. "I suppose, if we searched the house . . . Why? Do you think someone might try to claim this is forged?"

"I've no clue," said Manning. "If what she says here about the wax and runes on the will is correct, it all seems rather airtight. And she specifically mentions the possibility that someone else might try to contest the will. Hm. One could make an argument either way, about that. It'd be a convenient thing to put in such a letter if you *did* forge it."

"I didn't!" Violet snapped.

"Or if you asked her to write it—and the will—under duress or coercion," said Manning. He shrank from Violet's increasingly stormy expression. "I'm not accusing you of anything. I'm trying to anticipate what this could be about. Magical inheritance is hard to argue with, but some aspects of unmagical law still come into play."

"He's right," said Edwin unexpectedly.

None of them had ever been called to a hearing at the Library before. Manning ran them hurriedly though the basic procedures. At a quarter past the hour, one of the Barrel attendants knocked on the door and told Violet that they were ready.

"I will be accompanied by my full legal team," said Violet haughtily.

Jack was half expecting himself, Robin, and Edwin to be denied entrance, but the attendant shrugged and ushered them all down the hall. They went through a normal set of doors, this time, wider and taller than those in the foyer.

The room was windowless and circular. It held a dais with a long bench, behind which three men sat, and two wide desks with a few chairs each, facing the dais. A courtroom configuration. Two men stood at the leftmost desk, heads bent over a folder.

The walls were pale yellow, lit by plentiful lights in glass keepers set in brackets, and the ceiling was the night sky. Not just painted either. Above their heads was a soft, inky darkness within which a single constellation shone huge and bright, taking up the whole of the space within the ring of walls.

"I was expecting books," said Violet. "I thought this place was called the Library."

"It is," said Manning and Edwin together. Edwin went on, "The constellation is Libra. Scales, for justice. The stars are called the Librae, and the name evolved over time."

"I hope we're not keeping you from anything more important," said Walter Courcey.

Edwin's head snapped around as if on a string.

Robin's fingertips went steadyingly to the small of Edwin's back. Violet only looked curious; she'd never met Walter. It had been a long time since Jack had. Time had ironically brought the Courcey brothers closer in appearance. Walter, one of the two men on the left, looked like a version of Edwin drawn in a more confident hand.

"Courcey," said Robin in absolutely neutral tones.

"Blyth." Walter smiled. "Not that the Assembly isn't always *delighted* to cast an eye over our pet foreseer, but I don't recall seeing your name on the summons. Nor yours, Win."

"Nor mine," said Jack, before Edwin could make the mistake of reacting. He prodded their group towards the empty desk. "And yet here we are. You seem to be in a hurry, Courcey. Why don't you move us on to business?"

Walter stepped away from the desk, taking up a position in the centre of the room, and gave a nod of respect to the men on the dais.

"Miss Violet Debenham," he said.

Violet lifted her hand as Manning had instructed. The bracelet of runes melted again into the disc of purple wax, which Violet laid on the desk in front of her.

"Thank you for answering our summons," said Walter. "As Senior Advisor to the Assembly, I will convene this affair, which will be heard by Assemblymen Cowling and Singh, and Deputy Chief Minister Prest."

Jack knew two of the names. Bertrand Cowling was of the same dusty generation as half of the House of Lords: a drawn, white-bearded man with a permanent frown and fussy little eyeglasses.

Singh, he didn't know, although the man was exchanging nods of acknowledgement with Edwin. He looked younger than the other two on the panel, with strong features beneath a dark red turban and a thick Sikh beard without a hint of grey.

"Lord Hawthorn," said Richard Prest, meeting Jack's gaze with a hint of bluster. "What a pleasant surprise. I'd understood that you no longer involved yourself in magical affairs."

Jack's mother had brought him up to speed on Assembly politics during his visit to Cheetham Hall. Prest was an acquaintance of Lord Cheetham, though not a close one. He'd served two terms as Deputy Chief Minister and was expecting to be elected Chief Minister this time, as the current holder of that office was old and ill enough to have already stepped down if it weren't an election year. Clearly Prest was trying to calculate if Jack was still an influential Alston or if his black-sheep status made him safe to antagonise.

"I make exceptions," drawled Jack. Let the man chew on that one.

"And both sides have a magician to stand dicentis," said Walter.

Manning gave a little bow, as did the last man in the room, who now stood alone behind the second desk. He was a middle-aged

chap with a bare dome of scalp pushing through thinning dark
hair, and he shuffled his papers incessantly.

"*Are* there two sides?" asked Violet, who was either impressively uncowed by this room full of men or was doing an excellent
job of acting it. The line between the two was often unclear, with
Violet. Manning tugged at her sleeve, encouraging her down
into a chair, but she shook him off. "I see another dicentis over
there, but I can't see *whose* voice he is."

"Mr. Evers stands for an involved party whose identity need
not be disclosed in this initial hearing," said Walter.

"Like hell," said Robin indignantly. Singh winced a little.
Edwin dragged Robin down into a chair, more successful than
Manning had been with Violet.

There were only four chairs to each table. Jack remained
standing, deliberately radiating the impression that he was not
in the habit of fetching his own furniture. Prest cleared his
throat at Evers, who hastily brought across one of the free ones
on his own side.

Jack took a seat. Violet whispered, "Bravo," under her breath.

"Who's the Indian fellow?" Jack asked Edwin in a murmur.

"That's Adelaide's brother-in-law—her sister Catherine's husband," said Edwin. "Manraj Singh. I've met him once or twice."

"He volunteered for the panel," said Manning. "That's why I
was late, Miss Debenham—I was trying to find out who was sitting. Normally Assemblymen have to be hauled onto hearings
like this via roster. And Mrs. Kaur—"

"If we could begin, Courcey," said Prest loudly. "I understand this is an inheritance matter?"

Walter Courcey informed the room that doubt had been cast
on Miss Violet Debenham's inheritance of the estate belonging
to the late Mrs. Taverner, née Lady Enid Blackwood. Mr. Evers
produced the will in question, which was presented to the panel.
Violet let Manning deliver her letter to them as well. The Assemblymen pored over the documents for a few minutes.

"Seems in order," said Cowling. "What's the issue?"

"There is reason to believe," said Evers, "that this is an *early* version of Lady Enid's will, and a more recent one may exist. With different beneficiaries. You'll note," he added, over Violet's sound of outrage and Manning's sudden paging through one of his books, "that both will and letter are dated several years ago."

"Reason to believe?" said Manning. "What reason?"

"Conversations the deceased had with other family members," said Evers. "Including the party I represent."

"It's Aunt Caroline, isn't it? And after I—" Violet cast a look of hatred at Walter, but stopped talking. She'd made a generous gift of money to her aunt Caroline Blackwood and cousin Clarence, but she'd done it on the agreement that Clarence stop cooperating with Walter himself, who'd pressed Clarence into trying to wheedle information on the knife out of Violet.

"I am not here to provide full evidence at this time," Evers went on. "Merely to establish an intent to challenge."

"If you have no evidence to present today, then why was this hearing called?" Singh had a deep, fluid voice with a strong accent.

"Quite simple." Evers cast a glance at Walter as if for reassurance. No wonder Violet was being so ornery; she was familiar enough with theatre to recognise that this was a piece of it, and Walter Courcey was its choreographer. The only question was what it was designed to achieve.

Evers went on, "I propose that Miss Debenham vacate the property known as Spinet House while her inheritance is under challenge."

"There it is," muttered Robin.

There it was. Manning, who was clearly getting the measure of his client, put a hand out to prevent Violet's next angry outburst.

"Ridiculous," said Manning. "You propose to kick her out onto the streets?"

"Miss Debenham is rich in friends," said Walter silkily. He gave their crowded desk a pointed look. "I'm sure she will be offered hospitality while this matter is worked through."

"More to the point," said Evers, "it will allow a neutral party to search the house for a more recent will, if one exists. I'm sure you will agree that Miss Debenham can't be trusted to locate it herself. It would be in her best interests to destroy it if found."

Edwin looked almost sick as he stared at Walter. Even Jack's stomach sank. He got to his feet and waited for silence.

"This is a farce," said Jack, making firm eye contact with Prest. "Why would Lady Enid not have lodged her most recent will with her solicitors and asked them to destroy any previous versions?"

"It wasn't with solicitors," said Evers. "It was found in . . . a drawer of her desk, after her death." He'd noticed the trap Jack had laid, but couldn't do anything about it.

"A perfectly common practice with magical estates such as Spinet," said Edwin promptly. "And the argument about recency stands either way. The house would provide the correct will."

"What a *busy* legal team you have there, Miss Debenham," said Walter. His voice sharpened. "Do you deny that you're currently searching Spinet House for something?"

Manning looked perplexed, and this time didn't manage to stop Violet. She snapped, "If you're so keen to spy on us, then I think you also know by now how *unfriendly* Spinet can be."

Jack had an unpleasant memory of the wardrobe in that upstairs room and the sound of tearing flesh.

Walter said, "Are you making threats, Miss Debenham?"

Disapproving looks from the panel. Violet had enough sense not to open her mouth again. And—

"This is all a bit pointless, isn't it?" said Robin.

He had the ability to centre attention when he wanted to. He was standing, giving the panel one of his disarming, placating smiles. "Here's how I see it. We know that the Magical Assembly gave their blessing to the search for the Last Contract. So either everyone here is *fully* aware of what we're searching for in Spinet House, or you're not, and Courcey's relying on all these half lies and double meanings to make Miss Debenham look untrustworthy. When *he's* the one who wants to use this contract to steal magic from everyone he can."

What might have been a ringing silence was spoiled by Cowling breaking into a burst of dry coughs. Singh's eyebrows had climbed closer to the edge of his turban.

"*Well* then," said Violet.

Edwin was giving Robin a look as if he was speaking another language. Manning looked, understandably, extremely lost.

It was a bold move. It was a characteristic move; Robin was straightforward to a fault, and both he and his sister believed in dragging things out into the light. Jack just didn't know if it was the right move for this situation.

"We are aware of this . . . proposed undertaking regarding the Last Contract," said Prest stiffly. "*I* was not aware that word of it had *spread*."

"It's George Bastoke's pet project," said Robin. "And Mr. Courcey's here, too. And I'll wager they aren't telling the Assembly exactly what they've been doing in the name of it."

As if one or both of the names had been a signal, Walter cleared his throat and drifted back into the centre of the room. He didn't look angry or ruffled.

"There's no need for such dramatics," said Walter. "As the Deputy Chief Minister pointed out, the search for the Last Contract was fully endorsed by the Assembly. It is a vital legacy of British magic, and it was wilfully stolen by a group of women who didn't know what they were doing. Of course we are making every effort to recover it." He looked right at Edwin. "Perhaps Sir Robert wasn't going to mention that I had to interfere personally, when my brother tried to keep the coin of the contract for himself. And he still managed to inherit a magical estate for his efforts. Just as Miss Debenham here claims to have done. How *convenient*."

Edwin had lost some colour under his brother's direct gaze, and he didn't have much to lose. This battle was turning the wrong way, as battles often did when two sides were working with different maps. Jack's nerves knew it. His temples and the back of his neck were beginning to tighten.

A similar feeling had clearly struck Violet's dicentis, whose composure cracked into outright panic. Manning scooped his books shakily into his arms and said, "I'm sorry, I—I don't know—just wait—" and scurried towards the double doors.

"*Manning,*" Jack barked at his retreating back, but to no avail.

An incredulous smile crossed Walter Courcey's face. The Assemblymen looked nonplussed. Evers looked like he'd prefer to follow Manning out of the room.

"Courcey," said Cowling. "What on earth is going on?"

Walter sighed. "We do have reason to believe that Miss Debenham has inherited the knife of the Last Contract along with the rest of Lady Enid's estate. If these objects can be considered private property at all."

Edwin gave a small hiss of breath. Jack realised why as soon as Walter continued:

"In fact—it occurs to me—even if Spinet House and the rest of its contents are confirmed legally hers, Miss Debenham really should be required to hand over the knife. Along with, of course, any other pieces of the contract she might currently possess."

"Any other . . . ?" Prest frowned at Violet.

"Do make up your mind, Mr. Courcey." Violet had found her poise. "Am I in illegal possession of a private inheritance, or am I hoarding public property? It seems to be whichever gets you what you want."

Singh's frown had deepened too. "Indeed. Courcey, if the point of this is an inheritance hearing—"

"You're right," said Walter. "We've wandered from the point. But I can't allow these accusations to muddy the waters. I can assure you all that we're nowhere near knowing *how* to use the Last Contract to pool the power of many magicians. Which, I will remind you, is an *important goal*. We don't know precisely what darkness is gathering on the horizon for the magicians of Britain, but we do know we should all be working for the common good. Not selfishly hoarding the keys to power."

"Selfish?" said Robin. "You and Bastoke are the ones turning murderer in the name of power, Courcey. You tried to *kill Edwin.*"

No poise there at all. All of Robin's hatred bubbled up like bile, and the effect on the panel was obvious. He sounded desperate and looked unstable. It was unfair; he had every right to be. But this wasn't that kind of battle.

Walter let Robin's untidy emotion sit there like a spreading pool from where an untrained puppy had messed on the rug. Jack pressed his lips together and tried to think. In the pause, however, Edwin stood with enough force that his chair skidded on the floor, and marched stiff-legged to confront his brother, face-to-face.

It was a terribly brave act and Jack was almost certain it was going to make things worse.

"Hit me," demanded Edwin.

Walter let out a brief, incredulous laugh. "I beg your pardon, Win?"

"*Fuck*fuckfuck," breathed Robin.

"Go on. You have my consent. Lift a hand and try to hit me. Let them see you *can't,* because you're under blood-oath. The same oath that's the only reason the Assembly has access to Robin's foresight in the first place."

Walter exchanged a look with Prest. Then looked back at Edwin, in whose face the hurt of the past was blossoming like a bruise. And Walter, like Jack, had always enjoyed knowing exactly where to press down. A hint of self-disgust curled up within Jack. He despised Walter Courcey and always had.

"Don't be absurd," said Walter gently. "You're my brother, Edwin. Why would I want to strike you? Why would I ever need to give blood-oath *not* to hurt you? We're family. Our parents' blood is in the soil at Penhallick. It means something to me, even if it doesn't to you."

That was more than pressing a bruise; it was twisting a knife. Edwin flinched.

"Robin, *stay put,*" Jack growled without even looking over.

"You're evading," said Edwin. A thin, whip-crack whisper.

"But perhaps it doesn't mean anything," said Walter. "You had to go off and get your hands on another property instead. Just like Miss Debenham over there."

It was like that Oscar Wilde story about a painting: Walter Courcey looking calm and reasonable on the exterior, forcing all of his own viciousness to appear on Edwin's face as Edwin fought to keep his balance in front of the brother who'd tormented him for their entire childhood.

"*Stop* it," Edwin hissed. "Stand there under a truth-spell and declare you haven't let this project of yours run to kidnapping, torture, and murder."

"There's no such thing as a truth-spell," said Walter. Even Jack was tempted to gasp at that. Walter had used a truth-spell on Edwin, when trying to get the coin.

Edwin looked molten with indignation and lifted his hands to begin a cradle, even without string.

The panel's reaction was instant.

"*No* unauthorised magic in the Library!" snapped Prest. "Have some respect for this institution, young man!"

Jack was contemplating just hauling the lot of them out of there before any more damage could be done—respect be damned—when the only person to so far escape the fiasco made an abrupt reentry.

Overlapping footsteps came from behind them as Arthur Manning strode back into the Library with another person by his side.

"*Kitty?*" said Edwin.

Now accompanying Manning was one of the lovelier women Jack had ever seen, with a wealth of blue-black hair, glowing brown skin, and an elegant profile. She held a few leaves of yellowing paper.

She was also extremely, visibly pregnant.

Even Jack, who was usually in favour of throwing convention out the window, felt a stab of startled displacement. One didn't usually see women outside the house when they were this far along. Cowling had turned red; Prest's entire face was folded into an expression of deep discomfort, and he seemed unable to make his gaze focus on the newcomer.

"Ahmph," said Cowling. "I *say*. Hardly the place to be—my dear madam—"

"Catherine." Singh's tone was faintly querying.

"Good afternoon, my dear," said Catherine Kaur. "Assemblymen. Evers." A slight, masterful pause. "Courcey."

Edwin managed to stop staring at Mrs. Kaur and escaped back to the desk. Manning joined them.

"I was going to tell you," Manning murmured. "Mrs. Kaur practically trained me. She was never allowed to stand dicentis, but she did a lot of work with the Coopers. She knows some parts of magical law better than anyone. She'd heard about the hearing and dug up the papers on inheritance law for me. I thought she might still be in the Barrel, and"—a helpless nod to where Mrs. Kaur was making her slow, swaying way up to the dais—"she was. Is."

And she might have prodded her husband into volunteering for the panel so there'd be at least one semi-friendly face. Or at least one not actively primed against them.

Mrs. Kaur apologised for intruding and somehow managed to give the impression that Arthur Manning had *not* in fact ducked behind his teacher's skirts, but called upon her as a research assistant. She then unfolded her pieces of paper and laid out a concise summary of a case heard in the Library some forty years ago, where a magical estate in Wiltshire had been the subject of a tedious inheritance dispute. It included a brief note that the current residents, including one of the disputing parties, were deemed able to remain in place during the nearly six months that the case dragged on.

She punctuated the whole with the occasional wince or hand in the small of her back. Jack wanted to invite the entirety of Parliament into this room to learn by example.

He didn't know much about Catherine Kaur. She had worked with the Coopers. And then stopped working with them and moved to a different role, in a different part of the Barrel. He wondered why—and wondered if it had coincided with his cousin George assuming control. The Coopers weren't an army, but they were damn close to one, and Jack knew how armies worked. Atrocities were committed first and legitimised later, if the high brass were forced to acknowledge them at all. Perhaps Prest and the Assembly didn't know what George had been doing on their behalf, but Jack was quite sure they preferred it that way.

Walter Courcey looked livid during Mrs. Kaur's speech. But he didn't yank on any of Evers's strings when the dicentis stammered: "Well—in that case—no objection to Miss Debenham remaining in residence, although the challenge may still be brought—shall discuss with my client—"

"Yes, yes," said Prest impatiently. He levelled a disapproving look at Violet. "I must say, some of the accusations made today have been very concerning, Miss Debenham. Very concerning indeed. But I shan't argue against precedent if it exists in this specific case. Singh? Cowling?"

The other Assemblymen agreed that Violet's eviction was unnecessary. Cowling, too, was now frowning at Violet as if he suspected her of bad behaviour but hadn't been able to personally catch her hand in the biscuit jar.

"Dismissed," said Walter shortly. He stalked very close to their desk on his way out of the room, probably to intimidate Edwin further, and Jack had a fleeting wish that it'd been a bad leg day. If he'd brought his stick, he could have tripped the bastard.

"Thank you, Mr. Manning," said Violet. "I doubt that was what you expected out of your third time standing dicentis."

"Not exactly, no," said Manning. "If I'm to stand for you again, Miss Debenham," he added, with a sudden flare of personality, "I hope you decide to fill me in on the pertinent context."

"It's a matter of what's safe to know," said Jack.

Manning looked at the doors through which Walter had vanished, made a complicated face, and took his leave of them. After this, the unmagical Inns of Court would probably seem a blessed relief.

"I think," said Mrs. Kaur, "that I, too, will avail myself of the safety of ignorance. You can have Addy catch me up on anything you think I should know."

"Thank goodness for you, Kitty," said Robin. "Not to look a gift horse, et cetera, but are you really sure you should be—ah—" He went pink and abashed in the face of a long stare from Mrs. Kaur.

"I am expecting, Robin, not infirm. Glad to be of assistance, Miss Debenham. Edwin, you owe me a letter about that book I lent you."

She sent a smile up to her husband on the dais and left. The rest of them reappropriated the preparatory office, where Violet cast a muffling spell on the room and Edwin added an auditory illusion of indistinct conversation. Nobody asked if the precautions were necessary. Edwin's hand shook as he produced an odd one-handed cradle for the illusion, but he didn't reach for string.

"Well," said Violet, hurling herself and all of her skirts into one of the few chairs. "Did anyone else notice that that was a complete setup? *Not* just Aunt Caroline trying to get her hands on the goods."

"They may not have talked to your relatives at all," said Jack. "They didn't need a challenging party to stand there. Just Evers."

"Evers reading off Walter Courcey's script," said Violet.

"Walt wasn't exactly hesitating to speak for himself," said Edwin. "*A darkness hovering on the horizon.* He's sure there is something coming—he said it when we were at Sutton last year. Billy Byatt said it too."

"Crisis," said Jack, "is an excellent justification for the seizure of power."

Edwin shook his head. He had the twitchy expression that meant he was connecting ideas and was about to show you a pattern. "It was in the Grimm's letter. *The dark that's coming.* That's more than false justification, surely? Robin, have you . . ."

"You know what I've seen," said Robin. There was a terribly naked fear in the way he looked at Edwin now. Edwin flinched.

"Yes. No," he said. "All right. That's—that's hardly relevant to British magic as a whole. But I wish I knew what the Grimm meant. About that, and about the Last Contract itself. And how Dufay's song ties into it."

"Add them to the list," said Violet irritably. "Shall I recite it? We still don't know how to get hold of Lady Enid's knife, or if it'll be snatched out of our grasp by the Assembly once we do. We don't know what kind of spell or ritual Bastoke's people are planning once they have the whole contract. We haven't even decided how to hide these items, or otherwise prevent them from being misused if we get our hands on all three."

A depressed silence followed this, delivered as it was in Violet's most Shakespearean tones.

Jack cleared his throat. It was as a good a time as any to explain his suspicions about the equinox gala at Cheetham Hall and George's plan to use the gathering of magicians to steal power with the contract—so he did so.

"And if you were hoping to call upon official help at any point in this," Jack finished, "then today's been a good illustration of how *that's* likely to go. Now we're all liars and troublemakers, and probably thieves as well."

More silence. It was broken by Robin.

"Cheers ever so, Hawthorn. You can always be relied upon to lighten the mood."

It was two days later when Alan made it to Spinet House again. He turned up in the early afternoon, having told the sub-editor that he was going out chasing details for a story that would appear in the Saturday edition.

In fact, the story was done. He'd ground his way by candle-light towards the small, dark hours for the past two nights, and only partly made up for it by napping at his desk in the *Post*'s office instead of going home for dinner in the middle of the day. Hunger he could ignore, but his temper became a sullen cat of a thing when his sleep was snatched away. And while lighting his second candle the previous night it had struck him that magicians didn't have to pay for candles or gas or lamp oil at all, what with their glowing balls of light, and he'd been so furious at that injustice that he'd broken the nib of a pen. Nibs also cost money.

All in all, Alan was not feeling well disposed to anyone who lived in a magical Bayswater mansion and had nothing but leisure time on their hands.

Luckily for both of them, Maud Blyth was difficult to be angry at.

"It's just me today," she said, flitting into the drawing room to greet Alan. "Edwin and Robin are at the Home Office. Violet had a last-minute invitation to a luncheon with Lord and Lady Albert—I suspect they want her to be eccentric at people and talk up the opera company. And Hawthorn is at his club."

"Which club?" Alan inquired out of journalistic habit. The *Post*'s readers were extremely interested in details like a gentleman's club memberships.

"The Reform," said Maud, excellent source that she was.

The most progressive club that was still full of aristocrats. Of course. Alan's annoyance gave an enjoyable lash of its tail.

"If Edwin and Violet aren't here, I suppose there's no point me staying to play canary. When should I return?"

"No, stay!" Maud waved him back down onto the settee. Her eyes gleamed with her military-general look. "I should catch you up on what happened at the Barrel when Violet went to her hearing."

She did so. Alan felt his eyebrows climbing his face.

"So, Edwin's written back to this Grimm person, whoever they are, and in the meantime he and Robin are combing the office for previous Grimm letters—though, er, it sounds like everyone who had the job before Robin and Addy threw most of them in the bin—in case there have been other useful clues about the Last Contract. And nobody's tried to break into the house in *days*," she added, "which Edwin and Hawthorn are grim about, because they think it means Bastoke's people are going to go ahead and legally challenge *anyone* holding a contract piece, so they don't need to keep trying to get into the house and find it before us." A gulp of breath. Occasionally Maud's mind wrote cheques that her lungs couldn't honour.

"I hear this house isn't a shabby fighter on its own accord," said Alan.

"No, indeed." Maud turned her martial gleam onto him. "So it'll be perfectly fine if you and I go for a little expedition, won't it?"

Visions of menageries danced warningly through Alan's mind. "What sort of expedition?"

"Edwin was digging up what he could find about Alfred Dufay himself—the magician who wrote the orrery song—and it's said his ghost *haunts his own grave*." Maud-the-medium gave Alan no time to react to this. "And I'm no use twiddling my thumbs here in the house, and after all, Robin had a vision of me standing at a grave, and I *won't* let it be any of ours."

"You want to go and ask the ghost of this dead magician about the Last Contract."

"Yes! Or at least find out if he's there at all, so that Edwin can come and ask *better* questions."

"And if Bastoke's people are watching the house and decide to corner you for information on the cup when you leave? I can hold my own in a back-alley fight, but not against magicians."

"I don't know where the cup is hidden." Maud grinned proudly at him. "None of us do except Violet. We agreed. Spinet's more protective of her than anyone, and she has the most magic anyway. And she's a wonder with her illusion disguises. All she has to do is use the tunnel to the Underground, and she can step onto a train looking like someone else entirely. So, you see! If one of Bastoke's people got their hands on me, I *couldn't* tell them. Even under a truth-spell."

"That's . . . sensible," said Alan. His wariness had been replaced by something more complicated. But Maud was quite clearly doing this with or without escort, and hell—it wasn't like he wasn't *curious*. "All right then. Let's be off while there's daylight."

Maud attracted more glances than he did on the Underground. She wore the specific hat and blue coat that Robin had seen in his vision, and no doubt they were nothing special by her own wardrobe's standards. But she looked as though she should be in a motorcar or a private cab, not down here where most of the men had the same shabby-respectable garb as Alan. A wizened woman in faded black gave Alan a gimlet of a stare when he took the seat next to Maud's, as if suspecting him of being importuning.

Maud happily began to pass on to Alan some information— learned from Edwin, naturally—about the history of the London Underground's construction. She learned the names of the young boy and girl sitting on the next row with their mother, and also learned their opinions on picnics (favourable) and ants (less so). Alan had never seen anyone strike up a conversation with strangers on the Underground. As usual, Maud was a law unto herself.

They came up onto the street into a hot summer afternoon. Alan felt more able to contribute to the conversation when he wasn't being eyed from all sides as too common for his companion.

"How are the university plans, Miss B? Maud," he amended at her playful frown.

"Suspended," said Maud. "But Robin says I've stuck to the idea for long enough. He's given his word that I shall go. And—Violet's said she'll loan me the fees." She said it with only a short falter. The Blyths were happier than most toffs Alan knew to talk about money.

"Still a shameless trollop, I see," said Alan.

Maud was a safer bet for teasing than Edwin. She laughed and hooked her cotton-gloved hand through the crook of his arm. "That's me. No, I—I still want to go, desperately, but it feels less urgent than it did. Perhaps because I'm not running *away* from so many things now."

Alan had the unkind wish to drag her to his own house to meet Bella, to show her what a girl looked like when she had *real* problems to run away from. Hell. He shouldn't have let himself tease her, shouldn't have invited this intimacy of manner, no matter the ease of Maud's company. He didn't fit into this world. He wasn't *there* to fit in.

At first glance, the cemetery was nothing special. Alan would have walked right past it if he'd ever had cause to come to this corner of London. Apparently it was one of a few that were often used by magicians.

On second glance, it absolutely crawled with stray cats.

"That's promising," said Maud.

"Did Edwin say where exactly Dufay's grave is?"

"It's not too large, at least," said Maud, meaning *no*.

They were looking for something from the last century, so Alan could skim his gaze past the ancient or fresh-looking stones. Most of them were of the former type. Flowers were scarce, and many graves well overgrown, their headstones shawled with moss.

Marco Rossi had faithfully paid his funeral insurance, so at least Maria had been able to hold her head up and bury him in a good Catholic cemetery. Alan visited the grave every year: a simple stone amongst a sprawl of crosses and angels. Less of that here. Very few stones above waist height, and only a handful of boxy aboveground tombs. Alan saw only one other person on the paths, a stout, white-haired man paused at a grave halfway along the row they'd just come down.

Beneath the unclouded sun Maud looked uncomfortably warm, even after removing her blue coat and carrying it over her arm. She kept rubbing at her forehead as if it ached.

Alfred Dufay's grave turned out to be one of the grander ones. A rusted fence ringed the site at ankle height, and the stone had an elaborate border pattern. A tortoiseshell cat with a missing ear was asleep on the grave. Alan was more inclined to put that down to the warmth and angle of the sun than any ghostly presence.

"*We are man's marvellous light,*" read Maud. It was engraved beneath the name ALFRED DUFAY and the years 1798–1861. No biblical homilies. Nothing about whose beloved son or husband or father Dufay had been. Just the lines from the song.

"It's the right Dufay, then. Do you feel anything?"

"I feel like I've been plunged into the steam room in the *Lyric*'s Turkish baths. But I suspect that's just the weather. Mrs. Navenby was anchored to the locket—I had to touch it." She frowned at the gravestone and began to tug at the finger of a glove. "I suppose—"

And then she stumbled sideways and into Alan, as if she'd been pushed. Her coat fell to the ground and she tripped on it. Alan put out a hand to steady her but snatched that hand back again when he saw her face.

The wrongness of it lurched in Alan. Somehow Maud's round-cheeked, friendly face was taking on menacing angles, as if glass objects were shifting beneath a piece of taut linen. It settled into a deep frown.

Alan swallowed hard. "Mr. . . . Dufay?"

For a horrible moment Alan thought Maud had *yowled* without moving her lips. No—it was the tortoiseshell, awake and with all its hair standing on end. It swiped once at the edge of Maud's skirt and then bolted. Alan couldn't spare attention to see where it went. Maud's head tipped to one side and then the other as she inspected him. She looked barely human. Worse than birdlike.

"*Ha—arm*," Maud said, or possibly *hard*, or some other word that sounded like half-chewed gristle in her mouth. Her lips dragged back over her teeth. The next sound was no word at all but a pained, feral growl, and she lunged right at Alan with her fingers in claws.

"Bloody hell! Maud!" Alan had hold of her wrists. She wasn't strong, but whatever had control of her body was determined, and probably cared less than Alan did if some of Maud Blyth's tendons were to snap. "Can you bring yourself back?"

"*What*," she said hoarsely, and writhed. "*Wha—at*."

Definitely not Maud. And not seeming much like a gentleman who'd been alive a century ago, either, unless he'd died of something *very* unpleasant and his mind had gone beforehand. Alan should have asked more questions.

"I've seen you do this, Maud," Alan said between gritted teeth. "You swapped back and forth, easy as you like. And I don't know who *you* are, but you can *piss off* and let her speak for herself."

Maud blinked at him. What happened next reminded Alan of the trick where someone whipped away a tablecloth and left the setting: a sense of shifting, along with a sense of dangerous motionlessness. The angles of her features changed yet again.

"*Oh my*," she said, and gave a long, rich laugh that raised the hairs on Alan's neck even more than the growling had. It was intelligent, mature, and malicious. And it was still not Maud. "*Room for everyone, darlings, wait your turn—*"

Maud bent at the waist as if kicked. Her arms dragged out of Alan's grip and she staggered backwards two steps.

"*—no*," she gasped.

"Maud?"

She straightened, gulping for breath, flushed red and look-ing—no other word for it, really—haunted. "They're so much stronger," she panted. "With Mrs. Navenby I could—"

And she was gone again. The next voice spoke a version of English that was nearly another language entirely—the one after that did nothing but spit obscene vitriol about women—the one after that could barely speak at all for coughing and wheezing, and managed to fumble Maud's hat from her head, leaving her hair a pin-tugged mess.

The one bright side to all of these fucking, fucking ghosts seemed to be that no single one of them could maintain hold of Maud for long. Alan had a dreadful vision of a dead lecher tak-ing Maud's body on a ride around London like a stolen bicycle.

The *downside* was that there were enough of them that they just kept coming. Despite Alan's best attempts at calling and encouraging her, Maud didn't resurface again.

What was this doing to Maud? What was *Alan* supposed to do? Dragging her out of the cemetery seemed the simplest ap-proach, but whenever he tried to touch her, she either flinched or flailed or tried to hit him, or—oh, *wonderful*—burst into loud, wailing sobs and crouched to curl herself into a ball like a hedge-hog being poked with sticks.

"Jesus, Mary, and Joseph," said Alan.

"Oh dear," said a mild voice behind him.

He spun. For a moment he saw the stout, white-haired man from earlier. Then the man cradled a spell, and the illusion dropped. The magician who stood there was also stout and elderly. But now familiar.

"Miss Blyth isn't having the best of days, is she?" said Seraph-ina Vaughn.

Alan looked from Maud—still crouched, hugging her knees, and emitting the occasional whimper—to Mrs. Vaughn, the last surviving member of the Forsythia Club. The one who was working begrudgingly with Bastoke's people in order to find the Last Contract, because she believed in their plan to pool magical power.

Mrs. Vaughn had been on the *Lyric*. She and Alan had never spoken directly before.

There didn't seem much point in pretending.

"You're following her, then," Alan said.

"I could have been following *you*, Mr. Ross."

Alan ignored that. "You thought we were going to dig up the knife in a cemetery?"

"I am past making assumptions about where the others hid their pieces of the contract," said Mrs. Vaughn calmly. "Mazes and parrot cages. Why not buried in a grave? Though I'd have thought walking into a cemetery like this one, knowing oneself a medium, would be a piece of risk-taking too far even for the bold Miss Blyth."

As if to illustrate her point, Maud began to cry again, in the stifled manner of a child torn between terror at attracting attention and the sheer unbearable size of their emotion. This particular ghost seemed to have gained a firm foothold. Alan crouched to put a hand on her shoulder, trying to murmur the soothing nothings that penetrated this sort of weeping fit when Tom was having one. He glared up at Mrs. Vaughn.

"Are you just going to stand there, ma'am?"

"Should I be involving myself?"

"It's in your interests to keep Miss Blyth safe and sane," Alan said. "Everything she's doing is to *find* this bloody contract that everyone wants. I thought your lot were all about that. Making other people do the dirty work and then swooping in like magpies to collect." Bitterness seeped into his voice.

Mrs. Vaughn lowered herself to one knee with the aching slowness of age. She frowned at Maud.

"I can't say I know how to fix a possession. I can try a general negation. And a few other things."

Only when the first spell washed over Maud did Alan realise he'd invited one of Maud's enemies to inflict God only knew what kinds of magic on her, without interruption or supervision. It wasn't as if *Alan* had any idea what these spells were.

Christ. Too late to chase the woman off now.

None of them seemed to have any effect anyway. Mrs. Vaughn looked increasingly annoyed, in the same way that Edwin had when failing to drop the warding on the oak door. Eventually she cradled a spell that looked like pinkish spun sugar and held it in front of Maud's face so that it was sucked into the girl's nose on her next tear-choked inhalation.

Maud sniffed a few more times and yawned widely, and then her eyelids dropped shut and she keeled over to lie motionless on the gravel path.

"What did you do?" snapped Alan.

"She's asleep," said Mrs. Vaughn, straightening and brushing dirt from her skirts. "There. Your problem has been solved. Now I suggest you get her out of here."

"*How?*" Alan gestured to the prone body of Maud, substantial in her layers of clothing, and then to his barely taller self. Before Mrs. Vaughn could claim that this was not her problem—he could *see* that approaching in her smug, round face—he went on, "If you're helping, then help. Fetch someone. A doctor. A policeman. *Anyone.*"

Mrs. Vaughn raised her eyebrows at him and turned away. It was neither refusal nor agreement. Alan, watching her amble towards the street, figured he had a coin-toss chance that further help would actually arrive. He didn't dare to leave Maud alone. Nor did he know how long she'd sleep.

Less than ten minutes by his pocket watch, it turned out. She stirred right from unconsciousness into terror, struggling to get upright but tangled in her dirty skirts, and Alan lunged to help her stand.

"Maud. Miss Blyth. Maud, it's all right—you're all right now."

"I can't. I can feel them, and—oh, I'm *so* hot—" She sounded exhausted, ragged. "No," she whispered, and despair took hold of Alan again.

"Maud?"

"*You shan't take me*" came snarling out of her throat. "*You shan't,*" and thin fire erupted on Alan's jawline as she lashed out with surprisingly sharp nails. Alan hissed with pain and nearly tripped himself on her blue coat, still abandoned on the ground, as he got out of range. He lifted his hands in conciliation.

"I won't hurt you. Or take you anywhere—please—"

"*Lies,*" she hissed, and went for—Jesus, his *eyes*. Alan managed to twist away, winning only a shallow scratch across the temple. He hovered out of reach, warily watching the bleak violence of Maud's expression and her trembling posture.

His own body had switched from helping to surviving. Knees loose, hands ready to dart and block. He'd fought girls before, the street-forged ones with hard faces and fears smaller than their hunger. This was—he didn't know what this was.

And the only thing to stop it was sleep.

Alan muttered his first real prayer of the last decade, to whichever saint looked out for strong-willed girls and desperate thieves in far over their heads. He came in at a weaving angle and swung his fist precisely at Maud's head.

It was a blow designed to stun an opponent and end a fight before it could worsen. It certainly stunned Maud. She dropped like a rock, for the second time in less than an hour, and once again lay senseless.

Alan ran through a few of the more outright heretical oaths he knew, any one of which would have his ma boxing his ears. Perhaps he *would* have to leave Maud here while he fetched help. Why had he let her talk him into this?

"Oi!" came a shout.

Alan looked up to see a blue-uniformed man approaching. It was the first time in his life he'd ever been relieved to see a Scotland Yard copper.

That pleasant feeling lasted all of five seconds. It evaporated as soon as the man barked, "You! Get your hands off that girl!" and broke into a run.

"Jesus fucking Christ," Alan muttered, and braced himself for things to get messy.

10

"A pity," said Jack. "I was rather hoping they'd put you in a cell."

Alan Ross's entire face shouted how much he wished he could respond to that with a great deal of uncouth language. "His lordship is joking. His lordship has a *unique* sense of humour." His accent was as polished as Jack had ever heard it, clearly for the benefit of the policemen in the room. Several scratches stood out pink and angry on his face, as if he'd been separating fighting cats.

"I am joking," allowed Jack. "Maud."

"My lord," said Maud, with a meekness that sat even more poorly on her than restraint did on Ross. Her eyes were red-rimmed, her hair a disaster, and her dress dust-stained and creased. At least *she* had not been handcuffed.

Jack's pleasant afternoon at his club had been interrupted by a message that there was an apologetic Scotland Yard constable begging a moment of his time, with a wild story about his young ward being assaulted into unconsciousness by a man who claimed first to be her friend, then a hired attendant. All very fishy. Both man and girl—once she'd revived—had begged the police to fetch Lord Hawthorn, who would clear up the situation in no time.

Jack was looking forward to the day when he could escape back to his previous life and stop being summoned to apply the grease of his station to Maud Blyth's disasters.

"As I said, my lord," said a blue-uniformed man whose face already showed the strain of having been in a room with the full force of Maud's Maudness for some time. "This . . . individual . . . claims to have been hired to watch over the girl."

"Because I have *violent fits*," said Maud. "I keep telling them, my lord, that Mr. Ross was only trying to protect me from harming myself."

Violent fits. Harming herself. An old, old fear curled a sly hand around Jack's heart. For a moment he couldn't speak at all. Then he mastered it.

"Remove the cuffs," said Jack. "My ward does indeed require constant supervision, and I would personally vouch for the virtue of any young woman in Mr. Ross's company."

Ross's face wiped itself clean of expression and he stared at the ceiling.

Jack got them out of the station amid a flurry of apologies and harrumphing and *The whole situation seemed very irregular, my lord, I'm sure you understand*-ing. He heard the rest of the story in a cab back to Spinet House. Some of the cold fear fled, though it left frosted fingerprints on the underside of Jack's ribs. Possession, not madness. Or—anything else. And Maud seemed entirely herself now. Ross's face was the worst casualty.

"Why didn't you send for your brother?" Jack demanded.

"She wasn't awake for the first part of it," said Ross. "I played the highest card we had. Earl's son trumps baronet."

"So the fits of violent madness were your idea."

"My reputation is already in tatters," said Maud. "It can stand it. And it was quick of Alan to think of it."

Jack admitted the truth of that. He delivered Maud to the front of Spinet House, where she directed a semi-hopeful look up at him.

"No," Jack said. "*You* can explain your brilliant plan, and what happened, to the people who love you. And you can deal with all their yelling yourself."

"Violet will yell. Robin won't," said Maud glumly. "He'll look hurt and worried. It'll be awful."

"Good," said Jack. "You deserve it. Goodbye, Maud."

"Ill-bred cad," said Maud, but one of her dimples popped into

view and she went inside readily enough, leaving Jack standing
with Ross on the street.

"You really are," said Ross. "Actually, I think the breeding
contributed. You can *afford* to never have learned to be pleasant."

"I've yet to see any evidence you've learned it either."

"I might be a perfect lamb when I'm not being provoked by
you lot," said Ross. "You wouldn't know." He rolled his eyes
when Jack made a disbelieving sound. "When we met on the
ship you were holding a gun in my face, Violet was threatening
to mess about with my memory, and you all already knew I was
a thief." Like a stone thrown through glass burst that wicked,
uneven smile. "There didn't seem much point in pretending to
be *nice*."

"And now you're pretending?"

Ross hesitated. Finally, lethally—"I don't think you want me
to be nice, my lord Hawthorn."

Jack's breath didn't stop. It might have . . . paused.

"Besides—in my position, you figure out pretty fast who's
safe to push. Whose bark is worse than his bite." The smile
grew deadlier. Jack took a moment to curse Pete Manning, and
Ross finished: "You've a very good bark, your lordship—a huge,
rough, throbbing bark—"

"Stop that," said Jack. His tone surprised even himself: low,
commanding.

"—but I haven't yet seen you bite."

"Perhaps if you asked *nicely*."

It hung between them, developing its own weight and shape.
Their bodies swayed apart and together like a small tide.

"You've earned that hazard pay today," Jack went on. The
words came out, dragged by that tide. "I refuse to have you interview any more of my relatives, but I can offer you dinner."

"Dinner," repeated Ross.

"At my townhouse. I planned to dine there tonight anyway."

"*Dinner.*"

"Quid pro quo," said Jack, "if that helps your pride."

"You don't give a toss for my pride."

"Dinner and as much arguing about politics as you wish. Or if you'd rather keep yourself warm with the knowledge you *declined* a dinner invitation from an earl's son—"

"Piss off." But Ross didn't move. His face was a taunt. Jack waited, and eventually Ross said, clipped, "You know I can't change for dinner."

"Then I shan't either. It'll be informal."

"All right." A pause. "Thank you."

The exchange about biting throbbed in Jack's skull all the way back to his Mayfair townhouse, where Makepeace batted nary an eye at the prospect of an unexpected guest and put the machinery of dinner in motion. They ate in the smaller, more intimate dining room. Still—

"Informal my arse," muttered Ross, twitching as a footman flicked out his napkin. He stared around him at the table setting.

Jack was on home turf and therefore in an easier mood. "I haven't eaten here in weeks. Let them make the most of it."

Ross inspected a fork. "I suppose they polish the silver on Tuesdays even if there's nobody about to see it."

"Should I kick my staff out onto the street when I'm not in residence?"

"Pay them the wage, but let them do what they like with their time," said Ross. "Or are you afraid they'll become *educated above their station*? Here—when was the last time you had enough time and energy to read a book? For leisure or self-improvement?"

The footman he was addressing—Metcalfe, the younger one—gave Ross a startled, pained look, as if they'd both failed an unspoken test.

Jack cleared his throat. "Mr. Ross here has an irrepressible interviewing instinct, and I have deprived him of subjects. He's a journalist."

"Actually, I'm a jewel thief." Ross lifted the glass of wine to his mouth and paused before drinking. "Got my eye on all that silver."

Jack caught Makepeace's poker face, within which amusement gleamed, and indicated that they would prefer to dine in privacy and would ring when ready for the next course. Conversation would be easier without Ross needling the staff.

Once they were alone, he said to Ross: "I'll wait until you're leaving the house and then make a charitable show of giving you the candlesticks."

"I didn't have you down as a humble man of God," said Ross. "And—ah. You didn't have me down as someone who might've read Hugo."

"One assumes you learned all those long words somewhere."

The rhythm broke, and one of those sharp, considering looks replaced it, but Ross made the visible decision not to take offence. He merely shrugged. A miracle. Perhaps it was the wine.

"I was at a charity school, and that was the longest book in my teacher's collection. All about God and forgiveness and poor criminals bettering themselves through faith." The sharp look took on an edge of irony. "He was *thrilled* when I showed an interest. Less thrilled when I thumped it back down onto his desk a week later and went on about how the boys with the barricades had some good ideas which needed better execution."

"Guillotines," said Jack. "As I suspected. Nobody threw Hugo at my head until Oxford, and I can't say I enjoyed it. Was this the norm at those charity schools?"

Ross shook his head. "The school in our area was half funded by the church, and half by a philanthropic society. The masters there had the radical notion that teaching the poor to *think* would *not* tear apart the fabric of society. I was bloody lucky. Luckier still that my family let me stay as long as I did."

The Education Act made school attendance compulsory only to the age of thirteen. Where money was scarce, most families would encourage paid work after that.

Ross went on, "I was Mr. Voight's pet project. He had dreams of me winning a scholarship to university. The perfect poster boy for the ragged schools and their potential."

Impossible to miss the bitterness in his voice.

"What happened?"

"My pa died." It landed like a slap. "So I took what I had and I did the best I could with it."

"How old were you?"

"Fifteen." Ross raised his impossible dark eyes to Jack's in the candlelight. There was something more complicated than defiance there, and in the way he gripped the knife and fork of Jack's everyday silver dinner service.

"And now you're cornering earls in Parliament and demanding their opinion on the budget," said Jack.

"*Now* I'm in the fox trap of the lower middle class," said Ross. "D'you know what my brother Emilio wears to his worksite? Yesterday's clothes, mud stains and all. Nobody gives a rat's arse what he looks like. Look around you in the City sometime, Lord Hawthorn. Hundreds of the men you see can barely afford to wear a clean shirt every day, but it's *expected*. And they have to pay for rooms close to their place of work. And it's twice as tough if they have a family to provide for. They are terrified, to a man, of slipping below the line."

Most charity works were dedicated to improving the lot of the truly poor. Starving orphans, struggling widows on the street. Jack hadn't considered that there might be a need to improve conditions for the average banker's clerk.

He said, "You've never struck me as terrified."

Ross gave a harsh, incredulous laugh. "I've been below the line. I know I can survive it. That helps. But no, I'm clinging just as hard. I like using my mind rather than my hands. I like that I won't be useless by forty from backache or worn-out knees, and I like that men born into houses full of *silver* hear the long words I use and will give me a few more inches, a few more moments of their time, so I can keep my family's heads above water."

He spoke with an intensity that reminded Jack of Catherine Kaur, speechmaking in the Library: an ebb and flow that demanded your attention. In Ross's case he could have been taught oratory at that charity school, but Jack suspected it was

simply natural passion. Jack wanted to push back, to leap into
the rhythm, but he swallowed it and left silence like an invitation.

"I am terrified *all the time*," said Ross. "I am terrified that
my sister's daughters will grow up and go into service and then
get thrown back onto the street when their bellies start showing
the evidence of a rich man's greed, my *lord*. That happened to
Bella. And she and Caro wouldn't have ever found positions in
the first place if I hadn't forged references for them."

Finally, he shut his mouth. Glanced around. The dining room
was still empty but for the two of them.

"I'm enjoying my meal," said Jack. "I'll call the constables on
you after the dessert course."

"So much for the candlesticks." Ross ate a mouthful of food
and then said, sharp and defensive: "You already know I'll
steal for them. I stole *opportunity*. If the world were different,
I wouldn't have had to, but it's the way it is, and so I've been
scared my whole life and angry for even longer. It's exhausting.
You have no bloody idea how exhausting it is. Some people get
exhausted out of the anger early, because they need all their energy simply to stay alive. As I said, I was lucky." His smile was
a thin line, a rope thrown disdainfully across a dark crevice,
serving only to highlight just how wide and fundamental that
distance between them was. "I had enough fuel to keep the anger alive as well."

He certainly had. All along Jack had been drawn to it, that
angry, needful flame that filled the lantern of Alanzo Rossi. It
made Jack want to reach out and endanger his fingers.

So Jack said, "I've felt like that," because he had. "I'm sure
you'd say I've less to be angry about."

"Maybe not," said Ross. "But you sure as hell have more options when it comes to what you can *do* about it, when you've
power and wealth enough to want for nothing."

Jack gave a *fair enough* tilt of his head and reached out to ring
for the next course. He didn't think Ross had given him any of
that speech as part of the quid pro quo. It had been a challenge;

it had been, Jack suspected, the first time Ross had been allowed to speak his full mind in front of an aristocrat without fear of reprisal or unemployment. The very fact that Jack was *safe to push*—that, bizarrely, lay heavy as gifted gold in his hands.

So over the next course he gave Ross some of his own biography in return. He could only talk *around* Elsie's death, forming her shape in a blank space on the page. And he didn't mention magic. It was second nature in this place. Jack's Mayfair staff were unmagical apart from Makepeace, who kept secrets as superbly as he kept the downstairs in order.

But Jack told Ross about his own schooling at Oxford, and then—an awkward leap across the blank space of Elsie—serving for a while as an officer of the Royal Army, in the Boer.

"And back in England, as I'm sure you know from Miss Debenham, I went about gaining a reputation as a disreputable old-fashioned rake."

"Only a reputation?" said Ross. He hadn't interrupted, or spoken much at all. Those interviewer's instincts, no doubt. The source was talking; let them weave their own rope.

Jack let his mouth curl. He was feeling mellow and daring. He let the pause hang between them and grow hot.

"More bark than bite," he said softly. "But still enough bite to be getting on with."

When dinner was done, Jack showed Ross the upstairs library. Such as it was.

"It's not really a library," he warned. "Certainly not by Edwin's standards."

"It's not a room full of books?"

"It's a study."

Ross rolled his eyes. His hostility had all but vanished with the meal, but it was creeping back now as he climbed the stairs and trailed his hand across the green silk damask on the walls, as if daring Jack to scold him for besmirching its beauty with his working-class fingers.

He was going to be disappointed there. Jack needed the company of very few people to be content, and enjoyed the stillness of solitude. Even more so after the weeks spent in Spinet House. And yet, letting the turbulence of Alan Ross step into the heart and hearth of his existence had been—exciting.

Perturbator, Jack thought. It was like Violet's tuning fork, struck against his wrist. He thrummed with something patient and large.

In the study he lit the lamps and closed the door to keep in the warmth, turned around the chair at his desk to sit in, and waved an inviting hand at the single wall of floor-to-ceiling shelves. Ross might enjoy judging a man by his book collection as much as Edwin did.

"A library," said Ross, with finality. "I know one when I see one. You—" He stopped.

Jack smiled to himself.

Sure enough, Ross fixed on the half shelf of thin purple pamphlets and crossed to them as if drawn by a beacon.

"You keep them on *display*?"

"Most people won't recognise them from the spines," said Jack. "And I don't use this room for entertaining."

Ross turned. His gaze was dizzyingly dark. "Do you want my thanks for inviting me in?" He swept a bow. "An honour, my lord."

"The honour's mine," said some of tonight's wine, out of Jack's mouth. "I should ask you to sign them."

Ross straightened at once. Now he raised a hand, half-protective, to touch the booklets, and his shoulders took on a familiar angle. Edwin was like this about some of his invented spells. The artist both wanting and not wanting to be perceived.

"They're only filth."

"I didn't peg you as modest."

Ross's mouth twitched. He touched the books again.

"Tell me about them," Jack said. The atmosphere of the study found those notes of command in his throat and roughened his voice with them. "Tell me about the Roman."

Ross didn't look wary this time. He leaned back against the shelf containing the work of his own mind. "I told you I started at eighteen. We needed the money so Caro could give notice. The place she was in—she didn't have Bella's problem, but the housekeeper was a bully and the lady of the house even worse. It got us by until she married and became Dick's mouth to feed." A mirthless smile. *And so.* The arithmetic of living on that exhausting edge of survival.

"Why write about men with men?" Jack asked bluntly. "If it was all about the money, I'd have thought you'd choose the larger audience."

To his surprise, the smile became a real one. "I tried that first. Tried to get my hands on what was popular and copy the style. It was rubbish. I hated it. And then one day I threw a tantrum and wrote what I wanted, and the printer got it into the hands of an *esteemed collector.*" Ross pronounced the words mockingly. "No idea who. But he paid in advance for a few more. Word got around after that."

Not a large audience, but an appreciative one. And willing to pay handsomely. Jack couldn't remember who amongst his limited list of like-minded acquaintances had dropped the first recommendation into his ear. The memory of *reading* it crawled luxuriously down his nerves as he watched Alanzo Cesare Rossi, the Roman, slide a purple booklet from the shelf and crack it open.

"He liked the classical bent of the first one," said Ross. Pages fell beneath his thumb with a rhythmic whisper. "The anonymous sponsor. More of that, he said. Masters and slaves. Rent boys and gladiators."

Jack's body was heavy where he sat, his limbs full of more blood than usual. The first few Roman books had shared that setting—thus the nom de plume, he'd assumed—but quickly spread to cover other time periods. Other fantasies. All with that dark, sparkling heart of things taken and claimed.

"You said you wrote what you wanted."

He hadn't managed to inflect it as a question; nor entirely as a statement. There was a long pause. Ross wasn't smiling any longer.

"Don't dance around," said Ross. "You don't give a toss for manners when it suits you not to. Don't change on my account. You want to know *why*. So. Ask."

"Why is this what you write?"

Ross nodded, a surprisingly patronising motion from someone a foot shorter and seven years younger than Jack. Someone whose life Jack could have easily bought—*had* bought, he thought with a trickle of heat, remembering the cufflinks and watch he'd pressed into Ross's hands.

"Because *this*," said Ross, lifting the book, "is safe."

"I'll remind you of that if you're ever arrested for obscenity."

"Safer than the alternative. Or perhaps you think I'd come to no harm at all, risk *nothing*, if I were to go in search of rough-handed soldiers and cruel dukes and tell them that what I really fancied was being tied up and fucked and pretending that I didn't want it."

All of Jack's blood tried to converge on a single point. Heat gripped him, and he shifted in the chair. Ross's glance took it in, mocked him for it, and returned to skewer his face, all within moments.

Jack said, "If you tell me you've never been fucked, I'll say you're lying about being the Roman after all."

"One of the best pornographers I know is a fifty-year-old virgin spinster who looks like she's never had a dirty thought in her life."

"You dared me to ask," said Jack. "So *answer*."

That lighthouse-flash of emotion appeared. For a second Jack was convinced that Ross had changed his mind about this, whatever it was. That he'd shove the book into place and walk out of Jack's study and back to his own life.

"Yes. I've tried, once or twice. To go looking for more." The book tapped against his hand. "But not many men of your sort recognise the line between real and play. And it's just my luck that the appeal is right on that line."

Jack knew what he meant. His body was shouting for him to stand, to use his height and the force of his presence. To see that extraordinary face turned *up* to his, hating the necessity of it, alive with dislike and desire, here in Jack's house surrounded by the evidence of Jack's wealth. It was a cruel thing to want. He wanted it so much it was hard to breathe.

But more than that, he wanted Ross to feel safe enough to keep talking. So he stayed in his chair.

In Jack's silence, one of Ross's wicked half smiles appeared like a reward for Jack's restraint.

Ross said, "Ask me if I've been paid for it."

"Ask? I only have to look at you. Men would bankrupt themselves."

Surprise bled into Ross's face. His body was an angle, his shoulders tipped forward as if he wanted to move but a rope held him back by the waist.

Jack said, deliberately, "Should I tell you to name your price?"

Ross did turn and replace the pamphlet, now. He ran a hand through his curls.

"Fuck you all the way to hell, Lord Hawthorn," he said quietly. "This would be so much easier if what I wanted was *you* on your knees."

"You don't?"

"In an ideal world, yes. I'd love to see you driven to your knees. *Politically,* I'd fucking enjoy that."

Anticipation, always an optimist, had begun to work Jack's desire to a higher pitch. He wavered between pushing it aside and surrendering.

He said, "And actually?"

Ross barked a laugh. "In reality, I think if you forced me to my knees and fed me your prick, I'd come untouched before you had a chance to find out how deeply I can take it."

Jack had known, but he hadn't known. It had been hanging

like misted petroleum in the air between them. And Ross had made a vicious struck match out of his honesty—had said *I* and *you*, and dragged them out of the hypothetical and into the real.

It was the most arousing thing that Jack had heard in his life. But it wasn't an invitation.

"Oh, and don't you hate that," he murmured.

"*Of course I do.*" A wave of irritated shame rose right into Ross's face, and too late Jack realised that what he had here—a full collection of Ross's fantasies, and the knowledge of the author's identity—was even more than the political, social, and financial power he already held over Ross. It was a secret that nobody else had. The least safe of all.

Jack had to hand some power back. Not money, and not magic, but a secret in return. One that would mean something.

"I wrote you a letter."

"You—what?"

"I wrote a letter to the Roman," said Jack. "Perhaps five years ago, now. I gave it to the man at the shop in Charing Cross and told him to send it back along the chain. I've no idea if it ever reached you, but—"

"It reached me."

"Are you sure? I didn't exactly sign my name."

"How many letters do you think the average anonymous scribbler of illegal pornography gets?" said Ross. "I've only ever had the one. I thought it was a fucking joke, until I read it. Now I could probably recite it. Or reproduce the writing exactly. Mother of God. That was *you*?"

Jack spread his hands. That letter had been one of the most sincere and impulsive acts of his life, born from an odd sense of fair play. Someone had created something that had crept under his skin and found a blissful nerve; he wanted to tell them so. Now he felt uncomfortably as though he'd peeled back that same layer of skin.

"Don't recite it. I've no idea what I wrote. All manner of rubbish, no doubt."

"No." Ross's posture had shifted. "It meant something, to hear from a real person. It made it all seem less tawdry. It was—a kind thing."

And Jack wasn't going to ask how few kindnesses this man had received in his life, that a page-long letter telling him what he surely already knew—that he had a gift, and was using it well— would rank so highly.

That shift became movement. Ross came to stand closer to Jack's chair. Not too close; Jack would have to stand, to touch him. He hooked his thumbs into the waist of his trousers. His voice, level and honest a moment ago, became a low and electrifying taunt.

"So now I know the kind of filth your tastes run to. You want an excuse to treat someone like dirt? Is that why I'm here? A boy from the gutter, invited into the grand lord's house and shown everything he can't have?"

Jack had been expecting a thank-you. Perhaps even a sincere one. Anger rose faster than sense within him, and he was on the verge of spitting out a denial when he caught the expression on Ross's face.

He stood up. Ross took a step back, instantly. He did have to raise his face to hold Jack's gaze, and it did look as though it annoyed him to do it. In lamplight the fresh scratches on his jaw were stark. It was impossible to tell where the dark-rum brown of his eyes stopped and the pupils began.

Ross had said that Jack wanted for nothing. False, so very false. He didn't *need* this, no; he'd arranged his life and his heart so that he needed no one else. But *want* was another thing entirely.

Jack put his left hand on Ross's shoulder, and a muscle in Ross's neck tightened, and Jack was almost sure. Almost.

Carefully, forcefully, he pushed. Ross took three steps back for every two of Jack's forward. Beneath Jack's hand his shoulder was bony and hot, and he made no attempt to pull away. When his heel and hip hit the bookshelf again, his gaze cut to the side for a considering moment: registering that Jack had walked him right back to where he'd been standing. Right where the Roman booklets took up half a shelf in a purple block. His eyes flicked back to Jack, and now they were full of that half-wild taunting, as if they'd collected it along the way.

You dared me to ask.

Jack said, as if bored, "You're here because I *can* have anything. Anything I want."

Ross's lip curled. "Of course. You toffs are all the same."

Now he was daring Jack to stop asking.

And Jack knew there were reasons he'd considered this a bad idea, but right now he couldn't remember a single one.

So he did exactly what he wanted, which was to put his free hand in a proprietary way at the front of Ross's trousers and press down.

Ross gave an abrupt shudder. His eyes fell closed, which did nothing except show off the thickness of his lashes. He bit down on his lip in a way that was either involuntary or the most studied impersonation of it that Jack had ever seen. Either way, it called up an answering violence inside Jack's own mouth.

"Hm," Jack said. As if about to start haggling down the price. When Ross opened his eyes again and shot him a glare, Jack shifted his grip, rubbing with his thumb. The fabric of Ross's trousers was worn, soft and giving to the touch, and hid very little.

"Fuck you," Ross muttered.

"What was that?"

"You—*oh*shit—you heard me, your lordship."

Jack's other hand was still holding Ross by the shoulder. By now he knew Ross wasn't going anywhere. So he used it to force the man's chin up instead, finding that glorious eye contact again.

"Smart-mouthed guttersnipe, aren't you?" he said. "Go on. Tell me what you think of me."

Ross shuddered again under the next demanding caress, but kept his eyes open this time. His hips pushed into Jack's hand.

"I despise you," he whispered. "I resent your very existence. You're an unremitting prick."

"Tell me you hate me."

"I do hate you."

Jack trembled with how much his own cock ached, along with strange, hungry parts of him. The backs of his shoulders and thighs. The small expanse of skin where his hand cupped Ross's jaw, subtly rough with evening stubble. He leaned even closer, until the scent of body heat rose intoxicatingly into his nostrils.

"Tell me you want me anyway."

Ross made an angry sound in his throat and tilted his head up. He rose onto his toes, and he was hot and hardening under the heel of Jack's hand, and his mouth came close to Jack's ear.

"*No.*"

A barrier in Jack broke. One hand slid past Ross's ear to tighten in his hair and tug sharply, and the other slid around the man's hip to his arse, where the wood of Jack's shelves shoved painfully against his own knuckles. He didn't care. A patrol full of riflemen could have opened fire on the other side of the room and he wouldn't have fucking cared, because he had a thigh shoved between Ross's legs now and Ross was rubbing against it, all spite and heat. Ross's hands formed claws on his chest, and Ross's face was close to the base of Jack's neck. Jack took a moment to be concerned for his major blood vessels, then decided he didn't care about that either.

His body jolted as Ross shoved him away.

Jack pushed back, harder. A furious moan came from Ross as he sagged against the shelves. His mouth was half open and his shoulders rose with his breaths, tension and cock-daze in every inch of him. Jack wanted to devour him whole. He reached for the collar of Ross's shirt, and—

"No. Stop."

Jack's hand fell at once. He sucked in warm air through his nose.

He waited for Ross to step aside, to seek an escape, but it didn't happen. There was no fear at all in Ross's posture. Just surprise, in the arch of his brows—swiftly covered, but there.

And no sound but the both of them fighting to control their breaths.

"Ah," said Jack. "Did you think I wouldn't?"

"You've read my scribbles," Ross said roughly. "*Stop* and *no* aren't often heeded in that kind of scenario."

"Did you not want me to heed them?"

A ludicrous question in most circumstances. It seemed a sensible one now. Ross raised a thumb to drag down his own lower lip in a maddening, considering motion.

"I assume you have a name as well as a title. Though I've not heard anyone use it. Not even your pa."

"Why would I use it, when I have people who can say 'your lordship' like it's coated in dirt?" He let that lie there a moment. "It's John. Jack, more often. Jack."

"All right then. If I tell his lordship to stop, he can ignore me as he pleases. If I tell *Jack* to stop—he'd better pay attention, or he'll end up with a knee in his knackers."

Anticipation rose again and mingled with the frisson of hearing his name in Ross's mouth, the intimacy claimed boldly and unasked.

"Any other rules in mind?"

"Don't kiss me."

"Do you mean—withhold it, even if you ask for it?"

"No, I . . ." Ross searched Jack's face. Jack didn't know what he was hoping to see, or not see. Some of that hard boldness seeped away. Ross said, slowly, "It's fine if I ask for it."

Jack shrugged. He wouldn't hold a grudge for rule-setting. In that moment he'd probably have accepted any condition if it meant he was allowed to put his hands back on Ross's body, and he was uncomfortably suspicious that Ross knew it.

That, too, was power.

Jack stepped in, closing most of the distance that Ross had put between them. He let his voice drop and darken. "It's not the first thought I have when looking at that mouth of yours, anyway." A lie. All he could think of now was kissing it. "Fuck, you're a bloody devil."

Ross tossed into the gap between their faces a smile of lumi-nous and infuriating beauty. "I'm a guttersnipe, me. Probably trespassing. I don't know any better."

"You need to be taught," said Jack, hoarse, and they were away.

Now he was more in the mood to punish than tease. He un-buttoned Ross's trousers and reached into his drawers without further ado—smothered Ross's first strangled noise with his other palm, then gripped the angle of Ross's neck.

Ross hissed through his teeth. "Is that all, then?"

"You'll take what I give you," said Jack.

"And won't complain?"

"Oh, complain all you like." Jack had the warm length of Ross's prick in his hand now. He gave a couple of short, rough pumps within the confines of Ross's drawers. "It'll make no dif-ference to me."

"Christ you fucking rat's arse shit-heel bastard," said Ross in a low rush, but his eyes closed and his head thudded back, and his breath was coming as fast as Jack's ruthlessly working hand. A firestorm of lust had Jack entirely enclosed. Surely it'd be vis-ible if anyone watched, pouring off him like magic or smoke.

"Tell me again how you don't want this," Jack said, filling it with disdain. "Against your lofty principles, I'm sure, to be reduced to a toy for a lord to play with."

"Fuck you, *fuck* you," gasped Ross. "No—please—"

His hands were gripping Jack's arms. His cock was pushing back in little shoves, eager to be handled. He smelled like ink and wine and damp skin, trapped here where Jack wanted him. When Jack ran a thumb over the tip of that rigid prick, it was wet with need.

Pleasure rippled through Jack to know that he could easily bring Ross off like this, standing up and clothed, with another minute and a few more carefully chosen words. And even more pleasure to know that he could stop.

So he did.

He released Ross's prick without warning. Ross made a

guttural noise of complaint. He reached out, and Jack's prick throbbed with anticipation of a similarly rough grip. As if reading his mind, Ross merely traced with two fingertips the line where Jack was uncomfortably pressed against his own trousers. A thin skewer of fire sank deep into Jack's belly. He managed to hold back a grunt.

Ross's fingers traced back again. The motion was calculatedly wary, almost shy. "So, my lord. I suppose you want me to do something about *this*."

"I saw that face." When Jack took hold of Ross's jaw again there was nothing shy about it. He made his grip rough, grinding skin against sharp jawbone. "I saw your tongue flick out, there. I think you'd like nothing more than my prick in your mouth. But I'm not interested in what you want. Don't forget that."

Pushing his thumb between Ross's lips was a calculated risk. It got him a bite, painful but well short of breaking skin, and a warning of a look. Jack drew his thumb out fast enough to catch on the corner of Ross's mouth, and moved before Ross could react. He drew Ross with him across the room, not slowing when Ross stumbled, back to the desk where he'd been sitting.

"Clothes down, and bend across the desk." The scene from the book, read on the train, landed in his mind as if seared there. "Or do I need to hold you down and do it myself?"

Ross exhaled. It was the moment in which he stopped second-guessing. Jack could see it as if it were being narrated for him on a page. And Ross—miracle of miracles—did exactly as he was told, shoving his trousers and drawers down to bare himself from waist to knees. Jack caught only a glimpse of Ross's rigid cock, and the thick line of black hair leading down to it, as Ross turned. He moved Jack's blotting pad aside with a fastidious motion before he bent himself across the desk.

Just like that. Jack could have done anything to him.

He did nothing. He looked at the cheeks of Ross's arse and swallowed past a dry mouth. He waited until the thud of blood in his own ears settled. In the quiet he heard one of the clocks of the house, somewhere, striking a quarter hour.

"If I'm only here for the view, I'll go elsewhere," said Ross unsteadily. "I—" He cut off, with a sudden ripple of muscle, as Jack set a deliberate hand just above his buttocks. Ross hadn't the plush flesh of some men, but his skin was hot and smooth.

"Even if you're only here for the view," said Jack, "you'll stay where you're put."

He unbuttoned his own clothes and pushed them down a similar amount. His cock was as hard as if he'd been stroking himself for half an hour, and he allowed himself one torturous brush of the tip down the tight cleft of Ross's arse.

"Fucking hell," said Ross, his accent thick. "The only devil here's you."

"Beg me for it."

"In your fucking dreams." Ross's back was an arch, his elbows planted squarely in the leather writing surface of the desk, and he gripped the opposite edge. "You want it, *take* it. I won't make it easy."

"But you'll love it all the same." Shadows sang under Jack's skin. It *felt* like a dream. He'd fucked plenty of people in his life, women and men both, and nothing had ever reached this level of heated unreality. He wouldn't have been surprised to wake up hard and gasping in his own bed, having conjured this entire scenario from sheer want. "And I believe I made it clear. You're here for my pleasure, not your own. So hold those legs together, good and tight."

Not often had he wished he was closer to the truly dissolute old-fashioned rake that his reputation suggested. Perhaps that rake would keep oil in *every* room in the house, instead of only the bedroom. Jack hadn't even planned to enter his study tonight, let alone fuck someone's thighs in it.

Edwin would have a spell for this situation. Jack swallowed inappropriate laughter at the thought, and simply spit a few times in his hand instead. He was wound so tight that he wouldn't last long.

The feeling of pushing his cock between Ross's legs, right up against the drawn-up heat of the man's bollocks, was incredible.

He didn't bother to take it slowly. He was playing at selfishness, after all. He went as hard and quick as he wanted, keeping firm hold with both hands on Ross's hips. Ross jerked and cursed, his shoulders shaking.

"Tighter," Jack growled. "If you can't do it, I'll use a belt to hold them together, and perhaps I'll use it on this pert arse first. To remind it who it belongs to."

"Jesus *Christ*," said Ross, almost conversationally, and came on the desk.

Jack almost didn't realise it had happened, except that Ross's body shook and clenched in a way that dragged him even closer to his own release. And then he realised that the shake was turning to ragged laughter.

"Look at that," said Ross, muffled. The dark head had dropped further. "Made a mess of your fancy desk."

Jack dug his fingers tighter. Every slide was agony now. Suddenly he, too, wanted to burst out laughing. He felt light and far too warm.

"Don't—worry. I intend to make you clean it up."

Ross made a strangled hiccup of a sound and Jack's orgasm raced through his body. When the roar of pleasure had burned itself out, he came back to himself, curled like a parenthesis over Ross, and took two awkward steps back in order to haul his clothes back into a semblance of order.

Ross also pulled up his clothes and refastened them. Colour darkened his cheeks and a large hank of curls fell over his forehead as if it, too, were bloodlessly limp with the aftermath of pleasure.

Jack was ready for more insults, or for obvious regret. But Ross met his eyes, and what passed between them landed on Jack like . . . recognition, perhaps. A deeper version of it than before. Jack had the unfamiliar urge to say something to prolong this encounter, even though it had obviously reached its proper end.

Ross looked at the doubled mess on the leather surface and then back at Jack, who did laugh, now. He located a handkerchief in his pocket and handed it to Ross.

"You should do your own bloody cleaning," said Ross. "Work's good for the soul."

"Only for the poor," said Jack. "I read that in the *Morning Post,* so it must be true."

Ross made an obscene gesture and then cleaned off the desk. He considered the damp, crumpled ball of the kerchief, and Jack braced to have it tossed in his face, but Ross made bold eye contact and slid it into his own pocket. A sluggish surge of leftover desire filled Jack at the sight.

"Thief."

"Arsehole."

"People I've fucked are usually invited to call me Jack, actually. Regardless of context."

He watched the invitation being weighed as Alan Ross weighed all gifts: as if suspecting them of being hollow and containing Greeks.

"All right then. If you ever take a belt to any part of me, Jack, then I'll bite your fucking prick off."

"Duly noted."

"I've never given anyone I've fucked my real name."

"Julius Caesar," said Jack dryly. "I recall."

A brief smile: one of the real, uneven ones. "I suppose you could call me Alan. Only among friends, mind. If you have any."

"Go fuck yourself," said Jack. But he was too well sated to make it sound anything but fond.

11

It was much harder to make the name *Jack* stick to Lord Hawthorn than it had been with Maud, or Violet, or Edwin. Even *Sir Robert* was sliding into *Robin* in Alan's mind, from hearing the others talk about him.

Jack. It was a name like the slap of fingers against skin. Thoroughly unmagical, and unadorned by status.

Alan was going to transform his lordship into a simple Christian name if it killed him. He needed as much equal footing as possible now that things were . . . complicating themselves. This was only another person, as Alan was a person. Treading the same ground. Breathing the same air. And, at least for today, working towards the same goals.

Jack. Alan repeated it over and over, letting his gaze snag where the man in question lounged in Violet's largest armchair. Sensation wormed through Alan when the blue eyes held his with unhesitating interest. He jerked his gaze away at once, but stubbornness forced it back. He wouldn't lose this fight, whatever it was. It wasn't his fault that the well-bred Lord Hawthorn— Jack, *Jack*—was failing to do the polite thing and ignore Alan's presence as if nothing had ever passed between them. No surprise. He didn't care for manners unless they suited him. Hadn't Alan said as much the previous night?

Belatedly Alan realised that Edwin had asked him a question. "Sorry?"

"You brought it with you?"

The rosary. He pulled it from his pocket and handed it over. Edwin and Violet would try to get through the oak door in the spinet room today. Lord—*Jack* was here because runes had something to do with doors and his family had something to do with runes. Alan was here because Edwin had a theory about the rosary and perturbation.

"It's the combination of beech and rowan that's interesting," said Edwin. "I've found out some more about rowan. It's barely used in magical contexts at all, because it's a muffler. It makes any magic less strong, *less* useful."

"Like the dampening pedal on a piano?" said Violet.

"Exactly like," said Edwin. "And beech has a concentrating effect on magic. Using the two together makes no sense unless the opposition is the point. And your mother had you use this in a ritual?"

"Hail Marys and Our Fathers. Nothing magical about them," said Alan. "You say them over and over and you use the beads to keep count. And then, if you're five years old, you get bored of the prayers and just play with the wood because it feels nice."

Edwin pulled the beads through his fingers as if he could turn himself into a wood-taster. He went to the desk where the diagrams of Spinet House lay, and carefully tore a strip from a large piece of paper. Then he flicked the fingers of one hand until the pads glowed white and pressed his thumb to one end of the strip. It acted like glue, binding one end of the paper to the other. He brought the resulting paper loop back to Alan, who took it.

"There's a mathematical—well, it doesn't matter. See how I twisted it before I stuck the end down? It means that this loop has only one side. You could draw a line with a pencil, and it would keep turning inwards and meet itself."

"Look at that. You've learned to use visual aids, Edwin," said Jack.

"Robin likes books to have pictures," said Edwin evenly, and the corner of Jack's mouth gave a twitch.

Alan looked back at his loop. "What does this have to do with the rosary?"

"I think . . ." Edwin made a gesture like a figure-of-eight on its side. "Handling these woods, at an age when most magicians are starting to show their power and have their lock ceremony, gave your magic nowhere to go. The beech kept it flowing, and the rowan turned it back on itself, locking it away until there was no way for you to draw on it even if you'd known to try."

"Wait," said Jack. "Are you saying Ross is a magician?" His lordship hadn't been present when Alan explained about the cracked plates and his mother's panic.

Edwin made a *this is imprecise* face. He settled on "Was. You had the *potential* to be a magician, and it was suppressed. That explains Guignol's case studies, though I'd have to reread them to find out if there was any specific mention of wood. Or, er, Catholicism."

"Was," said Jack harshly.

The past tense, applied to magic. His eyes met Alan's again.

Alan wanted to snap at Edwin—*Stop giving me more things to have in common with this man.* He'd already been inside Jack's house, eaten from his table, laughed at his humour and touched his books and—Sainted Christ—spent onto his furniture, in the grips of an arousal so desperate and all-consuming he hadn't thought his body capable of it.

And then gone home with a spunk-stained handkerchief in his pocket and brought himself off with it, all over again, to the memory.

He shouldn't have given in to this. For all sorts of reasons. But most prominently: he had the urge to apologise to Berto for throwing stones about unwise liaisons. At least if you kept to fucking men of your own station, there was no likelihood of one partner being in vastly more trouble than the other if you were arrested for it.

Lord Hawthorn could ruin Alan's life. He could stand up and accuse Alan of indecent behaviour, and even if Jack had personally sucked the cocks of every man in the courtroom, Alan Ross would still be the one to go to prison. Not an earl's son and heir.

Last night had been an act of unforgivable self-indulgence. Alan was gambling his life and his family's security on Jack being a mild and decent person; the sort of person who wouldn't carry a grudge, wouldn't lash out in revenge, if he ever had reason to be angry with you.

Which, *ha*.

And even knowing that, even throttled by the tightening knot of his own mistake, all Alan could think about was doing it again. The memory of Jack practically hurling him from one side of the room to the other—Jack's filthy thunder-rumble of a voice—the heavy perfection of Jack's body behind his, thick cock shoving between his legs—all of it made Alan's own cock tighten anew and his chest turn to molten butter.

That was its own sort of disaster. For a while this morning Alan had entertained a futile hope that once would have been enough to purge that need from his bloodstream. To prove that a flesh-and-blood encounter would never live up to fantasy—especially the fantasies one took the time to wrap words around and set down in text.

Instead, it had worked in the opposite direction. Now Alan knew that this man could match him in terrifyingly tempting ways. Last night had only broken the iced-over surface of what he might dare to want from a partner like that. There was so much more, darker and riskier, in the depths.

Alan was fucked in so many ways.

"*Hawthorn*," said Edwin, jolting Alan back to the present moment. "If you scare my perturbator away by being your usual bastard self, we will never find this knife and you will be stuck here *child-minding*, as you put it, forever."

Violet picked up the loop of paper, which Alan had set down on the settee between them. "Let's return to business. Is this what happens when anyone else's magic touches him now?" she asked. "It—loops itself away?"

"I believe so," said Edwin. "Not to the same extent, obviously. But magic looks for paths. It replenishes itself in ley lines in the earth. And every path in you, Alan, is carved for diversion." With his string, he cradled a pale green spell. Goose bumps spread over Alan's forearms in memory, but Edwin held the magic within the pattern of string. "This is the chilling spell

I used on you before. Don't imagine a shield, this time. Think about that loop of paper. Think about the magic as something that—twists away. Yes?"

The spell broke over him, and Alan imagined himself as smoother than skin. Ice, or porcelain, or a polished, glossy surface of wood. Anything that tried to find him porous would instead be diverted gently away.

It was still cold. And Christ, it took effort—as soon as a stray thought snuck in at the side, muddying the image he was building, the cold intensified.

Still—"Better," he said, when Edwin was done. "I think."

Edwin was frowning. "I can't tell. Too subjective. Violet, one of your illusions, perhaps?"

Now Alan was the one to have no idea if it was working. He couldn't feel the illusion as he could feel cold. He stood there and thought about carved paths and loops of paper while Violet cast a spell and then walked around him in a circle, hands raised, making thoughtful noises.

"He looks a mess," said Jack.

"You're so helpful, Hawthorn," said Violet. "It was a mess on the *Lyric*, too, but it's worse now. Whatever you're doing is working, Alan. I think."

"Feels like running uphill," said Alan, breath catching unpleasantly in his chest, "so it'd better be doing something."

"We won't tire you out on experiments," said Edwin. "Let's try the door."

They went to the spinet room. The oak door remained visible to everyone, a fact which sent a satisfied light into Edwin's face that almost made him handsome. Whatever he'd done last time, to stabilise the door's appearance, was still working.

The warding on it was still working too.

"How do you get through any of the other doors here?" Jack asked. "If one rule gives you a doorknob for those . . ."

"Music," said Violet. "They have it carved on the frames, if you look." She sat at the spinet and played a one-handed tune. A humming sound came from the dark red door—jarrah wood—as it took up the same tune. And between one moment and the next, the door had a brass knob.

Alan went to look. On the topmost edge of the jarrah door's frame he could see the five lines of a musical stave and a short series of notes.

"If you're counting on me to see what's on the oak and then *hum* it, I won't be much help. I can't read a tune. Do you have a music-taster, along with the one for wood?"

"It's engraved? You could do a rubbing," said Jack. "Charcoal and paper."

"Let's see if he can get close enough, first," said Edwin.

So Alan took step after cautious step towards the oak door while the warding-dread tried to drown him. If he concentrated hard . . . it might have been no more than hopeful imagination, but perhaps he could feel something after all, pathways within him carved slowly and thoroughly like a scar constantly re-opened with the same knife.

Even the idea hurt. He was dimly aware that he was clutching his chest as if to keep its contents from spilling out. But the hurt brought everything into focus, and all of a sudden he *knew* that when he touched the wood-taster to the door, last time, it had been too *much* power trying to escape down channels that were too narrow to hold it. So it had flooded out into him instead, and nearly burst him, until it found a new path through Violet.

Feeling like he was walking a tightrope above a storm-raging sea, Alan walked up to the oak door and looked at the frame.

"No music," he said. "Only stars."

"What?" said Edwin.

"*Stars.*" Alan lifted a helpless hand and made the fingers twinkle. His head ached. He was losing what little mastery he had over the warding's effect on his nerves. He wanted to run a mile away and then empty his guts. "A whole—row of them."

"Violet," said Edwin sharply, but Violet was already saying, "Yes, yes, give me a moment—I have to do it by ear—"

A few false starts—the notes falling like broken glass on the throb of Alan's head—and then it sang out in the room. The orrery song. Alfred Dufay's song.

The storm carving through Alan's body vanished all at once. Exclamations came from behind him; the warding had dropped for everyone, then. And the oak door now had a doorknob exactly where a doorknob should be.

Unfortunately, it was still locked.

"What d'you think?" said Alan, now light-headed with the absence of pain. "Another song to make the keyhole appear?"

"It might only open to the owner," said Edwin. "The rose parlour in Sutton is like that."

But rattling the knob did Violet no good either. She frowned. "Hawthorn, your turn to contribute. How do the runes in the Barrel work?"

"I don't know."

"When will you stop being contrary, Jack?" Edwin snapped. "It's stopped being impressive. We all know you wish you weren't here. Now it's only tiresome."

Jack was leaning on one of the other doors, arms crossed. He seemed unable to exist without something to lounge in or against. He'd also chosen as his backdrop one of the paler woods—Alan couldn't remember most of the names—which made his dark brown hair look almost black, and his eyes like chips of iridescent glass. His waistcoat was of emerald green with rows of stitching that gave it the impression of scales when the light hit it.

His lordship sent Edwin a level look that did nothing to dispel Alan's thoughts of snakes. And then made Alan abruptly remember which category of people were invited to use the name *Jack*. The idea splashed in his mind and rearranged some things. Alan bit his lip against laughter.

"Believe it or not, Edwin, my very presence here means I am resigned to seeing this thing through. Yes—my mother's grandfather designed the rune system that controls the Barrel's doors. I've no doubt it was a difficult, time-consuming project, and it's hardly been passed through the generations as a bedtime story." Having delivered his squashing-down, Jack's posture loosened.

"It'll be like your library-indexing charm. Every room in the Barrel marked and named. What the doors need to know is which two rooms are being linked, and whether a person has permission to pass through. The rune will be a shorthand for those cradles. A defining clause and a pass clause. That's all the theory I can give you, and it may not even apply here."

By Edwin's face, that was more than he'd expected to get.

"If we have to know a defining clause that's only visible *inside* the room that we *can't get to,* then it's an impossible riddle," said Violet irritably. "Lady Enid clearly wanted this secret to die with her."

"But the house wouldn't," said Edwin. "It's not old enough to work like that. And you *did* inherit. You have the right to every inch of this space." Some of that light was back, animating him. "Hawthorn. Can you give us a rune for a basic opening-spell? Would standard spell notation work?"

What followed was some more scribbling in a notebook, producing a pattern like an exploded spiderweb, at the end of which Violet attached the looping *VAD* that was her signature.

On the verge of cradling a true spell, Violet looked at the paper and then at the door. She swallowed. A crack appeared in her poise. "Edwin. You made blood-pledge with Sutton, didn't you?"

"Yes, I—you didn't?"

"No. I was named in the will; the house accepted me. And you're right. It's young, they built it with new magic. Not the old traditions. I don't know if anyone has ever given blood to this house willingly."

A feeling stirred in Alan as if hauled up from the well of his childhood, from the years when he believed in God and the saints and the powers of heaven and hell. At Mass, the sound of the chant was like standing knee-high in black water, shivering with delight at being overwhelmed by something larger. A power that was strong enough to hold you up when you were too tired to do it yourself, or hold you down when you were too restless to sleep.

Magic wasn't religion, but it was a world of power, and a hungry shard of Alan wanted to rage for his own thwarted inheritance. To hurl himself against it until it carved him open along those childhood channels. Blood, if that was what it took.

"Fuck," Violet muttered. "Edwin, you do it, please."

She held out a hand in Edwin's direction, and winced when Edwin cradled something that left the side of one finger oozing red. A visible breath hauled her head upright.

"My name is Violet Anne Debenham. I accept this inheritance, and I . . ." Still wincing, she used her bleeding fingertip to trace the rune on the door. "I make blood-pledge with Spinet House and with its land."

"Mine to tend and mine to mend," said Edwin. "Mine the pull and the natural right."

Violet repeated it. And then added, in a rush, "I'm sorry I've been—afraid. I truly am sorry. I know you've been doing your best. Thank you."

Her hand fell from the door.

And the door clicked open.

The room was small; perhaps two-thirds the size of the downstairs parlour with the large string instruments. No spinets in here. No instruments at all, although Alan wouldn't put it past this house to suddenly start flinging clarinets at one's head.

Sunlight and faint city noise streamed through a single window with its curtains looped back—a real window rather than illusion, going by the faded patches on the floorboards. The wallpaper was pale yellow with tiny white flowers. All the furniture seemed a little too large for the scale of the room in a way that managed to be cosy instead of cramped. There were a great many fat embroidered cushions. The air was soft with dust and lavender, with age and quiet. And—

"Oh," said Violet. "This is where she kept the boxes."

They sat along the window ledge, adorned small tables and

display plinths and the lady's dressing table with its delicate chair and large mirror. Some were round, some square, some in the shape of hearts or many-pointed stars. They ranged in size from that of a matchbook to one—set on the floor and topped with a lace doily and another, smaller box, as if wearing it as a hat—that more rightly deserved to be called a *chest*. Like the doors in the spinet room, like every piece of wooden beauty in this place, they ranged in colour from palest cream to ebony black.

"James Taverner made boxes for Lady Enid as courting gifts," said Violet. "And then made her another as an anniversary gift every year they were married."

The air took on the weight of that as they looked around.

"This feels like either a bad dream or a fairy tale," said Jack. "I'm waiting for an elf to appear and tell us we have until sunset to find the one golden pin in all these boxes."

"Silver, not gold," said Edwin. His string was around his hands. "I wouldn't be surprised if Lady Enid had the idea for this place from Mrs. Sutton's rose parlour. And let's hope . . ."

He cradled a colourless spell, which he held as though balancing a soap bubble between his palms before tossing it away. After a few seconds, he inhaled sharply and looked at his hands, still raised in front of him with the string.

"It's a fossicking spell," he said. "It doesn't care how magical something is, only what it's made from. Here." He led them over to the dresser.

"Those again," said Alan in surprise, looking at the silver hand mirror and hairbrush.

Violet picked up the brush to inspect the pattern on the back. "Mrs. Navenby said that Flora Sutton gave a set to each of them. What else, Edwin?"

Edwin frowned as if listening to a faint sound. The next piece of silver was apparently in a simple rectangular box atop a high corner table. Violet carried the box into better light, where it proved to contain a thick bundle of letters tied with fraying pink ribbon, and a silver photo frame, very tarnished, with a sepia-toned photograph of a grinning young man with a gap between his front teeth.

"I'd forgotten they had a son," said Violet. "I—it's awful, but I can't remember his name. Lady Enid didn't talk about him. He died young. Before I was born."

Again, Alan wanted to run far away, but this time it had nothing to do with magic and warding. He didn't like what they were doing here: standing in a dead woman's heart and pawing through the remains of her life in search of secrets and power. Even walking through a cemetery with Maud hadn't felt this intrusive.

Even more than that, he wanted to run from the feeling of camaraderie that wrapped itself around him, seductive as a soft bed after a long day, the longer he worked with these people. It was starting to feel like he belonged there, respected and liked and allowed access to all these secret histories. He couldn't afford that. And he didn't want to afford the hurt that would come when it ended.

"Could the frame *be* the knife?" Violet asked. "Mrs. Sutton changed the coin into rings."

"And the rings turned back to a coin with a rectification spell." Edwin cradled again and applied it to the picture frame. Nothing happened.

Edwin's fossicking thumbs led them next to a rounded box of very pale wood tucked beneath an armchair. Inside it was . . . another box. This one was made of silver, with pearls inlaid in the lid. Violet lifted it out gingerly, and Edwin cast the rectification, but it remained a box rather than a knife.

Inside that one was—

"Another wooden box," said Jack. "Who'll take a wager that there'll be a smaller silver box inside?"

Violet cracked the lid. Jack would have lost the wager. The box was lined with red velvet, and inside it was a many-folded square of paper and a long lock of brown hair. Another keepsake from the dead son, perhaps.

The piece of paper, when unfolded, held two lines of hand-inked music. Violet blinked at it for a while, hummed experimentally, and said, "I don't know. It looks like the start of a transposition exercise. The same tune in two keys."

"Edwin, Violet," said Jack. "Do you remember your lock ceremony?"

"Yes." Edwin looked up sharply.

"What did the box look like?"

"Which box?" said Edwin. "For storage? I never saw it. The ceremony was at Penhallick. My parents had the lock sent to London for registration at the Barrel."

Violet agreed that she, too, had undergone her lock ceremony at her family home. This was an aspect of magical culture that Alan already knew: at the first sign of showing magical ability, children had a lock of hair cut and sent to a room in the Barrel, where the locks could then be used to determine the location of any registered magician in times of peril. Robin and Adelaide had used it to locate Edwin, with Mrs. Kaur's help.

"Our father took myself and Elsie in person to the Barrel, after ours." It was the first time Alan had heard that name from Jack's mouth. "They took us to the Lockroom and let us put our locks into their storage boxes." He nodded at the velvet-lined box. "They looked like that. Exactly like."

"But if . . . oh. *Transposition.* Oh, that's *genius.*" Edwin looked torn between laughter and tugging his own hair out. He looked around at them all. "The good news is, I know where the knife is."

Alan's heart gave a painful skip. So. What he'd come here for was mostly accomplished. That was a *good* thing, it was, it was.

He said, "And the bad?"

A smile lurched into existence on half of Edwin's mouth. "How do we feel about stealing something from the most magical location in England?"

12

Jack spent half of the following day at Westminster having conversations about the People's Budget, unable to shake the echo of Alan's voice in the back of his head while he did so. He then dropped in on his Mayfair townhouse, where Oliver was engaged in determinedly refreshing Jack's wardrobe and cataloging its defects, to keep his word to his mother.

Jack's illegitimate half brother was a pleasant boy. Too anxious-to-please to be genuinely sunny, but decent, and with a professional fussiness that was the stamp of all well-trained valets.

And Oliver oozed magic; there was no doubt about that. In the guise of preparing him to be a useful part of Spinet House's defences, should they be attacked again, Jack began filling in some of the gaps in *that* part of Freddy Oliver's training. Such as it was. Or . . . wasn't.

Edwin had a passionate lecture tucked away about how strong magicians tended to be sloppy magicians, because they never needed to be painstaking in order to make a spell come out as they wanted. So they brute-forced through the basics and learned more elaborate or complex spells only if they were curious and methodical or their family put the effort into having them taught.

Walter Courcey might fall into the sloppy category, but George Bastoke didn't. And neither did Jack himself, son of a Bastoke woman who'd insisted on her children being taught perfect control. Watching Oliver grow up with untrained Alston strength must have invoked a war between Lady Cheetham's tact and her practicality. Jack was surprised she'd managed to hold off on taking charge of the boy's education until now.

Once the magic lesson was done they returned to Spinet. Jack had Oliver make some adjustments to one of Jack's old dinner suits, so that when Alan turned up to Spinet House with half an hour to spare before the dinner gong sounded, Jack could have the mean pleasure of saying: "No excuses this time, Master Cesare. You're changing for dinner."

Alan looked from Jack to Oliver and then back to Jack.

"If you bought me a suit of clothes, I will throw them out the window," he said flatly.

"I wouldn't dare. They're castoffs. Fit only for the rag bin. Or you."

Oliver made a noise of outraged pride, but all of Jack's eyes were for the way Alan's face came alive with challenge. For a hot, mad moment he wanted to give Oliver the evening off and personally peel Alan Ross out of that ink-stained shirt and the plain brown suit that was fighting to make him look pedestrian, anything less than extraordinary, and was failing miserably. *How the hell does anyone get any work done with you in the office?* Jack wanted to demand. No wonder his editors were happy to let him roam the streets and drop in only for deadlines.

"Your castoffs? I'll swim in them."

"Oliver would be a poor excuse for a magician-valet if he couldn't adjust a suit to fit," said Jack, and Oliver's red hair bounced happily.

"I took a guess at the sizing, sir, but I can do the final touches once it's on."

Alan winced, probably at the *sir,* but Oliver's earnestness seemed to be a weapon he hadn't armed himself against. He submitted to being led upstairs to Jack's own room, and sat down to dinner in what might have been the first suit ever to fit him properly in his life. He looked well groomed and lovely and radiantly grumpy about the whole business.

Maud and Adelaide showered him in compliments. Violet took one look at him and turned to fire a gleefully suggestive expression across the table to Jack.

Don't, Jack cradlespoke at her.

She returned something with the vague meaning of *hungry and obvious about it,* and before Jack could say anything turned the flick of her fingers into beckoning for the platter of boiled vegetables, which the cook had mercifully smothered in a cheese sauce.

Conversation was light until dinner was over, but the atmosphere was tense. Everyone knew tonight's business. Before an offensive strike came the planning stage. Jack was no military historian, but he had enough practical experience to know that an hour of strategy could go into every key minute on a battlefield.

And a second of unexpected chaos could throw hours' worth of strategy out the window in an instant. But that wouldn't win him many smiles if he mentioned it.

Finally, Robin tapped his glass and cleared his throat. The dessert course had been removed and the table now contained only drinking glasses, stained napkins, and everyone's guidelights. The guidekeepers were cunningly blown glass orbs frothing with caught air bubbles, tinged subtly green, which gave the room an underwater look.

The servants had melted discreetly away. All of Spinet House's staff knew that *something* was afoot—the many nocturnal break-in attempts rather gave that away—and Maud had refused to lie to them, but too much information would still be endangering. So Violet had simply said that there was something valuable of Lady Enid's in the house that many people wanted to steal, and she wasn't going to let it happen.

"Stand for speeches, Robin," said Adelaide.

Robin smiled at her and pushed to his feet. "There's no point speechmaking to thank you all for coming, or to compliment the food. Let's be frank. We're here to discuss—"

"*High theft,*" said Maud delightedly.

Edwin stood too. "Well. Yes. We think that Lady Enid visited the Lockroom at some point and made a switch, removing someone's hair box and substituting the knife of the Last Contract."

"She made the Assembly do the hiding for her," said Violet. "I adore it."

"Ironic, then," said Jack, "if the Assembly has been ripping up carpets and killing people in order to find something that's been under their noses all along. It seems risky, as hiding places go."

"The Barrel is a crossing point for ley lines," said Edwin. "Even more so than Sutton Cottage, and in fact they have a line in common. Think of it like Underground stations. I suspect that's why that site in London was chosen for the Barrel in the first place. I'm not certain that the knife is there," he warned. "Mrs. Sutton said that a piece of the contract would create a heavier footprint on the ley lines, if hidden in a place of power, and that's how Bastoke's people suspected she had the coin in the first place. I would have thought they'd have found the knife even *more* easily if it was somewhere as magic-dense as the Barrel. But it's still the best lead we have."

"Edwin went to see Kitty Kaur today," said Robin. "She knows the Barrel better than any of us. We aren't telling her everything, Addy. I don't want her and Singh put in a difficult position if things go wrong."

"If we're caught stealing from the Barrel, after what happened at Violet's hearing? Yes, that would qualify as *going wrong*," said Jack.

"Then we don't get caught." Maud reached out an absent hand and took Violet's. "Edwin, Robin? Do you have a plan?"

"So far what we have is a list of problems," said Robin. "But thanks to Kitty, it's at least an accurate list."

He and Edwin took them through it, Edwin with the help of a notebook in which he'd written everything that Mrs. Kaur had told them.

Every visit made to the Lockroom to register a new magician— or to use one's hair to locate them, though this was much rarer—was entered in the record book. Full name of requester, full name of the magician whose box was added or fetched. The same enormous ledger had been in use since the Barrel was built. It should therefore be possible to see if Lady Enid had made a visit to the Lockroom, and whose box she requested in order to make a switch.

"It could have been her own, her son's, her husband's—anyone's," said Edwin.

"Edwin has a charm which can search the record for Lady Enid's full name," said Robin.

"Possibly," said Edwin. "I'm still working on it."

Robin's face was as good as a shout of adoring support from the sidelines during a rugby match. Edwin gave a tiny eye roll in return, but also stood straighter.

They moved on to the next page of Edwin's notes, which appeared to be a depressing list of reasons why this was a doomed folly. Not everyone had permission to access the Lockroom, even if they knew the rune that defined it. Most of those who could were attached to the Coopers. Who worked under George Bastoke. And Mrs. Kaur's own permission had been revoked ever since she was "threatened" into helping Robin access the room.

And even if they managed to make it into the Lockroom, any request they made to view and retrieve a box would be permanently logged with someone's full name. The records were only reviewed weekly, but it was near-impossible to falsify them.

"Stop looking like you've all washed your faces in mud. We must have *some* things going for us," said Violet. "I'm getting very handy with illusion disguises, for one thing."

"Robin and Edwin and I could come up with a reason to visit almost any department in the Barrel, with the liaison work," said Adelaide. "Robin and I have pass-tokens, and we know that Hawthorn can enter. In fact, most of us can get past the warding against non-magicians. It's only . . . Maud and Mr. Ross who can't?"

"A firm hand can get anyone in if necessary," said Robin, grinning at Adelaide. "You had to drag me over the threshold the first time."

"Am I likely to *be* necessary?" It was the first time Alan had spoken since dinner ended.

"We know Violet's illusions don't work on you," said Edwin. "And I don't imagine we'll need a perturbator for this. Especially as the effect you have is unpredictable."

"Fine by me." Alan's eyes flicked to Jack, then away. "The only other relevant skill I have is lock-picking, and it doesn't sound like that's what you need for those magical doors."

"I can help!" said Maud. "What can I do?"

"*You* should be chained to a bedpost and made to stay home," said Violet, "after that stunt you pulled in the cemetery."

Maud coloured, half anger and half—Christ, Jack wished he didn't know this—something else. Violet had indeed yelled at Maud after her unfortunate adventure in being multiply possessed, and Maud had yelled back. Maud and Violet went in for that sort of thing with great vigour, because making up after a fight was one of their favourite activities—another thing that Jack wished he didn't know, and which he only *did* know because Violet was apparently incapable of conducting her affairs without a friend to chew them over with. In her usual wildly inappropriate fashion, she had decided upon Jack as that friend. Three years in a Bowery theatre had made Violet far more comfortable discussing sex than most ladies of Jack's acquaintance.

In this particular instance, Jack had walked in on them . . . making up. Which he had informed Maud was natural justice being served for her bursting in on Violet and himself on the *Lyric*. And then he went off to try to scrape the image out of his memory with whisky. It was the first time in years he'd been tempted to get his hands on some lethe-mint.

Now Maud set her chin and turned to Edwin. "Is there some way you could make everyone evacuate the Barrel, so that it's empty and nobody sees you getting into the room? What would happen if some kind of danger arose?"

"There's a general exit rune," said Edwin. "It will get anyone, through any door, back to the main foyer. People would use that if something went wrong. But . . . evacuate? Due to what? A building full of magicians could deal with anything as simple as fire."

Maud frowned. "A threatened explosion?"

"Gunpowder, treason, and plot," murmured Alan. "Difficult to fake convincingly, that one."

"Besides, unless we can find a way to cheat the runes, we'll still need someone else to get us into the Lockroom in the first place," said Adelaide.

"Robin," said Edwin suddenly. "No. I don't think—"

"It's worth a try." Robin was tugging a ring from his finger. He set it down: wooden, like the ones that Violet used when she built illusions. "My visions helped Maudie on the *Lyric*. And you know I can direct it sometimes. I've been inside the Lockroom, so I know where to start."

The ring turned out to be made of rowan. Edwin had hoped it would keep Robin's increasingly painful visions at bay. Foresight wasn't magic, but it seemed related enough that the ring had been helping.

Edwin looked unhappy, but it was hard to dissuade a Blyth with an idea in their head. Robin closed his eyes and took slow breaths, rubbed his palms together as if trying to warm them, and—went still. Jack had only seen Robin Blyth in the grip of foresight once before. It was unnerving. His eyelids slotted open. The hazel eyes thus revealed were unfocused and glazed.

It lasted less than half a minute, and then Robin blinked several times and raised a wincing hand to his temple. A breath left Edwin like a quiet breeze.

"I don't know," Robin said, frustrated, before anyone could ask. "It was—bizarre. Chaotic. Dark clouds, and flashes of movement in the clouds. I *think* it was indoors, but I don't even know if it was the Barrel at all. And everything was shaking like a photo apparatus tossed around in a storm. Not much help. Sorry."

"Are you sure we can't leave the knife where it is?" said Adelaide. Worry creased her face, looking at Robin. "If it's all chaos and uncertainty—is there really any harm in letting it stay hidden?"

"And if the other side finds a way to make the triangulation work and finds it first?" said Edwin. "I haven't had time to plan for that scenario yet."

"We should," said Violet. "We should plan for it. Or—what if we *did* let it happen?"

"*What?*" said Edwin.

"What if Robin had the right idea at my legal hearing? Put it all out in the open, for everyone to know. Walter claimed they'd only use the pooled magic of Britain's magicians for the common good. What if we held them to it? If we had the entire Assembly on board, not just Bastoke and whomever he has in his pocket. We could insist that they needed the consent of everyone—a vote—before they did anything. Or . . . insist that they built a ritual that used the bloodlines of the Three Families but would exclude anyone who hadn't given *direct* consent."

"Insist how?" said Edwin, but he caught his lip between his teeth, thoughtful. "I—I suppose, in theory, pooling power isn't *inherently* dangerous. Only doing it without consent or oversight."

"It is dangerous," said Jack.

Everyone turned to him. His throat was tight and hot.

"Once magic has been drawn out of someone and mingled, there's no guarantee it goes back in again untainted. Or. At all."

"Does it need to go back in? I thought the whole point of magic was that you used it and then it"—Robin waved a hand—"refreshed itself. With time. Or else you'd never be able to do more spells the next day."

"Normally, yes," said Jack. "But—" And that was it, he was about to explain how he knew any of this, and the secret-bind flared to sudden, terrible life on his tongue.

Jack couldn't help the sound he made. He at least made sure it was short.

"Hawthorn!" Maud dissolved into concern. "This is about what happened with Lady Elsie, isn't it? And your cousin?"

"Oh, Christ," said Edwin. He sat, heavily, and rubbed his face. "Hawthorn, we *need* to know what you know, if it's about what Bastoke has planned for the contract. Especially now that the Dufay lead has come to nothing. It's absurd to have you sitting there like a book that's been glued shut."

Jack swallowed a gulp of water and slammed down the glass. "What a delightful fucking image, Edwin. And how *do* you intend to force the pages open?"

Edwin flinched but held Jack's gaze. Edwin was not kind, and neither was he weak, despite his appearance. Edwin would pin Jack down like a butterfly to a collector's board and do whatever it took, if it meant finding the answers he needed. And if it was for the *greater good,* Maud and Robin might let him do it.

Despite the water, Jack's mouth felt like it had been scoured from the inside. He wanted to spit. He wanted to leave this table, this room, and climb aboard a ship bound anywhere but here.

"By tricking it," said Maud.

"What?" said Jack.

"Magic is far less clever than people. Robin's oath to report his visions proves that." She smiled at her brother. "We're both very good at telling the truth in stupid ways."

They were. Jack had seen Maud tell a stunning number of lies without actually telling them. It was all about the shape of things.

An idea rose.

"Edwin." Jack snapped his fingers at the notebook. "I need a pencil. I'm going to draw you a section of my family tree."

"Why—"

"For *no reason,*" Jack nearly snarled.

Maud laughed. "That's it! Sarcasm is exactly what might work."

It didn't seem like it could be that simple. Jack couldn't convince himself that his sister's name on his tongue would do anything but sear it.

But he took a piece of paper torn from Edwin's notebook, and Edwin found him a pencil, and Jack drew his mother's side of his own family tree. Mary Bastoke. Two brief lines connecting her to Frederick Alston, Lord Cheetham, and more lines down to the names John and Elsie. His hand shook and his mouth dried further as he sketched a quick, erasing line through *Elsie,* then skipped up the paper. His mother's parents. His mother's older brother, the second John on the page; he leaned weight through the lead, writing the name more heavily, and did the same for the line down to the name George Bastoke.

He underlined his uncle and cousin's names, trying to think of his hand as something separate to himself, and then set the pencil down.

"Ask," he said. "I'll tell you some lies."

He wasn't surprised that it was Maud who spoke first.

"So, my lord. May we assume that you maintain *excellent* relations with your"—she consulted the paper—"uncle? And your cousin."

"I have the utmost respect for them both," said Jack. "We've kept in frequent contact over the past sixteen years. It pains me *extremely* that my uncle passed away some years back, after being in very poor health since—" But despite his trying to speak quickly, as if to outrun the racing hounds of the secret-bind, he couldn't finish the sentence once it tipped towards truth.

"Since," echoed Edwin. He traced the thick lines that Jack had drawn. "Don't try to nod. Just tap on the table if I'm wrong. Bastoke senior and George were both involved in what happened to Elsie. And it had something to do with pooling magical power." His voice, too, sped up and nearly stumbled. "Even then, that's what the Bastokes wanted. They were trying to draw on someone else's magic. And of course they'd try with you and Elsie—direct blood relations, who out of anyone would seem to have magic to spare."

"Did these people kill your sister?" said Alan quietly.

Hearing it filled Jack with the sort of wild, despairing anger he hadn't felt in years. The anger he'd been hiding from when he refused to follow his mother through the gate in Cheetham's gardens. He couldn't repress a small shudder. Did John kill Elsie? Yes. No.

"Too big," said Maud, watching him. "Someone try a specific."

Violet was pale, but she said baldly: "Did one of them push her off the roof?"

Alan made a small jerk of a movement, then subsided.

Jack exhaled. No secret-bind kept him from speaking about that event in particular. Only a deep reluctance to touch it, even in passing. He'd walled this memory away and hoped he could thereby make it vanish.

"No. She'd been . . . secluded, for the months leading up to it. Unwell. And even though I didn't have magic, I *felt* what happened to the Cheetham land when—" He closed his eyes. It didn't help. He flattened his voice utterly, as if he could wrench himself away from his body and let it, piece of flesh that it was, speak the words without his having to feel them. "I don't have any reason to believe that anyone else was there, or that anyone else caused it. When she jumped."

"We all knew she'd been unwell for a long time," said Violet. "But nobody knew exactly what happened. You said magic goes back in *tainted,* or . . . not at all."

"Oh, bloody hell," said Robin. "That's what happened to your magic?"

At least it was Robin. There was sympathy on his face, but it was the firm kind that Jack could bear. Jack didn't nod. He didn't tap the table either.

"And Elsie's?" said Edwin.

Jack managed a convulsive shake of his head before the bind punished him for it. Even if he could have explained it in the face of his parents' ever-more-desperate questions, back when it first happened, he wouldn't have known where to begin. Elsie never lost her magic the same way that he did. But she was lost to him and lost to the life—the brilliant, unprecedented life—that she should have lived.

"They obviously didn't have the Last Contract to use." Edwin stared at Jack as if at a live coal fallen from the grate. Clearly imagining the horror of being what Jack was. "That might have been what went wrong."

Jack couldn't answer that. Perhaps his magic and Elsie's had truly mingled, and perhaps they hadn't. His uncle had determined that they would never know. He had a sudden and very sharp image of splintered, blackened fingernails, and was abruptly done with this. It wasn't helping.

"I can't tell you the details," he said. "You will, as daunting as the prospect seems, simply have to trust me. Trust me that this is too dangerous for anyone to be allowed to experiment with it. And even if it wasn't—George and Walter and the others have killed several people to make this possible. Do you really think they'll step back with a shrug if the majority of British magicians decide to withhold consent when asked? Violet?"

"No." Violet looked flattened. "Fuck."

"So we're decided," said Adelaide. "High theft it is."

The planning took them further into the night than any of them expected. Edwin ended up with a list of further questions for Adelaide to take to Kitty, with apologies.

Maud kept sneaking hopeful looks at Alan, as if he might bestow gems of criminal wisdom upon them, but Alan didn't seem inclined to contribute. Nor was he needed to play a part in the scheme itself.

He didn't leave, though. At one point, when Adelaide and Robin were arguing over the location of a specific office, Alan slid Edwin's open notebook toward himself and tore out a few pages in order to sit there, head and shoulders bent over the paper, scribbling steadily away. Jack hoped like hell that what he was writing was journalistic in nature, because the idea of the Roman sitting across the table from Jack and openly working on a story about—about—

Jack wrenched his thoughts away from that and back to the planning at hand.

Violet offered rooms for the night to anyone who wanted

them, but Adelaide was expected home and Robin wouldn't let her go unescorted, and Edwin went where Robin went. And Alan said, "I like your house, Violet, but I don't think it likes *me* enough for that," and left by the front door with his head high.

Jack, yawning in the doorway with Violet, had an unnerving flash as if seeing sideways into a life that he might have had: marrying Violet, making her Baroness Hawthorn, and fare-welling their guests together after an evening party.

He glanced at her, luminous with her yellow hair and lavishly adorned blue gown. Perhaps she was imagining it, too, because she met his eyes and let out a tiny laugh.

"Lord Hawthorn." Alan was halfway down the steps. He gestured with his head down to the street. "Can I have a word?"

Jack followed. The nearest streetlamp was only yards away, casting dense shadows of leaves onto the stones of the street and making a pool of light that Alan stepped into. This conversation was to be private but not unseen.

Jack raised his eyebrows—*Well?*

Alan looked up at Jack and touched his fingertips to his own lower lip. Desire slipped through Jack at the sight, but most of him was a mess of feelings stirred up like the bottom of a pond. Anger and grief and loss were clouding him and would take time to settle again. And his fucking leg ached.

So he was not in the mood to be reminded of Alan Ross's mouth. He was ready to put the man down, sharply, when—

"How much did it hurt?" Alan asked. "When they put it on you in the first place."

Ah.

"It hurt," said Jack. "I don't know your points of comparison. And I am not about to start lovingly reliving it, if that was what you had in mind. No matter how much you might enjoy the idea of me in pain."

"I—don't." Alan's mouth twisted as if that had been difficult to get out. "I only wanted to say that I understand now what you meant about having reasons to be angry. The world's done a bloody number on both my sisters, but it hasn't killed them yet. I'd been wondering, if you had something like this, like magic, why you'd give it all up. Leave it behind. But it makes sense."

"I didn't give up magic." It was easier to admit here in the half shadows of night.

It gave me up. But that wasn't quite true either. Jack had been hurt and abandoned, and had wanted to hurt and abandon in return. Magic had been torn from him; and his twin, who was the best part of magic, as well. It had taught him a useful lesson about needing anyone or anything too badly.

And his decision had barely felt like running away. It had felt necessary, practical. Like exiting the ruins of a house gone to rot and dereliction.

"I suppose I've been building dream-castles," said Alan. "Can't help it. I keep thinking that if my family had power like this, we wouldn't have to be in service at all, and I wouldn't have to fight for connections to scrape my way into a better job, but that's not true. Your valet. Violet's servants. They're magical, but they're still in service."

"If you're looking for more footmen to question about their reading habits, you could come back tomorrow."

Alan huffed, halfway to laughter. "The plain fact is, the world's the world, and your title's still likely to do me more good than any amount of magic that might have been wrung out of me by a rosary. And yes, your lordship, I *do* hate that."

They weren't touching. Jack wanted to sip at that hatred and let it pour down into his fingertips. And yet he didn't want Alan Ross to hate *him*, except in ways that they both enjoyed. The knowledge jarred him. He hadn't cared about anyone's opinion of him for years.

But Alan Ross's opinions were deeply considered and strongly held, grown like hardy weeds in the difficult soil of his upbringing. If he judged Jack wanting, then Jack would deserve it.

"The world is the world," Jack agreed. "Most success happens through connections, no matter your station. There's no magical law of inheritance that means someone pulls out a drawer in their desk, when they retire, and there's a contract of employ-ment naming the ideal man for the job, handily giving his full name and address." Jack was hoping for another almost-laugh, but didn't win one. "People talk. People do favours. That's how it works."

"I know," said Alan bitterly. "Magical or not, people use one another."

A rash, aching feeling crested in Jack. He found the words *quid pro quo* behind his teeth and imagined spitting them out onto the ground, to be trodden into the dirt and forgotten for-ever.

"And I'm a card to be played, you said. So tell me what else you want. Use me."

Alan's silence had a suspicious cast to it. But he looked up at Jack, and swallowed. Ruddy lamplight played with the shadows thrown by his curls onto his forehead.

"You're writing me a blank cheque?"

"You'd tear it up and tell me to eat the pieces," said Jack. "And I know you have more imagination than that."

Perhaps Alan's cheeks darkened with blood. Jack wanted to put a hand there, to check.

"Use you. All right," Alan said hoarsely. "I will."

13

The office of the *Morning Post* was a piece of music played by an orchestra. Or perhaps Alan needed to resist Spinet House's influence and find himself some new metaphors. Either way— the office of a daily newspaper began slowly and then accelerated throughout the day, reaching its climax when the paper was put to bed in the evening and the steady racket of the printing presses, housed in wooden sheds in the dingy yard of the building, began.

Every story was an instrument: the political commentary, the notices and reviews of opera and theatre performances, the dispatches from foreign correspondents, the society pieces with their gossip dressed up in fusty speech. Each contributed to the sound of the whole.

It was midmorning and therefore relatively calm. That was the only way one could catch the *Post*'s editor for a leisurely conversation. Alan led Jack through a room crammed with typewriters on desks, only half of them in use at the moment, and towards Kenyon's office.

The sound of many people typing was a comfort to Alan, no matter how frenzied the orchestra grew as deadline approached. He'd grown up in a loud family and a series of dismally thin-walled rooms. It took a lot more than a bellowing sub-editor, directing spittle into the red face of a journalist who'd skidded in too close to deadline with a story five inches too long, to put Alan off his work.

"Sir?" Alan rapped his knuckles on the door, and Randall

Kenyon lifted his frown from reading to beckon him inside. "I've brought someone keen to meet you. Lord Hawthorn—"

"Yes, charmed," drawled Jack. He was carrying a stick today, something Alan had only ever seen him do once on the *Lyric,* and seemed to actually be leaning on it. He exaggerated that effect as he strode into the office and extended a hand.

His cufflinks had diamonds in them. Alan tried to look humble and non-murderous as his lordship's plummiest tones sailed forth.

"How d'you do. Kenyon? Wanted to meet you face-to-face, express my appreciation for the work you do. Read the *Post* religiously, of course. First one I pick up over breakfast."

"Well. I—delighted, my lord, of course. Thank you. Thank you."

Kenyon turned red above his moustache as he shook Jack's hand. When he'd first taken over the *Post* the occasional whiff of reformist thought had floated weakly into his editorials, but under Lady Bathurst's ownership of the paper he'd settled back into producing a solid Tory rag.

Unlike Lady Bathurst, he was easily cowed by titles. And unlike Lady Bathurst, he was *not* a personal friend of Lord Cheetham, and was therefore unaware that Jack's politics were those of a class traitor.

Alan had primed Jack like a cannon and was now ruthlessly firing him at the man. This was the last chance he'd get, while he and Jack were still engaged in the same business and while Jack still had reason to express gratitude with favours. It wouldn't last. Nothing did. Everything would change in a few days' time if they found the knife at the Barrel.

"And very good of you to give Ross here a chance to shine. Offering opportunity to the deserving poor. Shows an eye for talent as well as the editorial eye, hey?"

Baron Hawthorn patted Alan patronisingly on the shoulder and launched into an expanded version of the story he'd come up with in Westminster, complete with vague gesturing at both stick and leg, hinting at dire wounds. Good old Sergeant Ross had saved his life in the Boer. Much lamented. Been pleased to connect with Ross's only son back in England.

Alan couldn't remember if he'd ever told Kenyon that his father had been an ice-cream seller, but it hardly mattered. Reality was being overwritten through sheer force of aristocratic authority. Kenyon—both an ardent voice for the kingdom's military and an ex-Transvaal civil servant—gazed at Lord Hawthorn, Boer veteran, with increasing adoration. Alan swallowed a complex, wriggling mouthful of possessive feeling.

"—view it kindly if you'd help me keep an eye out for the lad's prospects," finished Jack insufferably. "I'm sure he's *acutely* aware of the privilege, and all that, working here at the *bastion* of modern political thought."

Alan managed to mutter something appropriate.

"Of . . . course," said Kenyon weakly. "Talented lad. Asset to the newsroom. Always thought so." His own sentences were falling into step with Jack's.

Jack reminisced about the war a while longer, made an on-the-spot donation of fifty pounds to the paper's ridiculous subscription fund to buy an airship for national defence, and trotted out the exact same arguments against the People's Budget that Lord Cheetham had used.

Kenyon was practically floating half a foot above the ground by the time he ushered them back out of the office. Several pairs of eyes snapped down to notepaper or typewriter as they exited, and the melody of innocent typing followed them out into the corridor.

"Jesus, Mary, and Joseph, that was even better than I expected," Alan breathed. "If he doesn't give me a sub-editor post by the end of the year, I'll eat my hat. Maybe even one of *your* hats. With all that stiff silk, it'd be harder to get down."

"Nonsense. I have full confidence in your ability to swallow stiff things," said Jack, in that appallingly cut-glass tone.

Alan choked on incredulous laughter. He told his prick, rather desperately, that this *wasn't the time.*

"Besides," Jack went on, before Alan could muster a caustic response, "when you then leverage the position for one at the *Sphere,* the man can hold me to blame."

"I don't think he'd blame you for slitting his throat even if you made eye contact the whole time," said Alan. "No, he'll moan at you about my fickle lack of gratitude, and you can agree that the lower classes these days lack all sense of loyalty to their masters."

The side of Jack's mouth twisted. He leaned against the wall and propped both hands on the silver head of his stick. The motion was casual, but the shift of his weight caught Alan's attention. Surprise rendered him ruder than he'd intended.

"Don't tell me you actually have a war wound."

"Nothing serious," said Jack. "The Lord Hawthorn who remembers his war service fondly and with pride will of course talk about it at every opportunity."

Alan laughed. "Hell, *he* was something, wasn't he? I could write a story about him." He was ready to put the thought away and pull it out again later, but Jack's gaze caught him like a fishing line and held him.

"What kind of story?"

For Christ's sake. Alan had never been asked to produce plot ideas while standing upright and fizzing with arousal.

"The kind of toff who'll waltz in here and throw his weight around like that wouldn't put himself out for nothing. Not for a gutter journalist like me. He'd do it because he expected something in return."

"Something," said Jack.

Too many emotions fought for attention. Alan was coming down off success and ignoring the ever-present groundswell of his guilt. He'd already made the mistake of fucking this man, hadn't he? He couldn't unmake it. He could only decide how much further he was prepared to go.

But writing was *work.* He didn't want to be the one coming up with the stage directions for something real.

"Yes. I imagine he'd be impatient about it too."

Jack looked briefly down the corridor as someone exited a door and headed away from them towards the street entrance. Then his attention returned to Alan. "And what precisely is the journalist offering?"

Deliberate; measured. Alan thought of how careful Jack had been, in his study, to be sure of Alan's desire before he let himself off the leash. Jack Alston was mocking and infuriating, and the existence of his station was a travesty, but he was—he wasn't—

Alan needed to stop thinking. He let himself be hunger, and shame, and little else.

He lifted his gaze.

"Use me."

An expression with claws and teeth rose behind the brilliant blue of Jack's eyes, visible in the way their corners tightened and a small sneer twitched beside his nose. He inhaled hard. "Come with me."

The limp, if there'd been one, was gone. Jack's legs ate up the corridor as he strode down it, rattling the handles of closed doors—opening those that weren't locked, and giving an impatient nod to anyone inside before closing them again. As if he had more right to be here than the people whose workplace this was. As if interrupting or inconveniencing them was nothing. Alan knew it was mostly an act and still wanted to punch him.

And it was unbearably arousing, because Jack was exerting the full force of his arrogance in order to find an empty room in which to let this play out.

They did find one. It seemed to be where broken chairs and old cabinets were put to think about their sins: gloomy, smelling of damp, and with the ugliest greenish carpet Alan had ever seen.

His lordship slammed the door behind Alan and crowded him back against it. There was no key to turn in the lock. Alan's heart snuck up his throat until he had to swallow hard to get it back down into his chest.

"You're right," said Jack. The sneer was in his voice now. "I'm not inclined to wait for what I'm owed."

"My lord. I don't understand—"

"I think you do."

Alan's mind kept looping on *no lock!* as his hands flattened on the door and his little finger banged painfully against the doorknob. He was spending a lot of time around doors lately. But none of his adventures in Spinet House could hold a candle to this.

A version of himself. That was what he needed, just as the man in front of him—broad and inescapable, close enough that Alan could see a shaving nick on his jaw and the exact shape of that broken nose—was a version of Jack.

"You think I'm that kind of man?" He let his voice shake. It would have shaken anyway. They were so close. Alan's body was alive and humming. "You think I'll let you have your way with me, in some kind of indecent—perverse—"

Jack didn't bother to reply. He smiled the cruel smile of a card-player about to take his opponent for everything down to the shirt on their back and lifted a hand to flick mockingly at a lock of Alan's hair. Then traced down the side of his face. Two blunt fingertips, barely making contact, but the touch sent shivers of sensation across Alan's cheek.

Then Jack pushed those fingers between his lips, without warning or ceremony.

Alan made a sound. It was stifled. He knew himself and his desires; he'd walked their boundaries pretty fucking thoroughly after nine years of being the Roman. If he'd thought about it specifically he would have agreed that yes, having Lord Hawthorn's fingers shove over his tongue and fill his mouth *would* be likely to send blood rushing to his cock.

He wouldn't have known the half of it.

He closed his eyes, because he could already feel and taste and smell the man in front of him, could hear the small, wet noises of his own mouth, and sight was going to be—too much. He shrank his world down to the insistence of those fingers and the way it felt to suck them and let his tongue explore. It was as if a string were tied to the base of his cock and the other end tugged hard whenever he swallowed. Brown light gathered behind his eyelids. His breath was hot and then it was forgotten, irrelevant.

"*Christ,*" Jack said, hoarse. "You want it so much, don't you?"

Alan coughed as the fingers withdrew. He cracked his eyes open and managed to glare. "*No.*"

"Nice try, Mr. Ross. I know exactly what sort of man you are. You followed me in here panting for a prick in your mouth, and that's what you'll have."

Alan could have resisted the push to his shoulder, but he let it bear him to his knees, his traitor mouth already watering further. The ugly carpet was surprisingly comfortable. Or perhaps it just beat wet cobbles. Or perhaps the rest of Alan's body was so warm with anticipation, howling with so much need as Jack took commanding hold of his hair, that he wouldn't have noticed if he'd been kneeling on spikes.

He let his hands rest on Jack's legs. The wool of those black trousers was incredibly fine and light.

A tug at his hair raised his face. He wasn't ready for it. The skin of his cheeks and forehead felt exposed, naked to the elements, to the wild sunlight and strange sleet that was the way Jack stared down at him now.

"Fuck," said Jack. It was soft and bruised-sounding. It didn't sound like an act.

Alan swallowed. Waited. Jack's fingertips rubbed against his scalp, sending a new and delicious set of shivers to join all of those already on duty. His lordship seemed reluctant to release Alan's hair for long enough to unfasten his own trousers and drawers.

So Alan did it for him. He wasn't unfamiliar with handling a gentleman's garments from this angle, though it had been a while. And Christ, he was motivated.

When he drew out Jack's prick, already halfway hard in his hand, there was a sharp inhalation from above him. Alan wrapped his fingers around the base and thought, hilariously, *silk hats.*

And then he did what he'd wanted to do since approximately ten minutes after first laying eyes on Lord Hawthorn, pistols and hatred and deadly peril be damned. He leaned in and took the very tip of that prick between his lips, savage pleasure filling him at how warm and vulnerable the flesh was as it filled his mouth.

"Now then, you little tart," said Jack. "I *am* going to use you, and I'm going to enjoy it."

A strangled moan parted Alan's lips and Jack took swift advantage of it, forcing them wider. Alan took him deep, eager, and gave a few hard sucks with his fingers still wrapped around half the length so he could control how much he took. Those few sucks were all he managed; then Jack tugged him off again. Alan shot a look up in silent query.

Jack looked merciless. He sounded parched. "I said *use*."

Because Lord Hawthorn was better than a psychic on a stage. He was something carved to Alan's specifications; hell, Alan had practically carved this man *himself*, with his pen, page after page and fantasy after fantasy. Jack had read them all. He knew exactly what Alan wanted. He was exactly what Alan wanted.

So Alan slackened his mouth and released his fingers, and let Jack move him back and forth as though he really were nothing more than a tool for Jack's pleasure.

Some people fucked to feel more present in the world; Alan, when he let himself fuck, did it to be *less* present for a while. To allow his grim grip on the world to loosen. He had to concentrate on being careful with his teeth, but the rest of him was lost in a dreamy web of painful pleasure—breathing raggedly around Jack's thrusts, his chin increasingly wet, his own cock rigid when he pressed a hand against it.

It seemed like no time at all before Jack was spilling into his mouth, with no warning beyond a thickening of taste and the palm behind Alan's head flattening out to hold him firmly in place.

That was definitely on the side of things that might be labelled *perverse*.

Alan finished swallowing. The pressure behind his head went slack and Jack's fingers were slow to unwind from Alan's hair when Alan pulled away. Pride struck a match in Alan as he tucked Jack's cock back into his drawers and did up the trouser fastenings, feeling oddly tender and finicky about it. Then he stood. He brushed at carpet dust on his knees.

Business concluded, Alan expected Jack to step back, but he was as close as ever. There was a thick, thoughtful pause while they looked at each other.

"To be fair," said Alan, "that *is* more or less why I followed you in here."

Jack's lips twitched. "Filthy whoreson brat."

"Overbred shit-sucking prick."

Jack laughed.

Some time ago Alan had tripped over the word *zephyr* in a book. By context it seemed to be a kind of gentle ghost, breathing both hot and cold at once. He felt that, now, in the minuscule space between them. He felt it when Jack ran his thumb over Alan's tingling mouth.

No kissing. Alan's own rule. Alan was a cup with water trembling at the brim, his senses were so full.

"*How* do you smell so fucking expensive?" he muttered.

"I'd tell you how much this cologne cost, but I'm worried we'll be back at guillotines."

Alan indulged himself, leaning forward and taking a deep breath. No flowers. Nothing sweet or edible. The layered, complex scent drifted smugly down his airways and made a permanent footprint for itself on his nerves.

"I don't even know what any of these scents are. It smells like a room in a palace where someone's just held an orgy."

"Your narrators stumble into orgies at a rate much higher than the average. The British aristocracy is not running around holding them at the drop of a hat. I myself have only been invited to—oh, four or five."

Alan stared, then realised he was being teased.

"Fuck off."

"I did think I'd been invited to one once," said Jack musingly. "It turned out to be a house party where we were all trapped in a room while the host's brother-in-law tried to convince us to invest in a terrible business venture."

"Sounds as though some fucking would have livened things up."

"It couldn't have made it worse."

Alan stopped fighting his grin.

"Speaking of which," added Jack. "I'm not done with you yet, Mr. Ross."

Alan's resigned prick became abruptly unresigned.

"I thought I was here only for your pleasure."

"And so you are." Jack's eyes crawled down him, and back up. "It will please me greatly to watch you bring yourself off right here against this door."

Blood filled Alan's cheeks. That—was not what he'd expected. But he found his own hand already squeezing himself urgently through the fabric, the other fumbling at buttons. Hm. Putting on a show was one thing, but getting spunk all over his precious work suit was another.

"Got a handkerchief?" he demanded.

"Oliver will harangue me if I keep losing them like this." Jack handed one over. It matched the one Alan still had at home: a wide square of fine cotton with embroidered initials. Alan took pleasure in crushing the impeccably folded creases, tucking it between his fingers and at the ready.

His breath skittered as he set his bare hand to his cock and gave the first stroke. This, he was going to manage with his eyes defiantly open.

"Of course you're hard already," said Jack. "I should have made you stay down there—I'm sure you would have loved rutting against my leg."

It was the disdainful Lord Hawthorn, who looked at Alan as if he wanted to kick him to the ground or eat him alive. Any thought of putting on a show flew out the window. It was all Alan could do to keep his knees from buckling as his lordship's

arrogant voice washed over him, lingering on how much Alan
enjoyed being used and all the other ways his lordship would
enjoy using him—

Alan was gone, loose from the world, and a braid of pleasure wove itself with vicious speed down his spine. He gave a
wrenching gasp and spilled into the handkerchief.

He'd kept his eyes open after all. The effort was worth it for
the way Jack's hands unfolded from white-knuckled fists at his
sides, and the look on Jack's face. There were clouds of dust and
desire in Alan's skull, mingling with that damn expensive cologne. To be *wanted* this intensely, by a man who could have
anything he bothered to beckon for, filled him with a hot jubi-
lation beyond anything he could have imagined. And Alan was
so very good at imagining.

It took him a moment to collect himself.

Then he wiped himself properly and, on impulse, held out the
handkerchief.

Jack gave a crack of laughter. It had a note of relief in it, which
punctured some of the tension and brought Alan the rest of the
way back into his own body. His gut clenched, reminding him.
Just this. Just this and they were done.

Jack took the handkerchief, folded it with delicacy, and pocketed it.

They got their appearances back in order before leaving and
parted on the street with a mercifully non-awkward nod, as if
between colleagues.

Which was what they were, now and for a few more days. They
had never been friends, and were lovers only in the technical sense.
No: pay attention to the clarity of your words, Alanzo. They had
been lovers. Twice. Past tense. And done.

Alan tucked his hands into his pockets. He had work to do,
but first he needed to walk for a while. Now that the clouds of
desire were dissipating in the sunshine of the street, the guilt
was creeping back, and he couldn't stop the thought dancing
through his mind:

What if things were different? What if I was allowed to keep this?

The world was playing a sick joke. Here, like a reward for all Alan's self-denial and hunger and hard work, was everything he wanted for himself.

The deserving poor.

Nobody got what they deserved. And things weren't different—they were how they were, just as the world was the world, and Alan had always known it. He couldn't afford to forget.

14

"Hm," said Adelaide, turning her face this way and that as she inspected it in a palm-sized mirror. "Do you know the number of shops in Mayfair I've been politely ushered out of with simpering remarks about *colonial tastes*? I've a mind to march back into all of them with this illusion on, try on ten gowns while loudly talking about my enormous inheritance, and then dismiss them all as not up to scratch and not buy a thing."

Adelaide's posture still spoke of deportment lessons, and her accent was as melodically educated as it had ever been. But the woman standing beside Jack, on the street a little way down from the Barrel, had white skin and mid-brown hair. Beneath her jacket, her shirtwaist had elaborate embroidery down the front and collar and cuffs: a dense floral pattern, which contained the runes required to anchor the illusion of a different person to the garment and whoever wore it.

"Bring me along on your shopping trip," said Jack. "I'll loom in the corner and look rich and unpleasant."

"You do that wherever you are," said Adelaide absently. She gave her reflection another long, complicated look before tucking the mirror away. "And I suppose I'm myself wherever I am. Unless I'm suddenly a pale English rose, in which case half the difficulty of my life is—gone. With just a few stitches and a flick of Violet's fingers." Adelaide's smile was strange and cool on that prim, pink mouth. "It's a queer thought. I'm not altogether sure I like it."

Jack's own illusion disguise was stitched into his necktie. Violet had merely fixed his nose and weakened his chin and turned his eyes brown. Even that much had given him a lurch of oddness, of being lost to himself, on looking in the mirror. Queer indeed. He had no idea how it would have felt for Adelaide, for whom appearance carried so much unavoidable weight.

He checked his pocket watch. Time.

"Ready, darling?" He offered Adelaide his arm. She tucked her hand through his elbow.

"Ready."

Adelaide's pass-token was in the woven bag she carried. They walked up the wide steps and through the huge doors, and were in the main foyer.

At once Adelaide clutched his arm more tightly. "Oh, look at that! Just like they describe, isn't it?"

Jack followed her gaze up to the glass-and-lead ceiling high above their heads, busy as it always was with the feet of crossing people. By the time he looked down again, Adelaide was exclaiming over the oak doors and the season-clock and the polished marble beneath their feet.

Her attention to detail reminded Jack to fold her jacket and his coat over his arm, as if prepared to carry them through the building. He made a show of surprise when one of the blue-liveried attendants stepped over with hands inquiringly outstretched.

"Much obliged to you," said Jack, handing them over. "Perhaps you can point us in the right direction? We've not been here before."

"By all means, sir. Do you know which office you're looking for? Is someone expecting you?"

"No," said Adelaide. "Oh, Tom, I told you we should have made an appointment!"

"I'm sure it'll be fine," said Jack. Perhaps he'd allowed too much of his natural tone to sneak in, there—the arrogance that was expected of Lord Hawthorn would be rudeness in a minor country squire. He coughed. "It's about our girl Rosie, you see. Her lock ceremony was just last week. Normally of course we'd send the hair down by post, but as we were visiting London anyway—we heard tell it's possible to bring it here ourselves, and watch it be put away in the Lockroom? Watch her be registered?"

"Rosie's our eldest," put in Adelaide, radiating goodwill. "It was such a proud day when her magic showed."

"Of course," said the attendant. "I'll fetch someone who can take care of you. Please take a seat, Mr. . . . ?"

"Pember," said Jack. "And this is my wife, Margaret."

Tom and Margaret Pember were deposited on a bench while the attendant traced a rune on a door, handed their coats through it into the cloakroom, and closed the door again. The next set of runes was more complex; the attendant turned the glowing doorknob and stepped through, and was gone.

According to Mrs. Kaur, there were three possible people who would be summoned to escort the parents of a new-minted magician for a lock registration. Jack and Adelaide waited a tense ten minutes before a stout man with buttery blond hair and a much-waxed moustache stepped out of a door, looked around the foyer, and then headed in their direction, smoothing back his already smooth hair as he came.

"Fawcett?" Adelaide murmured.

Jack nodded. He stood and strode forward, meeting the approaching man—Mr. Alec Fawcett, going by Mrs. Kaur's description—with a hearty handshake. He adopted what he hoped was the smile of a proud father and captured Fawcett's attention in introductions while Adelaide pulled a pebble from her bag and laid it on the floor beneath the bench.

"Maggie?" Jack called, after giving her enough time. "Come and meet Mr. Fawcett. He works for the Assembly."

"Mrs. Pember," said Fawcett, nodding politely when Adelaide hurried up to join them. "A pleasure. Congratulations on your little girl's lock ceremony."

"Thank you. I do hope we're not pulling you from more important work," said Adelaide earnestly.

"Nonsense. Nothing more important than registering a new

addition to magical society, is there? And you've come all this way. Let's give you a story to take home."

Adelaide made a tiny rueful face at Jack behind Fawcett's back as the man turned to lead them towards one of the oak doors. If they'd shared any cradlespeak, Jack would have told her not to be so sentimental. They would be inconveniencing the man, perhaps giving him a bit of a scare over nothing, but they weren't sticking a Goblin's Bridle on him. Or knocking him out and hiding him in a cupboard. This act of high theft was being run to Maud Blyth's rules of moral engagement.

Fawcett cradled, traced a complex rune, and then opened the door. The view through it was warm with wood and orange light. Fawcett ushered them both through and into the Lockroom.

"Oh my." Adelaide, who had been inside the Lockroom on illegal business only last year, clasped her hands. "It's so much bigger than I expected."

The Lockroom's rows of shelves stretched away into gloom. The air was still and quiet; untouched.

"Every magician who's come into their power since the Barrel was built," said Fawcett proudly. He pointed to the enormous map of the British Isles on the wall, pinned up above the high bench containing the room's ledger, and Adelaide hurried over with the keen air of someone determined to get their shilling's worth at an art gallery.

"Look at this, Tom," she insisted, and Jack joined her to inspect the impressively detailed but faded and unremarkable map. They needed to buy time for Violet to find the white pebble that told her which of the three expected men was in the Lockroom with them. Adelaide, ever practical, had also determined with Violet that a penny coin would mean someone unexpected, in which case Violet would need to improvise.

(Edwin had come up with three elegant and complicated ideas for charmed items, and three more ideas that were impossible because neither Jack nor Adelaide had any magic.

Robin had cleared his throat and said, "Er. Pebbles?")

"And this is the map that you can use if a magician is in peril?"

said Adelaide. "How thrilling. Could we see how it works? Not to spy on anyone, of course. I could name my aunt; I know she'll be at home in Bath."

Fawcett said, with the first hint of disapprobation, "I'm afraid not, Mrs. Pember. The magic of the Lockroom is not to be spent on demonstrations."

"Quite right," said Jack. "Why don't you—" But before he could ask for a tedious amount of detail about the huge ledger lying flat on the table, there was a loud knocking on the main door to the Lockroom. Adelaide jumped.

"What the devil—excuse me, Mrs. Pember," said Fawcett hurriedly. He raised his voice. "Who is that?"

"Mr. Fawcett? Alec Fawcett?" came an uncertain call. "Message for you, sir!"

Fawcett went to open the door. The tall redheaded woman standing on the other side leaned on its frame dramatically, catching her breath. Behind her a gloomy physical corridor curled away to the side. "Message for you, sir. Someone told me you were down here—sent me along from the staffing office—I'm sorry it took so long, sir, I've only been working here a week and I got turned around when they said to take the corridor down from the archives—"

"All right, girl. Take it slowly. What's the message?" said Fawcett.

"Something about your wife?" Violet, in her disguise, let her voice rise uncertainly.

Fawcett went still. "Helena?"

"Might be?"

"Is it—was the message from my house? The hospital?"

"I'm sorry, I was only told to fetch you—to come at *once,* they said—"

Fawcett cast a glance over his shoulder. Jack did his level best to look harmless. "If it's your wife, Mr. Fawcett, of course you must go. We won't touch a thing while we wait."

"I—yes, thank you. Will send—someone. To help you."

The door closed behind Fawcett and Violet, and Adelaide let out her breath.

"I was hoping it'd be him," she said. "A pregnant wife! Couldn't be more convenient."

Apparently Alec Fawcett and Manraj Singh had been gingerly bonding in the tearoom over their shared excitement and nerves about incipient fatherhood.

Violet would prove stubbornly unable to identify the person in the staffing office who had given her the message in the first place, and then would come to the realisation that she had the wrong name and was in fact seeking an Alex Mawson. And in the meantime, Jack and Adelaide were inside the Lockroom. Which anyone at all could open from the *inside*.

Less than a minute later, another knock came. This one was quieter and in a precise rhythm.

Adelaide grinned and went to admit Robin and Edwin.

"I thought this place had an underground feel, the first time, and I was right. This isn't just the basement, it's the *under-basement*," said Robin. "If we sneeze, we might disturb the foundations of the whole place. Huzzah for Kitty and her secrets."

"All clear?" said Edwin.

"All going to plan," said Adelaide. "Here's your record, Edwin. Get to work."

Edwin used his string to build an involved cradle into which Robin placed a scrap of paper with Lady Enid's full name. Then he directed the rest of them to stand clear of the huge ledger, splayed open on the table below the map.

Magic flowed forth and over the book like a breeze, lightly ruffling both the long black ribbon that lay in the open book and the very edges of the thick pages. The spell gathered and kept gathering: a whirlpool of rippling air now, tinged with stormy grey. Edwin was concentrating hard. This must have been taking a great deal of his magic.

The left-hand side of the book gave a sudden jerk. Edwin said, "*Got it*." His small storm of a spell sank into the pages, which began to turn themselves backwards as if flicked by a giant and impatient hand. Back and back.

And then, sudden as snapped fingers, the air was still.

Edwin rushed forward, still disentangling his string, and ran a finger eagerly down the page. "Enid, Enid—there! Look at that. She did request her own box. She used her married name to request it, but it's registered under her birth name."

"How do you think she got in?" asked Adelaide. "She must have needed privacy, like us."

"I could live to be a hundred and not know half of what the Forsythia Club could do," said Edwin. "All right. Ugh, Robin, can you—thank you."

Robin lifted a chunk of the pages in order to turn the book back to where the ribbon indicated the present day. It was unwieldy and looked heavy; the muscles in his forearms bunched where they emerged from his casually rolled-back sleeves.

"Show-off," murmured Adelaide.

Robin winked at her and let the pages collapse into place. Edwin ran his fingers through the motions of another spell, rehearsing, and then began it in earnest. This one looked simpler. A pen that lay in a holder in one corner of the table lifted itself into the air and hovered over the first column.

"Edwin John Courcey," said Edwin. There was no getting around someone's name going in the book. All that mattered was that they found the box and got out.

The pen wrote his name, and then the name *Enid Charlotte May Blackwood,* and then Edwin's hands glowed red and an answering red light sprang up, a ribbon reaching to the ceiling, in the gloom of the stacks.

"Your work, Edwin," said Jack. "You do the honours."

Edwin looked hectic with the pleasure of solving a puzzle. He muttered, "It still might—I might still be wrong," but he hurried away between the shelves and returned shortly with a wooden box in his hands.

Robin gave Edwin's arm a silent squeeze, and Adelaide made an impatient motion. Jack's pulse surprised him by picking up.

He wasn't entirely immune to a good puzzle himself. He con-
tented himself with leaning against the wall to give his leg a
break—it had been grumbling these past few days—and saying,
"Not to fault your sense of the theatric, Edwin, but we are under some time pressure here."

"Shut up, Hawthorn," said Edwin absently. He set the box on
top of the open record book and removed the lid.

This box was not lined with velvet. It was lined with a familiar beige substance, subtly textured.

"Cork?" said Robin.

"The only wood that's completely inert to magic. And I'd bet
anything the outer box is rowan," said Edwin. "That's why it
hasn't been doing anything to the magic in this place. And why
they haven't managed to triangulate it yet."

It lay innocently within its double prison of muffling woods.
A silver hair comb, which looked as though it might be part of
a set with the mirror and brush. But none of the other sets had
included a comb. And the silver was as bright as if it had been
polished just yesterday.

"Edwin." Adelaide put a hand over his and squeezed briefly.
Edwin, who seldom tolerated touch from anyone but Robin,
gave her one of his small off-centre smiles.

"Rectification," he said, and began the cradle.

The silver comb shivered under the rectification spell like the
surface of a flicked teacup. When it stopped shivering, it was a
small knife—a dagger, in fact—with a sharp-looking blade, and
a hilt with a flat pommel. In the centre of the pommel was the
simple design of a fern frond.

"Bother. Did anyone else remember to bring a sheath?" said
Robin, entirely poker-faced, and Edwin began to laugh. Robin
grinned and pulled both Edwin and Adelaide into a *huzzah-
we-won-the-match* kind of hug. Jack appreciated that no attempt was made to involve him.

It did mean that he was checking his watch, about to make
another pointed remark about the time, when the door to the
Lockroom opened.

Jack looked over. "Violet? How did you . . ."

Violet looked him grimly in the eyes and stepped into the room. She looked like herself, not the redheaded disguise she'd been wearing earlier. Her hands were pressed together, palm to palm, in front of her body. She was followed by three men, one of whom was holding her firmly by the arm. That man was unfamiliar; so was the one who followed.

Both of them turned their heads, deferential, as the third man entered the Lockroom. He was tall and dark-haired, and dressed as if the world would end if a hair fell out of place or a speck of lint marred his grey suit. His neat footfalls whispered against the floor.

"Well, now," said George Bastoke. "Once again, Courcey, you're better than a bloodhound when left to your own devices. I can't thank you enough. And you are, of course, all under arrest."

15

"Priez-vous, Hartley," George added crisply, before anyone else could speak. He pointed at Edwin. "On Courcey at least. And Blyth too, if he looks likely to punch anyone. And . . ." A flicker creased his brow as he looked at Jack, then cleared. "Ah. Hawthorn. Cousin, you're not looking entirely yourself."

The Cooper not restraining Violet was a wiry young chap with pale hair and the nervy air of a racing dog. He cradled the priez-vous and tossed it like a cup of water in Edwin's direction. Edwin's hands clapped together, palm to palm like Violet's. Meanwhile, George cast a negation, with an unfamiliar clause attached at the end, and walked up close enough to Jack that it was impossible to dodge as it washed over him.

Jack smelled burning first. Then he saw the first curl of smoke rising, as if from a cigarette smouldering forgotten between his lips—and then he felt the crawling, piercing heat against the skin of his neck.

"Hawthorn," said Violet urgently. "It's a targeted negation—it's going for the embroidery. Take off the tie."

Jack unknotted it hastily, pulled it clear of his collar and tossed it to the ground. The grey fabric was eaten through with embers and char where the runes of Violet's embroidery had been. Edwin had never been able to cast a negation strong enough to do that, when they tested it.

"You *have* been busy, Miss Debenham." George still held the negation between his palms. "Is there anyone else here wearing anything they shouldn't, I wonder?"

And he turned to the three people standing between him and

the ledger, and let the spell seep fluidly out until it filled half the room.

Adelaide's shirtwaist caught fire.

Robin shouted. Edwin jerked. Adelaide herself gave a startled scream and batted at her front and cuffs with her bare hands. Her embroidered illusion-runes were far denser than those on Jack's tie; there were outright small flames licking at the fabric and thread.

"Bloody— I can't do anything!" Edwin's hands spasmed as he clearly tried to start an extinguishing spell on instinct. "Robin!"

"Addy, hold still." Robin's larger hands should have been better extinguishing tools, but the runes rekindled themselves as soon as he moved from one patch to another. Adelaide emitted a displeased stream of Punjabi obscenity that seemed very odd coming from the mouth of a mousy white woman.

"Miss Morrissey, I presume. I prefer to see people truthfully," said George. "If that garment is carrying the illusion, then I suggest you remove it."

"Remove her *clothes*?" said Violet.

"Unless she prefers to wait for it to char into rags on her body?"

Adelaide had a murderous gleam in her eye as she hurriedly unbuttoned. Robin removed his own waistcoat. The other two Coopers had found reason to stare at either ceiling or floor, but George remained as patient and unmoved as a marble statue. Adelaide's chemise and corset had black specks on them when she flung the burning shirt to the ground and the illusion vanished. She hastily accepted Robin's waistcoat. It hung loosely on her, but at least Jack felt comfortable looking at her again.

"There," said George. "And now—the knife, please."

Nobody moved. Edwin's body shielded the knife and its box from view. Robin had his jaw set, and he stepped into George's way as George made for the table.

George stopped. That crease appeared on his forehead again. He and Robin were nearly of a height, though next to George's tailored appearance Robin—with his rolled-up sleeves, missing waistcoat, and pugnacious look—could have been a prizefighter George was inspecting before placing his bet.

"Sir Robert," said George. "Consider your situation."

Robin shot a glance at Jack, who shook his head. The last thing they needed was for the rigid potential in Robin's shoulders and arms to translate into violence. For an unmagical baronet in a room full of Coopers, even one with a superb right hook, that was only going to end badly.

Edwin clearly agreed. He said, colourlessly, "Don't give them an excuse." And stepped aside.

With a grunt of annoyance, Robin did the same.

George looked down at the knife, gave a brisk nod, and closed the box. It was small enough to slip into his pocket.

"Hartley," he said then, "where did you leave the journalist?"

Jack's heart missed its cue momentarily.

"Skulking in the corridor, sir," said the Cooper, who had now moved to shadow Robin.

George raised his voice. Not by much. George, like Jack, was accustomed to being obeyed without resorting to anything so vulgar as noise. "Mr. Ross? In here, if you please."

Alan walked in unescorted by anyone. His gaze met Jack's and leapt away quick as a whip. He settled himself against the wall next to the door, as if ready for the chance to slip back out again.

"But—you weren't meant to be here," said Edwin. "We didn't need you for this."

"Oh, no," said Violet bitterly. "It's even better than that."

"Indeed," said George. "This is exactly where Mr. Ross is meant to be. Where *I* needed him to be."

Beneath George's intensely polished exterior was a strong instinct for showmanship. A smile played on his face as he watched the impact of that on Robin and Edwin and Adelaide.

Jack had long ago trained his own face to hide more, the more he felt. Helpful for an army officer who was no more immune to fear than any of his men but needed to pretend otherwise. By now it wasn't deliberate. It simply set into place as he looked at Alan and his mind flew back over the last fortnight, searching for—what? Clues? Proof?

A truth: Alanzo Rossi hated anyone with unearned power who wielded it against others.

And another: Alanzo Rossi would swallow a great deal of what he hated, if it helped him support his family.

Someone had cracked an eggshell full of molten glass on Jack's sternum and had left it to trickle down between his ribs. It burned when he inhaled.

George went on, "Very careless of you all to have left him roaming around London after that voyage, without so much as a secret-bind, so that anyone could approach him with an offer of work." He tutted. "You see, Hartley, Rolfe? This is the sort of thing the Coopers exist to prevent."

"Yes, sir."

Robin managed two furious strides towards Alan before Hartley intercepted him with a cradle half-begun and raised warningly. Even then, Robin looked on the verge of barging right through him, but he stopped and glared at Alan over Hartley's shoulder.

"An offer of *work*," Robin spat. "And then you came and made Maud the same offer, and this whole time you've been playing the spy and reaping the rewards from both sides."

"The man's a common thief, Sir Robert," said George. "Were you expecting a shining diamond of integrity?"

Nothing shifted in Alan's face either. He looked sallow and tightly wound. One of his hands twitched as if about to clench into a fist.

"I don't understand," said Adelaide to George. "If Mr. Ross told you where the knife was, why didn't you come and fetch it yourself? Why let us go ahead with this entire scheme?"

"To catch us handily in the act, I presume," said Edwin.

"A happy extra," said George. "But no." He looked at Alan. "Well, Mr. Ross? Where is my cup?"

"Miss Debenham brought it," said Alan tonelessly. "Ask her."
Violet's hand went to her mouth.

"What?" said Edwin.

"*Fuck*," spat Violet. "Fuck you, Alan Ross, and fuck every generation of your fucking family and fuck us for *helping* you when you said you were in *need*."

The silent, burly Cooper holding Violet's arm—Rolfe—took a tiny step away, as if her obscenity might be catching.

"Miss Debenham." George held out an open palm.

"A note was delivered to me early this morning," said Violet to Edwin. "A note from *you*. It said that you wanted the cup on hand, just in case—that you might need it for an affinity spell. A last step in finding the knife, if it had been split into pieces like the coin was. The note said to bring it along, and . . . not to tell anyone."

"And you didn't talk to me about it?" Edwin all but shouted.

"It was written in *your hand*," she snarled. "Do you think I don't know it by now?"

"It was me," said Alan. Still with no expression in his voice at all. Alan, who forged references for his sisters, and who'd said of Jack's letter to the Roman, *I could reproduce the handwriting exactly*. Who'd sat at Violet's table as they planned all of this, writing with Edwin's notebook open in front of him.

"Miss Debenham, I won't ask again."

Violet's fists clenched and her gaze flicked to the door. She was more cautious than Robin, but her temper was worse when it was roused.

"Don't lose your head, Violet," said Jack sharply. "Hand it over."

Her angry look transferred to Jack and altered. For all Jack knew, he was about to be accused of working *with* Alan and George, given what Violet suspected about his feelings—*ex*-feelings—oh, to hell with it.

Jack said, "Ross is a dirty rat working for bigger rats, and he'll get what's coming to him in the end. There's no point fighting when the odds are so poor. We're all still alive and unhurt. Be sensible."

Violet swallowed hard.

"Fuck," she said again, now thick with misery, and rummaged in a pocket of her skirt. She pulled out a velvet pouch and then, at George's gesture, undid the drawstring to tip a small silver bowl onto his waiting hand.

The cup of the Last Contract had barely changed when Edwin cast rectification on it. The fern design had appeared, engraved on the inner surface, a circular pattern beneath the brim. Otherwise it was still a bowl, the size of one of Maud's cupped hands, and had spent several years inside the cage of a parrot called Dorian.

A proper smile spread across George's face as he turned it to and fro, then took the bag from Violet. Now he had all three: coin, cup, and knife.

They'd set out today to be ahead by two pieces and had instead lost all of them in a handful of minutes.

"Excellent work, Mr. Ross," said George.

"We're done?" Alan said shortly.

"Yes. You've fulfilled your end of the deal."

Alan pushed off the wall and came to stand in front of George.

"Waiting to be paid?" Violet shot at him. "Go on. Let's see you put your paws up and beg."

Even more colour had left Alan's face. Jack had seen this look on men approaching an unexploded grenade.

Alan said to George, with familiar defiance, "Do you need me to stick my tongue out, then?"

Jack found himself licking his lips. Alan had asked him— *How much did it hurt?*

Because George didn't believe in carelessness or mercy. He'd not employ an unmagical man and then leave him able to talk about it afterwards. Alan would have known that all along.

"No." George tucked the bowl in another pocket and began to cradle. The spell was a soft, sickly yellow in his hands. "I've had reason to find the loopholes in secret-binds recently. Myself, I prefer something a little more definite."

"What the bloody hell do you mean, *definite*?"

"Language, Mr. Ross," said George. "Don't let Miss Debenham drag us all into vulgarity. When was that voyage of yours?"
One finger moved, defining a clause. "Let's have the last four
months, to be safe."

"The last four months of what?" Alan's voice rose.

"Of your memory," said Edwin. He didn't even sound vindictive about it. He was eyeing the yellow spell with unease.

"What—no—" Alan tried to retreat. The oh-so-helpful Hartley got in his way. "That wasn't part of the deal."

"People lose their memory from knocks on the head every
day." George nodded at Hartley, who took Alan by both shoulders. "I'm sure your dear family will fill you in on anything
important."

Alan stopped struggling. Despite his exceedingly mixed feelings, most of Jack wanted to growl in dismay, watching the fight
drain out of that fierce, flawless face. He was abruptly certain
that Alan hadn't been paid a penny. George wasn't wasteful. He
didn't operate by quid pro quo when he could get the same results through other means.

"There," said George. "It'll be over before you know it."

He raised his hands to either side of Alan's head. Alan put up
his own hands as if he could fight it off, and his eyes screwed shut.
His lips pulled taut over his teeth. It didn't look like pain so much
as the effort it took to pick yourself up and keep fighting when
you were bruised in every limb and tiredness was hibernating in
your bones.

George frowned.

It occurred to Jack that if he were Alan Ross then he wouldn't
have told George Bastoke one single thing about the existence
of perturbators.

"Sir?" said Hartley.

"Not to worry." George drew himself upright. The yellow
of the spell brightened and pulsed around Alan's curling hair.
Alan's eyes flew open for a shocked moment. He gave a guttural
cough, as if spitting out seawater, and then collapsed in a heap
at George's feet.

The image flashed before Jack of a secret-bind slipping between his sister's unmoving lips. His body jerked as if struggling up from sleep.

George had Hartley drag the unconscious Alan to lie against the wall, out of the way—"Have him taken outside later. Leave him on a park bench, or in a gutter outside a pub." George then cradled another spell that took the form of glowing white chalk, and sketched a series of runes onto the nearest piece of wall. They shone bright and then disappeared.

"What does that do?" asked Edwin, who was still Edwin even when arrested and in peril.

"A summons," said George.

Jack caught Robin's gaze. The question was whether they ought to try anyway—whether desperation and numbers might let them overcome the Coopers before reinforcements arrived. They could open the door, but with Edwin and Violet hand-tied and unable to sketch runes, they'd be stuck navigating the Barrel's physical space.

"What do you plan to do with us now?" Jack asked his cousin.

"That depends on how cooperative you plan to be," said George. "The simplest path forward would be for all of you to make a voluntary blood-oath that you will never try to put your hands on the Last Contract again, or to interfere in any way with its use."

Violet, Adelaide, and Robin all spoke at once, variations on a theme of violent disagreement.

Jack didn't say anything. Neither did Edwin; he was staring at his hands as if he would drag them apart through force of will, even if it tore the skin bloodily from his palms. As Jack watched he raised his gaze to the map on the wall. He almost seemed to be staring *past* it, as Robin did when having a vision.

"No, I didn't expect you to like that," said George, meanwhile. "But the Coopers are not an unreasonable institution. The offer will remain open."

The door handle glowed and the door opened yet again. This time it admitted Walter Courcey and Richard Prest.

"Now it's a party," said Robin. "And nobody thought to bring the champagne."

A spasm of a smile happened on Edwin's face. At least part of his senses were in the room with them. His gaze was still miles away. And he hadn't looked over when his brother entered the room—that, more than anything, raised the hairs on Jack's arms with something closer to anticipation than fear.

"Deputy Chief Minister. Courcey," said George. "Do come in. As we were warned, an attempt has been made today to brazenly steal the knife of the Last Contract from this room, where the Coopers have been safeguarding it."

"Safeguarding?" said Prest. "I thought you were still searching."

"Need to know only, sir," said Walter. "You can see from today's unfortunate events why it had to be kept secret until we had all three pieces."

"We caught four of them in the room, with their hands on the knife," said George. "Miss Debenham—you remember Miss Debenham, sir?—had already lured away a loyal employee of the Barrel under some ruse."

"Yes, I remember. You're a disgrace to magical society, young lady. And to your family." Prest frowned severely at Violet. She managed a theatric bow in his direction.

"I *do* try."

"Would you like to tell me I'm a disgrace to my family as well?" asked Adelaide in her most gilded tones.

"My family's mostly dead," offered Robin.

"And mine already thinks I'm a disgrace." Edwin's attention was back in the room. "The feeling is mutual. Isn't it, Walt?"

Walter smirked. "Non-magicians, an ex-magician, and someone who can barely make a light in a dark room. It's not a surprise that you've been after the power of the Last Contract and doing terrible things to get it."

It was a spiteful slip in his calm, reasonable facade—but Walter was a bully at heart. He couldn't resist the urge to send out

tormenting prickles, especially where his brother was concerned. George cared far more to preserve the image of himself
as a true gentleman.

Now George picked up smoothly, addressing Prest. "We have
reason to suspect these villains, as well as Blyth's sister, were
responsible for the deaths of several people already, beginning
with Reginald Gatling and his aunt Flora Sutton, and including
Mrs. Elizabeth Navenby. As you'll recall, they have come into
several inheritances in quick succession. I wouldn't be surprised
if they somehow brought about Lady Enid's death as well, leaving Spinet House in Miss Debenham's hands."

Violet gave a strangled yelp of rage. "*You're* responsible for all
those deaths! And likely Lady Elsie's too!"

That made Prest blink. The two Coopers exchanged a puzzled
look.

George's gaze swung, unhurried and untroubled, towards
Jack.

The two of them looked at each other. Hatred soaked Jack
like petroleum. The hinges of his jaw ached with tension.

"Lord Hawthorn," George said. "You were there when your
sister died. Did I kill her?"

Jack could try his best, could shove his tongue out for everyone
to gawk at, but what difference would it make? The Deputy Chief
Minister had been brought here as a witness, and had already decided whose version of events to trust. And no secret-bind told
you who laid it. George could spin whatever story he wished.

Jack said nothing. There was no point.

"There," said George. "What happened to my cousin was a
tragedy. But the Alston twins were always somewhat unbalanced.
Wild magic. Not fit for proper use. Everyone knew it." A pause.
"I'm hardly out here blaming you for my father's death, Hawthorn, am I?"

To anyone else in the Lockroom that would have sounded
like a reasonable, if oblique, argument. The unfairness of it
lodged in Jack's throat.

George turned to Hartley and the other Cooper. "I think

enough has been said. Lock them all up. We'll get to the bottom of this plot."

"All right, Bastoke. Carry on, and keep us informed," said Prest. He paused as he turned to go, and nodded at the unmoving form of Alan. "What's wrong with that one?"

"A memory charm that took him a little too strongly," said George. "He shouldn't have been unbusheled in the first place, but he'll be no trouble in future."

And then a lot of things happened very quickly.

"Edwin's up to something!" said Walter, sharp, and—

A red ribbon of light gleamed from deep within the shelves, and—

"Robin," said Edwin, "a distraction, please!"

Edwin had been standing facing the ledger. He turned away from it now, and dashed with ungainly speed away between the shelves before any of the Coopers could react. His arms were free and separate at his sides.

"What—" said George, and Robin gave the bloodcurdling yell of an athlete with some rage to burn and swung an impressive fist directly at Rolfe.

The man's head snapped back in as perfect a piece of boxing form as a caricaturist for the newspaper could ever hope to capture. His grip fell nervelessly away from Violet. Robin didn't pause, but lunged at Hartley, who had begun to run into the shelves after Edwin.

So they were fighting after all. Jack felt a smile break his face. No time for strategy beyond *take out the greatest threat,* and the greatest threat was handily not far away.

He moved quickly over to George, took hold of his cousin's wrists, and forced them apart.

A nascent cradle of orange sparks disappeared. George tried to haul his arms out of Jack's grip, but Jack's favoured form of exercise since leaving the army had been singlestick. His grip was unshakable and his arms were strong, and George—

"You should have brought Morris along, George," said Jack. "Isn't this what he's for?"

George never lost his temper, and *George* employed people to be violent for him; Jack would swear he'd never been in a proper fight in his life. Which also meant he didn't know anything about defence and misdirection. His eyes slid to the side, over Jack's shoulder, and so Jack had enough warning to hurl them both sideways and around, as if they were dancing, so that he could see Walter with a spell built between his hands, about to cast it at Jack.

Jack's neck muscles tightened. And then Adelaide Morrissey, brown arms bare and Robin's waistcoat swinging as she moved, lunged in front of Walter's incipient magic.

Jack opened his throat to shout *no,* with a pure, sick rush of fear.

Walter made a noise instead. It was a short, stubbed-toe noise. Jack could only just glimpse him—Adelaide was mostly in the way, and Jack was still working hard to keep George's hands apart—but Walter looked baffled and furious, and lifted his fingers to inspect them. They had curled into claws.

"But—you're not—" Walter said.

"Aren't I?" said Adelaide, breathless, and kicked him between the legs.

The next sound Walter made was even shorter and more stifled. Jack and George both winced in unwilling sympathy.

"Oh, you *shit*" came from Violet, and then retching noises. Jack couldn't spare attention to see what had happened— George, apparently inspired, was now trying to kick *him* in the bollocks. In his periphery Jack saw a raised hand and his nerves yelled *grenade* without his consent, sending a splash of cold terror down his spine.

The raised hand was Hartley's. Robin had hold of his other wrist, holding it high above his head, but the young Cooper clearly had grit—practically dangling, he still cast the contents of his free hand in Jack's direction.

"Sir!" he yelled as he did so. George made another go at wrenching himself away.

The small glasslike bauble landed at Jack's feet and spilled out yellow smoke. The first tendrils rose to Jack's nose and all the air left his lungs at once. It was worse than landing hard off a horse. His chest refused to expand.

George wrenched again, and this time Jack couldn't hold him. He couldn't even breathe.

"All right, stop this," said George to the room at large. He lifted his hands to cradle.

Before he could, the British Isles flung themselves across the room.

It was the Lockroom's map-spell, designed for locating individuals; the map on the wall was now writ large and in white lines, on every wall and most of the ceiling. The lines turned a vivid purple and the map began to change, to merge and shift fast enough that Jack felt queasy as well as suffocated. Within it appeared one searingly bright line, running all across the ceiling and down the wall to a point close to the floor, like a vein of gold in a rock. Like lightning cutting through the sky.

"No," said Edwin. "*You* stop."

He came out of the shelves with a cradle in his hands and light crawling all over him. The light was the clean white halo of guidelights and electric, and bright enough that it took a moment to notice that Edwin was shaking as if in the grips of fever.

"Oh God," said Robin hollowly. "You made it work."

Jack managed to inhale for the first time in what felt like minutes. George, fast as ever, finished his spell and released it in Edwin's direction. Edwin jerked his wrist and—*something* appeared in the path of George's spell, sizzling it into nothing. All the light was concentrating between his palms.

"Give us back the contract, and let us go, or I will *unmake* you. I will tear your *cells* apart—"

The lightning line on the crazed map thickened and brightened, as if a crack were forming in the shell keeping an explosion contained. Edwin gasped raggedly, and the light in his hand grew brighter too. He did not look triumphant. He looked as if he'd been awake for three days under heavy fire.

"Mr. Courcey, *what* are you doing? You will stop that! Immediately!" squawked Prest, huddled near the door.

George tried another spell. Even Walter managed to drag himself upright and cast something, but this time their magic turned to sparking uselessness before even leaving the cradles. Dark clouds were filling the room now as if pouring from hidden vents, the light between Edwin's hands was brighter and brighter, and the map line began to writhe like a snake pinned down at both ends and tortured.

Even Jack could tell something was going very, very wrong.

Adelaide tried to take hold of Edwin's arm, and snatched her hand back. Jack took a half a step forward but never finished it. The floor gave a few tremors and then shook hard and fast like a dice cup.

Jack's leg gave out and he fell down. Walter almost followed suit but caught himself with a curse. Raised voices and shouts of alarm filtered dimly down from above them. Whatever Edwin was doing had stopped being contained by the Lockroom.

"All right, out!" snapped Walter, waving his hand at Prest. "Get out!"

Prest flung the door open and ran.

"*Idiot*," said Walter savagely. He limped over and closed the door again in order to cast the exit rune, hands shaking with haste. When *he* opened the door, it led to the main foyer.

At that point the writhing line of light abruptly shattered, a table leg broke and both table and ledger fell with a heavy crash, and between the thick black clouds and the fact that Edwin was now outright painful to look at, Jack's vision became more or less useless. He climbed warily to his feet.

He heard voices and shouts and questions and saw the outlines of moving figures. Some of them probably went through the door and out, because the stew of voices thinned to Robin's alone.

"No, not now—*not yet*." Robin sounded frantic. "Edwin, you can stop. Let it go. Please—please. One piece at a time, love."

An awful crack of stone sounded close above their heads. Dust fell onto Jack's face. A memory he'd have sworn he'd long ago set aside, one of the worst of the war, grabbed at all the nerves of his body. A high-pitched ringing burrowed into his ears.

He nearly lashed out with a fist when someone bumped into him, but managed to haul it back as he heard a female exclamation and felt the swish of skirts against his legs. Adelaide or Violet. He shoved whomever it was firmly in the direction of the open door, which was a dim picture frame showing frantically running people. Had George made it out? George had the contract pieces. Surely he'd be protecting them above all else.

Jack stumbled towards Edwin, face averted, and didn't bump into anyone else. He could still hear the steady rhythm of Robin's voice, though he couldn't make out the words.

"Robin!" he shouted, thinking of what Alan had done for Maud in the cemetery. "Knock him out!"

But he could barely hear himself; his voice and Robin's were both swallowed in a grumbling roar of rising noise.

All of a sudden the pressure of light vanished from Jack's eyelids. He swiped them free of dust, wincing as tears spilled down his cheeks.

Edwin was standing—*standing*, thank God, though leaning hard on Robin, pale and filthy and wracked by coughs.

Jack had hoped that Edwin managing to stop the spell, whatever it had been, would also stop this disaster in its tracks. But the clouds were taking on a reddish tinge like wildfire and the violent shaking was, if anything, intensifying. The stone of the floor and the wood of the walls were blurring, as if they were an illusion dying with the end of the caster's power. As if they were softening into mist despite the weight of the Barrel above them.

Unmake, Edwin had said.

"Time to leave," Jack snarled. He took hold of Robin's arm and dragged them to the door. The ground was uneven, as if potholed. Jack didn't dare look down to find out what the floor was turning into, in case it was happening to his feet as well. He got Robin and Edwin out into the crowded, noisy lobby with one good shove, and then—paused.

"Hawthorn!" said Robin.

Jack swore and turned back around.

It was barely a room anymore. It was an ocean storm: nothing but blood-sky and lightning and fear and fog. Dust coated Jack's nose and mouth as he plunged back in.

Part of him had wondered if Alan was faking the unconsciousness. If he'd managed to throw off George's spell entirely and had climbed to his feet when the door opened and was already streets away and still running.

But Jack groped along the wall, and it took only a few steps for his foot to hit flesh. He bent and hauled the floppy, heavy body into his arms and then over his shoulder. His bad leg cramped hotly as he groaned his way back to his feet.

Door. Nearly tripping again, as the floor heaved as if to vomit him up. *Door.* And *through*.

The main foyer of the Barrel was bedlam. Every door on the floor was open and people were running through, some with papers or cups of tea still in their hands. For a wild second Jack thought it was raining indoors. No—what was falling, in delicate, beautiful shards, was the glass of the ceiling. Jack flinched as some landed nearby and shattered.

He couldn't see any of the others, either his side or George's. He did what everyone else was doing: racing full-tilt towards the huge wooden doors out onto the street, which had been flung entirely wide.

Pain kissed his forehead with hot lips. His eyes were watering again, or else he was bleeding. That itch of liquid was suddenly the unbearable centre of his world. But he ran, and got himself and Alan out and down the marble stairs and onto the street.

Behind him, the centre of British magical bureaucracy continued to tear itself apart.

16

Alan's headache woke up almost before he did. It was a headache that demanded its own pillow on the bed; its own seat at the dinner table. It took a long, agonising stretch, in which opening his eyes was far too difficult to contemplate, for him to remember that he had other body parts below the neck, and to determine that none of *them* were hurting. Or perhaps they were and he couldn't tell. You stopped noticing a blister on your hand when you wrenched your ankle.

What the *fucking hell.*

Was he hungover? Men described the state of hangover like this, with haunted expressions and thinly veiled braggadocio. Alan had never drunk enough to find out for himself. He'd never been able to afford it, being unwilling to stoop to the kind of gin that would strip the skin from inside his mouth.

Had someone clocked him over the head in an alley? Best of fucking luck to them finding anything worth nicking in his pockets. Might well have taken his shoes, though. *Shit.* To replace them he'd have to dig into the money from—

From whom? From what?

Alan's eyes opened despite his skull's fervent wish otherwise. He was startled into it by the sheer unbalancing weirdness of getting halfway through a thought and having it slip from his grasp like a slimy fish.

He immediately wanted to close them again, but didn't. He wasn't in his bed at home. He hadn't fallen asleep on the floor of the *Post*'s office.

Alan was lying on his side atop a wide, soft bed with the kind of fiddly, curving bedposts that Caro used to complain about dusting. The pillowcase was slippery with quality beneath his cheek, sunlight fell through lace curtains, and there was a large man sitting in a chair by the bed and watching Alan with eyes like sapphires set in a statue of a snake. If a snake wore clothes worth more than Alan's annual wages, with heavy streaks of incongruous dust at the collar and all down the tops of his thighs. Trousers, rather.

Thighs, insisted an interested little voice in Alan.

The man had clearly noticed that Alan was awake, but he said nothing. His eyebrows, dark and thick, rose a little.

Alan's abused nerves were telling him, ludicrously, that to move an inch would be to invite an attack. Snakes were like that, weren't they? Couldn't see you if you didn't move. Or was it snakes that hypnotised you until you couldn't look away? That seemed about right.

Fuck, his *head*. His pulse had picked up, and the rate of the pain with it.

Finally the man shifted and sat forward, elbows propped on knees. (*Thighs.*) Up close his features were harsh, his jaw dark with shadow. He had a nose like a regal rock formation, a freshly scabbed cut on his forehead, and hair in a shade between walnut and ebony.

And how did Alan know what ebony wood looked like? And why was his mouth suddenly dry, his legs restless, at this man's proximity?

Jesus, Mary, and Joseph. Perhaps he'd fallen asleep while writing and dreamed himself into one of his own books. At least one of them began like this. If this man was a duke, it was all but certain.

"How much do you remember?" the man asked. A deep, cutglass voice.

Alan opened his mouth to say God only knew what, and a memory landed in his head as if dropped from a height. He remembered the *Lyric,* he remembered waking up on the floor of a cabin with a headache much milder than this one, and—

"Lord Hawthorn?"

An unrecognisable expression crossed Hawthorn's face. "And?"

"And wood, apparently." He kept his eyes on Hawthorn, convinced that losing sight of the man would cause the memories to slip away again. "I don't know. My mind's been chewed up by moths. What—what happened to me?" His voice cracked over the words.

"My cousin George used a memory-spell on you. And if I'm not mistaken, you did your level best to perturb it."

George. George Bastoke. A new memory, this one full of pain, punched its way between Alan's eyes and into his head. He found himself cradling one of his hands to his chest, curling his body around it.

"My head hurts like someone's been at it with a bloody hammer," he said into the pillow.

"Can you sit up?"

That deserved a glare, and Alan delivered it. Hawthorn produced a stoppered glass vial, removed the cork, and held it out.

"See if you can take a few sips."

Alan continued glaring.

Hawthorn's mouth twitched. He took a sip from the vial himself. "It's not magical. Just a tonic. It'll send you back to sleep, most likely, but it'll help the head too."

What was the worst it would do—kill him? *Then* his head wouldn't hurt. Alan took the vial and drank a mouthful. It tasted surprisingly pleasant, like watered-down honey and herbs. And he was indeed asleep again before he could bring himself to mutter a thank-you.

The second time Alan woke, his headache had retreated. It was occupying only a small attic rather than the whole bloody mansion.

The light had changed; the room was lit by an elegant gas lamp as well as a deep golden soup of sunset. Jack was still in the chair, still in his stained clothes. A full glass of wine and an empty plate lay on a side table, and he was reading a book bound in red leather.

Alan explored his memories of the past few months like someone gingerly handling an ancient scroll. Pieces slipped and crumbled. He remembered . . . Edwin handing him a loop of paper with one side, and the idea of channels carved within him by the rosary. Alan held that image and breathed with it, as he'd done when Bastoke was pouring that yellow spell around his head. It had *felt* like the perturbation was working. And then he'd felt nothing.

"I have most of it back now, I think." His voice was a dry ache.

Jack put the book down at once. "Name and year and Prime Minister."

"Asquith. Nineteen-nine. And my name's Julius Caesar."

Jack lifted a hand, hiding the shape of his mouth. "And mine?"

Alan automatically delivered one of the worst profanities he knew. "My lord," he added.

Jack stood from the chair. He tugged a bell rope to summon a maid, and ordered tea. They were in Jack's own townhouse, then. The style of this room fit with the parts Alan had already seen.

A slow, awful dread was winding Alan's guts around its hands. He did remember it all. He remembered the hatred in Violet's voice and the anger in Robin's, when his traitorous role in Bastoke's scheme had been made clear. He didn't have any memory of how Jack had looked. He hadn't had the courage to glance in Jack's direction at all.

And now Alan was . . . here. *How?* What had happened between Alan falling unconscious in the Lockroom and now?

Alan's tongue thickened and his heart thudded rapidly. However it had happened, he was alone in the heart of Jack's territory. Jack had ordered *tea,* as if settling in for a leisurely session of—what? Interrogation? A slow, masterful flaying with the edge of Jack's insulting tongue? Alan would prefer a hard beating with sticks to the way his betrayal squatted invisibly in the room between them, fouling the air and leaving him tense and miserable with nerves.

The tea arrived. Jack brought a cup and saucer to the bed and gestured Alan to sit up and take it. Perhaps this was where the poison was. Alan was too thirsty to care. Black tea, very sweet. It was the best thing his parched throat had ever experienced.

"So," said Jack calmly. "Did you fuck me as part of playing the spy?"

Arsehole that he was, he'd waited until Alan had a mouthful of hot tea. Some of it went down the wrong way. Alan choked, spilled tea onto his shirt, and contemplated tossing the rest of the cup in Jack's face.

God, he was so tempted to say yes. To drive a knife into this and let it die. But he hesitated too long.

Jack answered his own question. "No. I didn't think so."

Alan had learned a new method of lying from Maud Blyth: Don't say anything untrue. Keep your secrets in the gaps between your words. But he'd lied in action, he'd betrayed them all to the elegant monster that was George Bastoke, and now the weight of that sat leaden on his shoulders.

"I didn't need to," he said. "Maud and Violet—even Edwin—they all let me into the fold without thinking twice. I was trying bloody hard *not* to fuck you, as a matter of fact. Given that it seemed like the worst decision I could make."

"What happened to that plan?" said Jack, down in those dangerous registers of his voice.

"My willpower failed and I did it anyway. Christ, you're a smug prick." Nothing to lose. He might as well interrogate in return. "What *happened*?"

"To *my* willpower? I wasn't exerting any."

"To me. To everyone. What happened in the Lockroom?"

Jack told him. It took some time, and the growing horror of it got under Alan's skin until he couldn't sit motionless in the bed any longer. He got up and paced, and had more tea, and listened with gritted teeth to the disaster that was his own fault.

Jack hadn't stuck around to find out how much of the Barrel was still intact, but he'd sent a servant to that corner of London later, and the answer was: not much. The same servant then went to Spinet House, where nobody answered the door to knocking, but an hour later a note from Violet was delivered. The others were all safe.

Alan's legs weakened with relief to hear that, and he leaned against the bedpost. Something shaped like a prayer haunted the roof of his mouth. His back and one of his knees ached as if— well, as if he'd been dumped unconscious on a hard floor and left there, and then—

And then what?

We got out just in time, Jack had said. No specifics.

Alan might be small for a man, but neither Violet nor Adelaide would have the strength to carry him bodily out of a collapsing building. And from the sounds of things, Robin had had his hands full with Edwin.

A dangerous emotion broke in waves against the wall of Alan's will.

"You saved my life."

Jack didn't deny it. His mouth curved a little. "Next time I'll leave you to die, if your pride insists."

There was that cut on his head. And he'd sat here in those ruined clothes as Alan slept, and made Alan's tea perfectly, and Alan deserved *none* of it. Alan wanted to toss it in his lordship's face like a handful of hated diamonds.

The waves broke through, and they were scalding hot. Before Alan's common sense could raise even a feeble protest he was standing between Jack's legs, leaning down to grab hold of Jack's shoulder and shake. It was like trying to shake a lamp-post.

"What the devil—"

"*Stop* pretending you're not angry," Alan snarled. "It's—it's fucking *patronising*, is what it is, and I can't stand it."

Jack's free hand went to Alan's wrist, as if to remove it, and Alan lost his head entirely. He planted himself in Jack's lap; the chair was large enough that he could wedge his knees on either side of Jack's hips and rest his full weight on Jack's thighs. Jack went still. His pupils darkened and his mouth tightened. The air between them had the heady closeness of the hour before the heavens opened and flung down a storm.

"*I betrayed you.* You're furious with me."

"Yes," said Jack. His hand was tight around Alan's wrist. Alan could pull against it and never be free, and right now that was the only thing in the world that he wanted. The only thing that would help.

He hissed, "*Show me.*"

Contained fury bled across Jack's face. He snatched Alan's other hand and now his grip was circling both of Alan's wrists at once, holding them pinned, the bones grinding painfully against one another. Alan gasped. Jack's other hand was beneath Alan's arse, and before Alan could breathe again Jack was standing, bearing Alan's entire weight, and Alan was being flung hard back onto the bed, where he sprawled ungainly with surprise.

It knocked a laugh out of him: one he didn't recognise. Wild, snarling anticipation took him between its teeth. And then he lifted his head and saw Jack's face.

"Stop that," said Lord Hawthorn. It was flat and final, and far more an order than anything that had passed between them before now. "Don't you *dare* do that to me."

"Do what?" Alan asked. He didn't know what script they were playing from.

"When I fuck, it's because it's what I want. Not because I'm punishing someone, or too angry to be safe."

"Oh, untwist yourself, my lord. It's a game," Alan gritted out, pushing to his elbows. His own anger was turning ugly now. He had a sense of the floorboards vanishing beneath his feet, ready to dump him into the wine cellar.

"No, it isn't. Not like this." Jack stared down at Alan and a muscle jumped in his cheek. "Is this what you were doing at the *Morning Post*? You knew what you were about to do, so you used me as a rod to make stripes on your own back?"

The sheer disgust in Jack's voice was what did it. The size of his mistake began to sink horribly into Alan, and most of his crazed desire ebbed away beneath it.

"No!" He sat up fast. "I wanted that, and it had nothing to do with—hell, you have to know how much I wanted it. It wasn't punishment. It was a *reward,* and I knew I didn't deserve it, and I took it anyway."

It took several dreadful seconds. But Jack's expression relented, and he sat back in the chair.

Alan stayed in the bed. It seemed safest. "But you are angry. And you saved me anyway. Are you going to denounce me as a sodomite? Or leave it up to the others to decide what fate I deserve? Why am I *here,* if not to let you have your revenge?"

"I don't need revenge," said Jack.

"Why the *fuck* not!" yelled Alan.

His misery punched a brief hole in the conversation. Jack picked up the neglected wine and took a sip with an expression that said he wanted to throw back the whole glass.

Jack said, quietly, "Why were you working for my cousin, Alan?"

It was the first time he'd said Alan's name, for all that he'd been invited days ago. Not Cesare. Not an insult, real or playful. His name.

Jack went on, "Because I'd lay two hundred pounds on you not having a choice in the matter."

"There's always a choice." Alan hesitated, then reached out a hand in request, and Jack put the glass of wine into it. Alan took a good gulp. It was probably hand-squeezed by virgins on a moonlit mountaintop in France, but right now he just needed his nerves to stop jangling. "It was that Morris. He found me, and he's bad enough, but I've known thugs like him before and I think he realised that. So he brought me to your cousin George." Another gulp. There wasn't a great deal of wine left.

Alan said, "I could have *chosen* to let Bastoke drop a word in Kenyon's ear and have me dismissed. Or a word in our landlord's ear to have us kicked out onto the street. And that's not counting the other things they said they'd do, to . . . to everyone I care about."

George Bastoke had seemed bored by the very act of threatening. He'd laid out a list of things that magic could do to a person and earnestly suggested that Alan imagine them applied to his dear mother—his brother, his sisters—those charming little children. They'd done their research before Morris plucked him off the street.

Alan swallowed. His hand cramped and his mouth tasted sour. "Bastoke said, *You are completely at our mercy.* As if he was telling me the sky was blue. And he was absolutely fucking right."

"My wager stands. That wasn't a choice." Anger still sat heavily on Jack's features, but it had altered. "I'm sorry."

Alan waited. It didn't appear to have been a trick.

"You're apologising to me? *You're* apologising? To *me*?"

"Calm down—it won't happen again. I'm sorry you were put in this situation. That's all."

"If you had *your* way I'd have had my memory taken on the ship," Alan pointed out. "Peppermint, wasn't it? I don't know if I could have perturbed a potion."

"You already had," said Jack. "The sleeping charm Mrs. Vaughn put in my whisky should have had you out for days."

Alan absorbed that. He nearly pointed out that he shouldn't have drunk the whisky in the first place, but he was damned if he'd apologise for *that*. They'd not known each other then.

Not that Alan had dropped the habit of appropriating Jack's alcohol. He drained the rest of the wine and handed back the empty glass. It finally seemed to be calming him.

"Whatever Edwin and the others need to get the contract back, I'm on board. I'll help. Anything, if it'll make Bastoke and his people bleed. I hate them so much it makes me *sick*. Making me go begging for help, and then making me betray people who'd shown me nothing but kindness."

"Kindness and a prick in your mouth," said Jack, very dry, and Alan found himself abruptly shredded by laughter with his face buried in his hands. He shook with it, all the tension and dread of the last few weeks boiling to the surface, and he took a long time to stop. His rib cage kept giving little aftershocks and gulps.

A hand settled on Alan's shoulder. He lifted his head. Jack

was at the edge of the chair, his bulk awkward now that he was attempting to use it for something other than intimidation. Alan shuddered out a final breath and let himself be comforted.

"The others will hate me," said Alan.

"They're better people than we are," said Jack. "They'll understand."

"At least tell me *you* still hate me."

Jack produced a smile that Alan refused to translate. "I despise you, Cesare."

"Good."

After that Jack summoned another servant, this one to confirm that the baths—*baths*?—were ready, and then to ask Alan's address so that he could send his family a message. The offer to stay was not spoken, but Alan felt it hovering. He firmly wrote that he'd be home later that night, folded the letter into three, and handed it over.

There were indeed two baths drawn in the large bathroom that was part of Lord Hawthorn's suite of rooms. One of them was an absurd, claw-footed thing, properly plumbed and porcelain, with gleaming brass taps on either side of the faucet. The other was a plain metal tub that had clearly been fetched from elsewhere in the house. Both of them steamed. The room smelled of soap and a hint of Jack's deadly cologne.

"Easier to fill them both here than have the servants lug water down the hall," said Jack.

"Toss you for the big one," said Alan. "Though you'll have to lend me the penny." He looked around warily for the approach of Oliver. "Will I be attacked by valets again?"

"Contrary to popular belief," said Jack, who was already unbuttoning his shirt, "the aristocracy are capable of lifting a sponge to wash their own limbs. And I thought you might have an apoplexy if I offered you a bath attendant."

Alan made a rude gesture and began to work on his own clothes. He might not have cared if half of Mayfair trooped into this bathroom. Not just a hip bath but a full tub, with water that was actually *hot*? He wanted to sink into it and never come out.

It occurred to Alan, as he peeled off his sweaty, dust-covered shirt, that he and Jack had fucked twice and not yet seen each other unclothed. Cocks and arses had been uncovered just enough for business to take place. And now they were on their way to fully naked, and there was no real frisson in the air; no, Alan had squelched all chance of that with his earlier stupidity. Instead there was something stranger. Ease.

Which didn't mean Alan wasn't going to *look*.

Unclothed, Jack's size became the musculature of a man who stayed active, softened by the solidity of one who'd never gone hungry. A light carpet of dark hair coated his chest and the centre of his stomach, thickening further on his arms and legs. His body was irregular, in a strange way, like a sculptor had reached the final sanding and polishing but wandered away before they could be done. That broken nose, very obvious in profile—the heaviness of the thighs and shoulders—everything in proportion, and not precisely rough-hewn, but compellingly unfinished.

And with one obvious asymmetry.

Alan paused, distracted from his own undressing. "When you said a war wound, I assumed—I don't know. Something that left only a surface scar."

"The damage is mostly aesthetic."

"Aesthetic." Alan kept looking, as Jack didn't seem to care. The tangle of skin was like a landscape, forming sharp gullies over the large, uneven chunk of missing calf.

"It's a dull story by wartime standards. The muscle was mangled and got infected, and a hero of a surgeon went in and scooped out the rot."

"Ouch."

"I was deep in fever, so I can't remember much. But I was told later that if he hadn't been willing to maim me, I might not have lived." Jack stepped out of his drawers—eh, nothing new there, Alan had already seen *that*—and into the tub. The larger one, of course.

"You don't move like someone with that much damage." Alan

turned back to his own trousers. "And you don't use that stick of yours often."

"I worked damned hard to recover." Jack tipped his head back against the tub, arms stretched along its sides. "I resurrected my singlestick practice from Oxford. Good for balance and staying nimble. I won't be running any long-distance races, but I can walk steadily most days."

"Well. Thank fuck it wasn't your pretty face."

Jack's hand went to his broken nose. Alan crowed with laughter, which echoed in the tiled room. "Oh fuckin'*ell*, you're vain about the nose!"

"We can't all be oil paintings." Jack watched with unashamedly intent regard as Alan stepped out of his trousers. "When I first saw you, on the ship . . ."

"Yes?" Alan was expecting sarcasm. Something to hurt. Jack was very good at that, and Alan had just poked him in a piece of vulnerable history.

But Jack said, almost roughly, "I thought you were one of the loveliest things I'd ever seen. And that you'd stolen my best cufflinks."

Alan didn't know what to say to that. And didn't know how, without a quiet room and a pen, to put flattering words around the hard and greedy and incoherent *want* that had been his own reaction to seeing Lord Hawthorn for the first time.

He went to kneel beside the obscenely large tub, took Jack's face between his hands, and kissed him.

It wasn't a kiss of passion. It was a kiss of gratitude, for anything, for everything—for saving Alan's life. For believing in Alan's character when Alan had done little enough to prove it. For understanding *why*. For writing a sincere letter to a desperate boy selling smut to survive.

For finding him lovely, and being prepared to say so.

It lasted a few aching moments of Jack's lips moving carefully under his, and the stubble of Jack's jaw rough under his palms. Alan's chest squeezed. He thirsted to open his mouth and take in tenderness by the gallon. He made himself pull back instead.

Jack had that snakes-and-sapphires look again, and Alan wanted to steal it for himself and keep it forever.

"You said . . ."

"I know what I said," said Alan.

"Hm. I wondered why you made it a rule to begin with. The way you write kisses, they're—" Jack waved a hand. Drops of water fell from it. "Devastating. Obliterating."

"That's right. No real man can kiss like that," said Alan. "Better to keep the potential alive than risk disappointment."

He recognised that he was laying a challenge, and that it was a terrible idea. Sure enough, Jack leaned in again, his hand going to Alan's nape to hold him in place.

Alan said, "*Stop*, Jack," mostly for the pleasure of knowing that Jack would. His face felt warm with steam and silly contentment. He grinned and twisted himself until Jack's grip loosened and Alan could stand up.

"You're a natural tormenter, Cesare." Jack tossed a handful of water at him. "Clean off and go home."

Alan went to the smaller tub, finished undressing, and climbed in. His toes tingled hotly, but the water wasn't overwarm, and he could relax into its arms right away. He settled back and closed his eyes, fumbling lazily for the washcloth. Tonight he would be with his family again, and know he'd kept them safe. Tonight George Bastoke believed that Alan had no memory of magic, and therefore no reason to vow his own revenge; or maybe even believed Alan was lying dead in the ruins of the Barrel.

Tomorrow would be . . . more complicated.

But tonight, Alan ducked his head beneath the fragrant water and let it wash away the last residue of his shame, his grime, his secrets.

17

"Of course I told Spinet not to trust him anymore!" Violet practically shouted. "We're under siege here again, Hawthorn, and *he* handed us over to Bastoke and the Coopers, and for all we knew he was going to be leading them right down this tunnel and then *past* the wards because he's a perker—perber—oh, fuck."

And she burst, quite suddenly, into tears.

It had never occurred to Jack that Violet would be the sort of person to cry, unless it was artfully and to a purpose. He had the urge to retreat all the way back down the hidden tunnel that ran between Bayswater station and Spinet House.

He and Alan hovered now at the end of that tunnel, before the open door. Jack could have pushed his way through; Spinet's wards still welcomed him. Alan had paused on the threshold and muttered that he *did* feel something now, and it felt bloody rude to try to shove through it, considering the circumstances.

And then the house had sounded the melody of *friend* in loud disharmony with the unbroken note that meant *foe,* and Violet had come charging down with Maud's pistol in her hands to see who it was.

"Bastoke threatened his family," Jack said, instead of pointing out that Alan wouldn't have led anyone anywhere if George had succeeded in erasing Alan's memory and leaving him in a gutter. For George, it had been a staggeringly shortsighted plan. A waste of a brilliant mind he'd already coerced into being an asset. George was an elegant edifice of moral rot, but he did usually recognise talent regardless of class. Joe Morris was proof of that.

But then, George hadn't bothered to get to know Alan. Only to threaten him.

Maud appeared as if summoned by Violet's distress. She directed a green-eyed glare first at Jack and then Alan.

"What did you do to her?"

"Asked her to marry me," said Jack, losing patience. "Stabbed her with a carving knife. Violet, I won't stand here all day."

Violet made a wet sound that was almost laughter and scrubbed the back of her hand across her eyes. She looked pink and smudged.

"Up your arse, Hawthorn. It's been a beastly night and I've barely slept." She shifted to look at Alan, who'd stopped skulking in Jack's wake and come up beside him. He held himself as if braced for carving knives and pistols both.

"I'll answer any questions you have," Alan said.

"Answer them in front of everyone, then," said Maud.

"And I'm reserving the right to toss you both out a top-floor window," said Violet, but she put her palm to the doorframe. "Alan Ross is welcome in this house. For the moment."

The main staircase didn't flatten under their feet, and the music of alarm had faded to silence, but Spinet House had a wary feeling to it. Footfalls were swallowed by the air. Jack didn't bother to ask why everyone was gathered in one of the smaller first-floor parlours instead of the larger ones on the ground floor. Retreating to higher ground was a natural response to being under threat.

Robin lay asleep on the largest couch, his head resting in Adelaide's lap and those parts of his legs that didn't fit dangling over the other arm. Adelaide's striped grey skirt was unfortunately a similar fabric to the upholstery, which combined with her tired posture to give her the look of someone who'd sat long enough to be absorbed into the furniture. And Edwin paced. Back and forth with a book in his hands, occasionally turning a page, a motion that struck up a small echo of the past in Jack.

Edwin looked like a poor construction of himself. Surely he should have been the one asleep. He stopped pacing when Violet motioned Jack and Alan into the room, and actually swayed on his feet for several blank seconds before his face remembered a human expression.

Then he clapped the book shut. The sound startled awake Robin, who went from horizontal to sitting with comical speed once he saw Alan.

"All right, nobody start shouting until we've heard him out," said Maud hastily. She stood in the middle of the room as if to referee any boxing matches that her brother might be tempted to start. Violet planted herself in a chair and folded her arms.

"And why should we trust anything he has to say?" asked Robin.

"Fetch one of those truth-candles," said Alan.

"Which you can likely perturb at will. Because I taught you how. You're welcome," Edwin added in his cattiest tone.

"He didn't have to come back here at all," said Jack. "All of you be quiet and *listen*. And then you may shout."

Nobody in this room cared about Jack's title, but they were responsive to his officer voice when he wielded it with purpose. Edwin collapsed onto the space vacated by Robin's legs and made a wordless gesture of agreement.

Alan explained. He made no excuses for himself; nor did he let his fear and frustration show as he had last night in Jack's house. He just laid out what had happened. The atmosphere in the room, tight and hostile, relaxed by minuscule degrees.

"We know they like threatening family," Maud said when he was done. "Robin."

"Yes." Robin's body language had softened. One of his legs was pressed up against Edwin's.

"I didn't tell Bastoke a thing he didn't need to know," said Alan. "Not about that tunnel into the house. And not about *how* I was helping. I let him think you were happy to have an unmagical canary who'd simply walk into rooms first and take the brunt of any danger."

"So he didn't know what you can do," said Edwin. "Is that how you shook off the memory spell?"

"Yes." Alan paused and then said, stiffly, "I do owe you a lot, for teaching me how."

"How did they know to approach you in the first place?" asked Violet, edged with suspicion. "We were careful to keep you out of sight for most of it, on the *Lyric*."

Not careful enough, clearly. The gossips of first class had certainly known that the young journalist on board spent a lot of time with Lord Hawthorn and his two scandalous lady friends. And Morris was sharp.

Alan shrugged. "They may have only suspected. If I'd had more sense I'd have pretended not to recognise Morris, but he caught me unawares. Couldn't help it."

"If nobody is going to shout after all," said Jack, "I believe it's my turn to ask questions."

He had several. He'd busied himself last night arranging them into a list and ordering them, because he'd needed something to distract himself from the memory of pale olive skin stretching across Alan's collarbones; the way Alan's mouth had felt on his; the amount of restraint it had taken for Jack not to haul the man half-dressed into the tub and kiss him until he couldn't remember how to make words of any language with that too-clever mouth.

Unlike Edwin, Jack was not a natural list-maker. The distraction hadn't worked at all.

Now he turned to Adelaide.

"Firstly. Are you a magician?"

Something halfway between guilt and a grin took hold of Adelaide's mouth. She stopped tapping her ring against the arm of the couch and clasped her hands tight in her lap.

"No."

"Are you a perturbator?"

"No."

"Must I ask the next question?"

"It only worked because it was Walter," said Adelaide. Walter, who'd been about to hurl magic at Jack in the Lockroom when she'd thrown herself in between. "He's the one who made blood-oath with Robin. He can't harm any member of Robin's household."

"Household . . . ?"

"Addy asked me to marry her," said Robin. "And I agreed."

Jack was hard to shock. He still felt as if someone had tossed him a double handful of something entirely unexpected and difficult to grasp: live goldfish, perhaps, or blancmange.

"You're *married*?"

"Betrothed," said Adelaide. "My mother insists she needs at least until the new year to plan a wedding, and we agreed not to announce it until after Kitty's confinement."

Edwin didn't look as if he were wasting tragically away because the love of his life was pledged to marry someone else. He looked rather like he was suppressing laughter.

"I can't help noticing that nobody else seems particularly surprised by this," said Jack dangerously.

Adelaide laughed. "Robin ran it past Edwin and Maud first."

"And I told Violet," said Maud, in *obviously* tones.

"It was a precaution," said Robin. "When the attacks on Spinet House became more frequent, and Addy made it clear she wouldn't keep her nose out of things—ow, thank you—" His apparently affianced bride had pinched his leg. "Edwin had been thinking about how magical estates define families and households, and whether a blood-oath might do the same. An engagement is an oath too."

"And last month my parents told me outright that if I didn't produce a husband soon, they were going to choose one for me." Adelaide slid a fond look at Robin. "So I marched right into the office at Whitehall the next day and said we should do it."

Jack now had fifteen new questions, but they could wait. Adelaide was protected from Walter in the same way that Maud was. That answered his initial one.

"Fine. Next question. *Edwin.*"

Edwin looked uncomfortable. "You know I've had theories about using the ley lines to solve the problem of distance. If a magical estate can enhance an individual's power locally, then a ley line might be able to carry that enhancement. Yes?"

Jack remembered an extremely dull lecture on this subject being delivered over breakfast, and cursed himself for not paying better attention at the time. "You drew on Sutton Cottage? From *London*?"

"The trick was forcing magic to flow from London to Sutton first," said Edwin. "A catalyst, to open the channel. I managed a one-handed cradle to escape the priez-vous, then used the map charm to find Flora Sutton. Her hair was still in the Lockroom, and she's buried on the Sutton estate. The Lockroom's map charm is enormously powerful. I simply . . . tried to piggyback onto it and see if Sutton would notice that I was horribly angry and needed help. That's the best way I can explain it."

"Hell," said Jack, equal parts appalled and impressed. "And it worked."

"Far better than I expected," said Edwin. "I think I got tangled up in half of the Barrel's own magic as well."

"You nearly *killed yourself*," said Robin.

Edwin shot him an unhappy look. Robin returned it.

"All right, what is this?" Jack said. "You two have been picking at the lid on this fight like a damn scabbed knee for weeks, and it's clearly important."

"Robin—"

"I keep seeing him die," said Robin.

Maud made a small noise of distress, and Adelaide went still.

"The first vision I had was nearly a year ago, at Penhallick House. And they've been happening ever since. It's always different, never one event set in stone. The visions like that are *possibilities*. But they kept happening. It started to feel like I was summoning them simply by dreading them so much."

"That's why you wanted the visions stopped," said Maud. She

went and sat at Robin's feet and touched his hand where the rowan-wood ring was.

"That and the headaches," said Robin. "All right, now we're all aware of that cheerful little fact, does anyone else have anything to share with the class?"

"Edwin," said Violet. She tapped her wrist.

Edwin was looking even more drawn, and had taken possessive hold of Robin's other hand. He released it now and split a glance between Alan and Jack.

"Coopers have been banging on the door here since yesterday. Violet and I spent the entire night reinforcing the wards—or rather, she did. I was well and truly drained. And this morning an envelope addressed to me came through the mail slot, and no, I shouldn't have opened it, but I was exhausted, and all I could think was that we're waiting for the Grimm of Gloucester to write back." His voice was flat. He tugged back his cuff a couple of inches to show a purple bracelet of runes like those that had accompanied Violet's summons to the Library. "Apparently, the fact that there is no longer a Barrel hasn't stopped Bastoke and the Assembly from issuing something that's both a legal summons and a direct order for my arrest. It hasn't . . . done anything to me. Yet."

"We're all now officially dangerous radicals engaged in a plot to dismantle British magical society," said Violet. "Not even I've managed to destroy my reputation that thoroughly before. Well done, Edwin."

"Sod off," said Edwin tiredly. "Forgive me if I need some time to adjust to our entire community believing us to be violent criminals who *destroyed* . . ." He trailed off. "The Office should make a report about it, Addy. The Prime Minister will need a cover story for why an anonymous building in Farringdon is now a pile of rubble."

"Secret military chemical experiments," said Adelaide. She smiled slightly at Alan. "Or it was gunpowder after all. An anarchist plot."

"You can't go to the Home Office, Edwin," said Robin firmly. "Nowhere you usually go. You're staying here."

"We can still get in and out through the Bayswater tunnel," said Maud. "That's something."

"And we still have disguises." Violet made a face. "We know Bastoke can negate them, but at least he has to suspect someone in the first place."

"Good," said Adelaide. "Make me a new one, please. *I'm* going to the Home Office, and then I'm going to Gloucester."

A ringing silence followed that. Adelaide clasped her hands elegantly in her lap. She looked, even more than usual, as if she were on the verge of correcting someone's table manners. "You were right, Edwin. Now more than ever, if there's someone out there who knows about the Last Contract and how it might be used, and how we might prevent it, then we need to know what he—or she—can tell us. I'll check one last time for any mail. And then I'll go and find the Grimm myself and write down everything they know. Or stuff them into my luggage, if I must."

More silence. Jack was no longer surprised that Adelaide Morrissey had proposed marriage to a baronet. She should probably be *running* the Home Office.

Alan had been quiet during this discussion, as if he still expected to be thrown out of Violet's top-floor windows if he reminded them of his presence. Now he cleared his throat.

"I don't mean to piss on a good plan, but—are we still at the stage of *preventing*? Now Bastoke has all three pieces of the contract, how do you know he isn't using it as we speak?"

"He could be." Edwin, with something to explain, looked marginally brighter. "But I think it's unlikely. One of my problems has been how you could possibly use it to steal from a smaller number of magicians, and . . . I don't think it's possible. It's a definite contract, and it's the bloodlines of the Three Families who are defined. And from what you said, Hawthorn, one assumes we'd feel it—Violet and I—if our magic was being drawn on." He nodded at Jack. "I think you're right to suspect the equinox gala. Ley lines notwithstanding, distance may still be an issue in how difficult this is. If there's any sort of ritual involved, it'd be sensible to do it when there are as many magicians as possible in close proximity. Hell, I'm almost tempted to let Bastoke and Walter *try* to use the contract," he added bitterly. "Let them suck up as much magic as they want, if it feels anything like what I did with Sutton. They can tear themselves apart with it."

"And have them accidentally *unmake* Cheetham and half the magicians of Britain in the process?" said Jack. "I think not."

Violet ventured, "Could Walter have been telling the truth, at my hearing? They haven't actually figured out how use the contract yet?"

"If that was the case," said Adelaide, "the clever thing to do would be to get their hands on someone even cleverer."

The room looked at Edwin. Edwin looked at the runes on his wrist and pressed his mouth into a line.

"*No,*" said Robin, nearly a snarl. "That's it. We'll go to Sutton Cottage. You'll be safe there."

"What was that about *nowhere I usually go*?" said Edwin. "That's the first place they'd expect."

"It has warding against magicians!"

Edwin paused. "It'd only be moving the siege to a stronger fortress. But it would buy us time to work out what to do and see if I can get these runes off."

"What are you planning to do now, stop your *own* heart?" Robin snapped.

"Robin," said Adelaide, a clear note of warning.

Several people began to speak at once. Jack raised his voice to cut across them.

"Come to Cheetham Hall."

He succeeded. The first notes of argument fell away, and everyone looked at him.

"It's my parents' land," added Jack. "They have control over guest-right, and we can tell them—well, as much or as little as we decide."

"Go to the very spot where this party is taking place?" Robin demanded.

"Yes," said Jack. "We stop letting ourselves be besieged. We arrive at the field early and set up an ambush."

"I like it," said Maud, to Jack's utter lack of surprise. "Either something happens at the gala or it doesn't. Either way, it gives us time to come up with a plan, on friendly ground, and for Addy to talk to this Grimm in the meantime."

"Edwin," said Jack, moving over to the couch, "show me that summons."

Edwin met Jack's eyes as he extended his wrist and gave a tired creak of a laugh.

"What?"

"I'm remembering the last time we tried to involve you in removing a rune-curse on someone's arm."

Not one of Jack's finest mornings, all told.

"Don't tempt me to un-involve myself," he said, pushing down Edwin's cuff. "*I* remember how peaceful my life was before it was invaded by Blyths and hangers-on."

Now it was Maud's turn to laugh. She gave Jack an affectionate look from her position on the floor. Intolerable. Jack was never going to rid himself of any of these people.

"And I don't think this is a true curse," he added to Edwin. "My mother should be able to negate it, if we get you to her quickly."

That settled things. They were moving this circus of disasters to Cheetham Hall.

Violet and Maud were in their element when given the chance to arrange some theatre. They disappeared somewhere in Spinet House, arguing about the most convincing way to make it look like they were all staying safe inside during the weeks before the equinox gala. Apparently Violet would create some illusions of twitched curtains and nighttime silhouettes, and anchor them to the window frames. She and Edwin then planned to go—carefully disguised—to Maud and Robin's townhouse and set up some similar tricks, after which all four of them would head to Cheetham.

Robin and Alan and Adelaide were poring over railway time-tables, calculating when Adelaide might make it to Gloucester and what routes she might take south afterwards; and several other routes that various people could take, leaving London at different times, that would obscure the fact that they were all converging on the same point.

And Jack was alone with Edwin Courcey for the first time in nearly five years.

They were in the master bedchamber on the second floor, with its impressive windows looking out onto the Bayswater street. Violet and Maud slept in here. Jack was trying not to look at anything too closely, after making the mistake of recognising one of the little jars on the dresser. It was bad enough having Violet regale him gleefully with tales of her bedroom escapades. He didn't need to know that she was also familiar with Whistle-thropp's under-the-counter range of imbued products.

Jack expected to be plunged right into the technical detail of magical wards, but instead Edwin gave him an uncharacteristi-cally direct look. Prolonged eye contact often gave Edwin the air of a man straining to hold a weight steady.

"I want your honest opinion, Jack. Do we keep Ross involved? Robin and Maud are most of the way to forgiving him already, and . . . Violet's house likes him."

Unspoken: *You and I aren't kindhearted people. We should see things clearly.*

Jack didn't know if he could. He was full of his own com-plex potion of anger and forgiveness. He thought of how Alan had looked when he realised Jack understood his reasons: flayed open by exhausted relief, shadowed with that gorgeous linger-ing defiance.

Physical attraction to someone—that, Jack could handle, even at the extremes that Alan brought out in him. But he seemed to want impossible things that belonged nowhere near the bedroom, or even reality. He wanted to crack open his rib cage and place Alan Ross inside it, the better to warm him with Jack's own blood.

Not that he planned to admit that. Certainly not to Edwin, of all people.

"It seems I stand dicentis for the man in his absence," Jack said, keeping his tone light. "I say we keep him. He's sharp and resourceful and motivated, not to mention how useful the perturbation might be. And if you're asking if I trust him not to turn coat if his family is threatened again—well, how does that make him any less worthy than the rest of us? How would you behave if it were Robin?"

Edwin didn't reply. But his lips moved, and finally he nodded: verdict reached, matter closed. He pulled out a notebook and gestured to the window.

"Now, Violet's the best person to do the house wards, but I think I can add a misdirection," he said. "Not quite the same targeted warding that Sutton and the Barrel—had," with a wince. "That's recognisable, if you've felt it before. I want something subtler for the front of the house. *Discouragement.* And we haven't time for me to grow it into geraniums in the window boxes, but I'm sure I've read about anchoring runes that will release magic into a spell like that over a long period."

Edwin looked expectantly at Jack. He'd refused to sleep until this was done, claiming that it'd be easier if he simply wrote the runes down before Jack left, and then applied them later when he'd rested and had most of his magic back. So he still looked like boiled horseshit, and it gave Jack another strange flick of nostalgia. Edwin used to look like this all the time.

These days, Robin and Adelaide and even Maud would drag Edwin away from books and make sure that he ate and saw sunlight. He would never have Jack's figure, or Robin's, but at least he looked like a healthy slender man instead of a skeleton someone had unearthed in an attic.

Jack took a breath. Runes could wait. This conversation wouldn't be any easier if he put it off.

"Do you truly think you're going to die?"

Edwin fumbled the pencil. "What?"

"Because I've known soldiers who are so convinced of their death that they start hurrying it along. And that's dangerous for everyone around them."

"You think I *want* to die?"

"I think you hate the idea of things you can't understand and control, and if the opportunity came up to make it fast, painless, and meaningful—to sacrifice yourself—you'd be tempted."

For a long moment Jack wondered if he was about to be punched. He'd have allowed it out of sheer novelty.

"Mrs. Vaughn told Maud that using the contract would require blood," said Edwin at last, unwilling and quiet. "It seems unlikely that something as large as transforming it, putting its potential for misuse truly out of reach, would require anything less."

"It doesn't mean the blood has to be *yours*," Jack said. "Must I point out that you're no longer a foul-tempered librarian with no friends? Granted, the first two are still true. But there are people who'd grieve you."

"God, you're an arse," said Edwin. "And of course I know that. Robin refused to *let* me only have one person." He seemed as unnerved as Jack by the fact that they appeared to be having a conversation about emotions.

"Let you . . . ?"

"I always thought about it the other way around. If one day Robin rushes into danger too far and too fast, if he ever does something heroic and stupid—I'd still have Maud and Addy. And Kitty, and Violet."

"Not presuming on my account, I see."

"I wouldn't dare," Edwin shot back. "If I did lose Robin, it'd destroy me. But at least there'd be people around to pick up the pieces. And the same for Robin, if any of those visions come true. We can't be one person alone, or two alone. Not and be prepared to risk anything. And we have signed up for a fight, Jack," he added dryly. "Even you."

Jack was now in the awkward position of having gone fishing for a piece of emotional immaturity so that he could stamp on it, and having instead hooked some evidence that Edwin had thought this through further and more intelligently than him. He cleared his throat.

"So long as you're not planning any heroic stupidity yourself."

"Not if I can avoid it. I really *don't* want to die. I thought I might, in the Lockroom." A quick shudder creased Edwin's chin. "It didn't feel meaningful at all. Only terrifying."

Jack settled himself in the window seat and looked down onto the street. His leg felt full of blood. He'd been standing a long time. "I remember how it felt, being on Cheetham Hall's land and able to draw on it for support," he said. "It never felt like too much to handle."

Never until the day he couldn't talk about.

"No," Edwin agreed. "When I'm at Sutton, even normal English magic is easier. But it's especially easier to manage the different techniques that Flora Sutton and her friends used." He set the notepaper down on a cushion and leaned against the wall. A relaxed lecturing stance. "I keep coming back to the idea of magic carving paths in us. Like ley lines in the land. Magic goes where it knows, where it's already been. Learning new techniques feels like I'm making new, *wider* paths, so I thought . . ." A wry not-quite-smile. "I thought I could handle more. At first, in the Lockroom, it felt like the most natural thing in the world. And then it felt overwhelming. I was trying to use the wrong paths, the *wrong* language—I had only my will. And not enough of that, in the end."

It wasn't a lecture. It was closer to a confession. The only other magician around was Violet, who was new to this kind of responsibility; Edwin had played with Jack and Elsie as children, had visited Cheetham Hall when Jack's relationship with it was uncomplicated and joyous and full. Edwin wanted to say this to someone who might understand.

"Modesty doesn't suit you, Edwin," Jack said. "*Not enough*

will. Bollocks. You're probably the most bloody-minded, de-termined, and intelligent magician in England, and you're a lot more enjoyable to be around now you've realised it."

Edwin stared at him. Then, flatly: "I didn't know you knew how to give compliments."

Jack let his mouth twitch. The breeze scudded clouds across the sky and shook the green leaves of the plane trees lining the street. A woman in a nurse's cap and apron pushed a large per-ambulator down the footpath.

Edwin added, "And *you're* certainly a lot easier to take in small doses. Though I still wouldn't call it enjoyable."

"Your opinion counts for nothing," said Jack. "You have no taste."

"Yes, I've often suspected as much."

That won Jack's attention again. A hint of challenge gleamed in the pale sky-blue of Edwin's eyes. "But it turns out," said Ed-win, "there are people in the world who don't think that spend-ing time together also means fighting over every little thing."

That was a direct stab, neatly under a rib. Jack had always enjoyed a good fight and the challenge of trading insults. He'd grown up knowing himself loved; either there was affection be-hind an insult, or it simply didn't occur to him to take it se-riously, because he'd never bothered to believe anything bad about himself. For a long time he'd assumed, as children did, that his experience was the only one. That everyone else also treated conflict as a game. The best and most personal cut won, but none of it *meant* anything.

After Elsie's death he didn't bother to learn new patterns, simply became more deliberate about them. It was easy to shove the world away, to make them hurt as badly as he was hurt. He already had the knack for it.

It had taken a regrettable amount of time for Jack to realise that for people like Edwin there *was* no self-belief to act as a shield. For Edwin the insults had been real and raw and grind-ing him down since the beginning of his life.

The nurse and her charge crossed the street. A motorcar crawled past, metal gleaming in the sun.

"I didn't treat you particularly well," said Jack. "You have my apology for that, for what it's worth."

The silence from Edwin was gratifyingly thick. Jack could have bottled it.

"I certainly didn't know you could *apologise*."

"I've no idea why you stuck around."

Edwin coughed. Jack glanced at him; his cheeks were slightly pink.

"Not to inflate your hideous ego, but there were occasional compensations. But mostly, I didn't know what I actually wanted. I didn't know it was out there until I fell over it. Now." Edwin pulled his cradling string from his pocket and began to demonstrate the kind of slow-releasing clause he wanted to anchor to the window. The emotions part of the conversation was closed.

Jack picked up the pencil and began to sketch some components of runes.

He was turning around within himself a private resolution that if anyone had to die for this nonsense—if Edwin's transformation or negation did require it—then it would be him. But Jack had grown past his old gift for melodrama. Everyone had someone who would grieve them. Jack had promised his father, on returning from the Boer, that he wouldn't deliberately put himself in harm's way again.

He thought of his mother, who'd only just been granted his company again—thought of Oliver, who needed guidance—and thought of Alan. Who'd never needed Jack at all, but *wanted* him, in that artless and ferocious way that Jack found so devastating.

It'd destroy me, Edwin had said, of losing Robin.

Jack had already been destroyed by a loss once. Instead of letting anyone else pick up the pieces, he'd taken them away on his own and let them heal at strange angles.

But he *had* healed, while he wasn't looking. He'd been sitting on a folded-under limb so long it had gone numb. And then, when forced to run, he'd found it perfectly capable of bearing his weight.

Jack Alston might not have magic, but he was moving through the world again, and had people relying on him again, and it was blood rushing back into the numb flesh of his feelings. Forcing him to live.

18

"This was a terrible idea," Alan said. He stood on the doorstep of his own house with misgivings kicking him in the chest. "I've changed my mind. Go away."

Perhaps Jack would have obeyed and turned on his heel. More likely he would have found something sardonic to say. Alan would never know.

The front door opened inwards without his touching it, and his sister Bella stood there. They startled in guilty unison. Alan felt his face fall into exactly the narrow-eyed look that Bella was giving him, as they both tried to work out what the other was feeling guilty about.

For Bella, who stood with their ma's old coat buttoned over her belly like an ill-fitting tent, the answer was obvious. Alan got his oar in first.

"You're leaving the house?" he demanded.

"*Shh,* Mamma's napping. What're you playing at, dawdling on your own step? Who's this?" Bella shot back, pink with annoyance. She craned around him to look at Jack, her face changed colour, and her knees performed a reflexive servant's bob.

"I asked first," said Alan. He could feel Jack's amused gaze on the back of his neck. "What were you going to do, sneak out to the greengrocer's and tell anyone you met that you've been eating too many sweets?"

"Soffgh," said Bella. Alan snickered. That had started as *sod off,* and she'd tried to swallow it. Her face sagged. "I want some air that's moving faster than a slug. I'm *so hot.*"

"Mr. Ross," said Jack patiently, "are we preventing the young lady from leaving? Or shall we perform introductions inside?"

"Who *is* this?" Bella hissed in Italian, complexion shifting yet again to something in the tomato family.

"What's that? Caro? Bella? Who is at the door?" came floating down the stairs. It seemed Mamma was no longer napping.

"Sainted Mary," muttered Alan, and got them all inside the grimy brick-fronted place and the door closed while Bella fought her way out of the coat and bundled it into a ball behind the coat stand. The entryway was gloomy and stifling—late summer had spitefully turned from pleasant to hideous—and their ma's eyesight was poor enough that she wouldn't spot it.

There was nothing wrong with her ears, though.

Alan and Jack had argued about this yesterday, and argued some more about it today. George had last seen Alan memory-less and possibly dead in the collapsing Barrel. Perhaps he would strike Alan Ross, blackmailed traitor journalist, completely off his mental list of things to concern himself with.

Perhaps he wouldn't.

"What would it matter now if George does find out?" Jack had said. "You've served your purpose. You've no magic and no power over him. Even if he somehow discovers you're at Cheetham, he'll assume I dragged you back into things to spite him."

"But why do *you* need to *visit*?" Alan returned, and couldn't drag a good answer out of him, and it wasn't until Jack was sitting at their kitchen table with an air of impeccable courtesy that Alan realised what this was. Jack was simply being nosy. He'd seen Alan's workplace, he'd heard half the secrets of Alan's past, and now he felt entitled to waltz into Alan's house and play the lord with his family.

Alan should never have kissed the bastard at all.

The official story, for the Rossi family's benefit, was that Alan had been inside that anonymous office building. When it collapsed he must have had a bad knock on the head, because he couldn't remember anything about why he'd gone inside in the first place. And a very kind ("*Ha.*") aristocrat had heroically pulled him from the rubble and saved his life, and now his lord-ship had decided to show an interest.

The Rossis understood that. Showing An Interest was some-thing that toffs did from time to time. Especially the women. They might turn up with charity baskets and make appalled noises about the damp or sit by the kitchen stove and ask how much you spent on fuel and how much on food, and maybe you told them that our Emma worked in a big restaurant kitchen and snuck broken rolls out the back door when times were tough, and maybe you didn't, because nobody who wore that much lace on their clothes could be trusted, not really.

Jack had not brought a basket, but he had stopped at the bak-er's on the corner and bought a dozen buns. Alan's ma boiled the kettle for tea, Caro came in with Lizzie on her hip and Tom underfoot—Emily wouldn't return from school for hours—and the natural cowing effect of being in the presence of Lord Hawthorn lasted all of ten minutes before Alan's relatives were shouting happily over one another.

Indeed, the Lord Hawthorn in the room was very different to the one who'd charmed Kenyon. This man was clean-spoken and curious and displayed an eloquent Liberal sympathy for the conditions of the working poor. Even the taciturn Dick came out of his shell and was made to laugh, and Maria Rossi kept patting Jack's hand and telling him that he was an angel sent by the Virgin Mary to rescue her Alanzo.

Alan chewed angrily on his mouthful of bun.

"I'm leaving town for a few weeks again, Mamma," he said, when a lull presented itself. "More of that advertising work. For the railways, this time."

It was the easiest excuse. He'd told Kenyon that Lord Haw-thorn had invited him to the country to write an in-depth so-ciety piece on Cheetham Hall and the ball that Lord and Lady Cheetham were holding there—a *very* exclusive event—and Ken-yon had agreed instantly. Hell, a few more posh parties and per-haps Mr. Shorter would take Alan for *Tatler* after all, though if he had to start reporting on polo matches he'd die of boredom.

If he returned from the country at all.

Alan's rash anger, his desire to leap in and help, was curling fretfully at the edges now that he was near the dear flame of his family. What if he *did* pretend to have forgotten magic, and returned to his own life? What if he refused to get involved in the fight against a power-grabbing plot that might do harm to a lot of magicians, of which Alan *was not one*?

The sweet bun had gone ashy in his mouth. He set it down.

Alan spent his life raging about his own lack of power to change anything that was unfair about the world. He wasn't a politician. He couldn't vote on the People's Budget; he couldn't even write in favour of it, so long as he was at the *Post*.

But he could, perhaps, do something here. Not just for Violet and Edwin, whom he'd betrayed, but for all the magicians who didn't have money and station and their own beautiful magical houses. They deserved even less to have their power taken away from them.

The world had given Alan Ross a rare chance at an unselfish act. And it just so happened to have hooked into it the opportunity for revenge against the men who'd hurt him and used him and threatened his family as if they were nothing.

"Do you read Alanzo's newspaper, your lordship?" His ma had somehow managed to get Jack talking about Alan's job. Nobody in the family was illiterate, but Alan's ma had never read the *Morning Post* nor met anyone who had.

"Mrs. Rossi, I can say with certainty that I have read every word your son's ever written. I hate to think of the stories the world would have been deprived of, if I hadn't been there to save his life."

Alan coughed on a mouthful of tea and, for the second time in a handful of days, considered flinging the rest of it in Jack's face.

"In fact," said Jack, standing up and giving Alan a pointed look, "I've been promised that I might see the first draft of the next one. Your study's upstairs, Ross?"

Just one little cup of tea in the face. Just one. Alan tried to think of an excuse to refuse, but couldn't. He showed Jack to the narrow set of stairs, and went to follow him, but Bella grabbed his arm just as he began to climb.

"'Scuse us, your lordship," she said, and dragged Alan two yards away. She lowered her voice to a demanding whisper. "Are you *really* going to write about the railways?"

Alan's heart gave a skip of wariness. But Bella's eyes darted meaningfully towards Jack and she said, barely audible now, "You're not going off to be—*kept*?"

Alan stared at her. He would have been less surprised if she'd stood on her head or given birth to an ostrich egg.

"I took a delivery from Berto," Bella muttered, "and it was all wrapped in paper but the string was loose, so I opened it—"

"*Bella!*"

"And I only read a few pages, but—oh for fuck's sake, Al, I'm not a green virgin," she said, gesturing to her belly. "And Mamma might be happy to believe you've never had a steady girl because you're too busy working, but you've never even *tried*, not when we were little and not now. The girls in this neighbourhood look at you like you're a fresh apple and they'd stab each other to take a bite. You barely notice."

And she'd chosen *now* to have this conversation. Alan glanced frantically up the stairs. Jack was now out of sight. Loose in Alan's house. Fantastic.

"You can't tell Mamma," he said, instead of bothering to fight.

"Madonna santa, of *course* not." Bella knew as well as he did the endless moaning and prayers for his soul that would result.

"I'm not going off to be a bloody rent boy," said Alan. "Can I—"

"Only this lord looks at you exactly like the girls do," said Bella, not budging, "and I know you think you have to wade through shit so the rest of us can stay clear, but—you *don't*, you stupid arse. Not this."

Her eyes were too bright. Alan cursed himself. Of course Bella, whose life had been dragged into ruin by a rich man's attentions, would fear this for him.

"You don't have to worry. I can take care of myself," said Alan firmly. "And if his lordship lays so much as a finger somewhere it's not welcome, I'll punch him in the nose myself. I swear."

"Good. You might knock it back into shape," Bella said, and giggled.

By the time Alan reached his attic room, Jack was standing by the narrow desk, running his fingertips thoughtfully over the surface. Jack was too big and grand for this room. He made it look tinier and shabbier.

"You're out of luck. I haven't any drafts," Alan said spitefully. It was a lie. He had three half-started stories, pages curled up in the red-and-yellow cocoa tin that was his filing cabinet, and all of them featured a sardonic lord with dark hair and blue eyes. "You've seen the place. I hope it's as much of a hovel as you expected. Now leave."

"They're obviously very proud of you," said Jack, as if Alan hadn't said anything.

"I meant it."

"So did I."

Silence. Alan gave up and went and sat on the edge of his bed, which would have fit Jack about as well as Violet's couch fit Robin. The old boards creaked beneath Alan's meagre weight and the thin mattress sagged. He was acutely aware of the haphazard pile of thin coverings, very different to the single thick, warm blanket that had adorned the guest bed in Jack's house.

"My ma's glad I bring in enough to pay the rent. But they don't understand what I do, and it makes them uncomfortable not to understand."

"Bullshit."

"*Don't* pretend you know anything about us," Alan snapped. "You've been here half an hour. And Bella already thinks you're here to change my occupation to prostitute. She understands *that* well enough."

Jack looked genuinely startled. Then he laughed and his posture changed. Fuck, Alan shouldn't have said anything. This was a room of hard angles, and Jack's low voice shook it like thunder on the horizon.

"And how much am I paying you?"

Alan shook his head. The game didn't belong here. None of Alan's fantasies ever played out in this room. The cabins of pirate ships, yes, or the bedrooms and window seats of grand manor houses, or the dungeons of castles. Even if all went perfectly at Cheetham Hall, Alan would still have to live here, write here, exist here.

And if he had to sit at that desk and dwell in the memory of something gloriously real taking place beneath this low, slanted roof, he'd be starving and aching forever.

Alan rubbed a hand over his face. He said, because the exchange with Bella had put it into his head and he needed a topic as far from fucking as he could manage—"Did you ever hear of sin-eating?"

A pause. Jack had packed away his thunder when Alan didn't respond to it; his voice was normal when he said, "No."

"Welsh folklore. I read about it in one of Mr. Voight's books. It seemed familiar at the time, even though there's nothing Catholic about it. Someone would be paid to take on the sins of the freshly dead and leave them free for heaven. I read that and thought, right. *That's* what I'm for."

Alan had never been the oldest son or the coddled baby. He was the different one—the clever one. He'd barely been surprised when he was the invert one as well.

He used to have nightmares about being forced to eat stones until his feet sank into the earth, then knees and then hips and chest as he kept getting heavier and heavier, the weight shoving him all the way down to where the fires were.

He said, "It was simple enough. After my pa died, I was a forger and a thief and a pornographer, and it meant everyone else could stay *respectable*. And then one day I stopped believing in God. Like that." He snapped his fingers. "So I told myself, well, that's something, now stop believing in sin as well. Just drop it on the ground and leave it behind. I thought—I thought it'd be such a relief."

"But it's hard to rid yourself of something you've been swallowing since you were too young to be revolted by the taste," Jack said softly.

Alan eyed him in case this was another filthy joke. It didn't seem to be.

"Yes."

Christ, he was so tired, and Jack was so unbearably solid. If Alan went over and hit him, or flung obscenity in his face, or leaned his forehead against Jack's sternum—that stupid broad chest clad in expensive wool and silk and cotton—Jack wouldn't shift.

Alan had never needed to lean on anyone. It was intolerable that he now kept turning out the pockets of his soul and finding caught in their seams the desire to let someone else take his weight. The desire to be held, even kissed.

He couldn't bring himself to ask. And Jack would only do it if Alan asked him to, and it was Alan's own rule, but for a moment he hated Jack passionately for obeying it.

Luckily there was something he could ask, and would. He could squash his pride when it wasn't for himself.

"I want to ask you a favour. I know I don't have the right. I know you don't owe me a thing now. Take it as a chance to lord it over me, if nothing else."

A long look. Alan was uncomfortably aware that Jack saw through all of that.

"When you put it like that, how can I resist?"

"I'll do whatever I can to help. I meant it. But if this ends badly for me, I want you to tell my family, and take care of them. They're all I have." And he was all they had, which was too obvious to point out. This was a much bigger favour than an interview for the papers. Alan clung to the memory of Jack, mocking and cruel on the *Lyric,* saying: *You didn't ask for enough from me.*

Now Alan was asking. Alan would fucking beg.

"Tell them what? Perhaps your train came off the rails?"

"Yes. Tell them it's an insurance payout from the railroads. Anything, but . . ." Alan swallowed. "They've been on the streets before. I won't have that happen again. I will *haunt* you if that's what it takes."

"That won't be necessary. You have my word," said Jack. He walked over, extended his hand, and shook Alan's, and not a hint of mockery spoiled the gesture.

19

Jack arrived at Cheetham two days after Edwin and the others. Adelaide was still in Gloucester; Alan was still in London. Both were expected within the week.

Before leaving Spinet, Jack had written a letter for Edwin to carry to the Countess of Cheetham, begging her hospitality and her silence and explaining . . . not a great deal.

Ask Edwin to explain everything, he'd written. And then, awfully—*Ask him to answer all the questions that I can't.*

It was unfortunately not the sort of task that Edwin was suited to, but he did enjoy explaining. And he had the support of Maud and Robin, both of whom could handle difficult conversations with near strangers with the ease of a waiter handling an armful of plates.

For all its necessity, the letter felt like an act of enormous cowardice. A sharp lump of salt developed in Jack's throat as his luggage was transferred into the house by Oliver and Cheetham Hall's footmen. He climbed the front steps.

"Blake," he said, greeting the butler in the entry hall.

"M'lord."

"Is Lady Cheetham—"

"Thank you, Blake," said Lady Cheetham.

Blake slipped wisely away. The front doors closed, cutting off a sharp slant of sunlight, and Jack stood alone with his mother. Her white hair was in one of its severe styles today, her dress sashed tightly and her throat girded with coral beads. The fact that she'd had to arm herself to receive him made Jack feel like a smudge of grime on the world's boot.

"Edwin told you," Jack said, to be sure.

His mother's eyes turned for a moment to bleak gashes in her face. She came up to him, the layers of her petticoats a soft swish against the floor.

"Show it to me," she said.

Jack never thought of refusing. He arranged the words that had rattled unsaid within him for years, hollowing him out with their force, and which he never would say. *Your brother and nephew came onto this land when you were away. They tried to use my magic, and Elsie's, and it left me with nothing and Elsie with more pain than she could bear.*

Heat filled Jack's mouth like blood when he tried to speak. The pain was trying to climb down his throat. His eyes watered as he let his jaw fall open and his mother's hands cupped his face. She was nearly his height; she didn't have to crane to see the secret-bind where it would be glowing on his tongue.

"I see," she said.

A bronze horse statuette hurled itself from its marble plinth and fell to the ground with a hollow bang. Jack pulled away.

"Polly."

"That's nothing, my dear. Half the wallpaper came off in the yellow drawing room when Edwin was explaining." Her smile was level. "No matter. I'd been meaning to redecorate that wing soon. I wish you'd shown me at the time, instead of letting me believe the two of you had finally done something too big and too dangerous to handle."

And that was something *she'd* never said, although Jack had always known she believed it. His father had raged at him for his silence. His mother had kept saying, over and over, that whatever it was, it didn't matter, he could tell them. He could tell them anything.

Of course it had looked like Jack's fault. Neither he nor Elsie would speak a word about it, and when she died he dragged himself away from magical society as if his conscience couldn't bear the reminder.

He said, "We're still hosting the gala. We must, if we're to intervene."

"Oh, yes," she said calmly. "I will extend guest-right to my nephew George and his friends. I will be the perfect hostess."

Lady Cheetham hand-fed orphaned ducklings and would walk out of her way rather than tread on a spider, and yet Jack wouldn't have been surprised if the silent half of that sentence was *and then I will tear out his spine.*

"Where's everyone else?" he asked. "I assume you've put them all to work."

"Paddling in the lake. The sea grotto's finished, and Violet has some beautiful ideas for a light show. We'll walk that way and let them know you've arrived." Her gaze swept up and down Jack's travelling clothes. "Let me change into my tramping gear. And put on some proper boots, my dear. Tell Freddy Oliver to do the same" was her parting shot. "I'm sure the boy's keen for some nice, fresh air after so long in the city."

And so Jack set out to walk the grounds of Cheetham with his mother and his half brother, the reason for which became clear halfway up the first hill when Polly began gently grilling Oliver on how his magical studies had been progressing. *Studies,* as if Jack were a university tutor she'd employed.

"Very well, m'lady, thank you. His lordship has me working on intensity and time-specification clauses," Oliver said, handling the words carefully. He demonstrated with a small light-spell, using the clauses rather than sheer power to make the light brighten and dim. It was good, tedious practice, and Jack had taught it to Oliver with an enormous sense of irony, remembering how much he and Elsie had groaned over such exercises. "Oh, Ma said you were building a folly! Can I look? I won't be long. Careful, sir, there's thorns," Oliver added, sparing an anxious look for Jack's shirtsleeves.

Polly sent Jack a satisfied look as Oliver's red hair bobbed away on a brief detour to the folly, a lurching stone hut with a dense thatched roof. It was indeed ringed with wild rosebushes clawing their way free of any attempt at order.

"You and the gardeners are outdoing yourselves," Jack said.

"If this gala is to be a disaster, at least nobody will be able to say it wasn't a beautiful one."

As they neared the lake, other changes became visible. The land works from Jack's previous visit had been smoothed out and completed; the balustraded terrace looking down onto the lake was now just the highest edge of a huge sprawl of vivid green lawn, dotted with neat stone-ringed islands of small olive trees and bright flowers. The land beneath the terrace, the entire northern edge of the lake, was now a sea grotto three times the height of the folly: a carved-out marvel of intricate dark stone, decorated with shells and rough mosaic tiles in shades of green and blue, like an undersea king's palace in a picture book. A path of white stones wandered around the lake's edge and then beneath a pink arch made to mimic coral, and into the depths of the grotto, from whence laughter could be heard.

Something bright ran across the lawn in Jack's periphery. He turned in time to see a feathery tail like a dropped golden necklace vanish between trimmed hedges.

"What was that?" asked Oliver, joining them again.

"Leo said we should get golden partridges to complement the peacocks," said Lady Cheetham. "He really should have specified that he was joking."

Jack's parents had been well suited—scions of well-born and extremely magical families—but had, he suspected, married more out of goodwill than grand passion. His father kept discreet mistresses and split his time between Cheetham and London. His mother ruled the Hall, absolute in her dedication to the estate she'd married and pledged her blood to.

And buying a flock of ornamental partridges that she knew perfectly well he'd never wanted was exactly the kind of joke that she'd consider to be a display of affection for her husband.

The white stones crunched beneath Jack's boots, providing a warning of their approach, and the coral-arch of the grotto soon disgorged Robin and Edwin, both soaking wet and breathless with bathing flannels clinging to their bodies. Edwin in flannels looked like a tourist postcard designed expressly to make fun of the English, and his bare arms had already turned geranium-pink in the sun, but he was smiling. There was a darker pink mark at the side of his neck. Jack transferred his gaze firmly back to Robin.

"How d'you do, Hawthorn," said the baronet in question. "If you're looking for the girls, they went for a walk to dry off. I should warn you, Violet's had five new ideas for illusions, ma'am," he added to Polly. "At this rate you'll be shipping her entire theatre troupe over from New York and installing them permanently on the grounds."

"Don't encourage her," said Jack. He looked back at Edwin. The purple runes around Edwin's wrist were gone. Edwin noticed him noticing and lifted the hand to twist back and forth.

"Thanks to your mother," he said.

"I think young Edwin is disappointed in me," Jack's mother told him as they left Edwin and Robin behind and took a looping course back toward the Hall. "I had to tell him that we Bastokes have never gone in for keeping thorough records when it comes to runes. It never seemed all that important to me."

"Give him a few hours and he'll drag everything out of you and write it down himself," said Jack.

"I think Mr. Courcey's very kind," said Oliver unexpectedly. "He's always interested in what I have to say. He asked about Ma's healing spells, and what kinds of magic were useful for valeting."

Edwin's magpie of a mind, always picking and collecting. A true interest in someone *was* a sort of kindness.

"He has some interesting theories about ley lines," agreed Lady Cheetham. "Leo sent word of what happened to the Barrel, and Edwin told me how it happened." She frowned at the toes of her boots. "I've always found the bond to the land very intuitive. And I suppose I'm used to it. It's such an *effort* to do magic when I go to town, now."

Intuitive. Jack turned that word around in his mind. Like most women of her generation, and even those today, Polly

Bastoke would have been given far less formal training than her brother. Runes passed casually down in the family. Spells for the domestic sphere.

"Shall we talk to the bees?" asked Oliver. He answered himself by breaking into an eager almost-jog, heading towards the hives. Jack vaguely remembered having that much energy at that age.

His step faltered with realisation. "You introduced him to the bees? Or was that Leo?"

"It was me," said Lady Cheetham. "It seemed . . . practical."

"Then—he *must* know."

Lady Cheetham shook her head. "He doesn't know what it means. And it doesn't have to mean anything."

"What do you mean, *practical*?"

Jack's mother stopped walking. Jack pulled to a halt beside her, blinking away the sunlight.

"Jack," she said levelly, "I will only say this once, and I don't intend to apologise for it. Nor do I wish to hear any apology from you, given what I now know."

Christ, there was a preface for you. Jack had the urge to loosen his knees and widen his stance, ready for a blow.

"We didn't know if you would ever set foot here again."

It hurt as much as he'd expected. She went on, "We had to plan for the possibility that you wouldn't. Oh, you will inherit. No question of that. Beyond our family's oath, there's that little matter of an entailed earldom." She smiled ruefully. "But you could be Earl of Cheetham from London—you could be Earl of Cheetham in the wilds of Argentina—and never come back here, and this place will need caretakers nonetheless. People who know it."

An apology tried to bubble up. Jack caught it easily. He had years of experience refusing to apologise for his decisions.

Instead he said, with care—"I didn't know if I would return either. It *hurt*, Polly."

"I know." She looked, for a moment, even older. "Does it still?"

They weren't talking about grief, which was its own pain and kept its own house. Jack, his feet planted on the land of the Hall, finally forced himself to direct his attention to it. During his last visit he'd been so full of emotion it had been impossible to tell truly what was him and what was the land, and he'd refused to stop moving for long enough to disentangle it.

When Elsie died the pain had been even more tangled up, but even magicless Jack had been unable to escape it: the scream of a place where one of its heirs had died violently, died full of magic that had been twisted and wrong for a year. He'd been running from that violence, and the way it felt like a raw wound, as much as anything else.

For a moment it was like trying to wield a gun or direct a horse, having not done it for over a decade. The muscles responsible for this had lost their memory. It was laborious. And faint, once he fumbled for the knack; far fainter than it had ever been. But the land was there, singing soft, the trees and the dirt and the house itself. It sent a hot sharpness through his chest and up into his nose, the closest to outright tears he'd come in years. Nothing about it felt *wrong*.

"No," he said roughly. "It doesn't hurt now."

Hope filtered into his mother's face. "I'm glad. It was—well, honestly, we thought about leaving as well," she said. "But Leo couldn't stand the idea of letting Cheetham sit with the damage until it went bad. He stayed for five years. Barely left the grounds at all. And then I told him I could take it in hand from there."

Jack felt nearly sick with the humbling enormity of what his parents had done in his absence. They'd taken on the huge, hurting estate as if it were a wounded wolf, ignored the clawing and biting that would have resulted from their blood-oath, and stayed until the edges of the wound knitted.

They'd have done the same for you, a voice of plain and remorseless sense whispered in Jack. *If you'd bothered to let them.*

And it should have been you *to do the mending. What kind of heir can you call yourself now?*

And still his mother walked the estate every day, granting

recognition to even the place where Elsie had died, no matter how much it hurt. Moving herself above the earth in patient patterns. Carving channels through repetition, just as Edwin believed that the point of ley lines was for magic to flow and renew itself. Magic. Bonds. Intuition.

For a moment Jack had the uneasy impression of a large idea that he might be able to touch, to make solid and understandable, if only he could reach in the right direction.

But his mother started walking again, down the slope to where the bees danced in the summer breeze, and Jack followed her, and the impression slipped away.

20

The summer abruptly produced one cold day, a promise of the autumn just around the corner, and of course it found Alan shivering in annoyance on the train platform with his fingers locked around the handle of his single battered case.

The train coming in to his platform screeched and yelled as it came to a halt, filling the air with brass noise. Alan didn't realise that one of the high whistles was coming from a human mouth until a man touched his arm and said, "Think that dark lassie is trying to catch your eye."

Alan looked down the platform to where the man indicated. Adelaide was hanging out the window of one of the second-class carriages, waving both arms at him. Her travelling-suit was a sober navy blue with white piping and her hat was plain good straw, but she looked younger and more undignified than he'd ever seen her before. Alan lifted a hand in response and went to join her.

"I'm so glad the timetables worked out," Adelaide said. "Gloucester *had* to be on the other side of England to Cheetham, of course, but at least this way we'll have company if we end up helplessly lost in the country lanes of Essex."

Alan didn't believe that Adelaide Morrissey had ever been lost. Surely she'd just give the geography a reproachful stare and it wouldn't dare inconvenience her further.

She'd managed a small six-seater compartment almost to herself. A tattered person of indeterminate sex, wearing at least three anoraks, was wedged snoring in a corner near the window with a bulging canvas bag clutched in their lap. Alan lightened his steps so as not to wake them. He wasn't one to judge the places people found to snatch a safe sleep. He wondered if they'd snuck on without paying at a smaller station, and if he could try to forge a ticket for them for when the conductor made his rounds.

The luggage racks were at the very limit of Alan's reach. It took one foot on the seat and a shove of grunting effort to get his bag settled next to Adelaide's pair of smart matching leather suitcases and an enormous hatbox.

"I won't be much use in the country," Alan said, sitting opposite Adelaide. Steam was rising from pistons and people on the platform were dashing to the train doors with a hand on their hat or waving merry farewell. Their companion continued to snore like a handful of marbles bouncing over cobbles, so Alan didn't bother to whisper. "I've not seen any of it."

"Really?" said Adelaide. "I thought you were a seasoned traveller."

"Ha," said Alan, dry. "The only train I've been on was the one to Southampton. Then right onto the *Majestic* for five days, and only a handful of hours in New York before I climbed aboard the *Lyric* to come home." He'd stuck strictly to advertising and gossip on the first leg of the voyage, daring to venture into the illegal arms of the business only on the way back. And when he'd sent his family off to the seaside, afterwards, he'd stayed in town to work.

All of his stories set in grand country manor houses were based on other people's books about grand country manor houses, and hefty nicking of details from the sort of society article that really *needed* you to know how many miles of ornamental hedges a place had, and where all the marble for the floors had come from.

"You might decide you haven't been missing much. Robin prefers the city," said Adelaide. "And I've never set foot on an ocean liner, myself. Never left England."

Comparing this poised, moneyed woman—the future Lady Blyth—to his own family was absurd. But for a wistful second there was something about Adelaide that reminded Alan so strongly of Caro he found himself feeling brotherly. It was the only excuse he had for why he said, "Were you all right, staying in Gloucester on your own?"

"How kind of you. I've never run into any trouble—I'm not a young girl anymore, and I find the trick is to look as unspeakably dull and respectable as one can. This helps," she added, her smile growing to a small grin as she lifted her hand to display the ring that she was forever tapping on things.

The once-was jewel thief in Alan sharpened at the sight. Dull, it was not. A plain gold band nearly groaned under the weight of an enormous oval-cut ruby ringed with seed pearls.

"You could certainly take someone's eye out with it, if they bothered you."

"Family heirloom. Lady Blyth's own wedding band. Maud was delighted to palm it off on someone else and not have to inherit it herself, or so she says."

Alan hesitated, then said it anyway. They'd all heard his weaknesses, his worst parts, laid bare. And even though Adelaide had been cool-mannered with Alan at Spinet House after the Barrel disaster, she'd clearly made up her mind about him in the interim, and was behaving with all of her old friendly ease.

"Could I ask you a question?" he said. "Something personal?"

Adelaide's interest brightened. She folded her hands, obscene ring and all. "By all means."

"Do you—are you and Sir Robert—" His nerve failed. Some interviewer *he* was.

"Do I love him?"

Close enough. Blood filled Alan's cheeks as he nodded.

"Yes. In the way Edwin loves him, and the way he loves Edwin? No. But they trust me to see what they have without wanting to interfere with it, and respect me enough to believe I know what I want. And don't tell him I said this, but Robin's a traditionalist at heart. I believe he rather fancies the idea of offering me the protection of his name, along with sliding me sideways into Walter Courcey's blood-oath."

"Protection?" Alan couldn't help smiling. "You don't seem in need of that."

"I see it as a way to get the things I want, without the things I *don't* want," she said calmly. "And I'm not like Violet. I don't mind marrying to make my family happy, and to stop them worrying about me." Her manner softened into seriousness. "And that's still a choice made from love. Would I prefer a world where nobody expects me to marry at all, or believes a man's name will give my life legitimacy? Of course. But that's not the world I'm living in."

"Give Maud a couple more decades and she'll make one," said Alan.

Adelaide laughed. "No doubt."

The busy train-silence reigned for a while. They were still within the city, a part of it that Alan had never seen, though the sky was enlarging as they went with the promise of fields to come. Adelaide looked out the window and tapped her ring. She was clearly going to let the subject drop, being too well bred to pry in return about Alan's views on love and marriage.

Thank fuck. He didn't know if he *had* any presentable views. He'd never been in love. Marriage for a man already supporting a family would be a burden rather than a duty. And the best he'd be able to do on the subject of desire would be to hand her one of the Roman books and stumble through the excruciating explanation of the difference between sexual fantasy and personal politics.

Best to steer things out of those waters entirely.

"Did you have any success in Gloucester, then?" he asked. "Track down this Grimm?"

Adelaide jerked her head back to look at him. She brought a hand to her mouth and inclined her head towards the pile of anoraks in the corner.

It took Alan a second to grasp her meaning.

"Really?"

"I'm so sorry! I didn't explain, did I? I assumed—never mind." She straightened her face. "I won't wake him for introductions, but this is the Grimm of Gloucester. Mr. Dufay."

Alan fumbled after sense. "The one who wrote the song?"

No, that one was dead. Alan had stood at the grave with Maud, where the ghost in question had failed to present itself and be helpful.

"His grandson. Or nephew, perhaps? He was vague about it. He is"—Adelaide sighed—"not *quite* as bad as the letters in person, but not a great deal better."

Well, she had threatened to drag the Grimm back in her luggage if she couldn't get the information Edwin wanted. Alan eyed the sleeping man with greater interest. Even folded into the seat corner like a bent wire, Dufay gave the impression of height. The mismatched anoraks fell to a pair of heavy, scuffed boots. The snoring had quietened, but the occasional ripping snort still came from an old, clean-shaven face with oddly delicate features, surrounded by poorly cut shoulder-length hair with the colour and greasy shine of cream.

"Looks like he should be living in a cave on the moors, doesn't he?" said Adelaide.

"Or like an old sailor determined to drink through the whole voyage," said Alan, eyeing the canvas bag and boots. "Can he help, then? Does he know about the Last Contract?"

"I'm sure he knows *something*. For the entire first day he wouldn't talk to me because I'm not a magician, so God only knows what he thinks the Office of Special Domestic Affairs and Complaints *is*, for all the years he's been writing there. Then I told him we knew where the contract was, but that we didn't have it anymore, and he raged at me for being *irresponsible*. As if it were my fault!"

Alan, whose fault it was, shifted in his seat. "How did you persuade him to come along, in that case?"

"It was his idea!" said Adelaide. "I was trying to explain what we know, or sort of know, about Lord Hawthorn and Lady Elsie and what Bastoke has been trying to do—and he heard the name *Cheetham Hall* and the next thing I knew, he was insisting that we leave at once. He's spent most of the journey asleep. I think he can do it at *will*," she added, eyeing Dufay dubiously, "when he doesn't want to talk."

And Dufay stayed asleep for the rest of the journey. Or at least did an excellent job of pretending at it. The moment the train shuddered to a halt at the Cheetham village station, Dufay's eyes cracked open as if a pair of chambermaids had raised the window sashes in unison. Those eyes were brilliantly, piercingly blue, and fixed with suspicion on Alan himself.

"We've arrived, Mr. Dufay," said Adelaide, nodding her thanks at Alan as he hoisted her hatbox in his free hand. "And this is Mr. Ross."

"Not a magician either," said Alan, who was feeling needled by that stare.

"Hmph," said Dufay, a light, throaty sound, and unfolded himself like a clotheshorse.

Thanks to Adelaide's timetables, there was a carriage and driver waiting at the station to deliver them to Cheetham Hall. Dufay didn't speak on the way, but nor did he go back to sleep. His attention was keen on the village and then the green-soaked countryside. Watching him, Alan had the sense of an ancient sponge, twisted and parched, that was being slowly rained upon and unfolding its full shape as the water took hold.

Dufay was first out of the carriage, surprisingly sprightly, when it delivered them to the front of the house. Alan and Adelaide took more time. Alan felt relieved that Adelaide, too, seemed to need a moment to take in the size of Cheetham Hall.

It was a glorified series of large boxes, Alan told himself. Grey stone and square, poised within the green unfolding of nature brought to heel. Huge windows stared down at him, their sight rheumed with clouds that interrupted the patchy blue of the reflected sky. The wind was softly cold, puffing Alan's hair into his face, and smelled of clean nothingness tinged with grass. Between the enormity of the house and the mingling of liveried footmen and women in white dresses spilling like a foam-tipped wave through the enormous front doors, Alan felt spongelike in the other direction. He wanted to shrivel up and hide.

Voices rose. The white dresses were Maud and Violet, dashing down the steps, and Robin and Edwin were behind them, and—

Alan's eyes stopped moving when he caught sight of Jack, with an abruptness that made it shamefully obvious to himself that he'd been searching. Jack transferred from clean-scrubbed steps to the fine gravel of the drive and came up next to Alan, and his eyes stopped too. Alan had never been looked at like this, with this hot pleasure in his presence that had such palpable, irresistible weight. It moved like an iron over his irritable nerves and uncreased them.

"You must be lost," said Jack. "We don't admit your sort here."

"I've come to nick the candlesticks."

The air really was intolerably clean. It was scouring Alan's throat from the inside. He let himself hold Jack's gaze for a moment longer, a greedy child clinging to a treat, before he transferred his attention to the chaos taking place nearby. Robin and Adelaide had their heads bent together, and Edwin was trying to catch the elbow of Dufay.

"What on *Earth*," Jack muttered.

"He's the Grimm," said Alan.

"Truly? Christ. We'd better have him inside. My mother can at least make him welcome before Edwin begins the inquisition."

But Edwin's urgent questions were rolling off the greasy anoraks like drops of unheeded rain. Dufay had his face uptilted, frowning as if remembering something. He looked in every direction, ignoring everything from Adelaide's prompts to Maud's attempts at cheery greeting.

The only person to win acknowledgement was the footman attempting to take the canvas bag. Dufay pushed the bag into the footman's arms, a motion of abrupt and startling authority, and straightened to his full cranelike height.

Then he bypassed the steps entirely and stalked off around the side of the house.

"Blast," said Edwin, aggrieved, and hurried off in Dufay's wake. The Grimm was moving with such rapid strides and an air of such purpose that Alan found himself, along with everyone else, following along like children in the wake of a street parade.

So Alan avoided having to be swallowed up by Jack's ancestral home for a while longer, as he was taken on a strange little tour of the grounds. They passed through a paved area twice the size of Alan's house, with trees like absurd lollipops in huge pots, and then across a moss-furred bridge and through a small forest of slender trees that towered green above them. Then up a grassy hill that was topped with a single tree almost too large to comprehend. It must be a trick somehow. Magical.

Alan had not planned to go for a brisk and confusing walk in nature. He was not sure nature approved of him any more than grand magical houses did. But he was damned if he'd fall behind. He hastened his steps to keep up with Jack, who gave Alan a look that wasn't exactly a comment about his height but had all the trappings of it, as if Jack no longer had to open his mouth for Alan to know when he was being teased.

Alan glared and did not open his mouth in return. He was too busy breathing through it.

When they caught up to the others at the top of the hill, Maud was red-faced with exertion and most of them were puffing at least a little. Robin wasn't. Robin had a swing to his arms and a light in his eyes like he was about to suggest a brisk jog down the other side and then a nice, bracing swim. It made him absurdly attractive and also made Alan want to slap him.

Dufay was walking in circles around the tree, fingers trailing on the bark. Each circle took some time. It really was enormous. Perhaps the same magic—or country air, or whatever it was— was responsible for Jack's size.

"Oh for—*Hawthorn*," said Edwin, exasperated. "Can you shed any light on why the Grimm of Gloucester is so enamoured of this oak? I can't get a sensible word out of him. And I seem to remember it has a name, so I assume it has a story."

"The Lady's Oak," said Jack. Dufay shot a look at Jack on his most recent circuit, frowned—at the ground this time—and disappeared around the trunk again. "It's a family legend. Apparently an acorn was planted here by the wife of the first lord to be granted the land, and she asked the tree to grow into a long-lived guardian who would look after the family forever."

"Oaks grow very old," said Edwin. He craned up at it and touched the single low branch as thick as a man that looped down nearby. "This one could be several centuries. Or more, or less, if magic went into the life of it. Was she a magician, that woman?"

Jack shrugged. "One assumes so. I can't even remember her name. Something classical. Phoebe, or Phyllis."

"Phyllis died for love and became an almond tree," said Robin. "What's that look for? I did read Classics at Pembroke, you know."

"No. No, widdershins on all counts. No magic worth speaking of in an almond. Better to stick with oaks. And you were supposed to guard *it*, not the other way around." Dufay's light, throaty voice came around the tree first, and then he appeared again.

Alan blinked a few times as if that would make sense of what he saw. Was there an illusion there, being perturbed? Nothing melted or wavered. The features were the same, even if their delicacy now looked distinctly feminine. Same eerie height; same layers of flapping, flowing clothes; same yellow-white hair, gleaming like whipped butter in spots where sunlight snuck through the oak's leaves.

And eyes the exact same heartrending blue as those that stared back at—him? *her?*—from the face of Jack, who'd turned pale as clean smoke.

"And I've never died yet," said the Lady.

21

It was a long, long conversation.

In fact, it could only be described as a conversation in the loosest sense. The terms *shouting match, interrogation, game of riddles,* and *recitation of a fairy tale* were all about as correct as one another. Half of it took place beneath the Lady's Oak, where the sun was diving slowly down the sky and the wind was picking up, and they probably looked from afar like a raucous picnic crossed with a debate session in Parliament.

The other half of it, at Violet's insistence once Maud's teeth began to chatter in the wind, took place in one of the smaller dining rooms in Cheetham Hall. Not because anyone had appetite. Simply so that they could all sit, and the half-complete story could be rapidly recited for the benefit of Lady Cheetham. And then picked up again with a renewed onslaught of questions.

At least Dufay's oblique and rambling manner of speech began to straighten itself out, as time passed, like someone tumbling back into the lost accent of their youth when encountering it spoken as an adult. Even so: Jack kept losing the thread of things, his mind whiting out, as he stared at her. Dufay's appearance shifted eye-wateringly between that of a scarecrow carved from a particularly severe turnip and an eerie, wintry almost-beauty. Or perhaps Jack's nerves were desperately seeking the beauty as a way to cope with the knowledge that a possibly immortal member of the fae was sitting in his house, shedding dirt and grass all over the furnishings, and claiming to be one of his ancestors.

His emotions gave up entirely when Dufay turned to him and said, "So you never bothered to ask what the name *Alston* means."

Polly's hand crept onto his and gripped hard.

A long conversation and a tale like a thorn bush. Some of it had the echo of a half-remembered story from childhood. When all the pieces had been held up to the light, brushed down thoroughly, and put together in a shape that made sense, the Tale of the Three Families and the Last Contract went something like this:

When the land was only slightly younger, and the fae kept one foot of their domain planted here, mortals had a choice. They could draw from the magic that was inherent to all living things, finding more of it in places where the renewing ley lines ran and crossed. Or, if they wished for more magic, or magic directed to a difficult purpose, they could approach a member of the fae and offer to make a bargain. An individual contract. The amount and direction of the magic clearly defined—as well as the cost.

And then the fae announced their decision to withdraw, to move the foothold of their realm into other lands and other worlds, and so one final contract was made.

It was made in silver. Not just any silver, but elf-silver: a piece that was ancient even by fae standards, its origins a story old enough to have shifted several times in the telling. The allstone was split into three objects to symbolise the contract made with the Three Families.

This apparently explained a lot of things that made Edwin very excited, such as why the contract pieces couldn't be detected by magical means—why they had such an effect on the ley lines—and why they could *be* so magical in the first place, when usually metal was much harder to imbue with power than something that had once been alive.

The cost of the contract was straightforward. The Three Families would be left with the ability to use this magic, which because of its fae nature would lend itself well to spells based in structure and contract. And in return, they agreed to be leaders of mortals when it came to responsibility towards the land on which they lived. Guardianship and stewardship. That, the fae considered, was what human leaders were for.

Violet said that in her version of the story the contract was made with three sisters of one household who then went on to *found* the Three Families. In the version Edwin knew, each family was from a different corner of the Isles and returned there with their magic after the fae left.

Dufay herself was supremely uninterested in nailing down a single truth. She did say that the families were the ones who insisted on making the contract on behalf of their bloodlines. Fae, who seldom bothered to reproduce, considered *contractual* inheritance far more important. Blood was what the humans brought to the bargain.

That, said Adelaide dryly, rang unfortunately true. The history of men was the history of them trying to acquire and hold property and power for their sons, and obsessing over a pure line of inheritance.

It made Jack think in a new way about the fuss and discomfort that Walter and the Assemblymen had shown over Edwin and Violet's inheritance of Sutton and Spinet, which had been inherited by contract law and choice. And in Edwin's case, no blood tie at all, beyond that which he made directly with the land beneath a hedge maze.

And so: the fae left. The Last Contract was hidden away in a place deemed unlikely to be disturbed, given the weight humans placed on symbol and belief. The Lady of the Allstone stayed behind, and planted an oak tree in the path of a deep-running ley line, and gave her name as both promise and reminder to the human man she wed.

And fae magic had been the heart and the root of British magic ever since.

"Which was *not* the intent," said Dufay irritably. She looked around the table like a nanny who'd woken from her nap to find the children imbuing their dolls to fight one another. "Of course our magic is superior and more elegant. But having the gifts of the dawn is no excuse to lose touch entirely with what you already had. *Careless.* Irresponsible."

Robin had produced and unfolded the letter that the Grimm of Gloucester had sent to his office. He ran his finger under a line, and Edwin, sitting next to him, looked sharply at Dufay.

"The gifts of the dawn and the wages of the dusk. That's what you were talking about?"

"And you wrote the poem," said Violet. "The song. Didn't you? Under the name Alfred Dufay."

Yes, it turned out. She had been various Dufays, male and female, for centuries, killing one identity in favour of the next. No wonder Maud hadn't had any luck in the cemetery. Alfred Dufay had never died, just as he'd never truly lived.

The poem, along with the spell-game for children, had been Dufay communicating her annoyance in the way that fae knew best: putting words into the world to be repeated and kept.

"I even made it rhyme," she said rather sulkily. "You like rhymes."

"So you had the ability to make sense in writing at some point," muttered Edwin. "Why become the Grimm? Why didn't you just come and *tell* us—magicians, I mean—that we were losing knowledge?"

Dufay gave Edwin a look that cast clear aspersion on his intelligence. Edwin coloured.

"I prefer," said Dufay, "to be left *alone*. Not to fix other people's mistakes for them. But"—she waved at the letter— "one day a magician told me there was a place to write, if you had complaints or suggestions about the way magic was intersecting with the non-magical world. So I did it the mortal way."

"And you had a *lot* of suggestions," said Adelaide.

Dufay gave them all the displeased-nanny look again.

Jack's mother removed her hand from his. His skin tingled coolly when she withdrew her grip. The cast of her face was troubled, but she gave Jack a firm smile.

"From what you've all told me," she said, "these ladies of the Forsythia Club may have made some discoveries about this."

"Yes," said Edwin. "Old magic, new ways to use it. Flora Sutton was convinced that ley-line magic should never have fallen out of use, though I don't know how far she took it. I've decoded nearly all her diaries now, and she never put things in terms of—or perhaps she did, but I didn't know how to *read* it. Dawn, dusk. The liminal times." He slumped, rubbing his forehead. Robin put a hand on his back.

Violet said, "I'm sure Lady Enid at least knew the song was important, given how she worked it into Spinet's doorways and charms."

"*I* wonder," said Maud, "how much Mrs. Vaughn knows."

That made them pause. The fourth member of the Forsythia Club was still a cipher. From Maud's account she was equally ruthless as the men she was working with, but had little respect or liking for them.

Alan stirred as if to say something, but hesitated. He collected himself and said to Dufay, "Edwin talks about the magic of magical houses—like this one—as a different language. Which one is that? Dawn or dusk?"

Dufay's booted feet drummed on the floor as Maud's sometimes did when she was made to sit still for too long. "Messy. Both."

"Of course it would be both," said Lady Cheetham. "Houses only become like this when inhabited by magicians. Magic done *in* the houses and *on* the land must contribute as much as any magic inherent to the land itself. And when I use magic on Cheetham land and find it easier, stronger, the extra power must be coming from something outside of myself." She shrugged. "Mingling and reciprocity. It makes perfect sense."

"Hmph. Cheetham might be particularly mingled," said Dufay, "because it has all of mine as well."

"Your . . . ?" said Lady Cheetham.

"Magic." Another drumming of feet. Dufay made a flicking motion with her fingers, like the very start of a cradle. "I thought some of it might return to me, being back here, but apparently not. No reciprocity *there*."

"You're not a magician?" said Maud. It was nearly a blurt, and Maud winced as soon as it was out. "I mean . . . you can't do magic? But you're fae."

"*I* am the fourth gift of the dawn," said Dufay. She tucked a greasy strand of hair behind her ear. "Myself through the oak. A symbol. The oak put my magic into the land, adding it to what was inherent, and putting it out of my reach. A gesture of goodwill."

"No magic, for all those years," murmured Lady Cheetham. Her hand twitched towards Jack's, but she didn't touch him again. Jack might have flinched if she had, with the raw familiarity twisting in him now. Dufay had magic, and lost it here, at the top of that hill.

How much more painful, though, to lose magic when magic was what you *were*? What was left then to define yourself by? Marriage, to someone who had what you'd lost? Children? Guardianship of a land abandoned by every other one of your kind?

No amount of money could have spurred Jack to ask *Was it enough?*

"Contract is contract," said Dufay. Her voice harshened. Now the throatiness had a birdlike quality to it. "There had to be a sacrifice. It was mine. And now it may have been for *nothing*, because not only have mortals left yourselves with only that gift, some of you had the stupid idea of taking it all for yourselves."

"We're the ones trying to stop it!" said Violet.

"Yes, so this one said." Dufay nodded at Adelaide. "Your attempts seem less than useless. Perhaps you can now explain *why* these thieves of the contract have not simply been brought up in front of the council and executed?"

An entirely new silence sprang into being.

"Ex-executed?" said Maud.

"You do still *have* a council of magicians?" Dufay demanded.

"The Assembly," said Adelaide, "ah . . ."

"They're the ones doing it," said Robin. "Or at least support-ing it."

Dufay's face set. "You choose your leaders terribly."

"That's a common human failing, all right," said Alan, on top of the beginnings of protest from the rest of the table.

"Then how *do* you intend to stop them?" asked Dufay.

More silence. This one had a depressed feel. Edwin slumped a little further.

"We were hoping you might tell us," said Robin finally. "But it has to be done. The cost of an act of power shouldn't be borne by anyone except the person who gains the most from it." He looked at Jack. In that moment, his steadiness was a gift. "If magic can't be drawn upon and combined safely, and with con-sent, then it shouldn't be combined at all."

22

The next two weeks were some of the strangest of Alan's life. And yes, he was including in that the time he'd spent on the *Lyric* being involved in such things as escaped menageries, theft of hair from corpses in ice rooms, and haggling over jewels and pornography with a hateful aristocrat.

"No, that's no good. I think you're making it worse," said Violet.

Alan opened his eyes and inspected himself in the huge gilt-framed mirror that hung on the wall of Cheetham Hall's library. He wore a waistcoat into which Violet had stitched one of her illusion disguises. The illusion was based on one of the Hall's younger footmen; Alan was supposed to look like the man's shorter brother.

Instead he looked like he had been in an unfortunate slow-motion accident that had altered the geometry of his features. And was still altering them. He couldn't help lifting a hand to support his left eye where it was slipping down his cheek like melting ice cream. Luckily, his cheekbone was exactly where it should be. And his eyes too. He closed them; that helped.

"Making me queasy," he said. "I'll try it again."

Alan, Maud had pointed out, was once again a potential ace to be played. Bastoke and the others would not expect him to be at the equinox gala at all.

There was, though, the matter of illusion disguises. His perturbation had gone from being useful to an inconvenience, and

Edwin now wanted to find out if Alan could suppress it at will. He'd suggested that Alan stop imagining channels and instead imagine being *porous*. Let the magic sink in and work. He'd even gone out to the grove of tall trees, which were apparently beech, and woven Alan a ridiculous crown of supple twigs and leaves, in case the magic-enhancing properties of that tree made a difference.

Jack had wandered past during that attempt, and his eyes had gleamed with the promise of fifteen comments about Julius Caesar that he was no doubt tucking patiently up his sleeve for when they would be most aggravating.

Now Alan breathed slowly. Yesterday it had worked, a little, when they tried it with the cold-spell. But cold was something Alan felt. He could grit his teeth and imagine himself letting the cold in through gaps in clothing. Illusions gave him nothing to build the effort around, and staring at his muddied reflection in the mirror turned his stomach.

Magic. Magic, flowing down the channels. If only he knew anything about rivers and lakes. There had to be some reason why their water didn't slowly sink into the ground like rain sank into gardens. He could imagine that and then . . . imagine the opposite.

"Any better?" he said through his teeth.

"Perhaps we should take a break," said Violet.

"Why?" said Edwin. "It's not working yet."

Alan released all his effort. He turned around from the mirror before he opened his eyes this time, and exhaled with mild longing at the greenery and sky beyond the room's one enormous window.

Violet made an exasperated sound and pulled off her rings to tuck into the velvet pouch. "Because not everyone enjoys being shut up in one room for hours at a time, and this is obviously taking *effort*. Keep at it if you wish, but don't let him push you around, Alan."

He was Alan again, not Mr. Ross—and part of the team,

rather than the hired help or a spy. Perhaps Dufay's revelations had distracted them all from any leftover mistrust. Alan knew when to count his blessings.

And Christ, what a relief it was, to let himself *enjoy* these people now. He didn't have to keep trapping any friendly thoughts like roaches to be crushed.

Violet swanned out. The word particularly fit her elegant neck and long nose, and the white frothy dress that seemed to be the female uniform for a country party at this time of year.

Edwin was in the window seat with a pile of books. He looked around the library as if wondering why anyone would want to leave it. Edwin Courcey could probably find himself at the North Pole and still be able to locate a library. He'd moved himself into the Hall's, immediately colonised the largest available table with books and papers in the manner of a bird lining a nest, then set about criticising the library's size and contents. Jack had told him with some amusement that the Earl and Countess of Cheetham did not go in for collecting magical volumes, and apart from a reasonable selection of fiction and poetry, many of the books on the glass-fronted shelves were decorative.

"Probably bought them by the yard, decades ago. Might not have cut the pages of some of them," he'd added carelessly.

Edwin had been rendered speechless. For all Alan knew, he still hadn't figured out that Jack had been casting well-aimed stones at his composure.

Now Alan removed the waistcoat and set it aside. "If we can't make it work, I could always attach an enormous false moustache with spirit gum."

A bit of a smile appeared. "Or bleach your hair."

"Fuck *right* off," blurted Alan, and—of course—heard a small creak of the library door and a step that paused in the doorway. Knowing his luck, Jack had appeared just in time to overhear that. Alan enjoyed knowing his lordship's small vanities, and had no intention of handing any information back in kind. The bloody beech crown had been bad enough.

In fact, the figure poised in the doorway was Lady Cheetham.

Alan's cheeks heated. At least Jack's mother had ten times his manners and would never admit to having heard such language from a guest.

"Your ladyship," said Alan.

"Alan, I was wondering if you cared to be stolen away to join Lady Phyllis and me for our walk?" The pause, too, was impeccably polite. "You're welcome to join us, Edwin."

"No, thank you."

She nodded. "Robin and Jack should be back from their ride presently."

No amount of guilt, good manners, or strong magic would get Alan onto the back of a horse. He was happy to leave that one to the aristocracy. But he was used to substantial amounts of walking in the city, and he was determined not to show the grounds of Cheetham Hall any fear or disrespect. Spinet House had *eaten* people, and it was tiny and young compared to this place. He'd go for walks if that would keep the Hall happy.

Alan escaped the library and went to change. He'd vaguely imagined that country manor parties involved only outfits of unnecessary quality and style. It had not occurred to him to bring *mucking-about* clothes. Lady Cheetham had cheerfully produced some old garments from when Jack was—well, an age that Alan found hideous to contemplate—and bestowed them upon Alan with apologies for the holes. That line of charity having been established with sophisticated stealth, small piles of loaned clothing suitable for every occasion had been appearing ever since in the bedroom that had been granted to Alan.

The ever-helpful Oliver, too, turned up each time to do one of his little make-it-fit spells. Alan had surrendered to the inevitable.

"Lovely, let's be off, then," said Lady Cheetham when Alan joined her and Lady Dufay, whose entire being screamed *mucking-about* even though she was an ageless member of the fae. *She* had refused all offers of fancier clothes. She had refused to be involved in the complicated process of planning and hosting a magicians' gala. She had even refused a bedroom in the

Hall, and had instead moved with all appearance of satisfaction into the folly.

She did enjoy a walk, though. And had submitted to being on *Phyllis* and *Polly* terms with her hostess.

The two ladies talked mostly about gardening, but they also took some interesting tangents off into the history of the house and grounds. Alan had taken to bringing along his notebook so that he could jot down details for the society story he was purportedly here to write. No doubt most of it would be a pile of benign lies about an unremarkable party. At least he could stuff it full of accurate details about the place.

Sometimes the history was *family* history. Lady Dufay had deliberately distanced herself from the line of her descendants, more and more so as time went on. Lady Cheetham could recite both her own family and her husband's back an easy couple of centuries. They seemed determined to talk it all out and meet in the middle.

"I think she's glad to have someone of her own station to talk to," said Jack, later that day. They were back in the library. "She likes to involve herself in other people's lives, but she's very much the local grand lady, here. And too aware of it to allow herself real friendship. She's been lonely."

"I like her," Alan said. "She's very . . . solid." His mental picture of the countess was always in Wellington boots.

"She was raised not to blink an eye if a prince and his retinue showed up demanding tea and lodgings."

"Wouldn't know anything about that, me," said Alan, letting his accent slip. "But most women in my neighbourhood are practically minded and strong like that. You make do with what you have."

"Is your mother the same?"

Alan chewed his lip. "Used to be," he admitted. "Less so now. She spent so much of herself keeping us alive when my pa died, before I could pull my weight. There's only so much fight in a person. If it never lets up, if they can *never* rest—it gets squeezed out of them, forever." He couldn't march back through the years and stop it all from happening; he couldn't pour back his mother's lost vitality or restore her eyesight. But what he wanted more than anything was to give her a life of real *leisure*—not just infirm helplessness and the constant worry that they'd slip back below the line.

Jack's attention was steady, the sensation of it on Alan's face as heavy and alive as it always was now. He didn't say anything. He nodded and leaned back in his armchair.

A half-finished game of chess sat on the table between them. Maud had been trying to coach Alan in the game, but Alan was now even more of the opinion that chess was a wonderful substitute for chamomile tea or a potion imbued to make you sleep. If he wanted an excuse to sit across from Jack so that they could insult one another at a leisurely pace for an hour, they could play cards.

And he wanted the excuse.

It had been nearly a fortnight, and they hadn't fucked again. Hadn't kissed. Had barely touched. All of Alan's half-formed ideas about indulging those manor-house fantasies, about normality being suspended and play allowed, had come to an ungainly . . . well, not a halt. A pause.

He was in Jack's house and Jack was the future earl and still magnificently, unbearably himself. But Alan had met Jack's *mother*, and Jack had fae heritage, and Jack and Alan officially knew each other too well now for this to revert to being an excellent and uncomplicated fuck.

Not that it had ever been uncomplicated. But it had been cleaner, before, with that protective coating of true dislike hammered over the desire.

The desire itself was as strong as ever. Alan woke most mornings with a stiff cock and didn't bother to keep his mind off Jack as he dealt with it. He was acutely aware of Jack's body whenever they shared space. But it didn't feel like torture. And for all that lust could dig its silent, violent teeth into him at the sight of small things—like Jack's fingers dwarfing an ebony chess piece, or the prowling way Jack had of crossing a room—it didn't feel *urgent*.

It felt like something was working itself out, a pot set simmering through a long afternoon, and Alan didn't want to disturb it early in case it spoiled.

"Hawthorn," said Edwin now, calling from his usual disaster of a table. Violet and Robin had cleared off one corner of it and were, in fact, playing cards; they glanced up when Edwin spoke. "Come and hear this out."

Jack got to his feet and went to the table to be explained at. Alan took the opportunity to relocate to the window seat, where he settled in to enjoy a pool of sunlight and the squabbles of magpies just visible on the circle of lawn within the gravel drive at the front of the house.

"I think," Edwin said, "we can turn the Lady's Oak into the Last Contract." He looked warily at Jack as if for comment, ridicule, or applause.

"Pleased as I am that you've learned to appreciate that most people don't care to be buried in fine detail," said Jack, "I will need *some* detail more than that."

"I'd been thinking about what Dufay said, about her and her magic being the fourth gift, and the oak being a symbol of it. It's not silver, but it is something both of the fae and of our world. And oak holds power very well. We know that."

"A giant oak tree's not exactly portable," said Robin. "Or easy to hide in a pocket or a maze."

"It wouldn't need to be hidden if it couldn't be *used*," said Edwin, more animated. "When I drew on Sutton through the ley line, everything became tangled up and slippery. You *can't* hold something that large in a way that lets you do anything useful at all. And Dufay said that the Lady's Oak poured her own magic into the magic that was inherent in the land already. So—we tie the contract directly *to* the ley lines. To the inherent magic. We combine them."

"Mingling," said Violet slowly. "Really mingling, this time. Edwin, that's elegant *and* sneaky. I like it."

"Enough detail for you, Hawthorn?" said Edwin.

Jack looked at him for a long while. Finally he said, "You'll know better than me if the theory is sound. But Robin had a point. So long as the contract exists, there will be people interested in trying to use it, slippery tangles or no. You're putting the weight of guarding it onto my family's shoulders. Permanently."

"I'd do it on Sutton if I could," said Edwin. "But there's nothing there with the same history, the same link with the fae. It has to be that tree. And I can help," he said quickly. "That beech grove could be used to enhance a warding, you could plant other trees with other properties—everything I know from Flora Sutton's notes, you and your mother can have it."

"Ask her," said Jack. "It's her estate, not mine."

"Don't be glib. It'll be yours eventually. And you're right— it's a long commitment."

Jack's mouth moved towards anger, then moved back.

"How would it work?" Alan asked. "What would you need to do?"

"I'd need the silver objects, all three of them, and a blood-oath of agreement. Not of every magician, I don't think. One descendent of each of the Three Families would do."

"So we still have to get our hands on the contract pieces," said Violet.

Edwin deflated a little. "Yes."

There had already been several conversations about how they might manage this on the day of the gala. A lot of suggestions had been thrown into the pot, ranging from the eminently practical to the absolutely wild. However, nothing could change the fact that a lot depended on the unknown choices that would be made, were *being* made, by Bastoke and Walter Courcey and anyone else on their side. And it was a little late in the game, Robin had pointed out dryly, to have any hope of infiltrating a spy of their own.

Another of those conversations began to hatch now. Alan stifled a yawn with the back of his hand—the sunlight was heavy on his face—and heard a distant hum of sound. An engine, getting louder. He leaned into the seat corner and watched as the magpies scattered. A green motorcar slid smoothly around and came to a halt at the base of the front steps.

"Are we expecting visitors?" Alan asked.

Jack broke away from the table to look. Alan pointed down.

"That's my father's car," Jack said, as the liveried driver climbed out from behind the wheel. "Mother didn't say we were expecting him. I should—"

He stopped. Two more men had climbed from the other side of the car. One had a flat cap like the driver's and moved with the deliberation of muscle. The other was tall and well dressed, and carried a walking stick not unlike Jack's. Sunshine winked on the golden top of it.

Alan's body yanked him from the seat and away from the window before his sense could weigh in on the situation. His heart gave a hard, unpleasant shrug and then sped up.

"Alan? Hawthorn?" said Violet. "What is it?"

"It's Joe Morris," said Jack. "And my cousin George."

23

Jack had never understood Edwin's urge to make a study of things. You saw more, you missed less, if you took in as much of the world as you could. Bringing your focus down to learn one thing in all its detail was a waste of the brief time you had.

And yet he had, it seemed, been engaged in a single-minded study of Alan Ross, because in this moment he knew exactly where to look for Alan's fear.

The study had not been academic. Jack knew that. He'd been watching for any hint that he was welcome. His offer of play in Alan's attic in London had been turned aside; Alan, who'd spoken about fucking Jack in terms of his willpower breaking, had clearly decided that it would go no further. Jack knew when he was being given an invitation, and when he was not.

But he had been looking, and looking—and now he looked at the subtle inwards curl of Alan's shoulders. He watched as Alan's eyes widened and consumed his face, the pupils tightening to dabs of ink in the brown.

Jack's teeth ground together. They were under attack. A new front, that was all.

"Stay here," he ordered. "In this room. All of you. Assume the worst—assume they'll search the house. Violet, Edwin, you'll need to—" He stopped. "Where are Adelaide and Maud?"

"Doing something with dresses," said Robin.

"Where?"

"I'll go," said Violet. She stood, already shoving rings onto her thumbs, and cradled an illusion that fell over her before Jack had finished another breath. Now she was a deeply freckled brunette in a housemaid's outfit.

"Bring them back here." Jack was already moving towards the door, inspecting the frame. "And then ward this door to high heaven. A turn-away if you can, Edwin."

"Where are you going?" Edwin demanded.

"To host our guests."

"Hawthorn—"

"I am not leaving my mother to manage this alone," Jack snarled. "And it doesn't matter if they know I'm here. *This is my home.*"

The closest rug, a long one patterned in red and blue, gave a sudden roll as if shrugging off dust. The tassels at its end flicked Jack's ankle. Jack swallowed hard, and his palm on the doorframe was suddenly hot, as if he'd slammed it there to trap his anger beneath. This was more than simply feeling the land's magic beneath his feet. His breath skipped in his throat. He didn't have time to think about this.

Violet was already charging out into the corridor and towards the back staircase. Jack looked at Alan for a moment that felt like dragging flesh across broken metal, and then back at the rug.

"Keep them safe," he said to the Hall, feeling utterly at sea, and closed the door behind himself.

George was with Polly in the front parlour. Jack wondered where George had been received last time he visited, and whether he realised that Lady Cheetham had demoted him crushingly from being received in one of the friendlier spaces where family would be seen.

Morris might have gone around to the kitchen entrance. Not knowing where he was gave Jack the same unsettling feeling as looking up from his desk to realise that the spider previously haunting a corner of the ceiling had now vanished from sight.

"Hawthorn," said George, when Jack entered. "I'd pretend this was an unexpected pleasure, but you can't expect me to be overjoyed to see you. Forgive me, Aunt Polly."

His Aunt Polly had had time to prepare herself. She gave a

courteous nod and shot Jack the sort of look she'd developed for occasions when the twins were being presented in adult company and were expected to *contribute.*

Jack trifled for a moment with the idea of telling his cousin to go to hell and fuck himself with Satan's largest white-hot poker. But he needed to know what George was looking for. He needed to keep George away from the others.

"I wasn't aware I should keep you informed when I visit my own mother," he said, with only his normal amount of rudeness. "What are you doing here? In my father's car?"

"Yes, Lord Cheetham was good enough to lend me the use of it," said George. "He sends his regards. Couldn't tear himself away from some frightfully important business in Parliament."

"What are you doing here?" Jack repeated. Rashness made him add, "Do you plan to arrest me?"

George's eyebrows rose, unhurried. "I'm here for a final conversation with our hostess, to inspect the preparations for the equinox gala. If you can bring yourself to recall—" He paused, clearly calculating how snide he could be in front of Jack's mother. "This event means a lot to me professionally, cousin. I expect the upcoming elections to be remarkable. This is not only a celebration, now, but a reckoning on the future of magic in this kingdom. It's a time for magical society to come together," he said, desiccate with irony, "in the face of threats. Both future and present. It's really an honour for Cheetham Hall to be playing host to such an important gathering."

"We were flattered you volunteered us," murmured Lady Cheetham.

Jack found his eyes on George's brass-headed walking stick, his mind outlining the series of movements that would be needed to snatch it and use it to smash in his cousin's teeth. For George the stick was a true affectation, one he'd assumed even before Jack returned from the Boer. Perhaps he thought Jack had decided to copy his style. He could believe what he wished.

In the face of threats.

Jack had said it himself, after Violet's hearing: crisis justified the seizure of power. The Barrel's destruction had been a horribly perfect event for the head of the magical police. But George had planned to lock them all up for theft and conspiracy anyway. They would have been scapegoats regardless. Edwin had just rendered things . . . dramatic.

"And I would hardly be so impolite as to arrest my cousin, Lord Hawthorn, in front of his mother," said George, as if aware of where Jack's thoughts had run. He gave Jack a small *we're chaps in this together* sort of smile.

Alan would have formed a puddle of seething rage. Even Jack felt a lump of clay in his stomach at how unfair it was. George knew power, cultivated power, and had made a life's study of how to amass it. The Earl of Cheetham's heir was not the sort of person who was easily arrested. Even by magicians. Consequences were for lesser creatures.

"I appreciate it," said Lady Cheetham. Her hands were unmoving in her lap.

"Aunt Polly, I commend your sentiment in wanting to provide a safe haven for your son," said George. "But what happened to the Barrel—what Hawthorn and his associates *did*—was extremely serious. A real tragedy. Magicians cannot afford to be at war amongst ourselves. We need order, and laws to abide by, or we're no better than animals."

"And Coopers to enforce it, I suppose," said Jack.

George's look became the point of a knife. "We do our part. Speaking of which—I don't suppose you can shed any light on where Edwin Courcey might be found? Or Miss Violet Debenham? Or any of the other criminals you so unfortunately chose to associate with?"

"No," said Jack.

George's small smile appeared again, but the knife behind it hadn't been sheathed. A spasm of real fear shook down Jack's spine. He thought again of Morris, nowhere to be seen. He thought of Maud's bruised face on the *Lyric,* and black runes crawling up Robin's arm, and Alan's grimace beneath the memory-charm. And three dead women who'd denied George their power for as long as they could.

"No," echoed George. He turned back to Lady Cheetham. "The gala, then. I'm impatient to see the finished grounds. I take it the sympathy markers my men laid are still in place?"

Lady Cheetham nodded.

George cradled a spell and then traced four quick, invisible runes on the corners of the low table, which would normally contain a tea service when visitors arrived. Today it contained only a vase in which a cheerful arrangement of dahlias and bell-flowers had been sitting, kept fresh by charms, for several weeks.

The vase and flowers vanished beneath an eruption of green and brown and blue and grey, arising from the table like boiling mud. It was the Cheetham estate: an illusion built in sympathy and showing everything from the gatehouse to the Lady's Oak itself, nearly a foot above the table surface. George looked at it for a while, nodding as if it were a prize-winning cake he'd baked himself, then cradled a quick negation to vanish it.

"Very nice," he said. "I'd like to see the final view from above the grotto, I think. For security purposes."

"Jack," said Lady Cheetham. She stood. "It's such a busy day, with all the deliveries we're expecting. Mrs. Sturt has been wait-ing on me already. Would you do the honours?"

Would Jack take George for a walk to the top of the lake, alone? George had not believed Jack's denial for a second. He might not arrest Jack and drag him back to London, but he still might turn to some of the Coopers' less savoury methods to make him talk.

Jack thought of the rug tassel thudding against his ankle. He exhaled.

"Yes," he said. "I can show George around, and show him back to his car afterwards. I expect he's far too busy to stay long."

"Thank you, my dear. George." And she turned, rigid as if she were carved from something, and left the room. Jack didn't think she was running away. He suspected she was removing herself from the temptation to take George around the vegetable patch, stab him with a pitchfork, magic him into fertiliser, and use him to cover the lettuces.

So Jack took his cousin up to the lake. He avoided the folly; he had no idea where Dufay currently was, any more than Morris, and had a sudden, alarming vision of the two of them coming face-to-face.

George went right to the balustrade and looked down onto the sparkling water, then turned a slow circle, taking it all in. The circular stone-edged beds of cornflowers and carnations, hydrangeas and lupins; the fragrance of phlox and honeysuckle mingling on the breeze. Olive trees silvered in the light, and small orange trees in white pots glowed with fruit. One of the peacocks strutted around near the top of the slope, picking idly at the lawn and occasionally shaking out the profusion of his tail. It was a triumph of the English country garden, with touches of Mediterranean luxury. And it looked now exactly as it would on the evening of the equinox—minus several magical flourishes of Violet's yet to come.

"What'll be done about the weather in the days leading up to it?" George asked. "It's not been a wet summer so far, but the last thing we want is to be squelching around on muddy grass."

It seemed a genuine question.

"There's a magician in the village who's coordinated weather-spells before. Polly will send for help if it's needed."

"Fiddly spells of power are a terrible headache to coordinate," said George. "It'd be so much easier if it could all be done by one magician, wouldn't it?"

"If I killed you now," Jack said, "I wonder how much trouble I'd be saving us?"

The wind ruffled the lake's surface. A series of ripples showed the invisible rolls of fish, and a single dragonfly darted out like a jewel dangled on a string.

George turned, revealing the motion of his free hand. He was rolling one of those magical glass baubles beneath his palm on the flat marble rail.

"Perhaps you might be fast and lucky," George said. "But we are on your land, cousin. A violent death here would hurt you and Aunt Polly far more than anyone else."

That answered a little more of the question as to why George had pushed for Cheetham as a location. Jack felt like Robin must have in Violet's hearing: suddenly very sick of talking around the important things.

"And whatever you're planning to do at the gala, with the Last Contract—are you going to pretend that won't involve violence?"

George picked up the bauble—purple, glittering like a bruise shot with silver—and held it as if considering its weight. "Perhaps not, if you and your interfering friends don't try to prevent what needs to happen. It can truly be a night of celebration. A coming-together of magicians."

"And their magic," said Jack. "Why are you here, George?"

"To make sure everything is ready," said George, gesturing with his stick around the grounds, "for a night that I intend to see runs perfectly. And more to the point—to give you a chance, Hawthorn, to see that this is happening whether you want it to or not." His voice lost some of its deliberate laziness. "Whatever wild magic Edwin Courcey has learned to do, whatever illusions Miss Debenham tries to dress you all in, I *will* have a counter. The Assembly is full of men I have worked with for years. They know me and trust me. They agree that given what happened to the Barrel, there should be a strong presence of Coopers at the gala. In case it's a tempting target for more . . . disruptive behaviour."

Jack said nothing. George wasn't foolish enough to give away anything important in a moment of hubris. This was a practical warning. George was trying to clear away a mess before it could be made.

George tossed and caught the bauble neatly. "There isn't much they won't allow us to do. Everyone's fearful. A strong leader is reassuring. And we will show them that all magicians can lend their power to such a leader, for the good of everyone."

Jack ignored the sound of that and focused on the shape. A ghost of satisfaction haunted the corner of George's mouth.

"So," Jack said, "does Richard Prest know he won't be elected Chief Minister after all?"

The ghost thickened into something almost gratified, then vanished. "The position isn't important. Whatever's coming—a war within ourselves, a new level of threat from the unmagical, or an evil we can't yet imagine—we can protect ourselves, and win. We only need a champion."

"Christ," said Jack. "That's it? That's how you see yourself. Magic's champion."

George faced him fully. Annoyance was visible only in the tautness of the movement; his clean, regular features were unmoved. "Stop being so naive, Hawthorn. What else is the *point* of the contract being carried by the family bloodlines, if not for this? Generations of magicians all patiently choosing the best partners, becoming more powerful. So that when a threat comes, someone is strong enough to stand up and face it."

A string thrummed within Jack, as if he were one of Spinet's doors and George had sung the right melody to pluck at some cruel and essential beliefs that Jack hadn't bothered to pull out and examine for a very long time. He'd left them buried along with the rest of his past.

He forced himself to hear the thrum. He was seeing his elegant, ruthless cousin in a new and unnerving light. George didn't see himself as a machinator and opportunist; that would be bad enough. No, he thought this was *fate*. Something he deserved. That string snagged savagely, and Jack couldn't keep himself from speaking.

"You and John couldn't stand that I was stronger than you, and Elsie stronger than all of us. No wonder you—"

Even with Jack speaking to someone who knew its secret, the bind wouldn't allow him any further. Jack's fingers went to his mouth and his breath paused at the pain.

"So it is still there," said George. "I had wondered. If anyone could lift it, it's the Courcey boy." A mirthless smile. "But loopholes or no, a secret-bind sticks. I only wish to God it hadn't been necessary."

"*Fuck* yourself," growled Jack.

"Truly," said George. "My father was eager for me to marry her, you know."

That was like having saltwater poured across the brand of his tongue. Jack's muscles all clamoured at once for something to fight.

"Our child would surely be the culmination of our lines," George said with the lilt of quotation. "But I knew that would be too long to wait. And I was right. Now, now"—he glanced at Jack's fisted hand—"if you do kill me, nothing will change. It'll only be someone else who steps in to take the reins. Walter Courcey, I expect." A small, fastidious face. "He's strong enough. A pity about that nastiness in his temperament."

He was right about that. He was right about a lot of things, except for the ways in which he was desperately wrong. Blood was what mortals cared about, Dufay had said. The fae cared that you made sacrifice for the power you bargained for. And that you took responsibility for the places where you dwelled.

A different fear crept over Jack. The contract, as Edwin had pointed out, was between two parties; it had elements of fae and mortals both. What would happen when George and Walter called on blood alone, and took, and took? What did they intend to sacrifice? They could hardly expect to kill anyone in the presence of hundreds of magicians and get away with it, no matter how many speeches George made about drastic measures.

"What you intend to do with the contract, it won't *work*. Not the way you want it to," Jack said. A desperate last attempt to make George see reason. "It didn't work—" Water came to his eyes as the bind, again, filled his mouth with fire.

George was sharp enough to guess. A new note entered his voice: black anger leaking out.

"It didn't work because we made the mistake of letting you take an active part in the spell. My father," said George, "was a strong and skilled magician. He would not have lost control of his magic in that way. It was you and your sister who *corrupted* it—probably out of spite, or because that blasted girl had never been taught to keep herself properly contained—and left him weak and ill, such that—"

George cut himself off. In the next instant the blackness was gone again, tucked away deep below his polished surface. So much for not blaming Jack for his father's death: it was manifestly obvious that George did. Or at least that Jack was the only person left whom George could punish for it.

"We're finished here," said Jack harshly. If forced to listen for one more minute to George insulting Elsie and rewriting past events to suit himself, he *would* resort to violence. "Collect your dog and leave my land."

He began to walk down the slope. After a few steps, George caught up to him, stick swinging easily in his hand.

"Are you *quite* sure you haven't heard from Courcey and Miss Debenham and the others?"

Fuck all of this. "I have not."

"Strange. I thought Miss Debenham might at least have sent you word about the fire."

That put a falter in Jack's step. His leg was fine. His guts squeezed out a slow drip of dread. George could be lying. George would say anything.

"What fire?"

"After all, you lived there for a while too. *So* much wood," said George, with a sigh almost of pleasure. "Ingenious, I'm sure, but really—an accident waiting to happen."

24

It was a tense and largely silent wait inside the library. Edwin had spent a lot of his magic on warding the door, and Violet was keeping hers in reserve in case Morris or Bastoke blasted through it anyway and had to be fought off. So they didn't cast a muffling spell, and all stayed away from the window and kept quiet. Adelaide and Edwin read; Robin sketched them while they were reading; Violet allowed Maud to trounce her in a slow and nervy game of chess.

Alan tried to write some more of his article but gave up after ten minutes of staring at a half-finished sentence. Jack had been sure that George wouldn't do anything to him, here on Cheetham Hall's land.

Alan had no such trust. Alan would put absolutely nothing past George Bastoke and Joe Morris. Alan was furious with Jack for locking them all away and deciding that he would go out to deal with George alone, and he was furious with how far this Jack was from the uncaring Lord Hawthorn Alan had met on the *Lyric*—and he was furious with *himself* for the ball of dread that sat like a snugly knotted necktie in the hollow of his throat. There was more he wanted from Jack Alston yet. So, so much more. It would be unacceptable for Jack to do something as arrogant and stupid as go off and be hurt or captured or killed.

The knock, when it came, was not on the door. It was an impatient triple-thump of a fist on the wall a yard from the door frame, and everyone's head rose rabbitlike at the sound of it.

"All clear," came Jack's voice. "They've left. Good work on the turn-away, Edwin, I can't even find the bloody door."

Edwin cradled a spell that must have dropped the turn-away, because Jack came through the door a moment later. Unharmed, by the look of him. Though his face was set in an expression that Alan had seen on his brother Emilio before he told them all, over their ma's sobbing, that they were being turned out of their dark, cramped basement rooms and onto the street. That expression meant bad news for someone.

For Violet, it turned out.

Maud made a sound like she'd been kicked in the side at the very idea of something happening to Spinet House. Violet went first ashen and then red. But the problem, as Jack pointed out, was that they didn't know it was *true,* and not even Edwin could think of a way to find out quickly. Modern technology would have been more useful than magic. Cheetham Hall was too old and the earl and countess too traditional to equip themselves with a telephone line.

They didn't wait long. Either through luck or design, Bastoke had timed his visit beautifully. A letter from London, addressed to Violet, arrived in the daily mail delivery while they were composing an urgent telegram to find out if anything had happened.

Something had.

The letter was from Mrs. Smith, Violet's housekeeper. Shaky dismay sang through the words.

It had happened the previous night. By the time the first of the domestic staff had awoken and sounded the alarm, the fire was already too fierce, and going in too many places, for it to be easily extinguished by either the staff or—when they arrived— the fire brigade.

Nobody had sustained more than minor burns or a bad cough from the smoke. Near miraculous, Alan thought. But—they were magicians.

Mrs. Smith had taken the liberty of drawing on the household fund to find lodging for those servants who didn't have family nearby. However, she wrote, Miss Debenham was urgently expected at the lawyer's office—insurance and cleanup and rebuilding had to be considered—and there were Scotland Yard officers asking probing questions about unhappy or careless staff, and arson—

"I will skin him," snarled Violet, flinging the letter down. "Both of them. All of them. I'm going to set *their* houses on fire, with them inside, and I'm going to keep them alive by magic until they're no more than pieces of twisted *charcoal*."

Alan looked at Maud, then wondered why he'd bothered. Maud was not Robin, who could be relied upon to gently tug his partner back from flights of fancy. Maud had a look on her face like she would cheer Violet on and then make cheese toast over the embers.

"I should never have left. I have to go back." Violet wheeled on Edwin. "If something that serious happened—it's my house, I inherited it, you *saw* me make blood-oath. I should have *felt* it. Shouldn't I?"

"I don't know." Edwin sat rigidly. "I—I thought I would feel it if anything happened to Sutton, but—"

"But your precious Sutton is warded against magicians, so nothing would!" Violet almost shouted.

"And Spinet wasn't warded?" Edwin returned. His rigidity flicked all at once to restlessness. He stood and began to pace. "They managed to burn down a magical house that would have been directly warded against both fire and unfriendly entry. That takes several magicians, and both determination and creativity. If they really wanted to get at Sutton—hell. Perhaps *I* should leave."

"*Nobody should leave,*" said Jack.

It was a whip cracked across the heads of the room.

He went on, harshly, "*This* is what they want. They attacked Spinet because they knew it would make us flee, if we were hiding there, or draw us into the open from wherever else we might be. You especially, Violet." A hard look at Edwin. "And you. You think Walter doesn't know that Sutton is your weakness as well as your strength?"

"Go to hell, Jack," snapped Edwin. "We're not children. Stop talking at us as if we were. And it's all very well for you to be so bloody high-handed—nobody's burned down *your* house."

"No," drawled Jack. "They merely plan to use it to stage an obscene power-stealing ritual."

"If Violet doesn't go and deal with the legalities of this mess," said Robin, "could they make another legal case to take Spinet away from her?"

"They don't need it anymore," said Jack. "They have the knife."

Robin was unmoved. "People like Walter Courcey don't do cruel things because they're necessary."

Violet made another incoherent sound and kicked a chair, which jolted a few inches across the floor. Then she put her hands apologetically on the back of it. Then gave an awkward hiccup of a sob, her face crumpling, and Maud went to embrace her at once.

"She left it to me," Violet said. "She thought I deserved it."

"You do, dearest," said Maud. "Of course you do."

Violet's voice was thick and painfully young. "I—I told it I'd take *care* of it."

Alan realised he hadn't moved since the letter was read. He was leaning his arms hard on the table, and one of his hands was tingling and numb. He sat back and shook them. Violet's guilt was like a cloak flung over his own shoulders. He'd forced Spinet House to give up its secrets and now—if he hadn't helped set the trap at the Barrel, if they all hadn't been forced to flee like this—

"I'll go to London," said Adelaide. "Tomorrow."

Everyone looked at her.

She shrugged. "Hawthorn is right. They're looking for an excuse to get you all out of the way before the gala. I've no magic; I'll only be so much help during the night itself. Disguise me and send me back and I'll act for you, Violet."

Violet wiped at her face with a lacy sleeve. She looked torn. "It'll be a bastard mess, Addy."

"I'm very good with messes."

Nobody argued with that.

"Addy," said Robin, "they might want Edwin and Violet the most, but they do know you're involved."

"Good luck to anyone trying to barge into my parents' house," said Adelaide. "And my grandfather is even better at lording his way through situations than Robin and Hawthorn, and he's spent half his life fighting with property-inheritance lawyers." She hesitated, then added: "And it's not only—look, Kitty's due any day now, and I promised her I'd be there if I could."

Alan thought with a pang of Bella and Caro.

"You're sure, Addy?" said Edwin.

"I'm sure."

"Thank you." Violet untangled herself from Maud to throw an arm around Adelaide. "That would—thank you."

So Violet wrote a letter nominating Adelaide to act on her behalf and Jack witnessed it, and then they did something magical with a wax seal and a piece of Violet's hair, which would apparently prove Adelaide's delegation to deal on behalf of Spinet House.

The day didn't improve much from there. The general mood remained angry and despondent. Edwin lost his temper with himself several times working on his complex spell to transfer the properties of the Last Contract to the Lady's Oak. Jack gave everyone a brief and depressing outline of George's intentions and threats, and then took himself off to the village for a meeting with the Hawthorn estate manager.

Alan shut himself in his room and wrote a story that was dark and fantastical even by his usual standards: an occultist who summoned a demon to grant him untold wealth but was unable to keep it constrained to his will, and instead became the demon's sexual plaything. There was blood in this one, and fire, and the sense of a punishment that couldn't be escaped. Alan waited for the occultist's pain and fear to turn to searing lust beneath his pen, waited for the moment when the narrator lost himself in the freedom of pleasure—but the story fought him.

Finally he put the pen down in puzzled irritation.

In his head was Jack's voice. *You used me as a rod to make stripes on your own back.*

Alan muttered a curse and ripped the pages out of his notebook and into small pieces. He wrote the Roman stories for pleasure and for profit, and yes, sometimes to vent his frustrations, but always from a place of hunger rather than real hurt.

He was here. He would do whatever it took for revenge: his own, Spinet's, and everyone else's. That was all he could do about it now.

After an early dinner full of short tempers, it was clear that everyone was on the verge of disappearing to different corners of the Hall again, or simply giving up on the day and going to bed. But Lady Cheetham ushered them all—even Lady Dufay, who'd eaten nothing but a large plate of rare roast beef drowned in horseradish—into the largest sitting room.

It was unclear whether this was going to be an encouraging talk, a lecture on good manners, or an excruciating parlour game designed to raise spirits. The butler, Blake, entered with a tray: a bulbous dark bottle with a cork stopper, and a set of crystal glasses no larger than eggcups. He set it down on a small table near Lady Cheetham's hand and was dismissed with a nod.

"Polly." Jack was doing one of his long-legged sprawls in his usual armchair, like a wet spider that someone had draped there to dry. His eyes were fixed on the bottle. "Are you sure this is a good idea?"

Perhaps they were to get horrendously drunk on expensive liqueur. Alan's interest increased.

"Everyone's nerves are close to snapping, and Violet has had some horrid news," said Lady Cheetham calmly. She removed the cork stopper. "In three days' time, my murderous nephew will be attempting a political and magical power grab on my own lands. These problems will still be there in the morning. None of us is about to climb onto a horse or make any major financial decisions. So tonight we will *enjoy* ourselves for a few hours."

"Exactly how strong is this drink?" Robin asked, glancing at Maud.

Lady Cheetham poured the first cup. The liquid was pale greenish yellow. "Primrose wine, and not strong at all. But it's the imbuement on the primroses before steeping that has the effect. Traditionally," she added, lifting the cup, "you pay for your drink with a truth. Who will volunteer?"

"Can the wine tell if you're lying?" Alan asked, wary. He had purloined for a seat the enormous cushioned footstool that matched Jack's armchair.

"Honour system," said Jack. "Everyone gives their truth first, then you all drink."

"Fascinating," said Lady Dufay. She had agreed, when indoors, to swap her anoraks for an enormous blue-and-brown quilted dressing gown of Lord Cheetham's. She refused to relinquish her ancient boots. "It's a version of one of the guest-right ceremonies. Elf-wine *would* poison you if you lied about meaning your hosts no harm." She extended an imperious arm with a thin hand at the end. "There are mice in the folly. Truth."

"My apologies, Phyllis," said Lady Cheetham, delivering the glass. "I can have the groundskeepers lay warding charms. Or traps, if you prefer."

"No need. Don't mind them."

"Me next!" said Maud. "Violet, dearest, I have entirely lost that bracelet of yours with the turquoise and gold. You know how I am with losing things. I have been looking, and *looking,* but I think we have to assume we'll never see it again."

She accepted her cup with a grin of triumph.

Most of the truths were of that nature: small things, small confessions, rewarded with a glass of primrose wine. Alan could see why. Today had thinned their skin. Anything sharp or personal might make a wound through which too much could come pouring out.

Alan thought carefully and said, "I write fiction as well as journalism, under another name."

"How mysterious." Lady Cheetham twinkled approvingly at him. "Anything I might have read?"

Alan did not look at Jack.

"I don't think I know you well enough to say, your ladyship," he said, and took his glass. The crystal was heavier than the delicacy of the cups suggested.

Lady Cheetham looked down at her tray. Only two cups remained. "Who's left?"

"Me," said Adelaide. She stood, shoulders back. She might have been about to recite a poem. Instead she walked over to where Robin sat and Edwin perched on the chair's thick arm. "You two are to be *careful*. My parents expect a wedding, Robin, and if they don't get one they'll take it out on your corpse. That said . . ." She looked Edwin dead in the face. "Here's my truth. If *you* get yourself killed, I'll break the engagement myself."

Robin was a picture of shock, and Edwin was worse.

". . . what?" said Edwin weakly. "No. You wouldn't."

"Fetch one of your truth-candles and try me," she said. "I'm not a doll or a pet, to be left behind for comfort if you decide to martyr yourself. You don't get to use me as *insurance*."

Edwin clutched his glass like a lifeline. He glanced, for some reason, at Jack.

"Not to mention how the rest of us might feel if you died. How *I* might—"

She took a breath. Edwin had progressed to gaping unattractively.

"I'm going to hug you," Adelaide said, in what Robin called her maharajah's-daughter voice. "I won't if you say no."

After a moment, Edwin nodded. He even stood from the chair arm and gave Robin his glass of wine. He looked like he was readying himself for a blow, but Adelaide said, "Right," and folded herself around him. Edwin's face went into her hair. His hands trembled on her back.

Alan didn't know where to look. It was a private moment, but there was a reason Adelaide had done it in public. They were witnessing a promise.

Adelaide pulled out of Edwin's arms, smoothed her hair, gave
Robin a shaky smile, and went to collect her wine.

Lady Cheetham looked taken aback but recovered with
aplomb. "And *my* truth is that I have never had as lovely a
group of houseguests as this one, despite the circumstances."
She poured and lifted her own cup, lively and mischievous as if
decades had dropped from her age. Alan thought of Jack's comment about her loneliness. "Cheers."

The wine slid over Alan's tongue, whispering sweetness and a
sensation of walking out into the garden and inhaling hard. The
sweetness was restless. It flowed down through him, warming
him, and Alan felt a knot of muscle between his shoulder blades
soften like wax around a wick.

"Is it working on you, Master Perturbator?" asked Jack.

"Something is working." Alan smiled. "Is it supposed to feel
even *better* than this?" He'd expected everything to be fuzzy,
for his thoughts to slow, but he felt as sharp as ever. The room's
colours were brighter. All the tiredness and tension of the day
was sloughing from him. "Race you up to that bloody oak tree,"
he suggested, grinning a challenge at Jack, and Jack put back his
head and laughed. A long, true, rich laugh—different from the
short barks of amusement Alan associated with him. It seemed
infectious, because Maud started laughing as well.

Alan had only taken half his glass to begin with. Now he
swallowed the other half and tried to be porous, as he had with
Violet's illusions. Let it sink in. Let the magic work. It felt a
lot easier when he was relaxed and neither wary nor trying too
hard. He wondered if it was the effect, perturbed or not, of the
mouthful he'd already had.

He tried this theory out on Edwin, who had an arm stretched
along the top of Robin's chair now, and colour in his cheeks.
Robin had hold of Edwin's other hand and was tracing a finger
over its palm as if indulging in a new kind of future-telling.

"That makes sense," Edwin said. "Here, hold still."

He took his hand back, cradled without string, and batted the
ice-spell at Alan, who caught it as if it were a snowball. The cold

smarted in his hand, but he didn't care. It was like a delicious plunge into a cool bath on a hot day.

"Piss off," said Alan, laughing.

Maud was still laughing too. Violet had made an ark's worth of tiny, beautiful illusions shaped like exotic animals and was marching them over Maud's knees. Lady Dufay seemed to be telling an involved story to Lady Cheetham, barely stopping to breathe, and Lady Cheetham was shaking with quiet laughter as she listened. Adelaide was curled up in a corner of a chaise, taking pins from her dense pile of black hair and running her fingers dreamily through it, looking entirely content with her own company. Alan thought about what she'd said about marriage: that it would give her the things she wanted, without the things she didn't want.

And Jack—Jack was still looking at Alan, and the look was as good as a finger crooked in command. Alan's body, cracked open by the wine, filled up with yearning. He wanted to feel Jack's hand gripping tight in his hair, or simply brushing fingers back and forth against his scalp. This must be how cats felt. No wonder they rubbed themselves against your legs. Alan would do that too: he would sink to the floor, right here.

No. He looked away and deliberately let him himself rise above the wine's effect. He wasn't *that* shameless, and he laughed at himself for having the thought. Everything seemed worth laughing at.

Lady Cheetham tapped her empty glass against the dark bottle until she had everyone's attention.

"And now, I think," she said, "a game of Lady Macbeth."

Edwin groaned. "I hated that game. The twins always won."

"I'm sure we'd be delighted to play," said Robin. "What are we playing, exactly?"

"Lady Macbeth," said Maud. "Sounds very dramatic!"

"It's named for a chicken," said Jack. "It's a scavenger hunt."

They explained amidst general giggling. Lady Macbeth had been the champion layer of the kitchen gardens when Jack and

Elsie were very young. Their nanny at the time, needing ever more elaborate and exhausting games to tire out her charges, had taken a few fallen tail feathers of the hen and hidden them, and set the twins to compete in finding them.

By the time Edwin had been invited to play as a visitor, the game had become a cutthroat family tradition involving a list of possible things to be found. Lady Cheetham did a spell that inked a copy of this evening's list in tiny text on the backs of everyone's hands. Alan squinted at it. *Something red. Something completely useless.* And so forth.

Points would be awarded by the mistress of ceremonies for creative or humorous interpretations of prompts. Finding one of the three white feathers, which could be anywhere in the Hall ("Or the grounds," Lady Cheetham said, "within the radius that your guidelights will stick with you") was worth a full hundred points.

"Elsie would wait until you were heading back and then trip you with a charm and steal from you," said Edwin, but he was smiling.

"No rules against it," said Jack. A suggestion of a smile was on his face too—the first time Alan had seen one when his late sister was the topic of discussion. "Very few rules at all, in fact. Teams, Polly?"

"Choose your partners," she said magnanimously. "I've made sure you won't need magic to find the feathers."

The Blyths chose their partners predictably. Alan, teetering on the verge of more laughter, tried to convince himself that he would be less likely to make rash decisions like shoving Lord Hawthorn into the pantry and demanding to be ravished if he appealed to Adelaide to be his partner instead. But in the time he hesitated, she had already managed to pair herself off with Lady Dufay, and—

"I believe that makes you mine, Cesare."

Jack's hand appeared outstretched in his vision.

Alan tossed out the last of his reservations and let Jack pull him to his feet. The heat of Jack's grip sang on his skin, and he looked Jack balefully in the face.

"When will the wine wear off? How long will I feel like this?"

"Long enough for us to win," said Jack. "Come on. The others are ahead of us already. We can have that race to the Lady's Oak after all—let's see if the lights will go that far."

"How's your leg today?" Alan asked innocently.

"We'll find out," said Jack, and grinned.

He still had hold of Alan's hand and used it to drag Alan with him out the door. As soon as they left the room, the glowing balls of their guidelights appeared above their shoulders. Handy for explorations in the dark.

A quarter of an hour later, Alan couldn't tell if the primrose wine was still working on him at all. It didn't matter a jot. It was a warm night, and a fat half-moon beamed down from behind clouds when they were outdoors. He was breathless with running and laughter, and still felt like he could keep going until the sun rose. And between him and Jack that simmering thing was coming to a rolling boil, sending off hot flicks of sensation every time their eyes met, every time Jack's laughter poured itself into Alan's blood, with every small argument that felt like teeth scraping gloriously across skin.

Alan wanted Jack so much his bones were on fire with it. He was ready for the pot to spill over. Anything at all could happen after this game was done.

After a full hour, they'd found one of the three feathers—tucked almost out of sight between floorboards in the attic—and had collected in their pockets a pile of items for the list's prompts.

They were down in Cheetham Hall's long, narrow wine cellars, Jack tugging bottles free to peer behind them and laughing at Alan's explanation that Jack's shadow was the perfect solution to *Something taller than the tallest one of you.* Alan glanced at his hand, watching for the list to glow red and vanish—the signal that the game had ended—and heard someone shouting, "Hawthorn!"

Both he and Jack looked up. Maud and Violet were at the entrance to the cellar and hurrying towards them, guidelights bouncing gently along.

"Could be an ambush," Alan said. "You hit them with a stick, I'll run away with our goods."

"Where are those thieving instincts, Cesare?" said Jack. "I'll hear them out, and you pick their pockets."

"Deal."

"Hawthorn, finally," Maud said on arrival. She looked hectic and was clutching at her sides. "Oh, dear. Violet, I can't. I—" And she dissolved into giggles, through which she gasped apologies.

"Maud found a ghost," said Violet. In the dimness of the cellar, her guidelight rendered her hair the exact shade of the primrose wine. "We were around the side of the vegetable garden—there was a gate, and it wasn't locked, so we went looking for a feather in there, and Maud's voice changed—"

"Do you think a ghost would count as something useless?" Maud started giggling again. It had a breathless, hysterical edge now. "But we—she—"

"We think it's Lady Elsie," said Violet in a rush. "No. I—I'm sure of it. Hawthorn. Your sister is haunting your house."

25

The bottle Jack was touching shattered.

It was not a loud shattering, or a violent one. The glass simply fell apart, as if along pre-carved lines of weakness. Its contents trickled down through the bottle's shards, through the wooden grid and the many dusty bottles beneath, and began to seep onto the floor.

Jack looked at his fingertips. Two drops of red wine sat there as if someone had pricked him with a needle.

Violet's words were falling through Jack like stones through water. He fumbled after them. His heart was steady in his chest, and he wanted it to explode. He wanted to laugh. He wanted to tear up all the trees on the grounds, expose their roots, and leave them naked and smarting.

Your sister.

"Hawthorn?" said Maud. "I'll—if you want to speak to her, I can—"

"Be *quiet,*" said Jack savagely. He looked up. "I can't deal with this tonight."

Maud started to say something else. So did Violet. Alan was silent and still, his hand pressed over the pocket that held the feather they'd found. Something in Jack shuddered with absolute despair. Even then it was looser, lighter, than it should have been. He should have been feeling more.

"No," he said. To all of them. To all of it. "Tomorrow."

He walked out of the cellars alone, and up to his rooms alone, and undressed himself with numb fingers. The list on his hand glowed and died. His guidelight settled in its keeper and made

shadows of the room, and Jack lay awake in his bed as his buoy-
ant primrose happiness went to indescribable war with the rest
of his emotions. The curtains shivered with his heartbeat. The
air of the room pressed against his face. His ears rang with
nothing.

Finally the wine's effect seeped away from him, leaving the
heavy exhaustion of stretching out beneath sunshine on soft
grass after a lazy picnic lunch. Even the comedown was pleasant, with Polly's treasured primrose wine.

Still Jack lay there, and lay there, and thought about his sister
Elsie and the year before her death, and fell restlessly asleep only
a scant few hours before dawn.

Nobody disturbed him. Nobody woke him for breakfast or
knocked with a tray. By the time he stirred and called for Oliver,
shaved and dressed, and made his way downstairs, Adelaide had
gone—heading to London to deal with the ashes, physical and
figurative, of Spinet House.

There were two days left before the equinox gala. All their
existing problems *were* still there, despite those hours of brief
and uncomplicated happiness that Polly had gifted to them.

And Jack's dead sister might be a ghost. Might have been a
ghost all these years. He couldn't believe he hadn't considered
the possibility before.

You ran, hissed the voice of his shame. *You ran from the house
and the land, and from magic. You were running from her ghost
all along, even before you knew it might be able to speak.*

Jack gathered all the strength he had and went to talk to his
mother.

"It's your decision," Lady Cheetham said at once.

Jack swallowed the howlingly unfair wish that she would take
the decision away from him. He'd have resented her forever if
she'd tried. "Even so," he said. "Tell me what you want, Polly."

Lady Cheetham was quiet. They were in the conservatory,
which was gentle with light; it was a cloudy day, but not an oppres-
sive one. No sign that any magicians would need to be summoned
to keep away the rain.

"I would think," she said eventually, "that a ghost cannot be secret-bound. Curses end with death, and a bind is a curse. I want to know what it is that you can't tell me, Jack, about what my brother did to you both." She had the tense steadiness of someone walking a tightrope and knowing the cost if they were to fall. "But I do not *need* to know. It will not change the past. It will not bring her back. And part of me is afraid to know precisely what I failed to protect my girl from." She was wobbling by the end of it, tears thickening her voice.

"No," said Jack harshly. "None of it had anything to do with you."

"Nonsense. I was her mother," said Lady Cheetham. She reached out and squeezed Jack's hand, once. "Only you know what you want, and what you need. I leave it in your hands. I'm sorry."

Jack could hear voices elsewhere in the house. He wasn't ready for anyone else. He went out through the gamekeeper's pantry, into the breeze of the day, and let his feet lead him to the latched gate in the grey stone wall, behind which his twin sister had leapt to her death.

He stood in front of the gate for nearly a minute, fighting to breathe.

Then he turned away and went instead to the beehives. He stood in front of them, eyes closed, swaying a little on the uneven lawn. The rise and fall of their buzzing was like small waves breaking on the pebbles of a beach, washing the worst of Jack's fear away.

"I don't know what to do," Jack said aloud.

A twig broke behind him and he turned. Alan stood there, a dark shape against the green lawn, topped with wind-blown curls. Today he wore a dark red waistcoat that Jack had last fit into around age fourteen.

"You're following me now?" Jack snapped.

"Yes," said Alan. "I expect you're in the mood to fight with anyone who comes near, and at least I might enjoy it."

Jack didn't have a response that didn't prove Alan's point. He said nothing as Alan came and stood nearby, hands behind his back, to watch the hives curiously.

"Do they talk back?" Alan asked. "Oh—sod off, I don't know. I'm past assuming anything in this place."

"No, they don't," said Jack. "You talk to them. Give them your news. Elsie and I were introduced to the bees in the hour we were born."

"Oh." Alan leaned warily away as a bee came near his face. He glanced at Jack. "Introduce me, then."

It was somehow exactly the right thing to say. Jack bowed shallowly towards the hives and Alan, a beat behind, did the same.

"Hives and queens of Cheetham Hall," said Jack. "This is Alanzo Cesare Rossi, the bane of my existence."

"Pleased to meet you," said Alan. He made a motion of doffing the cap he wasn't wearing. "Sorry about your master's dreadful manners. *Bane.* They'll sting me to death at that rate."

"They're connected to the land. They know who I consider my real enemies."

Alan's shoulders relaxed. He allowed a bee to crawl on his trousers and didn't brush it away.

Then he said, abrupt, "Do you want to talk about it?"

Not really. But *not* talking hadn't helped either.

"What would you do, in my position?" Jack said. "Would you take Maud up on her offer?"

"I'm not in your position," said Alan. "Never will be. But I'd give anything to talk to my pa again."

"How did he die?"

"Pneumonia."

"Was it fast?"

A hint of hostility painted Alan's features. It was almost a relief to see something so familiar. "Fast enough."

"Mrs. Navenby's ghost was exactly how she was at the moment of her death. Same memories, same personality," said Jack. Now that he was talking, his doubts were firing themselves into the air like clay pigeons. He took aim one by one. "And she died suddenly, by magic. You have no idea what Elsie was like before she died. She'd been fighting the pain so long there was hardly anything left of her. And Mrs. Navenby said that to exist as a ghost, without a medium, was like being asleep. What if we wake her up, and she's in the same pain as before, and *I'm* the one forcing her through it?"

"And what if Maud can give her a voice, when otherwise she never would have had one?"

That was more than something to shoot. Jack's voice flattened to sheet metal.

"Don't try to manipulate me. Don't fucking *presume*. You didn't know my sister. You don't know what she'd want."

"Neither do you," Alan shot back, "until you *ask*."

"What do you care?" Jack snarled. A scream rang in his skull. For nearly a year he had let himself be dragged back into magic, back into this world, and now he wished he'd had Robin and Edwin thrown out of his townhouse before they could ever wave a curse in his face. "What gain is there for *you*, Alan Ross, to see this happen? There must be something. You said that philosophically you'd like me on my knees. So you're doing your best to drive me there, is that it?"

Silence followed. Even the hum of the bees seemed softer than before.

Fight! that scream in Jack wanted to burst out. *You said you'd enjoy it. Fight me!* He could see the fight in the deepening creases beside Alan's nose, in the lift of that sharp chin, and he thirsted for it.

He watched it rise and watched it dissolve.

"Go to hell," said Alan quietly, and walked away.

Jack made it another day before he broke.

It wasn't a conversation that did it. Everyone avoided him; Alan must have warned them off. Or else they figured, rightly, that if Jack could send even Alan retreating in anger then nobody else had a hope of a civil exchange. Jack collapsed into the relative silence with relief. This was how he'd spent the last decade of his life, after all: content with his own company, pleased to have a wide circle of unmagical colleagues and acquaintances but steering clear of the abrasive intimacy of family.

He took his meals on his own and went for long rides to inspect the Hawthorn areas of the estate, or for walks that deliberately avoided the route that his mother took.

He felt like a hollow log. If someone struck him he would ring with pain.

Returning from one of those walks, he saw Edwin and Violet, with Dufay and Lady Cheetham, standing beneath the Lady's Oak. The gala would take place tomorrow.

Jack rubbed a frustrated hand back and forth across the grain of his jaw. His anger had run nearly dry, and his inherited pragmatism was rising to fill its space. The others had been indulging him, giving him time, and now that time was up. Edwin would need him tomorrow. His mother would need him. And there was no way of telling what the world of British magic, or any of their lives, would look like after that.

George's visit had shaken something loose, and the space that Jack had been granted had allowed that something to settle into place to be inspected. Like his cousin, Jack had grown up thinking about his magic as something deserved—far more so than even his title and his wealth, which his politics had gradually led him to accept were representative of a fundamental flaw in any society that claimed to respect the humanity and wellbeing of all its members.

He *had* believed magic—his strong, wonderful, wild magic— to be his absolute birthright. It was why he'd been so angry when it was taken from him.

But perhaps nobody deserved to inherit this power either. Especially if they couldn't prove they'd wield it well. *Mine to tend and mine to mend.* It was there, the old bargain, but it had shrunk down to hide in words spoken only by landowners.

Alan would have something to say about that, Jack was sure.

And if Jack was going to accept the Last Contract onto this land in a new form, if he agreed to inherit more than just the title of Cheetham, then he needed to fully accept each piece of his past. And work, like his parents had, towards forgiveness.

His next step felt lighter.

He walked back to the Hall and found Maud, and said, "Yes. I want to speak with her, if you can make it happen."

If it had been a matter of speaking directly to a ghost, with no human medium in between, Jack might have been tempted to do it alone. Or at least with only his mother present. But asking Maud to keep secrets from Violet and Robin, to leave her without anyone to talk to about whatever might happen, was a step too unfair. They were all about to see this affair to its end. They deserved to hear how it had begun.

Enough secrets, enough silence, had been enforced around this already.

The high stone wall enclosed a square patch of lawn, well kept, ringed on all sides by a narrow bed of squat rosebushes. In the centre of the lawn was a large wooden swing seat, which Jack realised had been moved from its previous location beside a creek running along the southern border of the estate. One of Elsie's favourite haunts.

Jack caught the word in his mind and winced.

There were no other seats. Everyone sat, without a murmur, on the grass.

Everyone except Jack and Lady Cheetham, who remained standing, and Maud, who walked without ceremony to sit on the edge of the swing seat. She was a lot shorter than Elsie had been. Her toes barely brushed the grass.

"This is what I did last time," Maud said. Her steadiness was a rope in the storm of Jack's anticipation. "And then I felt it. Her, I mean. She startled me," she said apologetically. "Being possessed again reminded me too much of the cemetery. I didn't think. I pushed her off and we ran." Her weight bobbed the swing back and forth. "I'm sorry," she said to the air. "I'm here now."

Nothing. Nothing for long enough that Jack's tension began

to twist itself into disappointment. Perhaps it had been a trick of the primrose wine. Perhaps Violet had made a mistake.

And then Maud's shoulders jumped as if she were hiccuping, and she looked sharply down at her hands. She moved in a sudden scramble, nearly unbalancing as she planted her feet on the seat and stood up. She grabbed the overhead railing for support and seemed surprised to only just be able to grasp it. There she stood, riding the sway of the seat, the creak of its suspending chains very loud in the silence.

Jack's heart clenched. His mother had gone statuelike beside him.

"*No need to be sorry,*" said the ghost in Maud. Her voice was hesitant and almost a rasp. "*I dare say I was twice as startled as you.*"

And then she looked at Jack.

The name died in Jack's mouth. It would have been a question, but there was no question. He knew that smile, sudden as a summer flood, even when made by another girl's mouth. He found himself unable to say anything at all.

As always, his sister Elsie had no such problem.

"*Oh,*" she said. The longing there turned at once into a note of overwhelming relief. "*Oh, you've* lived. *I'm so glad.*" A pause. "*Pity you look like the wrong side of a camel. What kicked you in the nose, and why did you deserve it?*"

Jack's laugh felt like spitting out a mouthful of blood. "You can't talk," he said. "You're wearing someone else's entire face."

"*Jack,*" said Lady Cheetham, then lifted a hand to her mouth and laughed as well.

"Her name is Maud," said Jack. "The medium. She's—a friend."

Elsie hesitated. "*How . . . how long has it been?*"

Jack had steeled himself for that. "Sixteen years."

Elsie looked from Jack to their mother, and Maud's face tightened. "*Is Father—*"

"He's well," said Lady Cheetham quickly. "We're—we're all well, darling."

Elsie absently set her feet off-centre, bending her knees to keep the swing going. She looked without speaking at the others on the grass, pausing only for a blink of near recognition at Edwin. Maud's face went vague for a few seconds. But it was Elsie again when she looked back at Jack. She pushed some hair behind one ear in a gesture that meant Elsie wanted to escape from a difficult conversation that was her own fault. Jack's heart ached to see it.

"*Stop staring, lump,*" she muttered. "*I didn't think I'd see you again. Seemed better that way. I didn't want to have to— apologise. For leaving.*"

"No surprise there," said Jack. "You always hated apologising."

"*Oh, pot, kettle.*" She stuck her tongue out at him. Jack felt very young and very old, both at once.

"You never have to apologise to us," Lady Cheetham began, but one of Maud's hands went up quickly.

"It's me," said Maud. "She slipped. She's a lot less *definite* than Mrs. Navenby was. I think it takes effort, for her to keep hold of me."

"*Yes,*" said Elsie. Her voice was fainter again. "*It's like climbing a buttered pole. Sorry, Mother. Jack. I'm so tired.*"

Jack's world rose into his mouth. "Does it hurt?"

Her eyes closed. She took a long, deep breath, as if filling her lungs with the beauty of the afternoon. "*No,*" she said. "*Nothing hurts. And it's a different sort of tiredness to—before. This is like being close enough to falling asleep that you can't feel the shape of your body. But I can't wake myself further. Can't feel these toes even if I wriggle them.*"

"We'll let you sleep," said Jack, even though he ached to do nothing of the sort. To stand here forever and talk and talk. "But first—will you tell Mother—tell all of us—what happened under the oak? I won't bore you with the story," he said, taking refuge in irony, "but George plans to try again to combine the power of other magicians, and use it himself."

Elsie's expression darkened. She lifted a hand to her mouth

and made a silent *Oh* of realisation: no curse. No bind. No more silence. *"And you're going to stop him."* It wasn't a question.

"Yes," said Edwin. Elsie jerked her head to look at him. "Elsie, if you can tell us *exactly* what they tried, and how it felt . . . anything might help us, at this point."

She looked back at Jack. He nodded.

So Elsie told them. By the end of it she was slipping, as Maud put it, more frequently and for longer periods, clearly struggling to maintain her foothold in Maud's mind. But she laid out frankly what John and George had done, how they'd asked the twins to mingle their magic and then tried to use their shared blood to draw upon it. And what *she'd* done, when she felt the magic twisting and lashing out—when she heard Jack cry out, and panicked. She'd grabbed it all within herself and made the Hall help her hold it there, like a dam built in haste.

Jack couldn't say what he wanted to say. His tongue was heavy in his mouth even hearing it spoken about by someone else.

But he managed, before he could think too hard about it, to lift a hand and cradlespeak a sign they'd developed very young: a demand to *share*.

Elsie understood. Of course.

"It did want to be shared," said her fading voice. *"It kept trying to get out, Jack. To go back to you. But it was getting worse."* Maud's teeth bared in a quick twitch of a wince. *"By the end it was so bad—so not what magic should be—that I'm sure the shock of trying to absorb it would have killed you."*

"It killed *you*," Jack managed. He was wildly angry with her, and desperately glad to have even this part of her to be angry with. He remembered the bewildered abandonment he'd felt in the last months of her life, when she'd first refused to be touched by him and then refused to have him in the room at all, screaming and throwing things until he left.

Elsie faded from Maud's expression. It was five endless beats of Jack's heart before she found her way back again.

"No." Only a flicker of fire there, but fire nonetheless. "I

killed me. I'd told myself I would live with the pain forever if it kept it away from you. But I don't know if I'd have managed that either. It didn't matter. Another week and I'd have lost control of it. It had hollowed me out. The wall was so thin."

This was what Jack hadn't wanted: to make her relive it. The exhaustion and effort were catching at the sides of her voice now.

"It was one of us or both of us, Jack," said Elsie. *"I'm not sorry."*

Jack nodded, jaw tight. He turned to his mother and touched her arm. "Polly?"

Their mother wiped her face briskly. "I'm proud of you, Elsie."

She didn't say *I've missed you,* any more than she'd said it to Jack. She kept the door open for them to step through. That was all.

"I love you," said Jack, before he could lose his nerve.

Maud's nose scrunched in a final, heartbreakingly familiar expression. *"Ugh, very well. I love you, lump. Now, go raise hell on that bastard. And then come back and tell me about it."*

Maud climbed gingerly down from the swing. She raised an anxious look to Lady Cheetham, who thanked her and then drew her into an embrace.

Jack could see Edwin was brimming with five new theories about what it meant for magic to mingle and to go back into one person—for someone to ask their land to help them keep it there. Jack had just been scraped raw. He wasn't ready to discuss it in terms of theories yet.

He thanked Maud as well, and pleased colour came into her cheeks. Then he went back to his own room, uncertain if he wanted to lie down exhausted or do push-ups for an hour. He felt lighter again, with that night's terrible silence lifted at last. To have his twin given back to him, in this small way—to *have* her there. Perhaps not forever. But just to be able to sit there and know her at peace . . .

Jack sat on the edge of his bed and shivered restlessly. His eyes were dry and his mind moving too fast. He didn't want to sleep, or to walk, or to do anything that he could think of to do.

He wanted an illusion of Violet's that would take up all of his senses, so vivid he could sink right into it and forget himself.

Someone knocked on the door.

"What?" Jack said hoarsely.

"See, now I've met your ma, I *know* you got your dreadful manners from your pa," said Alan. "Must be the title. It ruins you. I always suspected as much."

If Maud had been a rope in a storm, the amusement Jack felt now was as good as an anchor. He sat more upright.

"I refuse to be insulted through a door. Come in and do it to my face."

Alan did so. He was still wearing that red-wine waistcoat that made his complexion sing, and he didn't look hesitant at all. He looked as if a decision had been put behind him.

The soft *click* as Alan turned the key in the door lock found a lace somewhere in Jack's body and pulled it abruptly tight.

Alan said, quick, "I meant it when I said I didn't enjoy the idea of you in pain. I'm sorry if what I said about Elsie, earlier, made that any harder on you."

Jack shook his head. "You were speaking sense."

Alan came over to him, still with no hesitation at all, and cupped Jack's face and tilted it up. The last time this had been followed by a kiss. Now it felt more like comfort. But there was still a promise there, in the closeness of Alan's body and the light scratch of his nails. In the way he released his breath when Jack set hands heavily on his hips to hold him in place.

In close daylight, Alan's hair looked like raven feathers. The deep brown of his eyes was breathtakingly even—not even a fleck of grey or yellow to break the intensity. Those eyes watched Jack thoughtfully, as if memorising him to capture in words.

"What do you want, Jack?"

People kept asking that of Jack as though it were easily answerable. Alan was asking it with the simplicity of invitation. His gaze said he'd give it if he could, and wouldn't if he couldn't, and Jack would always know the difference.

Only you know what you want, and what you need.

His hands tightened on Alan's hips. The man in front of him was solid and real and far, far better than an illusion.

"I want distraction," Jack said roughly. "I want something to consume me for a while."

"Hm." Alan's mouth made one of those crooked smiles. He stepped out of Jack's grasp. "Well. We are in this grand house of yours, after all. And for all that I've stolen this disguise, I clearly don't belong here."

He went to the dresser. Oliver kept most of Jack's things neatly packed away, but there was a leather travelling case set there. Jack could see only the back of Alan's head as he opened the case and picked through the contents.

"I'm only a thief. Was hoping I'd get away with it and vanish into the night. But you caught me in here with your best cuff-links in my pockets." He turned back and lifted an open palm, which glinted. His accent had slid downhill from the consciously educated one he used in company.

His expression said: *Well?*

Jack's breath was coming more heavily. The air between them was so tight, so rich with potential, that he wouldn't have been surprised to see a crackle of magic. A seam of lightning gold.

He stood. By the time he reached Alan and grabbed hold of the wrist extended in his direction, Alan had closed his fingers over his prize. Jack tried, none too gently, to prise those fingers up.

"There's no use being stubborn," he said. "I have you now. Hand it over."

"Go fuck yourself," said Alan, coming alive. He gave his arm a sudden serious wrench, using his body's weight to do it—Jack nearly lost him, but tightened his grip in time. "I'm not scared of you."

"As you pointed out, you are in my house." A sensation like a liquid shadow, like the burn of good brandy, was spreading beneath Jack's skin. His cock clenched. Alan's fingertips dug deeper still into his own palm, resisting, and Jack yanked him closer and leaned down to set his mouth above Alan's ear. Alan's whole body shivered.

"Nobody is coming to help you," Jack said, low and precise. "And I plan to teach you a lesson about what happens when someone tries to steal from me. Not *scared* of me, you arrogant brat?"

He pulled back. Instead of trying to get his nails beneath Alan's closed fingers, he lifted Alan's hand towards his own mouth and delivered a slow puff of breath, as if he could soften Alan's grip like a wax seal. Then he tapped his fingers beneath Alan's chin: mockingly, dangerously, deliberately gentle.

"Oh, we'll soon fix that."

26

Alan swallowed reflexively.

Luckily, the thief he was playing would have needed this moment, too, to reconsider the situation in which he now found himself. To feel the iron solidity of this lord's hand around his arm. To search that cold, brutal face for a single crack of weakness, and find none.

Alan needed the pause to tell his body not to climax on the spot. His entire hand still felt wreathed in the startling heat of Jack's breath.

"All right," he said, making it sullen. "No need for a fuss. I'll put 'em back. See?"

He released his fingers and the cufflinks fell to the floor. Jack shook him by the arm and Alan fired off a defiant grin.

"Go on then, my lord. Teach me your *lesson*. You think I haven't been thrashed before?"

"I'm sure you have," said Jack. "Clearly a repeat hiding won't make any sort of impression. No, I think we can do better than that." His free hand landed on the small of Alan's back and then slid down to take deliberate hold of Alan's arse, which he squeezed as if testing a piece of meat. Alan nearly bit the end of his tongue.

"What—what're you *doing*?"

"I know you've no education to speak of, common gutter-filth that you are, but I think you can guess." Jack squeezed again, this time using that hand to press Alan up against one of his thighs. He still had Alan's wrist captured. Alan nearly embarrassed himself by frotting against Jack's leg, but he put his free hand on Jack's chest instead, as if he meant to push away.

Jack, the absolute bastard, shifted his thigh just enough to make things interesting. Alan shut his mouth on a moan.

"There," said Jack, a low and satisfied rumble. "I'll tell you exactly what I'm doing, and what will happen to a lovely thing who has delivered himself so handily into my clutches. And I will use clear, plain words, so you understand." Another shift of his leg, this one more definite. "I will fuck you until you scream. And then I will turn you over and fuck you some more, and by the time I'm done, you'll remember nothing except how it feels to have my prick buried inside you."

"You won't," whispered Alan. Fucking *hell*. He should have been taking notes. "You—you wouldn't."

"You'll learn your place," murmured Jack, mouth falling to Alan's hair. The scent of him was all-consuming, the solidity of his thigh against Alan's cock an exquisite torture. "One way or another."

It took all of Alan's self-control, but he went still and loose, as if in surrender. He made a quick decision. He directed a grin down at the polished toes of Jack's shoes.

"Let go, my lord," he said, making his voice small. "I'll do what you want, but—please. You're hurting me."

Jack's grip on his wrist loosened at once. Alan shoved Jack in the chest and ran for the door. He rattled the knob a few times before fumbling with the key, and was clumsy enough with the race of his pulse in his ears, the glorious anticipation of capture, that he didn't have to pretend at dropping it. It fell through his fingers to the floor.

Before Alan could bend to retrieve it, Jack had him. One arm fell across his torso, holding his arms to his sides, and the other scooped beneath his legs and knocked his feet from under him as Jack picked him up like a troublesome sack of coal.

"*Fuck*," Alan said, breathless. It came out more impressed than he'd intended. He gave a token wriggle as Jack carried him back across the room.

This time, when Jack hurled him onto the bed and stared down at him, there was none of that true anger to be seen. Only vicious, hungry delight.

Yes. This was what Alan had aimed for: a fight that would engage all of Jack's attention, in the way he so clearly needed. And God in fucking heaven, did the weight of that attention burn sweetly. Alan would do anything for more of it. He would take Jack by the hands and drag them out further onto the cliff of this game than they'd ever been before.

The bedclothes were crisp and pale with a length of dark golden satin draped across the foot, and two round, gold-covered cushions set amidst an unnecessary number of pillows. The bed was not posted and canopied but had an elaborate wooden bedhead with inset panels of leather and brocade. Alan began to scramble back and to one side as if to try for another escape. A tiny part of him yelled that he was putting his *shoes* on the *good fabric,* and another part gleefully suggested he do it harder.

Jack caught his ankle and dragged him back, and before Alan could move Jack had one knee crossing the golden drape and then the other, climbing bodily onto the bed and using his weight to trap Alan in place.

Alan barely remembered to struggle. It felt unbelievably good: Jack's hands shoving his wrists down into the softness of the bed, Jack's knee planted with great deliberation between Alan's legs, with enough weight through it that the slightest squirm of Alan's pelvis was as good as having a hand to rub against.

"Look at you," said Jack. He was indeed looking down at Alan, and his voice fell between them like a line of dark molasses spilling from his lips. Alan's own lips parted. His hips twitched again against the wonderful unyielding pressure. "Your body knows what you want, even if you don't yet."

Alan flexed his arms against Jack's twin grips. No give there either. "Let me *up.*"

"No," said Jack. "You can't go anywhere. You can't run away.

You can't go and work, or steal, or even think. You have to stop, for a while."

The race of Alan's heart wasn't entirely desire now. Those molasses words dripped onto him, made him hear them. A fragile shape rose in his chest: hot saltwater and thin air and a quiet, irrational fluttering that was almost panic.

"No—"

Jack bent his head and growled, a few inches from Alan's mouth—"I'm not giving you a choice."

And then paused. There was a silence in which Alan could have told Jack to get off him, because he did have a choice. But he didn't want to do that. He didn't know what he wanted. His breath was coming in rapid rasps. He was almost afraid to blink, gazing up at Jack, needing something.

Jack's mouth twitched. His voice softened and became deliberate. "Cesare. My lovely sin-eater. You have to *stop*."

The mocking name had become Jack giving him an emperor's title, granting him power, even as the unstinting force of his body was agreeing to take it away.

The fragile thing in Alan cracked right down the middle. The saltwater crashed into his face, surging behind the skin of it, threatening tears. He swallowed hard, and then again.

"Alan." Jack released a little of the pressure on Alan's wrists.

"Don't you dare," Alan snapped, and Jack—thank God, thank God—put the pressure back at once. "Give us a moment. Bloody hell. I—didn't expect to be told something about myself I didn't know." That was it. The right words had found him. His breath steadied. "Stay with me. Keep me here."

"I have you." Jack's thumbs brushed firmly at the sides of Alan's wrists. "I have you, and you will lie here and take what I give you."

Alan said, fervent with gratitude, "I don't want *nothin'* from you."

"Anything," said Jack, chiding.

Alan spat in his face. Or tried. His mouth was dry. Jack laughed, a sound filled with burned-sugar edges, and bent to drop a kiss on Alan's forehead. Like the touch beneath his chin, at the start of this, the very gentleness of the action felt like a threat.

"And I don't care what you want. Now. I'm going to release your hands and take your clothes off. And you already know what happens when you try to run. This time, you will behave for me. Yes?"

Alan gave one last attempt at dragging his hands free, then relented. "Yes."

"You'll what?"

Exultant, hateful heat gathered behind Alan's breastbone. "Behave."

Jack removed Alan's shoes first, and then the rest of his clothes. No doubt his lordship was accustomed to another man assisting with his undress. In Alan it called up a turbulent mixture of embarrassment and arousal, which reached its peak when he lay completely naked. At least the summer had slunk back again, and this bedroom's windows must have drunk up the sun of the day. He was more than warm enough.

Jack, still fully clothed and now sitting on the side of the bed, set aside the last garment. He let his gaze travel from Alan's face to his feet and back again without changing his expression. A squirming feeling filled Alan's legs. He couldn't find a position that didn't feel awkward.

"You're welcome to dash out the door now," said Jack. "Show everyone what you are."

Before Alan could muster a response, Jack bent down and put his mouth to Alan's nipple and sucked ruthlessly hard.

The sensation, coming out of nowhere, punched through Alan. He nearly shouted, his torso jerking, his cock beginning to stiffen against his stomach. Jack's fingers scraped down his side, armpit to hip. Then Jack's mouth again, this time over his collarbone.

Whatever Alan had expected, it wasn't this: this series of devastating, deliberate touches, everywhere on his body but the length of his cock, where blood was tightening with every passing moment. His skin was alive, prickling with need, and he let

his whimpers of complaint get steadily louder. Jack watched him
as if he were an experiment, and left marks all over Alan where
he'd sucked blood to the skin, whispering filth in between. Only
a born tart would writhe like that. Jack would make it so that
the next time he released Alan there would be no begrudging
agreement. Alan would *beg* to stay in his bed.

"I won't beg you for a thing," Alan managed. "Not a fucking—
oh, *Christ*," his voice rising, as Jack took sudden hold of his
balls. Alan's cock was completely hard. He glared at Jack, un-
sure how to remain in character and still demand that Jack take
his clothes off *now* and do what he'd promised.

Jack seemed to hear it. He left Alan and undressed himself—
taking his time about it, casting the occasional satisfied glance at
the bed as if pleased with his handiwork. Alan wouldn't beg, but
he sure as hell wasn't going to move. Especially because Jack,
too, was fully aroused, and returned to the bed with a promising pot of lotion.

"How do I want you?" Jack mused. "I suppose it doesn't matter. I'll have you every possible way, eventually."

Jack could guarantee nothing past tomorrow, and they both
knew it. Alan still went hot all over at the thought. He barely
managed to catch the pot when Jack tossed it at him.

"Open that," Jack said.

While Alan did so, Jack took commanding hold of Alan's legs
and bent them up, planting Alan's feet wide on the bed. He gave
each globe of Alan's arse another of those possessive squeezes
along the way, and then set a hand flat over Alan's stomach.

"There. This way I'll see that pretty face as you're coming
around my prick."

Alan's pulse was thudding through his body and against
Jack's splayed palm. It was an odd sensation. He was going to
lose his mind looking at Jack's fingers. His arse was already
clenching around nothing. He didn't want this to be slow and
luxurious, or even painless.

"Jack." He held out the opened pot. "Don't take too long
with it."

A tiny nod of acknowledgement. Jack was businesslike and fast, one slick finger getting Alan used to the stretch. It had been quite some time since anyone else was involved in Alan's physical pleasure. Even longer since he'd been fucked by a real cock.

Jack slicked his own length, too, and a bolt of selfish pleasure went through Alan at the way Jack hissed. At the ravenous, overwhelming look in Jack's eyes as he knelt between Alan's legs.

"My lord," Alan gasped. Christ, he wanted to touch himself. Better if he didn't. He slid a demanding leg over Jack's thigh, getting their bodies closer, and Jack helpfully hauled the other one around, too, so Alan could have hooked his ankles together behind Jack's back if he wanted. Jack was a block of solid heat and Alan could feel the thick muscle of those thighs clenching, the push of Jack against Alan's opening. "I can't—you can't make me—"

"You're mine, little thief," said Jack hoarsely, "and you'll do precisely what I want."

And he took hold of Alan's thighs and dragged him, steady and inexorable, onto the length of his prick.

Alan shoved one of his own wrists between his teeth, because he could feel an unwisely loud cry trying to wrench its way out. All his attention was on the flare of almost-too-much between his legs, and the tight ripples of pleasure that dived straight for his spine. He had no leverage to struggle upright, with his hips lifted into Jack's lap like this, and Jack was setting up a rhythm that Alan could feel in the joints of his shoulders, his elbows, fuck, the top of his bloody *skull*.

You have to stop.

Alan's muscles relaxed and he let go of the world. Jack's pace was hard, his prick substantial, but it *did* feel luxurious after all—Alan only had to lie there and let Jack hold him where he wanted him, and enjoy being fucked.

He'd almost lost track of his own cock's existence, blissfully and blearily halfway to coming without it being touched, when Jack paused. Colour had suffused Jack's cheeks and throat, down across his shoulders and the very top of his chest. Alan stared at the muscles standing out in Jack's neck and wanted to climb him, claim him, *bite* him.

He clenched down deliberately, and Jack made a sound like an animal in pain. It was wonderful.

Jack's eyes glittered darkly and he took hold of Alan's cock in clear retaliation. It was Alan's turn for pained noises. He shuddered. All his nerves raced to wind themselves up.

"You're going to come for me, Cesare," said Jack. "Exactly when I say."

"No—"

"Yes." Inexorable.

It would have taken barely any pressure at all. Jack gripped his prick in the circle of thumb and forefinger and moved them rapidly back and forth, and—wisely leaning into the inevitable—said, "Now," just as Alan's body hurled itself over the edge.

It was like being wiped clean. Impossible to worry about anything, to feel tense about anything, when every molecule of the body was awash with pleasure like that. Alan sank deliciously back down from it and into awareness that he'd spattered his chest with his own release—Jack had taken *aim*, the bastard—and that the still-erect Jack had pulled out of him, leaving a sharp ache.

"What's the matter?" Alan asked. It sounded more like *wazzmadah?* He coughed and tried again. "All that talk, and you can't see it through?"

Giddy daring filled him. He would say anything. He would *do* anything. He looked at Jack's hard, reddened length and then right into Jack's pleasure-blown eyes, and licked his lips. "So much for my pretty face. You won't even get your precious prick near it."

It took a second to register. Jack went almost blank with surprise, and then bright with a danger that Alan wanted to burn up in like a moth. Jack leaned down and grabbed hold of Alan's hair, lifting his head with one hand—that *did* hurt, the new angle of his neck, but Alan wouldn't have tapped out for a fortune—and moved up his body, kneeling over him, using the other hand to work his prick hard and fast until his shoulders bowed and the white lines of his own release hit Alan's neck, and chin, and mouth.

Candle wax, Alan thought stupidly. His blood roared in his ears.

"Jesus fucking Christ," said Jack presently.

He lowered Alan's head again but didn't seem able to look away from him. Alan wanted to say, *I know,* but could only bring himself to stare back.

After a second Jack levered himself to the side and settled onto his back, and Alan managed to sit up. He pulled up his knees, then put them down again. His backside gave a mild twinge when he moved. He felt as if he'd been beaten for dust, hung in the sunshine, and then re-laid on a comfortable floor.

He also felt covered in the results of two spectacular climaxes, and had a halfhearted go at wiping himself clean with his hands. Then found himself hesitating before touching the bedcover, which was ridiculous given what had just taken place on it.

"We made a mess of you," Jack said, sounding far too pleased.

Alan leaned down and licked his way vindictively into Jack's mouth, wiping his hands all over Jack's shoulders and the dark hair of Jack's chest in the process. His lordship could see how *he* bloody well liked it.

He realised his mistake when Jack groaned against his lips and hauled Alan closer against him, and met Alan's tongue with his own, and Alan's senses flooded with the hot, indescribable scent that was Jack's cologne layered over the exertions of their bodies. Jack kissed like an argument. Alan slid his hand to the nape of Jack's neck and argued fiercely back.

The way you write kisses, they're—devastating.

Alan had two languages and would still have to invent another to properly describe the way it felt to kiss Jack Alston. What had begun as deliberately filthy was unravelling into something perilously close to tender. Alan was clinging to Jack now, his knee slung over Jack's leg. He could wrap himself around that thigh like a ribbon around a maypole, and be kissed forever, and be happy.

He was smiling at that image when they drew apart, and a mirrored smile appeared on Jack's mouth. He drew Alan in again for a lighter, quicker brush of lips.

Something moved in Alan the way he imagined worlds moved in the dark of the universe.

He tried to breathe around it.

"You're a wonder, Cesare," said Jack. "That was exactly what I needed. No, stay there," he added, when Alan began to move away. It was one of those aggravating casual commands, but for once Alan didn't need to push against it. His body was happy to flop back and obey.

Jack himself climbed off the bed and wandered naked towards a door connecting through to a tiny bathroom. Alan rolled onto his side and admired the view, both going and coming; Jack returned quickly with a flannel and a towel.

Alan held his hand out, expecting more flinging.

"I thought I told you to take what you're given," said Jack.

"I thought we agreed I'd throttle you if offered bath attendants," Alan shot back.

Being thoroughly fucked had been wonderful, yes, but this was a revelation: the surprising care in Jack's motions as he scrubbed and wiped both himself and Alan clean with the cool soaked flannel.

"This is an army thing, isn't it," said Alan, turning over when directed to. "Everything scrubbed and dusted and folded."

"And polished," said Jack. He circled the flannel over Alan's arse, idly running his thumb down the crack. Alan caught a noise in his throat and made a grab for the towel.

Once dry, he retrieved his clothes and dressed. Jack stripped the top cover from the bed in another efficiently military motion, and Alan drew one of the golden cushions onto his lap as he leaned against the headboard. He watched with a pang of disappointment as Jack's body disappeared again beneath trousers and shirt. That chest, and those thighs, and that cock. Forget stately homes: Alan could write articles about this. *His lordship Baron Hawthorn has a well-appointed figure, its architecture too rough to be described as strictly classical, dating back to the year*—how old was Jack, anyway?

Alan swallowed a laugh and set the cushion aside. "I should . . ." He tilted his head towards the door.

Jack paused on the last button. "Why?"

Alan cast a speaking look at the rolled-up, debauched bed-cover.

"Alan, we're in a house so full of inverts that Wilde could write a play about it, on my family's ancestral land. And there's still a while before we have to change for what will no doubt be an exhaustingly long dinner and strategy session." Jack came and stretched his legs out on the other side of the bed, sitting up, propped against pillows. "Another army lesson. Rest when you can. Stay."

He was probably right about dinner. Lord Cheetham and Bastoke were expected midmorning the next day, so tonight the final touches would be put on their plan for the gala: the ambush that would prevent Bastoke's ritual from ever taking place. A final snatched island of pretence and calm was a tempting thought.

Jack captured Alan's hand where it was fiddling anew with the golden fringe of the cushion. "I can tie you to the bed, if that's what it takes to make you rest in it."

Alan grinned and used his other hand to toss the cushion at Jack's face. "I look forward to it." But he made his own pile of pillows and slumped against them. Then shifted, restless. "Lying down in the afternoon. Doesn't feel natural."

Jack laughed. He still had Alan's hand; Alan hadn't seen any need to remove it from Jack's possession. Jack's own fingers slid against what Alan knew were distinct pen calluses, and a small constellation of dark freckles, and—

"What's this from?" Jack asked.

The white scar on the back of his hand. There was a matching one in the centre of the palm.

"That's—a reminder." Damn. He'd lost control of his voice. Jack looked at him sharply and managed to guess.

"Morris and George . . . ?"

Alan hadn't gone into detail when he first told Jack about his reluctant recruitment to the role of Bastoke's spy, but what was the point in keeping it secret now?

"Morris handed me a penknife and drew a rune on my hand. He called it a compulsion." He swallowed. His fingers curled tight within Jack's grasp. "They didn't stab me. I stabbed myself, when they told me to. And—" And twisted the blade, when he was told to. Alan swallowed a rise of bile. "And once the point was made, Morris healed me. Good as new."

Except for the scars. A reminder of who owned him, and what was at stake.

"Compulsion is difficult magic." Jack could have been Edwin, explaining a concept, except for the terrible flatness of his tone. "Hard to maintain for any length of time. And it must be very contractual, *very* specific, to work at all."

Ah. Part of Alan had wondered why they hadn't slapped such a rune on him and told him what they wanted, and set him loose. Simpler than coercion, surely.

And Alan hadn't known how to perturb anything purposefully then. There'd been just enough room to shift within the compulsion that Alan's terrified fingers had spasmed and released the knife the first time he set its point to his own hand.

Not the second time. Morris had put more effort into it then.

"They were," said Alan, "specific."

A pause. Jack kept Alan's hand folded in his as if the cufflinks or some other precious thing lay there.

"Maud is still hoping we won't have to kill anyone tomorrow," said Jack. "I rather hope the opposite."

Alan looked at his hand engulfed in Jack's. He said, coming to the realisation along the way, like a sentence that only revealed itself word by word as he wrote it down: "You're still the kind of arse who'll pick two fights before breakfast, but you've been desperate for someone else to look after, haven't you?"

"Someone else . . . ?"

"Because of Elsie."

Jack's expression began to darken, and Alan was ready to snap back. Then he read the darkness properly. It wasn't directed at him.

"Jack—you didn't *fail* her. It's obvious you'd have died for *her,* given the slightest opportunity."

He wondered if Jack would break to anger after all. Alan had stopped thinking in terms of presumption, when it was just the two of them; here he was, talking to this lord as if they'd grown up on the same street. But like the very first night in Jack's study, there was a gap along his nerves where the danger could have been.

Jack's arm, near him, was trembling.

"Oh, fucking hell," said Alan. He did what he'd have done for anyone else he cared about: he reached out and touched Jack's shoulder.

Jack leaned into it, and then kept leaning.

Alan swallowed a sound of surprise. All right then. He let his legs flatten so that Jack could shift further down, until the arrogant Lord Hawthorn was lying with his head propped on Alan's leg and his hands over his face. He wasn't crying, Alan didn't think. A storm long buried had been creeping closer to the surface since they'd come to Cheetham Hall, and Elsie's ghost had knocked down the last barrier keeping it at bay. Alan had no idea what to do about it. It didn't seem the sort of thing anyone could fix.

He opened his mouth, then closed it. Didn't seem the kind of thing words would help either.

Alan slid a hand into the dark walnut-wood of Jack's hair and left it there. Occasionally he moved his fingertips, soothing. Mostly he just sat and let the enormity of this, the fact that Jack was letting him see it, sink into him. Despite the gulf between their lives, they had this in common: neither of them was given to trust. Both of them had been twisted up by the plain facts of their existence. The past could turn you into a strip of paper with a single side, so that comfort and vulnerability slid away down invisible channels and couldn't be grasped.

Except, perhaps, if you bent your will towards unlearning your own history. If you let yourself soften and be porous. Even if only like this, in silence, and at an angle.

27

The last time Jack had attended the triennial equinox gala of British magicians was the year he and Elsie turned sixteen. Just old enough to attend, their parents said. As long as they behaved, they added, with rather less hope.

It had been held in a castle near the Scottish border, and Elsie had taken less than two hours to acquire a small regiment of similarly excited young magicians. By the time the sun rose, there wasn't much left of the castle's greenhouse. Lord Cheetham had apologised frostily and then lectured his offspring for the first hour of the long carriage ride home.

Jack thought about this as Oliver shaved him. He could remember that night with less pain than before: his father encouraging Jack to take an interest in politics both magical and not, the candles charmed against midges, the fireworks that had filled the sky at the deep midpoint of the night, the unrepentant dimples that always ringed Elsie's mouth when she led them into trouble.

George and Lord Cheetham arrived even earlier than expected. Oliver, stationed as lookout for the approaching motorcar, rushed into the breakfast room to let them know. Everyone set down cutlery on poorly emptied plates.

"Here we go," said Robin.

"Edwin," said Jack.

"I know." Edwin sent a faint smile at Robin and slipped out of the room. If all went to plan, that would be the last Jack would see of Edwin's face until this was finished. Alan had not even come to breakfast with the rest of them.

If the enemy didn't know you had a weapon, you damn well kept it up your sleeve for as long as you could.

"Well then," said Lady Cheetham, rising. "Let's find out exactly how much poison my nephew has been feeding my husband along the road, shall we?"

Jack squeezed her hand when she slipped it through his arm, and they walked out into the cool September morning with the others trailing behind them. Liveried servants were hurrying to gather as well.

No Morris stepped from the car this time; no doubt he'd be coming later, along with Lord Cheetham's valet and most of the luggage. His lordship did not travel lightly when switching residences.

Jack treasured the moment of raw surprise on George's face as George climbed the stairs and found himself greeted by most of the people he'd been searching for.

"He knows we're here and we know he knows," Maud had said. "Let's play this all out in the open."

"Give them precisely what they expect to see," added Violet, the theatre magician, "and their eyes will have less chance of straying to look at anything else."

Jack sent George a bland and hostile smile.

"Polly," said Lord Cheetham to his wife. "Hawthorn. This is more of a welcoming party than I expected."

"Leo." She stepped in to greet him. "Indeed. Let me introduce you to our guests."

"You see, sir?" said George. "I didn't want it to be true. However . . ."

Lord Cheetham's brows lowered. And there went the hope, which Jack had been trying not to nurture, that he'd have the time and space to explain this entire outrageous situation in a way that his father would understand. He still refused to believe that his father would have been part of this conspiracy from the beginning, condoning the cold-blooded murder of old women. But Lord Cheetham, stubborn and self-righteous Conservative peer, *would* believe in power being collected and used for

the good of all magicians. He might also believe that George
Bastoke, the model of strong magic and political acumen, was
the right person to wield it.

Perhaps Jack and Polly could still drag Lord Cheetham into
the walled garden, with a young medium his father had never
met, and try to convince him to listen to the voice of a ghost.
Perhaps the earl would even believe them.

In which case he would throw George directly off his land,
and the entire conspiracy would go into hiding and try again,
in secret, and whatever slim chance there was of thwarting them
would vanish into nothing.

"Polly," said his lordship. "I hardly wanted to believe—
sounded so unlike you, when George told me—you do know
what these people have *done*?"

"I invited Miss Debenham up here last week, to help with
decorations for the gala," said Lady Cheetham calmly. "She has
a remarkable gift. And Jack's friends, too—we've been quite the
cosy little party, and they've been invaluable in helping with our
preparations. This is Sir Robert Blyth, and his sister, Miss Maud
Blyth."

If anyone knew how to exude well-bred friendliness in a
frankly absurd situation, it was Robin and Maud. Even Lord
Cheetham murmured something reflexive and shook Robin's
proffered hand.

"The Blyths are not magicians," said George. "I hardly think
their presence at the gala is appropriate."

"I understand Sir Robert is a valuable unbusheled foreseer
for the Assembly," said Lady Cheetham in tones of surprise.
"Surely he deserves to attend."

Lord Cheetham's frown was undimmed. George put a hand
on his arm. "It makes no difference, sir. I have everything under
control. Although," he added, looking at Jack, "it does surprise
me that your little party of criminals is missing its ringleader.
Aunt Polly, will you still deny that Edwin Courcey is staying at
Cheetham Hall?"

"I will gladly deny it," said Lady Cheetham. "I haven't seen

Edwin Courcey for years. Shall we go inside, Leo? The staff have so much to do today. And you *must* be in need of refreshment."

A flicker passed over George's face as Lady Cheetham led everyone through the front doors. Jack fell in at his side.

"Left the bulldog in London, did you?" said Jack. "I imagine fancy parties aren't his cup of tea."

"He'll be where I need him to be," said George, and strode ahead.

Jack had thought the day might drag, but instead it raced. The Hall was a mound of activity and preparation. By late afternoon there'd been so much magic done in the house that the back of Jack's mouth fizzed.

He dressed early to give Oliver the rest of the evening off, squiring his mother around the party.

"And be careful," he said. "If anything looks like trouble, you take your mother and leave."

Oliver was too well trained to ask questions. He knew that trouble was expected and that Jack and the others had something clever planned, and he'd been firmly warned off interacting with Joe Morris. Other than that, Jack wanted him well out of it.

"Yes, my lord." Oliver delivered a final critical smoothing to the back of Jack's formal tailcoat. "Have you seen Mr. Ross?"

"No."

Oliver grinned. "Proud of the job I did on that one."

Now it was Jack's turn to firmly squash his curiosity. He went to his own mother's dressing room and found her almost ready, clad in elegant pale blue with a great deal of black gauze overlay and black lace flowers, with black gloves to the elbow. At Jack's nod, she dismissed her lady's maid, saying that her son could help her with her jewels.

Jack lifted the sapphires from their case. Necklace, earrings, tiara. Her wedding present from Lord Cheetham. She turned her back to him obligingly.

"I made a promise to Mr. Ross," Jack said, looking at the

white hair at the nape of her neck and the delicate clasp of the necklace. "I need you to fulfil it, if I can't."

He explained about Alan's family and handed her their address in an envelope; she gave him a look, but took it.

"If things go poorly enough that neither yourself nor Mr. Ross makes it through, I expect to have other matters on my hands. But yes. Of course."

"You know you don't have to do anything tonight, Polly. Be a hostess. Focus on protecting the guests and soothing the land if anything happens. Don't do anything rash. The Hall needs you."

The look intensified to a Look. "It's very sweet of you to want to protect me, my dear."

That was not agreement. Jack thought of her saying, of Elsie, *I was her mother*. He considered starting the fight about which of them was most allowed to die for the other, and resigned himself to losing it in the same breath. He leaned in to kiss her cheek instead.

He found Alan adjusting glasses on a table set beneath a twinkling string of lights that faded from one colour to the next. Shadows were long and the daylight was beginning to change. The first guests were expected at any time. Everyone had a task, and there was nobody close by.

Jack tapped Alan on the leg with his stick.

"I see you've accepted your station in life. And about time too."

Alan paused, turned, and dropped Jack a vindictive bob. For a beautiful artist's muse of a young man, he made a rather unfortunate girl. The shortness of his hair was disguised by a white cap, and he blended perfectly, no magic required, into the stream of black-and-white-clad maids who were putting the finishing touches on the preparations.

"If you tell me it suits me," said Alan, "I will stab you in the throat."

Jack swept a look up and down the black dress and white apron. "I prefer you in red. You look like an underfed magpie."

Alan returned the look. Jack's formal evening suit was also

magpie shades, but Oliver had ensured that the satin lapels of his
tailcoat shone like dark water against the ice-white of shirtfront,
waistcoat, collar, and bow tie.

"You look like a nightmare," Alan said softly. For a moment
his face was a portrait of hunger, and Jack understood exactly
what he meant. The pull of a danger you could inhabit and then
wake up from. "Be careful," Alan added.

"The benediction of the evening. You as well."

"Morris was wandering around the grotto and the lake earlier," said Alan. "Came within a few yards of me and didn't so
much as blink. Looks like underfed magpies aren't his type either. I ducked into the grotto afterwards to see if they're using
it as a hiding place, but it's clear. I suppose they think *we* might
be hiding Edwin in there. And," anticipating Jack's rather more
vehement repetition of the *be careful* sentiment, "I'm armed."
His hand dipped into a hidden pocket of the black dress—thank
you, Oliver—and emerged with a vicious little flick-knife.

"Borrowed this one from my cousin Berto before I left town,"
said Alan. "And the dress comes off quick if I need to run." He
lifted an edge of black skirt to show riding breeches. Something
else purloined from Jack's youthful wardrobe.

"Show me the cradles again."

Alan made four subtle shapes with his hand, one after the
other.

They were ready. There was no other benediction to give.
Edwin had been right: they'd all known they were signing up
for a fight. If Jack couldn't command his mother against taking
risks, on his behalf or anyone else's, he certainly had no hope
of it with Alan Ross. *I forbid you to be hurt. I forbid you to die.*

Useless.

Music floated faintly across from the direction of the Hall.

"Here we go," Alan said.

Sunset. Here they went. The Earl and Countess of Cheetham
would be on the Hall's front steps, where each arriving magician
would do a small act of magic—a light was traditional—and be
formally granted guest-right before being directed in through

the house to the grand ballroom. Tonight it was no more than a way station, where they'd be served glasses of punch dosed with a particular imbuement from Whistlethropp's to banish fatigue until the sun rose. Another tradition.

Jack met up with Maud, Violet, and Robin in the ballroom, and they toasted with their own cups of punch. Maud's eyes were keen and determined above her mint-green-and-silver gown. Violet's gown was subdued, for her: a remarkably tasteful pink that left her upper arms bare and which was intricately decorated with beads ranging from pale pearl to deep fuchsia.

"I think," said Robin to Violet, "I've had a vision about that dress. Wish I could remember it better."

"I'll wear it to your wedding," said Violet, taking his arm, "and we'll say it was that."

Jack led Maud out through the ballroom doors, down the back terrace, and out onto the lawn. The way from here to the lake was indicated by more of those glowing lights, strung up in the trees or from tall lantern poles where clean, white light glowed and illuminated the grounds. The magic that usually produced the Hall's guidelights had been redirected and gathered atop those poles; it wouldn't be needed indoors tonight.

The gentle slope of lawn and the large flat terrace filled steadily with people. The air smelled of honeysuckle and food and perfume, and even out here it faintly fizzed with the number of spells laid over the food tables to keep things fresh, hot, or cold as required. The maids and footmen had only to keep the tables stocked and the drinks circulating.

Maud turned her head at an offended peacock screech.

"I told Violet the peacocks wouldn't like the cheetahs," she said.

Violet was saving all of her magic for this evening, but she'd spent the past fortnight steadily at work constructing elaborate light-show illusions and then anchoring them to small oak-wood discs, which Edwin had shown her how to use as a power sink. Tonight her illusions required no magic from her at all. The oak-hearts would power them all night.

Already there were murmuring clusters of magicians gathered in various places to watch the show. An enormous koi fish soared in a slow, watery circle in the sky, giving off its own scarlet-and-gold light. A fairy-tale tower built itself from the lawn upwards, bricks first and then a rapid crawl of ivy and thorns. A pair of young men had already levitated themselves to window level, nearly twenty feet above the ground, to see if the tower was inhabited.

And there was a vivid illusion-menagerie featuring larger versions of the creatures that Violet had danced over Maud's lap on the evening of the primrose wine. The poor pheasants and peacocks—very real, and unbothered by the throngs of people—were indeed giving the big cats a wary eye and the occasional threatening yell.

It really was a triumph. Magical society would be talking about it for months, even if nothing more interesting or dangerous than a giant fish were to happen. Jack had been running from magic for so long that to find himself surrounded by a brilliant celebration of it was somehow more jarring than trying to escape a magical building dissolving in a magical storm. A tight collection of buried emotions was unfurling. He forced himself to ignore them.

Familiar and half-familiar faces were everywhere, many of them being whipped away so that their owners would not be caught looking at Jack. Even beyond the rumours that were no doubt swirling about the Barrel's destruction, nobody had seen Lord Hawthorn in magical society for years, and the rumours *there* were even better. Violet and Edwin had told him most of them. He'd lost his magic. He'd refused his magic. His sister had gone mad and he was halfway to following suit.

Jack heard the raised voice of Edwin's brother-in-law Charles Walcott, loudly denouncing the disgraced Edwin as a black sheep of the family—nothing to do with the rest of them, no, hang the very thought! Jack caught sight of the Mannings and exchanged a nod with Pete. Violet's *dicentis* Arthur Manning was there, along with two young women who Jack assumed were the bookish sister and the new fiancée.

"There's George," said Maud.

"Good," said Jack. "Keep him in sight."

George was indeed standing in a group of Assemblymen and their wives. Jack cast a quick look around. Robin and Violet—acting as the bait—would be keeping an eye out for Walter and Morris. Somewhere in this crowd was Edwin, disguised by an illusion sewn in white thread onto the white silk scarf draped over his tailcoat. Only Violet and Alan knew exactly what he looked like. And Alan was . . . there, busy behind another of the food tables, head bent. Jack let his gaze swing past without sticking.

The endless discussions and arguments had come down to this: they needed to know, before anything was done with them, which of their adversaries had the pieces of the Last Contract. Or where they had hidden them.

The contract was undetectable to magic. A fossicking-spell for silver would be all but useless in a formal sea of pocket watches and canes and cufflinks and tiaras and necklaces. And they were up against suspicious and powerful magicians, one of whom commanded a gang of men trained in suppressing any kind of threat to magical society, and all of whom would be extremely on their guard.

All they had to work with was that suspicion. And the fact that most of them were, indeed, extremely visible, with one prominent missing piece. Edwin. A missing piece who'd shown himself capable of greater and stranger magic than anyone knew he had, even if it had ended in disaster.

The plan, as Maud had put it, was to pretend that they'd already succeeded.

Robin and Violet had between them three exact replicas of the contract pieces, formed painstakingly in silver from Edwin's magic and Robin's memory for pattern. They had the hardest piece of theatre to perform: to bring these into the open, in front of Walter or Morris or both, and let them be *seen*. All they needed was enough of a reaction to determine if one of them, or George, was carrying the items. Or for one of them to hurry away to check on someone else or some secret hiding place.

The cradlespeak was for anyone to signal to Alan which person was most suspect, or which person should be followed. Simpler than magic, and faster than coloured pebbles. Alan would then pass that information on, via the same signals, to Edwin; both of them should be moving unseen by their enemies until the time came to act.

Edwin had been practicing a directed sleeping spell until he could cast it with one hand and no string. He would get up close to their target and use it.

Violet's next role would be to keep anyone else away, through illusion or defensive magic or simply having hysterics, while Edwin found and retrieved the contract pieces. Maud and Jack would run whatever interference was needed there.

It would be risky and tight. But they needed only a few moments. As soon as Edwin had the silver in his hands, Jack would ask the Hall to revoke the guest-right of their enemies, once and for all.

And then they would go to the Lady's Oak and transfer the Last Contract into a form that could not be carried off Jack's land.

Jack nearly swayed into Maud and caught himself on his stick as a man shoved bodily against and past him without so much as an apology. Jack turned to snap something and was distracted by the sight of Dufay, who was not wearing anoraks. Nor was she wearing a dressing gown. She was wearing—there was no other word for it—*robes*. As if this were a costume party and she'd come as the concept of spring.

She was attracting even more looks than Jack himself, and carried herself with twice as much scowling arrogance. Jack was impressed. Everyone would assume she was exactly what she was: an elderly recluse deigning to emerge only for the gala.

"George is keeping an eye on us in return. He's holding court. Lots of handshakes. This *would* be easier if all men did not insist on dressing exactly the same at formal events," said Maud. "At least the women—oh. She is here after all."

She wasn't speaking of Dufay. Maud had caught sight of Seraphina Vaughn, who was entering the terraced area with a look of suppressed pain on her face, as if climbing even the gentle lawn slope had been more effort than she wanted. The last member of the Forsythia Club looked around and clearly saw Maud, too, because she changed direction to approach them.

"I'd been hoping for someone to be loudly unpleasant to," said Jack. "And a harmless old woman, no less. Time to put some tarnish back on my reputation."

"I want to talk to her," said Maud.

"Maud. Do you need reminding of the fact that she tried to *kill* you?"

"Don't let her do it again, please," said Maud, and actually reached out her hand as Mrs. Vaughn approached, a determined portrait of greeting from a young girl to a respected old woman.

Jack took a half step around until he could keep an eye on George over the top of their heads. At least both Maud and Mrs. Vaughn were barely scraping his collarbone in height. They had not considered it likely that the men of George's conspiracy would trust Mrs. Vaughn to carry the contract pieces for them.

They might, Maud had stubbornly said. *It'd be a good misdirection of their own.* Of course she wanted to keep Mrs. Vaughn in sight too.

"Well, Miss Blyth?" said Mrs. Vaughn. "Hoping to convince me onto the other team at the final stretch?"

"Yes," said Maud.

Mrs. Vaughn gave a warm, creaking laugh that seemed to catch at her ribs. "I see. What brilliant story will you try to sell me?"

"One you've heard before," said Maud steadily. "Your whole life, in fact. Men have decided over and over again that you can't or shouldn't wield power, or should be forced to wield it in secret. Your father, your brothers, your husband. Are you going to let a horrible, self-important man like George Bastoke do it again? Because he will. You know he will."

That *was* a story. Half from the woman herself, and half from the tale that Mrs. Navenby's ghost had given them. Seraphina Vaughn's eyes flashed to hear it.

But she calmed herself at once and cast a glance over at George. "I have his word. Trite, but it means something to men like him."

"He killed his own cousin trying to steal her magic," said Maud. "His word is useless."

Perhaps it might have moved her, given another hour and all of Maud's powers of persuasion. But Mrs. Vaughn put a gloved hand to her side, grimaced, and then reached out with her other hand towards Maud's face.

Maud flinched. Jack put his hand at her back.

Mrs. Vaughn smiled like the cool decision of a falcon and patted Maud's cheek.

"What are you and your doomed friends offering me? Nothing. You're no better than any of those men, or Beth and Enid and Flora. You want to deny me this as well. I haven't much life left to me, Miss Blyth, and I *will* have the power I deserve before I die. Right out in the open."

George was bending his head to listen to Richard Prest. Movement stirred nearby. It was—yes, it was Morris, striding up to the group of politicians. George's magical thug was better dressed than Jack had seen him before, but he didn't wear the finery with any kind of comfort. George drew aside at once to speak to him.

Jack tilted his body to watch closely, heart rising into his throat. He saw George's hand move, in a single sharp motion, to his pocket. Saw George relax, recover his poise, and then speak intensely to Morris.

An answer. And the enemy were on their guard. Time to move fast.

"No use arguing with a lost cause, Maud," Jack said shortly. "Come on."

He drew them away from Mrs. Vaughn, walking to the edge of the terrace and finding a sight line down to Alan. Maud's silence brimmed with excitement as she kept her eye on George and Morris. Jack waited until Alan looked in their direction and then cradlespoke the symbol they'd come up with for *George,* disguising it in an adjustment of Maud's hand on his arm.

Alan turned away at once. So did Jack, steering Maud in a loop so that they'd end up close to George again, ready to leap in and contribute to the distracting chaos when the man collapsed.

Morris nodded and strode away again. Jack let him go and watched George.

"Come *on,*" Maud said beneath her breath.

Together they stood and watched the shifting group near the balustrade. This would still take time. Time for Alan to find and signal Edwin, and then remove himself prudently from the scene. Time for Edwin, whatever he looked like, to make his way towards George. A pity that Morris wasn't still there; Edwin could have taken them both down at once.

George cradled a spell with fluid grace.

Jack tensed his hand around his stick and softened his knees, ready to shove Maud behind himself, but George did not attack. Nor did he collapse in sleep.

George floated calmly into the air until he hovered above everyone's heads, a dark and confident shape against the lights and the sky.

28

It was a levitation spell. There must have been an amplification spell tacked on, too, because when George spoke, his voice was loud enough to be easily heard over the noise. He gave a brief speech of welcome, including a heaping of praise for his dear aunt and uncle, the Earl and Countess of Cheetham, who had produced such a wonderful array of spectacle.

"But I think we can do more," George added. "This is a remarkable evening in more ways than one, and we have a very great achievement of the Assembly's to unveil for you. An achievement that deserves a *particularly* special stage for its unveiling. We have this wonderful lake here, after all. It'd be a pity to waste it. In fact, I invite you all to come and stand upon it."

Admiring murmurs began to rise from the people closest to the balustrade. Jack frowned and got himself and Maud a bit closer.

"What is it?" said Maud, who couldn't see. The question was being echoed all around them.

"They're freezing the lake," said Jack.

At least eight magicians—Coopers, no doubt—stood at various points around the lake, working the same spell in practiced unison. White mist rose curling into the air, and white arrows spread out across the lake's surface from where each man stood. Each arrow of ice met its fellows and formed a solid, unbroken sheet. At the further edge of the lake, the ice was doing something more complicated: a raised stage, giving the whole thing the air of a theatre. Which of course it was.

"To allay any fears the ladies may have: we'll keep the air

warm enough, and it's quite safe to walk on without slipping," said George. "You have my word." And he sank back to earth, looking satisfied.

It was a spectacularly George thing to do. It wasn't enough for him to piggyback on someone else's triumph of hospitality: he had to make one for himself. And it was a pointed display of the level of magic that at present could be produced only by a group.

As invited, the mass of finely dressed magicians began an excited exodus down from the terrace and the grassy slope and around to the sides of the lake, where two gorgeous bridges of densely braided ice now led out onto the frozen surface. Jack and Maud were in the tail end of the crowd. Jack had lost sight of the others. He kept a steady pace, Maud right at his side.

This was the window for Edwin and Violet, surely. George had said his piece. For the time being, nobody's eyes were upon him.

Where most of the crowd was heading towards the bridge, Jack and Maud turned with unspoken accord and broke away from them. Instead they took the path of white stones that led back to the sea grotto, directly beneath where they'd been standing.

"Hawthorn," said Maud.

It wasn't quite a question. There was a thread of unease in her voice. It met a matching thread in Jack, which was then swamped by the rightness of their feet taking step after softly crunching step along the path of white stones, beneath the pink coral arch. This was where they were supposed to be.

They stepped into the grotto proper, and the unease flourished into outright fear.

"*Fuck,*" said Maud beside him.

"I completely agree, darling," said Violet.

Violet and Robin stood in the centre of the grotto, this beautiful, mosaic-ridden space glowing in sea colours with another string of magic lights. Neither of them moved more than their eyes towards Maud and Jack. Both of them were grim-faced atop the stillness of their bodies.

All of which was explained by the glowing strings that looped around their wrists, the other ends vanishing into the slender central pillar of the grotto: dark rock adorned with smooth green tiles and a ring of real pink-and-white seashells.

And standing by the other entrance to the grotto, watching Jack and Maud's progress with an expression of faint and malicious amusement, was Walter Courcey.

Fuck, indeed.

Jack felt his face shut down with anger and despair. Still his legs kept walking, as if his bones were working from a different script to his mind. As if someone had opened him up and engraved the runes of a compulsion there. He and Maud walked right up to the pillar, and their hands rose in unison towards it.

"Fight it, Maudie," Robin said urgently. "Hawthorn, if you can . . ."

Maud's hand trembled. If Jack knew her at all, she was fighting for all she was worth. It made no difference. The magic was too strong.

As soon as Jack's fingers touched the first shell, the overwhelming urge to do so vanished, as if he'd been yearning for a specific food and it had turned to ash on his tongue. He'd have hurled himself away, he'd have turned and charged at Walter Courcey stick-first, except that—as he'd expected—a fresh Bridle appeared around his wrist. All control over his body sank away.

"Very good," said Walter. "I must say, that worked even better than I'd hoped."

There was a silence in which Jack realised he was waiting for Edwin to ask the question. Edwin wasn't here. *Edwin wasn't here,* and neither was Alan.

Dry-mouthed, Jack asked it instead. It seemed as good a way as any to buy time.

"How do you make a compulsion work without words?"

"It's not *strictly* a compulsion," said Walter. "Well, I suppose it is. It's the Pied Piper. I hear you're familiar with that one." He sent a thin smile at Violet. "With the subject changed to an imbuement, thanks to the Vaughn woman. All it takes is a dab of powder on bare skin. And you have all made yourselves *help-fully* visible to the Coopers tonight."

Someone pressing against Jack in the crowd. Mrs. Vaughn touching Maud's cheek. Even with the layers of formal evening wear, it would be easy enough to brush gloved fingers against exposed skin if you were determined and quick. Then all it would take would be for someone to activate the Pied Piper on a single spot—such as this pillar—and bring the compulsion to life.

"And this is a neat little version of the Goblin's Bridle," added Walter. "Speech but no other movement, combined with a curtain-spell on the space, so nobody can hear or see what goes on." He nodded around the grotto. "I'm told the Coopers favour this setup for interrogations."

Jack gritted his teeth. Through the open-air windows of the grotto he could see the lake, the frozen surface now half-full of people, and could just make out figures moving on the raised stage at the end. Nobody at all would be watching the grotto; and even if they were, the curtain-spell was in effect.

"Oh, don't look like that, Blyth," said Walter. "Your tiresome blood-oath is still in effect. I can't harm you or your sister. Nor do I need to interrogate you. You know nothing of value to us—none of you do. We only need you kept tidily out of the way. Now, excuse me, I must see what's keeping—"

He was interrupted. Two people came in by the grotto's other entrance, one holding the other tightly by the arm.

Joe Morris. And, hands shoved together in the priez-vous, white scarf missing, and entirely himself—Edwin.

"Caught this one outside," said Morris. "The damn fool followed the others."

"Ah, Win." Walter's smile grew. "I had a feeling you'd show up eventually."

Edwin's eyes widened as he took in the scene. He didn't ask any questions at all. But he was clearly not under the same compulsion as the rest of them, because he tried to yank his elbow out of Morris's grip—failed—and then stood still.

"Oh, for God's sake, Edwin, why *did* you follow us? That wasn't the plan," snapped Violet, who was never at her best in a crisis.

"Forgive me," said Edwin thinly, "for needing to know why the rest of you were walking in the *wrong direction*."

Of course. Without Violet and the others as backup, he'd have been swarmed by Coopers as soon as he was seen going through George's pockets, even if he did manage to send him to sleep.

And without knowing where Jack himself was, Edwin also couldn't rely on their backup plan for if they failed to steal the contract pieces: let the ritual start, whatever form it took, and then have Jack remove guest-right as soon as the Last Contract was out in the open and visible. Difficult, and messy. Removing guest-right was unpleasant but not a compulsion on its own, and there was no telling what George might manage to do before it became unbearable.

Jack was still on his land, and could still speak. What would happen if he removed their guest-right now?

George would take the contract with him as he left, and potentially try to complete the ritual anyway as soon as he crossed the Cheetham border. Walter and Morris would likely take *Edwin*, and the rest of them would be just as stuck.

And *where the hell was Alan?*

"And very convenient of you to bring yourself," said Walter to Edwin. "Bastoke planned to use Blyth here to draw you out. But here you are, ready to volunteer your services."

"What *services*?" said Robin, nearly a growl.

Edwin looked resigned. "It is blood after all, isn't it? I couldn't see how you could make any of this work without it."

Futile, furious cold gripped Jack at the word *blood*. But Edwin was right. It was only what they'd expected.

Walter nodded. "At first Seraphina Vaughn believed the ritual would have to involve the sacrifice of three people, one from each of the Three Families, as a sign of how seriously magicians were taking the request for power. But we've realised there's no need for that. It's been so many generations—there's been enough intermingling that any British magician will have blood from all three."

Edwin had gone even paler but still showed no surprise. If Robin's gaze could kill, Walter would have been a smear on the floor.

"He's your *brother*. You're all so obsessed with blood— doesn't that mean anything?"

"Robin, you're wasting your time," said Edwin, but Walter spoke over him, suddenly ugly and sharp.

"*He* has no loyalty to magicians, or to our family. I'm hardly bound to show any in return."

Amazingly, Edwin let out a laugh. "Be honest, Walt. I beat you once and you still can't stand it. So. I suppose you're going to kill me in a corner somewhere, and Bastoke will pretend the power came because you asked the contract *nicely*?"

"Oh, no. It's important that this happens in public."

"In public? In front of everyone? These are normal, decent people," said Maud heatedly. "Most of them won't see *murder* as a means justifying an end!"

"You have a naive view of normal people, Miss Blyth," said Walter. "Public executions of dangerous criminals have always been well attended. They still report on hangings in the papers. That's not murder. It's the world being set right." He gave his brother a look that was chilling in its satisfaction. "But I wouldn't put our father and sister through that, Win. Don't trouble yourself that they'll have to watch you die. They'll see exactly what we want them to see."

Morris had been stolid through all of this, keeping his eyes on Edwin. Now he said impatiently, "Courcey. Mr. Bastoke will be waiting."

"There are still people on the bridges," said Walter with a glance out the windows. "And I'd hate for Win's friends not to know *exactly* what's going on behind the illusion that everyone else will see."

Edwin was right. This was about Walter enjoying himself.

Showing himself to be on the clever side. And drawing delight from Edwin's fear, just as he always had.

"Not three people, or three deaths. Three wounds. They'll be shallow and symbolic, as far as everyone will see." Walter made two slashing motions with his hand, and Edwin flinched. "And how *good* of Mr. Courcey here to volunteer, as repentance for what he did to the Barrel." A final motion, this one an outright stab. Walter's fist rested on Edwin's chest, over his heart.

"No," whispered Maud.

Edwin looked his brother in the face and his jaw moved, but he said nothing.

"So you kill him up on that stage and an illusion of him does a tap dance, I suppose," said Jack. He felt sick.

"Or faints," said Walter carelessly. "And we say the Coopers have locked him up for everyone's safety, and in a few years—who will remember? Who will care?"

Beyond the people in this room. Behind Walter's smile was the unspoken promise that they, too, would be locked up as criminals—or killed, or secret-bound, or memory-wiped. Whatever George and the Coopers found most expedient.

"If you go ahead with this—if you kill him," said Robin, white-lipped and flat, "I will destroy you, Courcey."

"Once we have the contract to draw on," said Walter, "you may *try* to do whatever you wish." He nodded at Morris. "All right. Time for the show. Strengthen that priez-vous on him, Morris. He's managed to get out of it before; I won't let that happen again."

Morris nodded and released Edwin long enough to do the spell. The tendons stood out on the back of Edwin's hands and he winced.

Walter said to Edwin, "And just to be certain there's no repeat of whatever extravagant nonsense you weren't strong enough to control at the Barrel: Morris will stand guard outside of this little cave, where he has a good view. The first *hint* of trouble from you, Win, and Morris will step inside and slit Blyth's throat. Foreseer or not."

"*Go to hell,*" choked Maud.

Edwin met Robin's eyes with a desperation that made Jack want to yank his own gaze away, it was so private and so raw.

Walter smiled at them all. "You'll notice I'm still not harming you, Sir Robert. I'm simply telling you a fact."

And he took Edwin by the arm and marched him out of the grotto. Morris followed.

29

Alan didn't know what was happening, but he suspected that something had gone spectacularly fuckity-buggerin' wrong. As his cousin Berto would put it.

He'd taken Jack's signal and passed it on to the disguised Edwin, then made a direct line to look busy near one of the food tables again. From here his role was flexible. Backup if needed. Running messages to Lady Cheetham, if for any reason they needed her.

He had hoped for something a little more hands-on when it came to revenge. But his family would prefer him alive to dead, and death was what he'd be courting if he threw himself unnecessarily into a magical fight.

There was also the prospect of *after*. After they reclaimed and transformed the Last Contract. Bastoke and Courcey weren't the sort to let themselves be thwarted without seeking their own revenge, and the longer Alan's involvement could be kept from them, the safer the Rossis would be.

Alan did intend to watch as George Bastoke was magically chased off Jack's land, though. Perhaps he'd throw something at the bastard's retreating back.

It was hard to miss George's speech, delivered from ten feet in the bloody air. Alan's heart beat hard as he stacked empty glasses onto a tray. The invitation down onto the lake—*onto the lake?*—had clearly not been extended to servants, and he'd look obvious hurrying after them now. Surely Edwin and Violet would be seizing this window.

Seconds turned into minutes. The crowd on the lawn was disappearing as all the magicians moved down and to either side. The air visible past the balustrade had taken on a thin haze like morning mist hugging the Thames.

There was certainly noise, but it was excited in a pleasurable way—not as if anyone had collapsed. Not as if any kind of fight were happening.

A couple of the other maids had taken advantage of this unexpected change in the party's plans to run up to the now-empty terrace. They were gazing down, leaning on the balustrade railing.

"Sod it," Alan muttered, and went to do the same. It was late enough now that the sky was fully dark apart from the glowing bulge of the moon, and cool enough that he was glad of the breeches beneath his skirts.

And down on the lake, it was winter. Pale bright light from more magical lanterns illuminated the scene, glimmering on ice-bridges and the solid, iced-over lake surface. The ice had the rough and sturdy appearance of a natural winter freeze, and none of the delighted throng appeared to be having trouble keeping their footing.

Inhaling the rising air gave Alan a strange, hard pang of childhood memory. His father opening the ice chests to haul out metal tins of ice cream, or solid blocks of ice to be chipped and shaved into treats. Chill mist wreathing Alan's face. The last time this memory had hit was in the ice room on the *Lyric*, when he was snipping a lock of hair from a corpse. This air was equally cold, as if giant-wafted fans were driving the chill upwards and away from the magicians.

George Bastoke strode up onto an icy stage at the other end of the lake. It was too far for Alan to make out his face, but that unhurried, long-legged gait gave him away.

"*Fuck*," said Alan, with feeling.

Where was everyone else? Down there, surely. Alan scanned for Violet's yellow hair and pink dress, or a glimpse of pale green that could be Maud. He had no hope of finding Jack in a crowd full of tall, brown-haired toffs in tailcoats. Especially when they were all facing away from him.

What the hell was he supposed to do? *I've nobody's hair to do a map-spell to find them*, he thought hysterically. Followed by: *And I'm not a bloody magician*. All he could do with magic was make it go wrong, and not even in usefully predictable ways.

"They're cutting it fine," said Lady Dufay.

Alan's tightly wound nerves made him yelp aloud in surprise. She'd come up noiselessly to stand next to him. In moonlight and magic-light her skin and hair almost had their own glow, in a way that was far more uncanny than it was appealing. She seemed to be wearing linen bedsheets and half a shrubbery.

"Thank Christ," Alan said weakly. "What's happened? Where are the others?"

"Does Courcey intend to send Bastoke to sleep in front of all this crowd?" said Lady Dufay with her usual air of criticism.

So she didn't know either.

A different chill went down Alan's spine as he spotted Lady Cheetham being escorted—and it clearly was an escort, given the men flanking her—to a spot where her husband already stood near the front of the crowd. Her ladyship gazed fretfully around. Alan could get to her, perhaps, if he kept his face hidden as much as possible. Pretend some emergency had arisen in the kitchens, or a guest had fallen ill. And *she* might be able to find the others. Surely through the land—she and Jack had both made blood-pledge to this place, hadn't they, so perhaps—

"The *bees*," said Alan.

He grabbed hold of Lady Dufay's arm through the draped fabric. The limb was thin and solid as a broomstick. "You know this place. Your magic's in it. Could the bees find Jack—Lord Hawthorn?"

He had her attention. She looked down at him with the wonderful, chilling fae-blue eyes that Jack had inherited even at the distance of generations. The deep lines of her face deepened further in thought. "Find? Yes. Can't speak to *show*."

That was enough for Alan. He realised after the first two strides that he still had hold of her arm, and released it hurriedly, but she was moving. And taller and faster than him, besides. Alan hiked up his skirts to his waist and once again he was racing in the Lady's wake: downhill this time, not up to the oak. He had a dreadful sensation like a fishhook between his shoulder blades, spooling out line as he ran away from the lake, away from where—surely—the danger was brewing and he was most needed. But this was the best idea he had.

He reached the hives, breathless. There was little sound coming from the wooden boxes, and only moonlight here to see by, but he couldn't see any stray bees either crawling or floating. Asleep. Did bees sleep?

Lady Dufay, arriving ahead of him, lifted one hand to her chest and inclined her body in a movement that made the bizarre drapery she was wearing flow abruptly into *rightness*. It made Alan's eyes ache.

Alan bowed too. There were words. Jack had spoken them.

"Hives and bees. I mean queens," said Alan. "Hives and queens of Cheetham Hall. You know me, and I suppose you know Lady Dufay. She planted that tree and started this family, and one of the family is in trouble. Probably." He gulped in air. The silence from the hives was unchanged. "You know who their enemies are, and you know I'm not one of them. I'll—promise you blood. I'll tell you all my secrets. Whatever you want. I need to find Lord Hawthorn."

Lady Dufay said nothing. Alan's lungs burned and he felt beyond foolish, standing here in the dark begging a bunch of insects for help.

A shadow rose slowly from one of the hives. Dark, silken movement against the backdrop of trees and night. Alan considered bowing again, wondering if he was about to be stung to death after all for the presumption.

The swarm flowed away towards the lake.

"Oh thank you thank you," Alan said, and followed.

The bees were nearly as fast as Lady Dufay, but Alan forced

himself to keep up. They led him and the Lady back the way
they'd come. Alan was starting to invent excuses for why a
skinny parlour maid would be chasing a horde of bees through
the crowd of magicians—was he an apprentice beekeeper, and
they'd escaped?—but he realised quickly that they weren't heading out to the lake proper. They were looping down to the sea
grotto, which Alan had checked earlier that day. The platform of
ice started several yards away, leaving a boundary of black lake
water and reeds that abutted the path and the grotto itself.

An abrupt yank at his sleeve stopped Alan in his tracks. The
Lady dragged him behind a hedge and put a finger to her lips.
Alan was too grateful to care about her customary *lord-what-
fools-these-mortals-be* expression. He leaned carefully out of
the hedge's shelter and saw Joe Morris, several yards away, gazing out across the lake.

Alan followed Morris's gaze. From here he could just see
the raised stage where Bastoke stood, now flanked by several
other people, and another man being led up there too. Fair
head. Edwin.

Bastoke was speaking, the tones of his voice amplified again.
Alan's thundering pulse let him hear only some of the words.
Blood stood out. *To serve all magicians.*

Fucking shitting Christ. That didn't seem promising. And
Morris was between them and the pink arch leading into the
grotto.

The bees, when Alan looked for them, had vanished. Pity.
He really would have given them anything in exchange for
watching Joe Morris be stung a few hundred times. His skin
was already crawling with memory and fear. His scarred hand
cramped hard around its handful of black skirts. Morris was
too loyal to be bribed or reasoned with. He cradled faster than
any magician Alan had come across, and inflicted horrible pain
without blinking.

What had worked against this man on the *Lyric*?

Theatre. Theatre and lies.

Alan's next breath shook. He smoothed the skirt and apron

back down, and adjusted his cap to make sure no short curls were escaping at the back.

"Your ladyship," he whispered. "I need a diversion. Go and be an eccentric old woman. As eccentric as you possibly can. And—get good and close to him."

Lady Dufay asked no questions. There was a new glimmer of yellow-white as a smile bared her teeth. And then she was sweeping around the hedge, her feet uncannily quiet on the stones of the path.

"What the devil—" Alan heard, from Morris.

"Good sir," said Lady Dufay. You could have seen your reflection in her voice. It was as if someone had taken Lady Cheetham and polished her for an hour. "Oh, my lord, is it you? Have you returned to me, as you promised? Perhaps I am ready to forgive you after all."

Alan dared a glance around the hedge. Lady Dufay moved like a drunken dancer, her robes swaying, and she recited an indistinct poem that had the awkward rhythm of the orrery song. Morris stood solidly in place, good guard that he was, and told the odd woman to go onto the lake with all the other guests. He was clearly reluctant to be outright rude—or physical—when he was trying not to attract attention.

The Lady fluttered closer, reaching for Morris's face, and Alan hastily inserted himself into the scene.

"My lady! There you are!" He tried for a soft, placating version of Bella's voice, and kept his face tilted well down as he hurried up to them. His shoulders felt like bricks, his body braced for magic or a blow. He kept his eyes on Morris's legs. "I'm so sorry, sir, she wandered away—I'm taking good care of her, I swear I am, please don't tell anyone—my lady, you're supposed to be with the others, on the lake—"

"Get her away," said Morris shortly. "Oi—" He finally took a step sideways as Lady Dufay cooed at him and reached out to touch his shoulder.

"She's not got all her wits," panted Alan.

"I can bloody see that."

Alan got himself in between the two of them. Close quarters. Right. His hand slid clear of his pocket.

Morris reached across him to try to keep the Lady at arm's length. His sleeve caught on Alan's cap and pushed it nearly off.

"What the—"

Now. It had to be now.

Alan spun, adjusted his grip on the knife, and flung his free arm around Morris's side as if embracing him. Holding him steady. Judging, the best he could through all these bloody clothes, where the man's lowest ribs stopped and unprotected flesh began.

He set the knife's point to that place and shoved in and up-wards with all the strength he had.

Alan had been in his share of ugly fights. The rule was that you ended them fast and in whatever way you could. This wasn't a scuffle over food or a prime stretch of begging space on the street—Morris wasn't the sort to take a wound as a warning, and Alan had no faith at all he'd be able to knock the man out cold.

Alan had never killed anyone before.

Morris grunted when the knife sank in. He sounded sur-prised.

Pressed up close like this, the heat of Morris's body was tre-mendous. Alan smelled sweat and copper. He couldn't feel his fingers around the knife handle. He yanked anyway, praying his muscles would cooperate, and stumbled back a few steps with the knife in his nerveless hand and finally, finally looked Joe Morris in the face.

Morris was staring back at him with the violence of a bottle freshly broken against the edge of a bar. Recognition bled onto the bottle's edges and, horribly, Morris gave three little coughs of laughter. Each one expanded the hint of darkness that Alan could see seeping out onto the white shirtfront from beneath the black of his waistcoat.

"Nice try, thief," Morris ground out.

And began, doubled over as he was, to cradle a spell. It took shape with searing quickness, pale blue and glowing. Alan had seen this spell before. He found himself glued mothlike to the sight of it as the cold acid of his own actions drained from his limbs and left him shivering.

Move, you bloody fool, he snarled at himself.

He darted forward with a clumsy swipe of the blade at Morris's fingers, but Morris was ready and took two steps back out of reach, now pressing the blue spell to the wound Alan had left in his side.

Healing. As he'd healed Alan's hand once the damage was done.

The spell sank in and was gone. Morris straightened up and stepped toward Alan, already cradling anew. His face was pale and shone with sweat, but he moved as if the knife had never been in him at all.

Lady Dufay moved faster.

The swoop of white fabric was like a swan taking off from the water. Morris growled a curse, and Alan flinched back, and when he recovered Morris was standing trapped with his arms held firmly out on either side, each wrist held in one of the Lady's hands. No way for him to cradle like that. He was still kicking backwards for all he was worth, trying to throw his captor off balance. If he cursed any louder, then the back row of the rapt ice-platform crowd would hear him.

Lady Dufay stood like an oak tree herself. She gave Alan an impatient look. "Well? Get on with it."

Alan's stomach clenched with such abruptness that he nearly retched. There was blood on the knife. There was blood soaking his hand. God, God. To do this *twice,* and to do it the second time to a man held helpless—even such a man as this, who had in his snarling face Alan's death and the deaths of his family, and the small scraping sounds of a blade against the bones and tendons of Alan's hand—

Sin-eater, Alan thought, numb.

This time he drove the knife into Morris's neck. The gush of blood when he drew it out was like warm water from a tap, purple-black in the darkness. Unreal.

Morris choked. Trying to say something. His eyes rolled, and his arms strained against Dufay's implacable grip.

It took a few awful bubbling breaths, and then it was over.

Alan wiped his knife shakily on his skirts and returned it to his pocket. He heard the scratchy thud of Morris's body hitting the ground as Lady Dufay released it, but he was too busy emptying his guts into the reeds to see it happen.

"Oh, settle down," said the Lady. Alan straightened to glare at her, but she wasn't looking at him. She knelt with a hand flat on the stones. "There'll be more of that to come, no doubt."

Yes. No doubt. Alan cast a frantic look across to the stage. The crowd had the quiet of an attentive audience. George's voice was still going. How long had all that taken? It didn't matter.

Alan ran through the pink arch and into the grotto.

As soon as he stepped across the threshold, there was a moment of stunned silence, and then four people began shouting at him at once.

Alan took in the scene—glowing strings, some kind of prison or tether, and none of them were *moving*. He shoved his fingers in his mouth and gave a single sharp whistle. That shut them all up.

"Tell me how to get you out of this," he said.

"Edwin," said Robin at once. "Is he alive? Have they—have they killed him?"

"What—" started Alan.

"I felt someone die," said Jack.

The land. Lady Dufay, soothing it. Perhaps she was still doing so, because she hadn't followed Alan in here.

"I don't think they've done anything to him yet. And that— that was Morris." Alan rubbed his palms on the blasted apron. "Morris is dead."

Another startled silence. Then—"Bastoke and Walter are *going* to kill Edwin, and it won't look like they have, they'll have an illusion up," said Robin, tripping over his words. "Forget about us, go and save him."

"On his *own*?" Jack said sharply.

"He can disrupt the ritual. Perturb it, somehow."

"Perturb this bloody Bridle!" said Violet. "If *you* touch the pillar, Alan, maybe it'll turn the spell in on itself."

"And maybe he'll be trapped too," said Maud. "Isn't there another way?"

Oh, fantastic. Another argument about magical theory. And the only clever one *wasn't here.*

"Wait—if Morris is dead," said Robin, "then this can't be something he was powering directly."

"If it's a trap, could he have laid it here this morning?" said Alan. "Left it for later. Like your illusions, Violet."

"They only work because of the oak-hearts," said Violet. "As Edwin keeps telling us, wood holds magic because magic clings to *life.* This is stone. How could it—"

"*Mostly* stone," said Maud, and Jack said at the same time, "The shells."

A single row of pink and white shells circled the pillar like a ring on a finger. Alan walked between his motionless allies and took hold of Jack's stick, which slipped easily from Jack's grasp when tugged.

He lifted the silver-topped end, took aim, and smashed it right into the closest seashell, which shattered.

The glowing strings blinked into nothing.

Maud's legs buckled. Robin grabbed at her arm and steadied her.

"Thank you, Cesare," said Jack. He bent and rubbed at his own bad leg. "I shudder to think what we owe you after this."

Alan held out the stick. Jack took it.

"Nothing owing," said Alan.

"We have to move," said Robin. "Hawthorn, I hope to God you have a strategy for us, because if not I'm heading up there to strangle them all with my bare hands."

"Violet," said Jack, turning to her. "We'll need a curtain-spell in order to move unseen, and likely a shield after that. And at least one good illusion at the same time, if you can manage it."

"I'm full to bursting." Violet looked radiant with anger. "I can manage all *sorts* of things."

Alan was sent up the other side of the lake, his apron hastily cleaned of blood smudges by a quick spell of Violet's. Nobody watched him as he scurried across the ice bridge on that side. He was a servant, after all. Even when he stepped up onto the braided side of the bridge, like a boy straining for a better view of a parade, he was spared only the smallest of glances and frowns from the magicians nearby. They had better things to look at, after all.

The ice was very cold under Alan's hands, but rough and solid as stone. He wasn't afraid of slipping. And now he could *see*.

Edwin was in the centre of the icy stage. He didn't seem too badly off, at first, except that he'd been stripped to the waist and was white and stiff with cold. He stood with both arms held helpfully out and down as if waiting for a valet to fasten his cufflinks. Someone had drawn a path of red ink down one forearm, a path that went meandering and liquid where it crossed the wrist and the hand.

His brother Walter stood next to him with a small silver knife in one hand and a silver bowl in the other. He traced the knifepoint delicately down Edwin's second arm, and a new line of red sprang up in its wake.

Edwin didn't move. Nor did he cry out. He stared out above the heads of the crowd. Alan watched the steady rise and fall of his chest. How much of this was real? How much of it was the illusion Robin had mentioned? The crowd murmured to one another. Nobody made any motion to help, or to stop this. The atmosphere was that of a huddled group watching a street performer, into whose cup someone had placed a shilling or a wristwatch. Any moment now it would appear again, or perhaps be transformed into a ribbon of silk. Any moment now.

To one side of the Courcey brothers and a few paces back stood Mrs. Vaughn, hands folded in front of her like an elderly schoolmistress keeping watch over her charges. And to their other side, much more prominent, stood George Bastoke.

Bastoke had a palm extended. Floating above it, turning in the light, was a large silver coin. He gave a nod of satisfaction, as

Walter caught the new trickle of Edwin's blood with the lip of the bowl, and broke into a new segment of speech. Alan didn't bother to listen after the first couple of sentences. It was about what he'd expected: sacrifice and power and coming into birth-rights, spoken with the rhythm of ritual, the cadence of Latin chanted at a midnight Mass. Alan half expected him to put the silver disc on his tongue and say something about bread and bodies, blood and wine—it would fit with the rest of this high-handed nonsense, wouldn't it?

Alan needed to be closer to have any hope of perturbing the illusion. He climbed down from the bridge and wormed his way around the edge of the crowd, head bowed, until he was nearly at the front. He didn't dare move too fast in case he caught the eye of anyone on the stage.

And *there* was Lady Dufay. She'd made her way up here, too, to Lady Cheetham's side. Like everyone else, they stood watching the obscene performance. Lady Cheetham—Alan peered around a large lace flourish of bodice, and a gentleman's beard—had a set expression. Alan couldn't see her hands. Could he get to her after all, and tell her that she didn't need to act, that help was on the way? Could he do it without drawing Bastoke's gaze? Damn, *damn*.

Bastoke stopped speaking. Walter Courcey lifted the knife and put the tip over Edwin's heart.

Some more murmuring arose. A young woman near Alan swooned strategically sideways into her partner's embrace, keeping her avid gaze on the stage.

And then nothing happened for a little while, as if the four on the stage were posed waiting to have their photograph taken. Alan stared hard and thought of flowing water, paper loops, but only managed to make the whole scene waver and blur nause-atingly. A very powerful illusion, this one. What was going on behind it? Where was—

A blur of black and white erupted from the crowd very close to Alan, charged up the steps to the stage, and then kept charging, right at Walter and Edwin.

Robin.

Over the crowd's fresh noise came a shout of alarm that sounded like Walter, even though the Walter on the stage hadn't spoken or even moved, and—"Rolfe," barked Bastoke, snapping the fingers of his free hand.

A bolt of golden magic flew from the front row of the crowd and directly at Robin, who had almost reached the Courceys.

It flew right through Robin and out the other side towards Mrs. Vaughn.

She didn't move any more than Walter had, but there was a new cry, short and irritated and female, and suddenly the scene . . . changed.

It was still Edwin and Walter and Mrs. Vaughn. Instead of serene, the old woman looked angry and off-balance, and was patting at her skirts as if to stifle fire. She must have been holding the illusion, and now it was dropped.

Now they could see what was truly there, and—"*Fuck*," Alan said, aghast. Audible dismay rose around and behind him like thunder.

Walter stood with the knife raised and his teeth bared. And Edwin—Edwin was not the resigned, anaemic figure with two thin cuts. He was heaving for breath, swaying on his feet, and his arms were a ravaged mess of blood.

It was hard to keep track of what happened next. Robin ran smack into Walter, who flinched and fumbled the bowl, and shifted the knife as if to drive it right into Robin's face. *Alan* flinched, despite knowing that this Robin was an illusion. And indeed the knife sank through Robin like mist.

In the same moment, an exact copy of Robin seemed to step out of the air itself, behind Walter and Edwin. His face was a map of fury and he was holding Jack's stick. He drew his arms back and swung it at Walter's head like a cricketer driving for the boundaries.

Alan was close enough to hear the extremely non-illusory *thunk* as it connected.

Walter reeled, sank to his knees, then collapsed on his side with bowl and knife clattering from his nerveless hands.

"Violet!" shouted Robin. He threw himself between Bastoke and Edwin. Bastoke, recovered from the initial shock of events, was on the verge of completing a cradle.

The curtain-spell dropped—it must have taken incredible concentration to keep it up while also manipulating that illusion of Robin—showing Violet and Maud standing at the side of the stage. Dark and glittering ropes of magic erupted from Violet's hands and flew at George Bastoke, wrapping around his body and limbs like covetous, angry snakes. His cradle died as his arms were forced to his sides. His face twisted in pure, outraged disbelief as he lost his balance and toppled to the ground like a felled tree.

The coin jolted out of his hand, rolled, and came to a halt against Walter's unmoving body.

Relief hit Alan like a cold flannel.

"Jack!" cried Lady Cheetham. "Oh—well done, darling."

Alan looked over. Jack had taken advantage of the chaos to surprise the front-row Cooper, Rolfe, and was roughly tying the man's hands together behind his back with—was that Jack's bow tie? Seemed to be. His collar was in chaos.

There were probably more Coopers around, and the hesitation of seeing their leader incapacitated wouldn't last long. Alan dashed for the nearest steps to the stage, already yanking his apron off. He got his teeth into the fabric and managed an uneven tear with the rough strength of urgency. Good enough. Two pieces instead of one.

"Arms," he panted, coming up next to Edwin. "Stop the bleeding."

Edwin was the colour of rotten milk, his eyelids fluttering, but he submitted to Alan tying the fabric tight around his bleeding arms. His skin was clammy and cold and Jesus fuck, there was so much *blood*. Robin had an arm around his waist, and it seemed to be the only thing keeping him upright.

Concentrating on this task, Alan was only just aware of Mrs. Vaughn running past them and falling to her knees by the unconscious figure of Walter Courcey.

"*Stupid*," she hissed, "you stupid man, how could you let them—"

She might wake him up by magic, Alan supposed, but what difference would it make? The ritual had been stopped. Nobody would be killing Edwin to complete it. And Lady Cheetham could keep an eye on them in the meantime.

"Alan."

He turned to see Jack, who took over the makeshift bandaging of Edwin's other arm with military ease.

"Go and see if you can find Freddy Oliver," Jack ordered him. "And his mother, Margaret. She'll be able to heal Edwin if anyone can. I'll get the contract pieces and we'll meet them at the oak as soon as we've explained things to my mother's guests. In fact, if she can—"

A high, short scream pierced the air.

Maud.

Alan jerked around as several more screams came from the audience, as if Maud had been in an echoing cave. The green figure of Maud stood—untouched, safe—with her hands pressed over her mouth and her eyes wide with horror.

She was staring at Seraphina Vaughn, whose hands held the hilt of the knife of the Last Contract.

And who had plunged that knife, deep and sure, into Walter Courcey's heart.

Time did something strange. Alan felt a tickle of wind on his face: cold air, moving up and away. His nose itched. The shouts and cries of the crowd were hollow and distant. No matter how many times he blinked, the scene was the same. Walter dead. Mrs. Vaughn, now tugging the bloodstained knife free of his body and setting it neatly on his chest as if signalling she was done with her meal.

"Why?" Maud said, small but clear. "Why would you—"

"As always," said Mrs. Vaughn, "I find I must do everything myself." She glanced over at them, and her gaze found Edwin. "If your blood was good enough to start this, boy, then your brother's should finish it off nicely."

"Maud, the *coin*," said Jack sharply, already moving towards the old woman, but Mrs. Vaughn cradled a spell and flung her hands wide. Both Jack and Maud flew back two feet and crashed heavily to the ground.

"I told you I will not surrender my chance," said Mrs. Vaughn. "You really should have listened."

She set the bowl on Walter's body. Placed the coin into the bowl. And then touched them both with the bloodstained knife.

"There," said the last member of the Forsythia Club.

And light erupted under her hands.

30

There was no coin, no cup, and no knife when the light died.

There was only Mrs. Vaughn climbing to her feet. In her hand was a chunk of silvery rock. The fabled allstone of the fae was less impressive than Alan had imagined: the size of a large apple, its shape was uneven and globular like a piece of candle-drip broken off from the taper. It was bright as if freshly polished, but it no longer gave off its own glow.

Mrs. Vaughn inhaled long and slow. Her satisfied gaze fell onto the stone.

"What's happening?" said Violet. "I can feel . . ."

"So can I," said Edwin. His voice was hollow. "It's *going.*"

Alan felt nothing at all. It was clear he was in the minority. The noise from the magicians on the ice was louder now, and small glimmers of colour sprang up everywhere—magicians frantically testing their magic as they felt it begin to drain from them. Many of them looked dizzy or ill. Even Edwin, who couldn't afford to look any worse, put a bloody hand to his bare chest as if feeling the wound that Walter had never had a chance to inflict.

"A little more light, I think," said Mrs. Vaughn.

She looked up, and her brow creased. She made no cradles, spoke no words, didn't even reach out her free hand to the sky.

Alan hadn't realised there was a layer of cloud cover until it began to draw back. Someone was washing the dirt from a grimy window or tugging at dust sheets draped over old paintings. Slowly the full brilliance of the night sky revealed itself:

stars and stars and yet more stars, spilled like powdered sugar across the dark. The moon hummed with fat, white glow.

"Fuck," muttered Violet. "That's good theatre, isn't it?"

It was. The alarmed crowd had fallen into the quiet of wonder. Into it, Mrs. Vaughn spoke, and her voice was as clear as if she stood directly next to Alan.

"You see? A piece of magic that might have taken ten magicians, or twenty, done by one alone. And that with only a fraction of the power that is yet to come." She continued to watch the sky. "Look," she said, a perfectly audible whisper. "That is what we are. We deserve to be seen. We *do* hide our light under bushels, and we are scared of unbusheling when we should celebrate it. The danger of being few has always been the risk that we will be punished and hunted if we are feared by the many. So. *Let* them fear us. What can they do to us, if we can do this?"

"Anyone have any ideas?" Alan muttered. There hadn't been a real plan for what they would do if the ritual was *completed,* beyond what Jack had drawlingly suggested: *improvise and pray.*

"The longer this goes on, the more magic she has and the less the rest of us do," said Edwin. He was still papery pale and leaning hard on Robin. "I wish I could *think.*"

Maud met Alan's eyes and a hand went to her thigh. Her dress, too, had been given pockets. Alan had never seen Maud Blyth look so utterly without light.

"If someone else can distract her—" she started.

"*I can't hold Bastoke,*" said Violet in alarm.

Alan turned, heart kicking into a new pace. The magical ropes that she'd produced were thinning and fading, and abruptly they disappeared altogether. George Bastoke climbed to his feet. The only consolation was that he, too, looked shaken and horrified as he stared at his hands. Magic would be leaving him like everyone else.

Still, he cradled a spell. His motions were tiny, and the white spark between his hands was barely visible, but it was there.

Fear tightened around Alan's throat, and he waited, trying to predict what Bastoke would do. Something to seize control of the situation, no doubt.

Bastoke moved behind Mrs. Vaughn with his hand half-hidden by his side, pinched the white spark between two of his fingers, and flicked. A motion that would be barely noticeable to anyone not on the stage. Alan was ready to dodge, but the spark floated towards Seraphina Vaughn, who now held the allstone in both hands and seemed to be savouring the moment while she decided what piece of wonder to commit next.

The white spark landed between her shoulders like a fly. Bastoke closed his hand into a fist.

Mrs. Vaughn swayed forward, then back. The allstone remained clutched in her own hands as she toppled and fell. It even remained in her hands as her body went lax, a look of indignant surprise on her face, directed up at the stars she had unveiled.

"Ah," said Bastoke. "A pity."

He leaned down and picked up the allstone. He did not seem particularly moved by the fact that his two most prominent allies were now corpses strewn in the centre of the stage he'd created.

"Fucking sodding fucking hell," said Jack.

Alan agreed. So, by their expressions, did everyone else.

"A pity," Bastoke continued, holding the allstone in one hand, "that a misguided old woman should believe *she* has the ability to wield all the power of British magic without consequence." Calm as ever. Almost sorrowful. Alan wanted to rip the bastard's smooth tongue clean out of his head.

"No sudden moves, Robin, *Maud*. Now, Edwin," said Jack, low and fast, "can the contract still be transferred to the oak, if we take it from him now?"

"I . . ." Edwin swallowed, eyes on Bastoke, who was telling the crowd that everything would be *fine. He* had this magic under control. *He* would not falter, his heart would not give out under the strain of it. "I don't think it matters now *what*

symbolises the Last Contract," Edwin said reluctantly. "It's
been reversed. The magic of the fae is—remaking itself. *Rectification*. Now the process has begun, it wants to be whole, as the
contract pieces are whole."

"He's right," said Violet, looking at her hands. "It *feels* like
that."

"Then what?" Alan demanded. "Surely we want it out of the
bastard's hands anyway."

"Yes," said Maud.

"He stopped Mrs. Vaughn's heart," said Robin to Edwin.
"Can you stop his?"

Edwin winced. "I'm almost drained. Haven't enough left to
nudge a leaf. Violet?"

Violet shook her head miserably.

Jack exhaled, long and slow, as if he were about to commence
lecturing them on their uselessness as troops. But instead he levered himself to his feet and walked forward, with no attempt at
either speed or stealth, to the front of the stage two yards from
Bastoke.

"Christ," said Alan. He went to follow Jack, but Robin grabbed
his wrist.

"No sudden moves," said Robin. "Let Hawthorn—let him
try. This is his land, and Bastoke is his kinsman. It might still
mean something."

"Cousin," said Bastoke.

Jack had his hands raised. He was also holding his weight
stiffly, as if feeling the lack of something to lounge against. His
leg. Just what they fucking needed.

"George," he said. "You've done enough. And you know
magic mingled like this—can't be returned." He spoke as if
avoiding potholes on the street. "Can't you feel it?"

"I have it under control," said Bastoke. The allstone—Alan
blinked. Was it truly glowing now? Were those yet more white
sparks dancing up from it, curling around Bastoke's hand?
The uneven surface made it hard to tell. Alan's mouth dried up

imagining one of those deadly white sparks flying onto Jack. Stopping his heart. Just like that.

Bastoke said, "I was—born to do this," and this time Alan heard the slightest bump in Bastoke's voice, too, as if he were fighting harder than usual for his elegantly unruffled tone.

Jack smiled the cruellest and least forgiving of his smiles. He and Bastoke looked like eerie bookends: two sketches of aristocracy done by someone with a keen eye and no interest in flattery.

"Nothing about your blood makes you more able to handle this than anyone else," said Jack. "If Elsie couldn't, *you* certainly—" And he stopped, lips firming with pain.

After everything, still, the bind.

He'd said enough. Bastoke's mask cracked a fraction with anger, and even as he opened his mouth to reply there was a sudden *whiteness* that slammed Alan's eyes shut and seared a glowing line across his eyelids. A stifled yelp from Violet. The beginnings of yells from down on the ice were drowned by something even worse: a deep, ugly, unbelievably loud *crack* that started in Alan's shoes and climbed all the bones of his body.

Alan forced his eyes open. That line of brightness still carved itself across his vision, glowing brown and white when he blinked. The crowd was a blur struggling to form in the well-lit night.

"Oh God," said Robin hoarsely. "The ice."

Another palpable crack, this time followed horribly by a lingering vibration. The movement of the crowd became fragmented. The ice was *splitting,* breaking into large pieces set adrift on the lake. To Alan's horror, one of those pieces was unevenly populated enough that its balance was off: it began, slowly, to tilt. People slid. And screamed.

Bastoke's mask had fallen further: he stared at the tilting ice in a way that said he hadn't intended to do that. He *had* lost control of the magic he'd pulled from the allstone. And was now losing control of his all-important audience, given that he was on the verge of plunging some of them into the water.

Maud cupped her hands to her mouth. *"Everyone off the lake!"* she screamed. Some of the closer people heard her, but her voice barely carried. She took breath to try again.

"No."

If the crack of the ice had set hooks in one's bones, this grabbed them and shook. It was Jack. His arms flew out to either side as if to keep back two walls that were trying to fall in on him, and his voice seemed to grind and grate.

No. That was the ground; the ice. The shake went on and on, and the screams of the crowd grew even more alarmed. Twin bottlenecks of panicked exit had formed at the bridges. Those people not stuck on fragmented islands of ice hadn't needed Maud to tell them to get the hell back onto solid ground.

And then the shaking stopped.

By now Alan's vision was mostly clear. He stared. The tilted part of the ice had—frozen, in fact, at its angle. It was tilting no further. Nor were any broken parts of the ice sheet moving against one another.

Finally, it was beginning to feel cold. The chill ached upwards from Alan's feet.

"I think—he froze the lake," said Edwin. "*Completely* froze it."

"Which *he*?" said Violet.

Alan stared at Jack's shaking shoulders and knew the answer. Bastoke recovered quickly.

"The danger has passed," he said in his magic-enhanced speech that carried across the lake. "I will not let you come to harm."

But there was wariness, finally, in his face when he looked at Jack now.

"Well, well, cousin," said Bastoke. "Where did that little trick of yours come from, I wonder? Do you intend to fight me for this?" He held out the allstone. The white light was stronger, and it flowed and pulsed—now illuminating the silver, now Bastoke's hand, as if magic were passing back and forth between man and stone.

Jack looked barely less shocked by what had happened. He

was putting even more weight on his good leg. His hands still shook as he made a cradle, and waited, and—nothing.

No magic. Whatever the trick was, he couldn't repeat it.

Relief shadowed Bastoke's expression.

"It shouldn't be fought over," said Jack. He let his hands fall. "It shouldn't exist, George."

That endless pulse of pale magic was faster now, brighter. When Bastoke smiled, Alan almost expected to see it come flooding out between his lips.

"Alan," said Maud, suddenly at his side. Her hand was in her pocket. "I—I'll need to be closer."

"You need a diversion," said Alan.

She bit her lip, bleak and determined. And nodded. Alan thought about animals racing through a ship and Maud Blyth dragging a thieving journalist into her quest. The only part of it he regretted was betraying her, and here he was, setting it right.

Alan unfastened the black skirt and removed the cap. He ran a hand through his hair, getting at the itch of his scalp. If he looked at Jack, he didn't know what his face would do.

So he didn't. He walked right up between Lord Hawthorn and his cousin Bastoke, and raised his best East End insolence in Bastoke's direction.

"Oi. Remember me, you pox-ridden donkey's prick?"

Shock was followed quickly by contempt. Oh, yes. Bastoke remembered. Alan kept on before Bastoke could gather his wits: "And if you're wondering where your pal Morris is in all this, I'll tell you: I cut his throat. He's *dead*. He won't be torturing people on your behalf anymore." Alan's heart sang wildly. He grinned. "Guess you'll have to get your precious hands dirty and do it yourself."

Bastoke's face creased into deep and thwarted annoyance. His gaze bored into Alan's and the glow around his hand had sparks of red in it now, within the white. Whatever was coming, it was not going to be as quiet and small as stopping Alan's heart.

Alan inhaled as if before a dive into water, and braced himself.

A metal sound clapped short and sharp in his ears.

Bastoke jerked back, suddenly slumped over and stumbling. His hand fell. The allstone tumbled from it and hit the icy ground, then slid. Bastoke made as if to fumble after it, but instead stopped and pressed his hand to the wound in his shoulder, grimacing in silent agony. The glow had winked out. Blood seeped through his fingers.

Maud lowered her pearl-handled pistol.

"*Maudie,*" said Robin, behind them.

Bastoke seethed in a new breath and tried again to bend for the allstone—Alan, closest, darted in and delivered two kicks. The first was to the allstone itself, and carefully aimed. The stone skittered across the stage to Jack, who trapped it beneath his own shoe like a schoolmaster ending a game of football.

The second kick was to the back of Bastoke's knee, collapsing one of the man's legs beneath him. Alan wasn't fool enough to stick around in hitting range, even with a man who'd been shot. He scurried back a few steps, giving Maud a clear line where she'd moved to Jack's side.

"Maud, cover him."

"Stay right where you are," said Maud, levelling the pistol at Bastoke.

Bastoke raised his head. He was on one knee, still clutching his shoulder, and all semblance of composure had gone from his face. His lips peeled back from his teeth, and—

"Oh Jesus Christ," said Alan.

A dragon's breath of white magic misted from Bastoke's mouth. More of it seeped from the wound on his shoulder, as if it had replaced his blood. It gathered between his hands when he brought them together. Fingers moving. A cradle. The magic was the hideous, cloudy purple of breath-starved lips.

Whatever power he'd pulled from the allstone before dropping it, he still had it.

"You—will *not* ruin this for me, Hawthorn," Bastoke ground out. "Not after so long."

His hands lifted towards Jack and Maud.

So, Alan thought. And then didn't think—only moved, once again placing himself directly in Bastoke's line of sight, just as the spell erupted forth.

A paper loop. O Madonna santa, let this work.

The magic hit Alan like a boiling wave of pain.

31

Seventeen years between acts of magic. Jack wondered if it was a record.

In fact, he was still wondering if what he'd done was magic at all. There had been no clauses, no careful construction of what he wished to do, no expression of it in the language of cradles. Anger and fear had opened their eyes within him and yelled, as one yells frustration in an empty room, expecting no reply.

Something had replied.

The *Hall* had replied.

If it was magic, then it was the sort performed by child magicians in the days before their lock ceremonies, when magic showed itself like a flash of light in the dark. Standing there with his hands thrown out, Jack had felt briefly, excruciatingly young. Aware of the ley line beneath his feet and even more aware of the Hall's distress: their guests, to whom they owed protection, had been endangered. Jack's awareness was dragged to that fact like soft skin across sandpaper.

And so he had filled up. That was the only way to put it. A creek bed, empty so long it had forgotten its purpose, suddenly found itself in full flood. The magic had gone down him and through him and did what he wanted before he could properly form the thought of wanting it. He'd saved lives, or at least altered the world so that they were no longer in danger.

And now Alanzo Rossi was saving his.

A noise punched from Jack's throat when the magic hit Alan, who bent double with a grunt. A bolt of humid purple erupted back in George's direction as if Alan had been a mirror and struck George right in the chest.

George crumpled to the ground. Jack did not particularly care if he was dead, though he supposed that someone should check. Later. Alan, the perturbator, had directed magic back at the caster.

"Alan?"

No response. The next moment, Alan, too, collapsed to the ground and didn't move.

Jack's heart tried to slam itself in three different directions. He took in the battlefield at a glance. The lake was frozen safe, and the crowd of magicians was neither silent nor yelling. George was down and no Coopers were coming out of the woodwork to display disastrous initiative. Walter and Mrs. Vaughn were dead. Maud had a gun and Edwin was still on his feet.

Jack lifted his shoe from the allstone. "*Nobody* touches this," he snarled to Maud, as the most likely to try picking it up out of helpfulness, and moved to kneel at Alan's side.

Jack should have revoked George's fucking guest-right as soon as they had the allstone away from him. But he'd had the fool thought that it would *hurt* more, be a more satisfying vengeance, to make George stand there bleeding and account for what he'd done, in front of the audience whose magic he'd stolen and whose admiration he craved.

So he hadn't spoken. And George had acted, and Alan had paid for it.

"Don't!" said Violet.

Jack's hand jerked back unwillingly before it could make contact. Alan's body had the tight curl of painful unconsciousness. His grimacing face glistened with sickly sweat, his hands were fists, and the occasional terrible breath rattled through his nose.

"Violet," Jack gritted out.

"This happened in Spinet," said Violet. She sank to her knees on Alan's other side. "When he couldn't perturb all of the magic

from a warding, he—absorbed it, somehow. It tried to escape
into me and Edwin when we touched him. Like we were sponges
and he was a pool of spilled milk."

"So what did you do?"

"Nothing." She frowned down at Alan. Light caught on tear
tracks, dried on her cheeks. "It settled down. Eventually. I think
it went back into the house."

"I'm *not* touching him with the allstone," snapped Jack.
"Even if it is where that magic came from. For all we know, it'll
make it worse."

Absorption of magic. He closed his eyes and, fumblingly,
reached for the Hall. Instead of stretching a disused muscle it
now felt like straining one taxed to the point of trembling. But
he tried.

*Will you take it from him? Take it into the ley lines, like Du-
fay's. Let it be taken in and untwisted. Fae magic into land magic.*

He didn't know if he was feeling anything or just wishing
that he did. Was Alan's body relaxing? Were his breaths coming
more evenly?

Violet touched Alan's shoulder hesitantly. She frowned, but
didn't take her fingers away.

"I don't know. It feels different—"

"*Lord Hawthorn.*"

A loud throat-clearing sounded, with impatience suggesting
it had been going for some time.

Jack looked up. Richard Prest, the Deputy Chief Minister of
the Assembly, stood there, along with another two men of similar age. One of them kept glancing at Walter Courcey's and Mrs.
Vaughn's bodies as if they might leap up at any moment.

Some of the audience had decided it was now safe to stop being an audience and demand answers.

"Lord Hawthorn," Prest repeated, frosty as his own misting
breath. "I trust you will explain what the blazes has happened
here, and *where our magic has gone.*"

Prest swept an illustrative arm out over the lake. Hands were
moving in cradles everywhere, with no spells coming to life. At

least two rows of people were crowded up against the edge of the stage, waiting with demanding eagerness to see how their leaders were going to fix this. Jack found his parents, their heads bent together in conversation that had the look of the few arguments of theirs he'd ever seen: his father abrasive and loud with anger, and his mother becoming increasingly calm and implacable in response. Dufay was still with them.

"*You* can all go—"

"Violet," said Jack, cutting her off. Much as he sympathised with her habit of stripping men with her tongue and would normally have sat back and enjoyed it, there were still plenty of ways for this night to go wrong. They'd need all the goodwill they could scrape together.

Alan's eyes were still closed. Violet's hand was tight on his shoulder. He could have been a boy in a fairy tale, fallen through a broken mirror and cursed with endless sleep. Jack had wealth and title and could do nothing for him at all.

Jack stood. He wanted to take the world between his hands and snap it like a dry branch, and Prest had handily presented himself for snapping.

"*Our* magic?" he growled. "Our magic was a gift of the fae, as you of the Assembly knew when you granted my cousin George and his allies your blessing to find the Last Contract. And now they have taken a magician's life and used that death to pull that gift back into the stone from whence it came."

"It's all in there?" said one of the men. His cheeks were nearly crimson with emotion above his greying moustache. "Then we shall have it back."

And he strode with purpose towards the allstone, which still lay abandoned on the ice where Jack had left it.

"Don't be a damned fool!" Jack tried to shove forward to stop him, but his bad leg cramped sharply with the sudden movement. He stopped with a curse to shake it out.

Meanwhile, Prest had hurried after his colleague and eagerly elbowed the man out of the way. "Leave it to me, Terrence. It's my responsibility. After all, *I* will soon be—ah, there we are—"

Prest straightened. The look on his face was already melting from hunger to horror.

"I—" he said.

Magic choked the air. Quite literally choked: the back of Jack's tongue was alive with a coppery taste and fizzing so hard it was like a new secret-bind being laid. Soon it became like trying to breathe in sparkling water. Jack's lungs stabbed and ached. Violet was having a violent sneezing fit. A large cluster of magicians, emboldened by the fact that several of their leaders had broken the unspoken barrier and walked onto the stage, were milling close as if to do the same. Most of them were now coughing.

Between Jack's eyes and the unveiled sky, the night took on an oily shimmer that pulsed in soft waves, like wind billowing a gauze so thin it was almost invisible. Jack's ears popped painfully and then went dull and pressured, his blood thundering up to his face as if he'd been hanging upside down for several minutes.

And then finally—it felt like finally, though surely it had been only seconds since Prest picked up the allstone—the shimmer began to thicken.

Breathing became even more laborious; Jack couldn't tell if the spots of light in his vision were magic or an imminent swoon. The air around and above them was puckering like a skin on hot milk, gathering and thickening and darkening along what Jack couldn't help but think of as an enormous *seam,* and he remembered all over again that this was the magic of beings whose reality was not a human reality. Who had removed themselves entirely from this world and, presumably, gone to another.

"Prest!" Jack shouted with a difficult lungful of breath. "Drop the bloody thing!"

There was no sign that Prest heard him. One of the noises that Jack was hearing now, past the painful pressure that dulled his ears, was the violent chatter of the man's teeth. Prest gripped the allstone as if it were the only thing keeping him alive.

Perhaps it was. Jack didn't care. Maud had probably reached her limit on shooting people, but *Jack* hadn't. He could—

"Give us a hand, Hawthorn," said Robin.

Jack turned in time for Robin to pass him Edwin's arm and half of Edwin's weight. The makeshift bandages were stained dark brown now, and Edwin's eyes were open and as bright as needles.

Then Robin strode calmly into that invisible storm of chaotic magic and punched the Deputy Chief Minister in the head.

As in the Barrel, he delivered it beautifully. Prest was out cold before he hit the icy stage.

The air returned to normal with the suddenness of snapped elastic.

The allstone rolled a little way and then stopped. It was the wrong shape to get too far.

Edwin, hand clawed around Jack's arm, gave a tiny hiccuping laugh. Jack understood why. As serious as the situation was, it was also taking on a faint resemblance to a game of rugby where the only rules anyone could remember were *tackle* and *grab*.

Robin, the rugby star, made no attempt to pick up the ball. He stood guard. He looked at the milling magicians who had prudently paused in their attempt to rush the stage and recover their stolen power.

"I think we'll all leave the silver lump full of dangerous magic alone for now," Robin said firmly.

"Did anybody bring a cork-lined box?" Edwin murmured. "Or do we wrap it in someone's skirt?"

"Perhaps we can still take it to the oak," Jack said. "The land might take this magic as well."

"I . . . don't like the idea," said Edwin. "It was worse for Prest than it was for Bastoke, and I don't think it was because Bastoke's the stronger magician. There's more magic in it now. It's *still filling up*. It would have begun with all the magicians here tonight, but there are so many more of them in Britain. And if the ley lines absorb it, who says we ever get it back?"

"I don't think you do anyway," said Jack. He didn't bother to soften it. He forced himself not to look at where Alan lay. "Not without—what happened to Elsie. You said it yourself. It's been made whole, and won't be divided again."

Edwin stared at him, eyes wide with dismay. Before he could reply, a startled yelp sounded—Maud—and turned to a sound of outright pain.

George was on his feet again. Bleeding and magicless, he had somehow managed to wrench Maud's pearl-handled pistol away from her. At least that was all he'd done: she was clutching her wrist, wincing, but looked otherwise unhurt.

The small, pretty weapon looked absurd in George's hand, though there was nothing laughable about the way he moved it back and forth between Robin and Jack as if unable to decide which of them he most wanted to destroy.

Jack felt—something. Not a change in the air, this time. Deeper and more internal, or perhaps more earth-bound, as if he stood with his back turned to a river and became aware of it flowing faster.

A delicate crack of light glowed on George's forehead and was gone. The gun had come to a halt pointed at Jack, and George . . . did not move so much as his finger where it gripped the trigger.

His face was ravaged by exhaustion and anger, his gaze poured hate at Jack, but he did not move.

"*This has gone far enough,*" said the Countess of Cheetham.

Her voice had sea-cave echoes. Jack stared at her where she stood, still close to the stage but not on it. She really had been keeping it all under wraps: all the hurt, all the grief, all the violence. Jack had never in his life seen his mother look like this. Nor, by the way he was staring, had Lord Cheetham.

She took a deep breath and was Polly again, though icy as the lake beneath her feet.

"George Bastoke," she said. "You will not lift another finger against me and mine. I revoke your guest-right. You are welcome no longer on the land of Cheetham Hall. You are decidedly *un*welcome."

Maud, always braver than anyone expected, came and took her gun back. George's fingers did not resist her, though his eyes darted to her with hate and fear. Maud gave him a thin smile and pocketed the pistol.

"There. Whenever you're ready, Lady Cheetham," said Maud.

A chunk of ice exploded at George's feet, and he was abruptly released. He swayed on his feet. And then he turned, awkward with pain, and ran. Jack could feel the land directing George as he fled, guiding his feet where it wanted him to go. Off the stage—the crowd drew back hurriedly to make room—and off the lake, not by the bridge but the closest bank where frosted reeds stood motionless. George stumbled across grass.

He'd moved out of the well-lit areas designated for the gala, so it was difficult for Jack to make out what happened next. Above the shadowy figure of George appeared a new shadow, like a small and shifting cloud. *Swarming*. It was drawing down, and closer.

There was a short, muffled cry as the shadows merged and became for a while a single, thrashing, collapsing shape.

And then silence.

Jack felt it as a knot of vindictive pain deep in the Hall's land tightened for a moment and then released itself and was gone.

"All right, I officially don't understand what's happening," said Robin. His voice cut loudly across the quiet. "Hawthorn— you froze the lake. Have you your magic back again? And Lady Cheetham still has hers?"

"Only them. Because of where we are," said Edwin.

"I don't think it's that simple," said Jack.

This was the shape he had been grasping at ever since his mother told him about repairing the Hall's hurt. He looked down at his mother, who now had the faintly embarrassed air of any hostess who'd been forced to banish a guest for bad behaviour. And he looked at Dufay, who was looking back. "The gifts of the dawn and the wages of the dusk. The ley lines belong to every magician, you said? Their magic was ours before the fae ever arrived in this place. Wages, not gifts. Every spell an agreement between a magician and the land."

He waited for Dufay to nod.

"Edwin. Do one of Flora Sutton's spells."

Edwin blinked at him.

"Think about drawing on Sutton, if that helps. At a distance. Just as you did in London."

"We're not even on the same ley line," said Edwin.

"It won't matter. Don't think about cradles—you've broken a priez-vous without them, haven't you? Think about that second language."

"I can't—"

"You can." Jack was far from as certain as his tone suggested. But it was the tone that was important when telling a soldier that he *could* strap on his helmet and go into a fight. Jack cut his eyes to the magicless, agitated crowd and added, quieter, "And if you can, then others might be able to learn."

Edwin was silent a few heartbeats longer. Jack didn't blame him. They were lucky Edwin had walked away from the Barrel at all, and Jack was telling him to replicate it.

Edwin closed his eyes. His grip on Jack's arm loosened, and he lifted his other hand. Several long, long moments passed. Several more.

"I *say*—" said someone in the stair crowd, in tones of complaint, and Violet shushed them harshly.

A tiny crease appeared in Edwin's brow. Lines beside his lips. He moved his fingers in a fluid motion like sleepy cradlespeech, set them to his bandaged wrist, and drew them along his arm.

Blue light followed in their wake.

When Edwin opened his eyes, more than the new furrow vanished from his expression, as if half of his pain had disappeared as well. Perhaps it had. That spell had the look of healing to it.

"Good, excellent, glad that worked, whatever it was," said Robin in a rapid undertone. "Now. Would someone like to tell me what to do with *this*?"

This was the allstone. Jack had the desperate wish to be back on a ship and able to throw the damn thing into the depths of the ocean, never to be seen again. But who knew what effect that much magic would have on *any* place. Leaving a mark on ley lines wouldn't be the half of it.

Jack looked at Edwin, and then at Violet—who was still seated next to Alan's unconscious form, and who cradlespoke *no change*. No despair; no relief. Jack was a lighthouse himself, now, spinning and seeking in the dark. He turned back to his mother and Dufay.

"If we can't reverse what was done to the Last Contract," he said, "then we will break it."

Dufay's eyebrows rose. She didn't bother with stairs, simply hauled herself up onto the stage by grabbing its edge like the pommel of a saddle. Her face was both more ancient and more girlish, and for once there was more curiosity in it than judgement.

She shook her sleeves into neat folds. Suddenly those robes did not look ridiculous at all, flowing white and green against the ice. Suddenly, despite the chaos and the blood and the rugby-match air, this was *ceremony*.

"And do you speak for all magicians, son of my line?"

For all magicians. The irony nearly choked Jack. He barely deserved to speak on behalf of his own estate.

He looked a question at Edwin that was trying very hard not to be a plea.

"It's your party, Hawthorn," said Edwin. With a strong unspoken edge of *you enjoy politics and I would rather bury myself in sand than speak in public.*

"Stop bloody waffling and get on with it, Hawthorn," came a loud Somerset voice from the crowd. "The wife's not enjoying this cold."

Thank God for Pete Manning. Jack turned to direct his best facsimile of his usual arrogant stare at where the man's voice had come from, and felt instantly better. Politics. Very well. George had been right about spectacle serving a purpose. Jack might have spent years building himself a shell of uncaring about other people's opinions, but ceremony needed a voice.

Jack nodded Robin out of the way. Perhaps it would be more

impressive if he attempted a levitation spell, like George had with the coin, to hold the allstone aloft.

No. Sod it. It could stay on the ground.

He had no magical amplification for his voice, either, but the crowd hushed quickly and he felt the intense pull of their listening.

"I don't know precisely what George Bastoke told you. But here is the truth: This stone is the Last Contract between the magicians of this land and the fae, and it contained—*contains*—all the magic they left for us, to be used by the few in the service of the many. That magic has been pulled out of you and is being pulled from every magician in Britain." He paused, not sure if he should say the next part, but he owed more than half-truths. And the secret-bind wouldn't get in the way here. "I do not know if it can be returned or regenerated. I do not believe it can. And as it is now, it can only be wielded by one person, and—such a thing should not exist. Even if it could be controlled."

They'd felt the lake crack. They'd seen what happened when Prest picked it up. The spectacle was already on Jack's side there.

Still. Politics was politics, after all.

Jack said, as dry and lordly as he could: "Would anyone like to express a dissenting opinion?"

Several someones got halfway there, Jack could see. Lord Cheetham certainly looked as though he were thinking about it. But Jack stared his father down, and Lord Cheetham slowly shook his head.

So.

"Now what?" Jack asked Dufay. It was more her party than his.

"I suppose one member of each family—"

"Oh, damn the bloodlines," said Violet suddenly. She stood from Alan's side and came up next to Hawthorn, all of her stage presence pulled around her like a brilliant cloak. "This is a fairy tale. It's all symbols. All we need is three. Come on, Edwin."

Edwin stepped up as if he'd been waiting for the cue. He was still pale, but far more alive.

"Lady Dufay?" said Edwin. "We wish to return the gifts of

the dawn. We have not upheld our end of the Last Contract, and this magic . . . no longer suits the society that we have become, headed by people who hunger for power to its own ends, instead of its use in safeguarding. We have changed too much. It's not your fault."

Jack would never have thought to put it that way. But Dufay's expression had hints of an ancient, bewildered pain, and he knew that Edwin was right. The fae had assumed that mortal society would remain exactly as it had been when they left. But the distance between those who had power and those who had none had widened, and the willingness of leaders to take responsibility—for land, for their own actions, for anyone else— had withered.

If it had ever been there at all.

Dufay said, "And if the darkness is coming for you?"

"You mean this *wasn't it*?" said Violet.

Edwin was unshaken. "Then we will need our own stars to see by. You told us that and we didn't listen." He took a breath. With his thin pallor and his own blue eyes he looked, fleetingly, far closer to a relation of Dufay than Jack ever had. He looked halfway fae himself.

Edwin said, "We, the magicians of this land, accept only the wages of the dusk. Everyone bears their own cost."

It sounded right. Scoop out the rot, Jack thought, and hope there's enough left to heal.

"I accept," said the Lady of the Allstone.

There was a long pause. The allstone itself did nothing at all.

"Now what?" said Jack.

"Unmake it," said Dufay. "I can't. It was—of me—for too long. And the wages of the dusk are not mine to draw on."

"Unmake. . . ." Edwin swallowed. "Yes. All right."

"Wait," said Violet. "Breaking the contract—we're not going to suddenly thaw the lake? Should we clear everyone off?"

"No," said Edwin. "Hawthorn didn't use *this* magic at all, did he?"

This time he closed his eyes only a moment. No inky storm

clouds boiled around him, and no golden lightning tore through their reality. But the spell gathering around his fingers was the Barrel's destruction in miniature.

Edwin Courcey picked up the Last Contract and it turned to dust in his hand.

From the dust rose a pillar of light that soared higher than the eye could follow, almost too bright to look at where it lay against the stars, like a slick of brilliant water catching sunlight where it crossed dark stone. It happened before Jack could finish a breath.

And when he did finish it, he was knocked back and off his feet. It felt like a giant hand, an unstoppable wind. It blasted out from the silver pillar, which was even now shimmering into nothing like a firework—like dust, in truth.

Nobody was left standing. The wind, too, died quickly.

And then there was stillness.

Jack looked around. A post-theatre kind of crowd noise was rising, although instead of the theatre lights coming up at the end of a play or a symphony, the opposite had happened. The tree-strung colours were gone, and even the bright lanterns that contained the Hall's diverted guidelights were dimmer. He wondered how much of Cheetham Hall's magic, that mingling of the two forms, would now be gone.

Everyone was climbing to their feet.

Everyone but Alan, who continued to lie unmoving.

Jack went over and knelt by Alan's side. It was more like a collapse of his knees. His chest was tight with anguish and he felt unmoored in time, as several of his memories fought to overlay themselves on this scene. The first time he ever saw this man, lying unconscious on the floor of an ocean liner's suite, having drunk from tainted whisky meant for Jack. Alan asleep in Jack's townhouse with his memory straining to pull itself back together.

Elsie curled up beneath the Lady's Oak, near death from building a wall around their broken magic to protect him. Then, Jack had called on the Hall for help dragging her back from the brink of death. It was the last act of magic that he had performed until this night—and like tonight's, it had been a magic performed entirely from instinct, running along a path older and deeper than any fae bargain.

He'd said, *Take whatever you need from me.*

Jack took hold of Alan's cold wrist and reached out his awareness one more time to the land, swollen and alive, beneath them.

This time he said, "Lend me what I need."

Despite everything he'd said to Edwin, he wasn't at all sure that this would work. For anyone, but especially for him. Breaking the contract had been so bone-shaking and final. And of all the magicians in Britain, surely Jack least deserved to call on the wages of the dusk. Jack who'd run away. Jack who'd selfishly heeded only his own wounds.

He deserved to pay for it. But Alan did not.

"I will pledge you myself, for the length of my life. *Please.*"

And felt himself begin to fill again.

Jack could have yelled, or wept. Relief choked his voice. "Don't you dare perturb this, gutter-brat. For once in your damn life, you will let me help you."

No panic drove this magic. It had to be deliberate, and Jack didn't have Edwin's months of practice breaking free of the mould of their training. A request would have to be enough.

He thought, *Wake up and be well,* and released his magic in a trickle that became a fierce surge.

Alan's head jerked and his eyes flew open, twin puddles of reflected moonlight. Before Jack could speak, Alan pushed himself to sit up. He looked bewildered but his arms barely shook. His skin warmed in Jack's grip.

Jack's gladness mingled with that of the Hall. Alan had bowed to the bees, and Alan had saved the heir to this land, and the blood in Alan's veins had their fingerprints, their magic, all over it now. Good. *Good.*

Alan looked around, squinting in the dim light. Sometime in the last minute the others had gathered and were standing close by, watching but not interfering. Jack hadn't noticed.

FREYA MARSKE

"Fuckin'ell," Alan slurred. "Don't tell me I was out cold for the exciting bits *again*?"

His gaze moved to Jack's hand still gripping his wrist. He took a deep, shuddering breath, and touched his sternum as if it ached, and his eyes widened.

"Jack—"

"Nothing owing," said Jack.

32

In the end it took more time to convince Edwin that he was *not* obliged to single-handedly teach every magician at the gala a new approach to magic before sunrise than it did to persuade said magicians to break with equinox tradition and leave Cheetham Hall early. Jack's mother managed both of these feats without dropping her smile. That was a kind of magic that Jack had never bothered to learn.

Perhaps it helped that the foundations of magic were already in pieces. Breaking a tradition that was mostly about eating and drinking and dancing for a solid twelve hours seemed nothing in comparison.

"It started as more than that," said Dufay, "the equinox *is* important," and then wandered away without explaining further.

"This is Flora Sutton's diaries all over again," muttered Edwin.

It was a little past midnight. The last guests had left. They had all begun to drift towards their own rooms but had found themselves lingering in the main downstairs hall as if chewing distractedly over an unfinished argument. The Hall's remaining magic seemed able to manage guidelights, once Lady Cheetham had shooed the servants off to their own beds with instructions that the cleanup could wait until the full light of day. The grounds of the estate were dark now. Only moonlit; only starlit, although some of that thin cloud cover had begun to drift back into place.

They'd moved the corpses off the lake, at least. Soon enough that ice would begin to melt.

Edwin continued, "She has some dense pages about different

kinds of magic being more suited to different seasons—I really thought it was based in agriculture, but I can tell that—"

"Edwin," said Jack. "You will not turn the remainder of this night into a theoretical magic lesson. Take your blood loss and go to bed."

"But—"

"Come on," said Robin firmly. He hadn't left Edwin's side, or stopped looking narrowly at him as though he might yet swoon. Or die. Jack wondered what tightrope of possibility and probability they'd walked that night, what path they'd found between Robin's visions.

Edwin's two symbolic deaths, and the halt before the third. His brother experiencing the third in his place. It did have a grisly fairy-tale shape to it.

Robin persuaded Edwin away to the wing that held their rooms, and Maud and Violet followed soon after. Alan, too, slipped up the main stairs; he caught his gaze on Jack's but didn't say anything.

Jack stood for a while in the shadowed marble of the entrance hall. He could hear movement distantly—small, friendly noises of footsteps and voices and things being moved and locked and settled. A winding-down. Jack didn't feel wound down. He felt as though he could walk the boundaries of this place for the next six hours, acknowledging and accepting the tremors of pain beneath his feet at what had taken place here tonight. Blood spilled, and lives taken.

He'd left his mother and Dufay to explain things to his father, and had no idea what shape that conversation would take. He was holding his long-trained respect and his half-formed adult opinion of Lord Cheetham like a carved statue that cast different silhouettes depending on which way the light struck it. There would be long, strange, difficult days to come. Jack was not precisely looking forward to them. But they were owed, and Jack would pay what he owed.

Freddy Oliver had gone back to the village with his mother, at

Jack's urging. Jack was already removing his tailcoat—he wasn't going to sleep, but perhaps he might read—when he let himself into his own rooms.

His guidelight slipped across the room to the keeper by the bed, where it increased in brightness and took on a golden tinge until the room was cosily lit.

On the way there, it illuminated Alan.

The part of Jack that enjoyed being right and was generally convinced of his own rightness tried to tell him that he wasn't surprised. But he was. Every large and dreadful thing that had ever happened to him in his life he had worked his way through, afterwards, alone.

It was a new experience, to want his solitude and then find someone intruding on it and be glad. A small gladness, like a mouthful of good wine, but world-shaking in its novelty. Not since Elsie died had there been someone whose company Jack preferred to his own.

Playing cards were arranged in a half-started game on the rug. Alan ignored them as he stood from his cross-legged seat. His own guidelight wavered and then blinked out; it would be in the bracket outside the door, waiting for him to leave.

Jack did not want him to leave.

They gazed at each other for a few moments. Alan was still wearing the top half of a maid's uniform, and riding breeches beneath. Jack risked Oliver's future ire by tossing his tailcoat across the chair drawn up to the writing desk and began to work on his cufflinks.

Finally Alan said, "I have to *write* about that party. Thank God I'm good at fiction."

Alan, the journalist, had downstairs efficiently dragged a description of what had happened while he was unconscious out of three different sources, all of whom had noticed and dwelled upon different things to Jack.

"Make it stretch," Jack suggested. "Use it as inspiration for the next Roman story as well."

Alan's glance was long and considering enough for the back of Jack's neck to prickle.

"Nothing titillating about a frozen lake and several murders," said Alan, but Jack recognised the tone. It was the opening sally. Jack, who'd made that dig about Whitechapel fishmongers when Alan first walked back into his life, was being invited to *haggle*.

So Jack smiled. "How about a daring young man in disguise as a parlour maid—his secret discovered—blackmailed into unspeakable acts by the heir to the estate—"

"I think I might steer clear of manor-house stories for a while. Besides," he said, suddenly frank, "wouldn't it feel odd? To read one of my books and know you'd inspired it?"

Jack pretended to consider that as he went to drop his cufflinks and collar on the dresser.

"To be frank, I think it'd give me a prick I could hammer nails with."

Alan choked on laughter and his posture relaxed. He crossed to where Jack stood, treading hearts and diamonds underfoot, and looked up at him from a close distance.

"Well, don't hold your breath. I don't want to share this with anyone else yet." It could have been a sweet statement, but for his hand landing deliberately on Jack's prick. Jack's breath caught. Heat swelled between his legs as Alan squeezed and rubbed.

"Hm," said Alan. "Couldn't hammer a thing with it yet, but you might raise a bruise."

Rising desire sent Jack's hand to Alan's nape, where he dug a fingernail in hard and watched Alan's pupils swell. He wanted to take his teeth to Alan's neck. To suck at that night-rough skin. Raise a bruise. God, yes.

The vision of Alan brimming with channeled magic, tense and unconscious with pain, swept across his mind unbidden. Jack forced himself to drop his hand and gather some damned unselfishness.

"It's been a long day. You should rest."

"*Rest?*" Alan took a step back, sharply exasperated. "I swallowed a glass of punch to keep me awake until sunrise, like the rest of you. I've no idea if I managed to let it work—bloody felt like it did, but that could have been the nerves. Or the small fact of slitting a man's throat." His voice thinned. "And then whatever *you* did to me made me wake up feeling better rested than I have in *years*. I could climb five hills, or write ten articles without stopping, or ride you ragged and then suck you until you were hard enough to have me again."

Jack crept a fair way further towards nail-hammering territory.

"So that's where I'm standing, Lord Hawthorn. If *you* want rest, you can bloody well say that." The tightness of Alan's eyes softened. His accent tumbled downhill in a way that sounded self-mocking. "I like you masterful in the bedroom, m'lord, but you needn't be ready to turn it on at any moment. I don't need you to want me every second of the day."

"I do," said Jack. "I want you so much it makes me useless." It was not even close to what he'd meant to say, but he didn't care. "I could fuck you three times a day and wouldn't feel I've caught up for a full year."

Alan's mouth and eyes found a smile of pure, startled pleasure. Perhaps this was what he'd looked like when he'd received Jack's letter to the Roman. So much of what they said to each other hid beneath sarcasm, as if the truth had to slither around a secret-bind. Jack enjoyed that. But he also enjoyed this: the look of Alan surprised by unadorned compliment.

"So," said Alan. "Now we're on the same page and all. Tell me more about these *unspeakable acts* the heir to the estate has in mind."

Jack took his leisurely time inspecting Alan, down to the toes and back up again. "I've changed my mind. You look more like a pirate than a maid in that getup."

"*Exploits of a Cabin Boy*?" Alan's teeth flashed. "That one sold well, I'm told. Not surprised you fancy the idea. The ruthless captain, summoning me whenever you've an itch to scratch, having me bent over a barrel with the rest of the crew watching me squirm . . ."

The challenge was there, full of laughter. Jack took hold of Alan's black shirt and dragged him close. He let his palms sweep down Alan's sides, past his hips, a little way down the tight cling of the breeches on those lean legs, letting the feel of them suggest the next possibility. "Or perhaps you're an insolent groom who needs to be taken for a thorough ride in the stables."

Alan scoffed. He kept his arms at his sides, but his groin swayed against Jack's for a spark-inducing moment. "A ride. I see. You don't want to do the work. Lazy toff."

"You're the one who said the words *ride you ragged*."

"Alliteration gets you hard. I'll remember that."

Jack delivered a light, warning slap to Alan's arse. More taunting space appeared between Alan's lips. His eyes were so dark, Jack could dissolve in them.

"Speaking of lazy," said Jack. "Last time, if I recall, you just lay there. Given you're so well *rested*, it's your turn to put some effort into it."

Jack's body was at an urgent hum that interfered with his sense of time. Maybe they lingered over undressing; maybe it was less than a minute before their clothes were on the floor. Maybe he remembered going to the dresser in search of the lotion they'd used last time; maybe he blinked and found himself lying flat and bare on the bed, with the pot miraculously in Alan's hand where he sat, equally nude, astride Jack's thighs.

Jack gazed at him, covetous. That smooth olive skin. Those startling dense patches of black hair—at his armpits, trailing down from his navel, and thickly gathered above his cock—that Jack wanted, deliriously, to shove his face against.

He didn't. He lay where he was and hissed when Alan, pen-calloused fingers lightly slicked, shifted forward so that he was holding their two pricks aligned together.

"I have a theory," said Alan, remarkably steady, "about the air in this place. Or perhaps it's the water. Everything that grows here is unreasonably large."

More sparks of heat shot through Jack's belly. Only Alan's

fingers were moving, sliding and teasing with the lack of real friction, but the sheer sight of Alan's cock growing to full hardness against his own was devastating. Jack put his hands on Alan's thighs to stop himself from grabbing hold of their lengths himself and forcing a faster pace.

"Unreasonably." Black gravel filled his voice. "Is that so?"

"A man could feel inferior," said Alan, not sounding like he meant it in the slightest.

Jack swallowed three different comments about the *inferior classes* and gave Alan's own cock a considering look. His stomach muscles tensed and jumped with need.

"Do you think I give a damn for how you feel? That pretty prick of yours is mine, too, now. You brought it out for me, and you're showing it off for me. Isn't that right?"

Alan's weight shifted with clear embarrassment. He muttered, "Yes."

"I didn't hear that."

A sparkling glare. Alan's fingers tightened for an agonisingly brief second. "*Yes*, my lord."

"Good boy," Jack said, squeezing his arse hard in return. "I intend to inspect my property more closely, then."

He pulled. Alan moved forward up Jack's body easily enough but didn't realise what Jack had in mind until his cock was nearly touching Jack's chin.

Then, gratifyingly, he made a cut-off sound—"*Ah.*"

This wasn't the first prick that Jack had taken between his lips, though the act wasn't one he'd ever had—well. A particular taste for.

But now, hearing the way Alan's breath changed to needy, rough bursts, and feeling the way Alan's thighs tensed and trembled beneath his hands . . . yes, perhaps he could learn to like this a great deal. The lotion tasted of nothing but a faint oiliness that disappeared quickly, and Alan's cock was a smooth, obedient weight in Jack's mouth. Jack, made ambitious by sheer lust, managed for a few wild seconds to take him deeper, and buried his nose in those black curls until the dense scent of Alan's body made his head whirl with arousal.

Then he found himself in the middle of a very unmasterful coughing fit.

Alan's thighs shook with something closer to laughter as he hastily withdrew, going back to his previous seat astride Jack's hips.

"Don't strain yourself, your lordship. We can't all be as gifted as me."

Jack wiped at his mouth and looked up. Alan wavered between smug and shivering, his neck gleaming with sweat and the planes of his face sharp as thorns. The pang of awe-soaked need that went through Jack was close to pain, as if he'd hurled himself upon those thorns and let them pierce his skin.

"And what a gift you are. Born to take my cock however and wherever I want to give it to you."

Alan grinned and leaned down. He whispered, the words a tingle of air on Jack's lips: "Then we'd better put that cock where it belongs. Before I decide to go in search of a better offer."

Alan didn't bother to prepare himself, but took a long, tortuous time about first applying more slick to Jack's cock and then sinking onto it, letting it work him open in tiny increments, controlling the pace with small movements of his hips. It took horrendous effort for Jack to keep his eyes open and not to swear aloud as that tightness engulfed him—slowly, *slowly*.

"Get on with it, brat," he gritted out, when it became clear during Alan's latest pause that this was now being done for effect rather than comfort.

Alan put his hands on Jack's stomach and dug in with all his nails. He gulped in air, looking half-drunk, but his grin found even more thorns.

"Make me, you posh twat."

And that was an invitation. Jack took hold of Alan's waist and forced him steadily down the rest of the way, watching him writhe, *feeling* him clench. And oh, the look on his face. One of

Jack's legs jerked involuntarily and his spine fizzed, a wave of almost-release trying to rise. He had to breathe it down again, forcing his muscles to relax into the bed.

His next slap to Alan's thigh was a lot harder.

"Now. Ride."

"You do realise," said Alan, "that I've never been *on* a bloody horse."

"The activities," said Jack, "are not exactly compar—" He lost the word to a groan as Alan raised himself halfway and then lowered fully again. One hand was steadying himself on Jack's stomach; the other he ran through his hair as he gave a breathless laugh. Christ, he was beautiful.

"I'd fucking hope not," Alan said, and began to move again.

The muscles needed for control were similar, though Jack didn't point that out. Alan was doing just fine. Jack couldn't keep from touching him, as if by keeping contact with Alan's leg—Alan's heaving stomach—the hard nubs of his nipples—he could distract himself from the blissful coil of pleasure that was tightening within him.

And the temptation of Alan's cock, too, proved too much. It was as pretty as Jack had said: dark with blood, a single sly vein making a prominent path, the foreskin shifting delicately when Jack took firm hold in the circle of finger and thumb. Alan sucked in air and began to shove his hips more erratically, more strongly, into Jack's grip.

"I—fuck," he said, stilted, and came between Jack's fingers.

Climax seemed to take Alan all at once and by surprise, every time. It was fascinating. Jack wondered what it would take in order to drag it out, how much care and observation would be needed to bring him close to the edge and then hold him back from it.

He intended to find out.

Jack swiped his hand across his stomach and then held it up to Alan. He'd never have done this with another bed partner. But there was a shelf in his townhouse filled by Alanzo Rossi's purple-covered, filthily creative mind, and Jack had stopped bothering with limits to the things he wanted. If limits existed, Alan would tell him so.

"Your mess," Jack said, full of drawled contempt. "Yours to deal with."

A muscle fluttered at the base of Alan's neck, and another beneath the subtle inverted V of his rib cage. His eyes were solid black as he took Jack's hand and proceeded to do as he was told.

If nothing else erotic ever happened to Jack for the rest of his life, he would be able to bring himself off to the memory of lying with his rigid prick buried in Alan's arse while Alan's tongue curled around his fingertips and explored the webbing between his fingers.

"Christ alive," said Jack hoarsely. "I won't share you with a soul."

"The crew'll be *so* disappointed," murmured Alan into Jack's palm. It wasn't a kiss, but wasn't unlike one.

Jack took his hand, free of mess, back. Alan didn't move from his seat. He stifled a yawn that might even have been genuine, and laughed when Jack pinched the skin of his leg.

"Did you want something, m'lord? I've had mine. You want me fucked any further, you'll have to do it yourself."

Jack's bad leg gave a twinge with how fast he moved, but it was worth it for the widening of Alan's eyes and the ungainly way he flailed as Jack flipped them over. Too close and impatient for further games, Jack simply shoved Alan's knees back, lined up, and drove down into him, finding that enclosing heat again. Alan gave a *hnnh* sound and then a panting exhale as Jack leaned all the way forward, covering Alan's body with his own.

And then a few more deep strokes, Jack's hand firm at the top of Alan's head and Alan's legs now wrapped around him, Alan's breath coming in hot grunts at the base of Jack's throat—

He managed not to collapse entirely when his release took him, a dervish of pleasure both dry and drenching at once, but it was a close thing. His limbs had gone to sand within his skin.

When he gathered himself to pull out and away, he didn't get far. Alan's legs tightened, holding him in place.

"I want to feel it," Alan said quietly. "This all right?"

Jack stared down at him—trapped between Jack's arms and skewered on Jack's cock, ravaged and sweaty and lip-bitten, the most arousing sight Jack could imagine.

"Cesare," he said hoarsely, "I am completely at your mercy."

One of those expressions like a stone thrown through stained glass passed over Alan's face. Uneven edges, colour and light. When he spoke, Jack wondered for a blank second if it was possible for a fuck to be so good it destroyed that part of the mind responsible for understanding speech. None of the words were words.

Ah. It wasn't English at all. Alan was speaking quiet, deliberate Italian.

He'd never slipped into the tongue before: not when Jack was at the Clerkenwell house, not when furious, not when consumed by pain. Not even in the throes of passion. He had utter control over who was allowed to see and hear this part of himself. And now he was showing it to Jack.

"—kiss me," he finished. "Is what the last part meant."

Jack's heart gave a hard thump. "And the rest of it?"

"I'll translate," Alan said, and drew Jack down.

Alan's kiss tasted of something sour and something sweet, and it was flecked with sharpness. Jack's tongue kept finding teeth, their chins scraped roughly against one another, and every drag of Alan's lips was as wicked as the way he smiled when he didn't care to make a good impression. But beyond the sharpness was something dizzying, an abyss of need with no bottom to it. Alan made rough, desperate sounds like he was dying. Like he would die if Jack stopped.

At some point Jack's softening prick did slip out of Alan entirely, and he broke the kiss to look an inquiry down at Alan. They'd ended up more on their sides, Jack's leg now heavy across Alan's body, Alan's hand buried in Jack's hair.

When Jack went to remove some more of his weight, Alan

grabbed Jack's topmost arm and pulled it over himself, keeping their bodies pressed together.

"Fuck, I love how big you are," Alan said. Again sounding pleasure-drunk. "Actually, no. I hate it." His sigh was palpable against Jack's chest. "Size *and* strength, station and wealth. All the advantages possible. Do you know how hard it is to believe someone won't use any of that against you? To put your heart in someone's hands, knowing that?" His voice was a mere breeze by the end, hardly audible over the sound of his fingers shifting Jack's hair against his scalp.

Jack had quite honestly had no idea that *hearts* were on the table at all.

But he'd shaken apart with his head in this man's lap and never once feared that Alan might speak a word of it or use it against him. This thing between them was weighty and alive and seductively, terrifyingly easy. They fit in ways they shouldn't ever have fit. Even when they fought, they fit—there was no mockery falling on soft, miserable ground as there had been with Edwin. Only the knowledge that any volley would be met and thrown back, brighter and better.

Jack could have said: *If there are days in the rest of my life when I don't have you there to pick fights with, they will be the poorer for it.*

I could walk into any room, anywhere, and always be glad to see you there.

He said: "I would take your heart between my ribs and guard it like my own. Is there any way I could make you believe it?"

Alan shifted to look at him. His throat moved, swallowing. Naked in Jack's arms he was as beautiful as frost-tipped grass, or a bruise left by loving hands on eager skin. Untrusting, because he had to be. Because despite all that was easy, there was still so much tipping the scales against them.

"I don't know," said Alan. "You're the magician. Is there?"

The instant denial—*I am not*—sprang to Jack's mouth, but died there. He couldn't say it. Not in this place. Not after what had happened tonight.

And so the next thing he said was a magician's promise, the familiar rhythm finding him easily.

"I'd put my blood into any oath you care to name," he said.

In fact—

"Come on." Jack untangled himself from Alan and sat up. He was still nowhere close to sleepy, and his blood was jubilant in his sated body. "Clean up and get dressed, and come with me."

33

Alan stole one of Jack's shirts and a woollen jumper. The clothes hung loose on him, swamping his hands, but his body hugged the heat of recent intimacy to itself as he followed Jack out into the grounds of Cheetham Hall.

The night was punctured by nature sounds that Alan had no hope of recognising. Cheetham Hall's guidelights were now too weak to leave the Hall itself, so Jack had hunted out a proper handheld lantern with thick glass walls, which cast a small golden pool onto their path up the hill and to the Lady's Oak.

Jack set the lantern by the base of the tree and seated himself on that low, looping branch that might have been grown for exactly that purpose. Perhaps it was.

Alan sat next to him, closer than he'd have allowed himself to sit before. He felt wildly, insatiably greedy for everything of Jack's that he was allowed to take, even if part of him still dug in its heels at the idea of taking a damned thing. This, though. The warmth of Jack's body bleeding through clothing and into his own.

He was so glad to be alive. His blood sang with it.

He tucked a foot up and wrapped his arms around the bent leg. The cold cleanness of the country air was no longer strange. Up here it had the faintest tinge of leaves, and of dirt, and strangely of pepper. The jumper he was wearing added only a vague wool-and-mothballs note; it didn't smell of Jack. His lordship's clothes were kept too meticulously for that. The garment was probably aired thoroughly between every wearing. Alan swallowed his ludicrous disappointment.

"What are we doing up here?" he asked eventually.

"This was Elsie's favourite part of the grounds," Jack said. "If there's a place here to make promises, this is it." He paused and then lifted his own feet, one at a time, to remove shoes and socks. His feet looked very white against the grass. When he spoke, it was still Jack's bored, deep voice, but he had a similar air to Edwin talking his way through a problem. "Like Violet in Spinet, I never actually put my own blood into this place. My parents did it when we were born—most families don't bother anymore. It was a choice made on my behalf. As we made a choice for all magicians tonight."

Perhaps no response or contribution was expected. But Alan had interviewed people who were cagey, and also people who were desperately waiting for the right question to be asked—for the truth to be uncorked.

He said, "Do you think it was the wrong choice?"

A long pause. Really quite long indeed. Jack shifted his bare feet. "No." He looked at the lantern and stretched out a hand as if to warm it.

The light throbbed and sputtered, and then grew. Within the lantern the flame itself was no larger, but the circle of illumination expanded and brightened until they sat within a cosy room of apricot-golden light. The night went on beyond.

Jack dropped his hand and exhaled slowly. The light shrank back.

"Every time it still feels like a mistake," Jack muttered.

"Don't say that where the tree can hear you," said Alan. "Your land might decide I should still be unconscious."

Partly joking; partly not. Jack had said it was Cheetham Hall who saved Alan—who drained the worst of George's twisted magic from him and woke him up hale and well. Jack's clear discomfort with his own magic aside, not a scrap of self-effacement lived alongside his natural arrogance, so it had to be at least partly true.

Alan had promised blood and secrets to the bees of Cheetham Hall. He didn't know what he owed them now that the place had saved his life. He had a new, uncomfortable sense of what Jack and Edwin and Violet meant when they talked about obligation to a place. He didn't want to remove his own shoes, in case he felt—anything. That would be too much to handle tonight.

"My land would prefer everyone to remain upright and non-bleeding," said Jack, very dry. "I'll already have to spend a lot more time here, to repair the damage from tonight's deaths, just as my parents did after—Elsie. And *that's* a choice." His voice firmed. "It's something I ran from, and I intend to stop running. I will inherit, after all."

If there'd been the slightest hint of martyrdom in his tone then Alan would have felt fully justified in punching him, but there wasn't.

"And after me, who knows?" Jack went on. "Someone who doesn't know the place as well. I should do what I can, before then."

Alan wrenched his thoughts to a stop in front of a large pile of his own assumptions. He thought about Robin and Adelaide. "You don't intend to marry? Produce an heir?"

"The last time I had this discussion, a rich American was attempting to hurl her daughters at me," said Jack. "You're welcome to try to sell me your sister, if you wish." He made an open, mocking gesture. "So far all I know is that she's not a virgin and she probably detests me, but we've already established that I'm quite keen on angry, dark-eyed Italians who fit those criteria. And I expect she's *far* better at housekeeping than you are."

"Sod off," said Alan. "You'd be lucky to have her."

He was trying not to laugh. Past that, an appalling surge of jealousy was making itself known at the very thought of Jack getting married, but he firmly dismissed it as absurd. He would never ask anyone to throw away responsibility to family. Not for anything. Certainly not for him.

"No doubt," said Jack. Some of the mocking glitter left him. "No. Even removing finer romantic feelings from the equation, I've never encountered anyone where I felt we could stand each other, even for duty's sake, well enough to live together. Let alone have a sensible partnership."

"I can't imagine why," said Alan. "What with your warm and accommodating personality."

Jack's thumb slid across the nape of Alan's neck with just enough fingernail to make it a threat. Alan shivered, distracted.

"Then who *will* inherit?" he asked. "The place is magical. Different rules. Could you choose someone? Like Lady Enid did with Violet?"

"If this were Sutton or Spinet, yes. But rules can't be dodged when it comes to earldoms. Without an heir . . ." He gave an amused huff. "Ironically, Freddy Oliver might do after all, but for the pesky matter of his being illegitimate."

"Oliver?" Alan was missing something. "Your *valet*?"

Silence. Jack had a peculiar expression on his face.

Finally he said, "He's my father's son."

"Oh." Alan couldn't help the expression on *his* face.

"Not through . . . unwanted attention," said Jack, reading his mind. "Well. To be frank, I don't know that for certain." It sounded effortful to admit. "I've always assumed Margaret Oliver was willing."

The spectre of Bella was in the conversation again. Perhaps Margaret Oliver had said yes because she'd known how much it would cost her to say no.

"Give the lord a prize, he's learning," said Alan. This still felt odd. Jack wasn't acting as though he'd shared a great and emotional secret. More as though it had simply slipped his mind.

"What?" Jack asked, in response to Alan's look.

Alan considered *Nothing*, but discarded it. If it was a fight, it was a fight. They knew what to do with those.

"I thought you'd have stronger feelings about having a half brother, given you've lost a sister."

No fight at all. Jack shrugged. "I thought I would too. But I don't need to know him like a brother. It's certainly not what he needs from me. The fact of blood doesn't matter much without the fact of growing up together."

Alan tried to imagine a boy showing up on the Clerkenwell doorstep and announcing himself a long-lost child of the dead Marco Rossi. Alan might have some feelings about it, but he couldn't imagine they'd be straightforward.

He steered back to the topic at hand. Freddy Oliver. Who'd been genuinely gleeful and proud of making disguises to fit, and who had strong opinions about shoes and neckties and which tailors his lordship should deign to frequent.

"You think Oliver would make a good Earl of Cheetham?" Alan said, not particularly tactfully.

"Perhaps not. But he learns fast," Jack said. "And he loves this place. And the presence of my former valet in the House of Lords would certainly throw a cat amongst the political pigeons."

Damn him, he was right. What an appealing image that was.

"So cheat," Alan said.

Jack looked a silent question at him.

"Not the magic. That's the part you care about, right? Picking the right caretaker for the land. Cheat the aristocracy part. Make Oliver legitimate."

"His mother . . ." Jack said. And then, somewhat strangled, "*My* mother . . ."

"Don't pretend he's your father's legitimate son. Pretend he's yours."

"Alan," said Jack. "I have no intention of marrying Margaret Oliver."

"Forge a document saying you did, and a birth record saying he's your son. Lodge it sealed it to be opened with your will. It won't matter until you're dead, will it?"

Jack looked at him unblinking for a few moments. "It's alarming that forgery is your first instinct," he said, "but I admire it."

"If the rules are stupid, sod the rules."

"It is helpful to have the option," said Jack, and finally laughed. "You are far too clever for your own good, Master Cesare." His hand lifted to Alan's face. Halfway to bending down, he stopped and raised his eyebrows. "Ah. Is *this* still a rule?"

"Yes," said Alan. "You have too much given to you without asking, your lordship. It's good for you to have something withheld that you want, and—fucking hell"—the shivers from earlier began a campaign to conquer every inch of his skin, starting at his cheeks and heading downwards—"I love how you look when you're wanting it."

Jack hovered exactly where he was.

"Though I suppose," Alan said, managing graciousness despite the drum of need trying to explode in his ribs, "you could ask."

A slow smile, absolutely ruthless, set up camp on Jack's face. *I've made a dreadful mistake,* Alan thought, as Jack's palm firmed on his cheek and Jack's mouth descended to within an inch of his own. Jack spoke like he was reading one of the most depraved scenes from Alan's darkest and dirtiest stories.

"I want to kiss you until your mouth forgets it exists for any reason but to let me taste it. I want to kiss you so well, and so long, that every narrator in your books will crawl off their pages and die from sheer jealousy." His lips almost, almost made contact. But didn't. He sounded like rough gravel and black tea full of sugar. "Will you let me?"

It was as bad as being made to repeat *Behave.* No: it was *worse,* which was genuinely fucking impressive. Alan's cock had a real go at showing interest all over again.

He nodded.

Jack had said that the Roman wrote kisses that were obliterating. And Alan had thought he wanted that: wanted acts he could dissolve into, to forget himself and the hard realities of the world.

He could not dissolve into this. Every part of him cried out to be more present, to feel *more,* to drag Jack against him harder, to take breaths and more gulping breaths of Jack's mouth and Jack's skin until that unnameable, expensive scent was part of his lungs. Until the path of Jack's lips and tongue from his mouth, across his jaw, briefly and hotly on his earlobe, was seared there for anyone to see. He was almost tempted to make good on his earlier threat: to get down on that soft grass and suck Jack to hardness again, and then bait him into shoving Alan against the solid trunk of the tree to be roughly fucked.

That did seem a mite disrespectful to the oak. Alan imagined Lady Dufay popping out from behind it with her most disapproving face. He laughed, breaking the kiss.

Jack winced as he straightened. "I should trade you in for a larger model. You're too short for this."

"There's nothing wrong with me. You're too bloody tall." Alan considered, then stepped up onto the branch just as Maud-as-Elsie had stood on the swing seat. He looked around. "Hm. I can see the appeal. Master of all you survey."

"Turning class traitor after all, Cesare?"

Alan sniffed and tried to imitate Jack's manner of lounging arrogantly even when fully upright.

"*I* am Lord Hawthorn, Liberal sympathiser and dues-paying member of the Reform Club. I believe in taxing my fellow wealthy men to educate the poor. And yet I have no quibbles with a system that means I own all of *this*"—he made a sweeping gesture around the estate—"while there are thousands of people in London—hell, tenants on my own land—who'll never be able to stand on so much as a rickety chair and say they own the place where they live. Never for the full span of their lives."

His heart beat hard into Jack's silence. It was a relief to have found that anger there, still, and to have drawn it defiantly out into the light.

Class traitor. That had smarted more than Jack likely intended. No matter how Alan felt about this man, no matter how well matched their ideals and their minds and their sexual tastes, they were still straining to clasp hands over a chasm of vast injustice. Lord Hawthorn needed reminding of that. And so did Alan.

"Too much given to me without asking," Jack said finally. "I concede the point, though will argue I have *some* quibbles. And I don't know the best solution—if it's law, or politics, or charity."

"Or guillotines."

A quick smile. "It was the point, in a way, of breaking the Last Contract. One object can't be the key to all magic. But magic also can't be about what land someone owns on paper, or it's the few and the many all over again. And nobody owns ley lines or the magic they hold. It's there for everyone to use, even if that's not in such large ways as the contracted fae-magic."

"Freezing an entire lake was fairly large," said Alan dryly.

"That *was* because of being on this land, I think." Jack nodded at the Lady's Oak. "The true spells of power will continue to need magicians working together, perhaps even more than before, and that's for the best. It should take agreement to achieve large things."

Alan wasn't sure what to say. He reached out and put his hand in Jack's hair, as he'd done earlier and also—God, was it only the previous night? It felt like weeks ago already. Jack leaned into the touch with no change of expression. Alan had an odd jolt of pride and triumph left over from childhood, when he and Caro and Emilio would crowd around the milk cart while the man was unloading and shamelessly bribe the patient old mare with crumbs of sugar stolen from their pa's stores. You had crowing rights all day if the horse's soft nose chose *your* hand to press up against first.

Alan stored that comparison away for a future time when Jack needed his arrogance deflated.

"In the meantime," said Jack, "as I am currently unable to divest myself of the land entailed to my future title, I can at least make it available to others." He glanced up at Alan. "You're welcome here at any time. Bring your whole family, if you wish. We've certainly room for them."

Alan tried to imagine his ma's horrified face at the Rossi clan being invited as houseguests to the Earl of Cheetham's estate. He brimmed with appalled laughter. His hand fell from Jack's hair and he lowered himself to sit again on the thick branch.

"I don't think so."

"And I'm sure Polly would take your sister Bella into service, once her child's born and weaned. If I can manage to restrain myself from marrying her in the meantime."

"She'd . . . *what*?"

"I'm told both of the Miss Rossis have excellent references," said Jack blandly. "I mean it. You should ask her. Polly."

"I should *not*."

"Then I will."

A trap. Alan glared. "Stop giving me things. It's a terrible habit."

"We Liberals are passionate about the redistribution of wealth."

"Fuck *right* off," said Alan, but he couldn't fight the smile.

"You know what to say if you truly want me to stop."

Oh, Christ. Wasn't that well aimed. All those advantages, wealth and size and position—and now magic. Yet Alan had the power to deny Jack anything, simply by saying his name.

And, which was even more enormous again: Alan trusted that Jack would honour it.

Jack added, watching him carefully, "Nothing owing. I meant it. Anything between us will always be gifts freely exchanged. And I won't give you a penny if you don't want it, but my connections and my name—"

"Your knack for bullying innocent newspaper editors—"

A twitch of Jack's mouth. "I want to see what you become when you're given the space for it."

It was another devastating nudge in the universe of Alan's soul. *I would take your heart within my ribs.*

Alan was the one whose job it was to put words around passion, and here he was being put to shame by an aristocrat. He had no idea how to speak aloud, to a real person, thoughts and feelings that were so real they terrified him.

Wrapping them up in Italian had been the best he could manage. *I would write you into immortality. I would trap you in ink and wear the pages next to my skin until they fell apart. Kiss me until I know you. Kiss me until you know me, and unmake me, and love me anyway.*

He touched Jack's mouth, instead: a single thumb run across the seam. Heat prickled hard in his nose.

"Oh, is that all," he said unsteadily. "Gifts freely exchanged? What the hell am I supposed to *gift* you, Lord Hawthorn? You don't need anything."

Jack's outstretched legs cast shadows in the lamplight that were even longer again. Night birds called close by. Past the dense leaves of the oak the sky still frothed with moonshine and stars.

Jack had followed Alan's gaze outwards to the sprawl of the world. He didn't look back again, but he put his hand over Alan's where it lay on the mossy bark of the tree. Not heavily. Alan could pull himself free at any time.

"Yes, I do," said Jack.

EPILOGUE

"If I had to choose a moment," said Robin, "I would say that I decided on Adelaide as the future partner of my life when she first realised I wasn't a magician and looked at me as if I were a particularly unintelligent species of dormouse."

Adelaide beamed and shook sandwich crumbs from her gloves. "For myself, I can't decide whether it was Sir Robert's mound of unpaid debts or his complete lack of interest in women which I found more appealing in a husband."

Violet choked on a mouthful of sandwich.

Jack, currently engaged in brushing fallen petals and rain-drops from the top of his silk hat, glanced up to catch the look on Alan's face. Alan was looking both delectable and annoyed, as he always did in formal garb. A few tiny white petals had caught in his curls.

"Thank you," Alan said, tucking his notebook away un-opened. "How touching. My wedding gift to you will be completely ignoring everything you just said and inventing some appropriate quotes for the article."

"Make sure to mention the dress," said Adelaide.

Alan gave her a long-suffering look. "That's why you had to stand around so long for Danny and his camera. If there's anything *Tatler*'s readership cares more about than how many titles were in attendance, it's what the dress looked like. Along with a reliable rumour about how much it cost."

"How vulgar," said Adelaide cheerfully. "Please invent a disgusting sum for that too."

With no female relatives currently drawing on his purse, Jack hadn't the faintest clue how expensive said dress might be. It was certainly impressive to look at. More and more women were choosing to be married in white, like the late queen, but the freshly minted Lady Blyth had chosen a pale gold that glowed against her brown skin, with enough ruching and lace to satisfy even *Tatler*'s hungry fashion pages, and a layer of red silk around the hem of the skirt that had been part of her mother's wedding sari.

It was April, and the grounds of Thornley Hill looked greatly relieved to be passing into the colours of spring. The seat of Robin's baronetcy was a small but remarkably handsome house in a pleasant corner of Kent, and Robin and Adelaide's wedding dinner was the first event it had been called upon to host for nearly a decade.

The newlyweds themselves had declared their intention to spend some quiet time together on the grounds before dinner, and daringly vanished with a bottle of champagne and orders delivered via Maud for a select group of people to meet them in the apple orchard.

Orchard was a kind word for the untidy cluster of trees. But the blossoms were wearing all the white that Adelaide wasn't, and there were oiled blankets laid on the damp ground—it had rained all through the morning—and a large platter of sandwiches under linen cloth, which Adelaide had fallen on with a famished sound.

"That reminds me. *You* haven't given us a wedding gift yet, Edwin," said Adelaide.

Edwin shrugged. He looked at ease, sitting close to Robin on the blanket, a sense of laughter lurking beneath the surface of his expression as there had been all day.

"Unless it's to be a pile of books you've no interest in, I'm waiting for you to request something," he said.

"Make me a snowflake," said Robin.

Some of the laughter found its way onto Edwin's mouth, and then out into the air. Even now, Jack could count on one hand the number of times he'd heard Edwin Courcey laugh.

"All right," said Edwin.

Edwin seldom used string for spells these days. He still worked slowly, and with concentration and care, and he still preferred gesture as a way to focus his mind. Most British magicians did.

Many were finding other ways, which suited them better.

The snowflake began as a small cloud of mist, hovering off to the side of the blankets. And then it grew. And grew and grew. Watching it create itself, layer after layer of patterned ice, put Jack in mind of watching a cathedral being built.

Maud herself, never one to sit still when there was an alternative, had been wandering dryadlike between the apple trees, occasionally drifting back to Violet to touch her hair or steal a bit of sandwich or continue a private joke. When the snowflake had reached her own height, she stepped up to it and stroked one glittering point with a fingertip.

"Oh," she breathed. "Violet—"

"No, darling."

Maud's huge green eyes turned onto Violet. None of them was entirely immune to Maud when she was putting effort into it, but Violet had more practice than most.

"But you don't—"

"Yes, I do. And no."

"Even if it's only an illusion . . . ?"

"We've only just emerged from winter," said Violet. "I am sick to death of snow and cold, and don't need to create a room full of it in the house, illusion or not. Ask me again in the middle of summer."

"I'd've thought we'd all had enough ice for a lifetime," said Alan. "Emily and Tom wanted to drag me ice-skating at Christmas, and I pretended to have a terrible flu."

"You're all terrible ingrates with no appreciation for beauty, and it's *my* snowflake," said Robin. "And I think it's marvellous."

Edwin smiled. After a moment, he leaned in and kissed Robin: quick and light, but with the rest of them looking on. That, too, was new. But today, of all days, it had a sense of staking a claim.

These days Edwin was splitting his time between Sutton, where magic still came easiest and he could devote his time to creating a variety of new techniques, and his permanent rooms in the Blyth house in London. He was busier than ever. The Magical Assembly had been split on whether to recruit the destroyer of the Barrel into the senior advisor post that his brother Walter had held, but Manraj and Kitty had gone around being devastatingly sensible at people until they had enough votes. If it had been hard to argue with Kitty when she was pregnant, it was nearly impossible when she was aggressively jiggling a baby.

Violet was spending a chunk of her fortune rebuilding Spinet House into something thankfully far more normal and far less anxiety-inducing to inhabit. Which would mean she could rent it out when she followed Maud to Cambridge later in the year, even though Violet herself had no intention of studying at a college. She and Maud spent half their time in ever-more-extravagant plans to create their own sort of female Bloomsbury set: a haven for girl magicians and artists and musicians and students.

Knowing them, they would pull it off with flair.

Alan, now lying flat on the blankets with his eyes closed—he'd kept himself and Jack awake long past midnight the previous night, exploring in detail a scenario for the latest Roman pamphlet, so it was really his own fault—also continued to split his time. He wrote society pieces for *Tatler* and concise commentary for the political pages of the *Sphere,* which currently showed a lot of illustrations of the ongoing debate in the Commons about curtailing the power of the Lords, following the rejection of Lloyd George's budget.

Jack lifted his walking stick, concentrated, and sent a small nudge of magic at Alan. He'd always felt more comfortable using a physical object to fight with, and Edwin had uncovered for him some ancient Germanic texts on the use of wooden wands. This particular stick had been a Christmas gift from Violet. Hawthorn wood. Remarkably good for magic, as it turned out.

Alan didn't open his eyes, but twitched and flicked his hand back in Jack's direction. The magic sank into Jack's chest with a pleasant fizz of sensation.

"Piss off, Jack," said Alan, a smile playing on his lips.

"You haven't asked me for a quote," Jack said.

"Don't worry, I'll invent one for you too," said Alan. He stifled a yawn and sat up, brushing petals from his waistcoat. "You had designs on the new Lady Blyth yourself and were furious when she turned down the opportunity to become the future Countess of Cheetham."

"Wait," said Adelaide. "I want to hear about this fictional proposal. I may yet change my mind."

"Married a few hours and jilted already," said Edwin. "Robin. Fight for your honour."

"I haven't any," said Robin amiably. "I let my sister run off and be ruined, remember? And I plan to be a thoroughly unfaithful husband."

"Very well," said Jack. "As my wedding gift to you, Robin, I will not steal your wife. In the society papers or anywhere else."

"Much obliged," said Robin.

"There is a real gift as well," Jack said, because it was ridiculous to feel outdone by a snowflake. "Beehives, and two swarms of bees, for Thornley Hill. They should be delivered next week."

"How do you deliver bees?" asked Violet with interest.

"With great care, and something to do with smoke," said Alan. "Apparently."

"It's part of making bargain with the land," said Jack. "Even for unmagical people. You talk to them. Announce things— births. Weddings."

Robin didn't laugh. He nodded seriously and looked at Edwin. "A bargain. Then let's do it properly. I think I remember how it works."

Robin climbed to his feet and went to the still-hovering snowflake, and touched it more deliberately than Maud had. His fingertip came away dotted red with blood.

And then Sir Robin Blyth, unmagical as he was, knelt down

and swore the traditional blood-oath to, he said, as much of the land as would have him.

"And, er, this is my household," he added awkwardly. "If you don't know that already. And my sister, and—my terrible black-sheep cousin, I suppose," with a grin for Jack. "And the people we love. There."

Jack shared a look with Alan. They agreed silently that this was *far* too much sincerity to be committed in public, but also that they wouldn't say a thing to ruin it.

"You too, Addy," said Edwin.

"I will if you will," she said, giving him a hand up. Edwin blinked but didn't protest. And they, too, shed their blood and put it into the wet earth and made a promise. *To tend and to mend.*

And then all three of them flinched a little, as if something had struck them.

"Robin?" said Maud at once.

"I don't know," said Robin. He looked at Edwin, who was frowning at his bleeding finger.

"I think it took," he said. "I think—"

"Yes, I think it did," said Adelaide, her voice strange. "Ah. Edwin?"

A pale light was flickering on her fingers: small but there. It vanished. Then, as Adelaide narrowed her eyes, it appeared again, brighter than before.

Silence.

"Bloody hell," said Alan.

"Indeed," said Jack dryly. "That changes things."

Adelaide dropped the light and put a hand to her shocked mouth. Maud lifted and stared at her own hands, her eyes also huge and considering. Edwin's face was a crowded portrait of ten questions being asked at once. He opened his mouth but didn't say anything. No doubt the questions were fighting for preeminence.

Before any of them could win, Robin put his hands on either side of Edwin's neck.

"Edwin," he said, in his most baronet tones. "Today, I want to enjoy some uncomplicated time out here with my family, and then go back to the house and be a good host. You can plan the complete reinvention of British magic—again—*tomorrow*."

After a short age, Edwin nodded.

"The country wedding of Sir Robert Blyth and Miss Adelaide Morrissey was a quiet, intimate affair," said Alan. He moved closer to Jack and plucked Jack's stick from his grasp. "No immortal fae in attendance, no healthy screaming from the bride's infant niece when asked if anyone had grounds to object, and no earth-shattering revelations about magic whatsoever."

"Your tongue for fiction is as smooth as ever, Cesare."

Alan's gaze caught on his and darkened, but he didn't pick up the easy bait. Instead, he continued running his hand consideringly up and down Jack's stick, caressing the golden-brown gloss of the wood in a tight, encircling grip.

Heat pooled lazily in Jack's belly. Alan didn't look away.

"I'll thank you to stop that filthy behaviour at *once*, Mr. Ross," said Violet, flopping down next to him. She used a shocked and quavery voice. "There are unmarried ladies present."

Alan went slightly red and fumbled the stick.

Jack laughed. He leaned back until his own hand was off the blanket, fingers buried in the wet grass. This wasn't his land. And yet all of this land was his, in a way, as it was every magician's. He relaxed into the faint, far-off throb of magic flowing, renewing itself as it went: paths lying full like floods, indeed, and no longer weak but there for the taking, as they all taught themselves how.

And somewhere far away on the ley lines was Cheetham Hall, and the sleeping ghost of Elsie—to whom Jack had told the story of the equinox and George's death, as she'd asked. And then let her rest.

Adelaide had now dragged Edwin back down to the blanket and sat with her head leaned on his shoulder, the two of them carrying on a conversation with Maud that sounded suspiciously like they were getting a head start on the reinvention of magic regardless.

Robin hadn't noticed yet. He was distracted by Violet, who was performing for Alan an unfortunately dead-on impression of the elderly vicar who'd performed the wedding ceremony. Alan, Jack's stick loose in his hand, had a wicked gleam in his eyes that said he was considering joining in—perhaps to play the part of Lady Dufay, who'd sat with Lady Cheetham beside Jack and Alan and muttered critical commentary throughout the whole thing.

Family.

Jack didn't have Robin's optimism. He wouldn't call this collection of beloved and fascinating chaos *uncomplicated,* nor did it stand much chance of ever being so. But—as Edwin liked to say, it was the way of magic. Broken items wanted to be whole. Sets yearned to be complete.

Twilight fell, and magic spread. Jack could feel it.

ACKNOWLEDGMENTS

Even more than the other two in the series, I think this book deserves some quick historical notes. Nobody with a speaking role on-page is a real historical figure, but Randall Kenyon is a fictionalised version of Fabian Ware, the editor in chief of the *Morning Post* in 1909. The *Post* was indeed owned by the Countess Bathurst, and they did indeed try to raise money for an airship to be used for national defence.

Pretty much everything around the People's Budget except for the exact aristocrats debating it is also accurate. People have been trying to drag a functioning welfare state into existence for a very long time, and other people have been throwing tantrums about it for just as long.

In building the life and background of Alan and his family, I drew heavily from the book *Round About a Pound a Week,* a piece of astonishingly detailed and practical sociological research into the lives of working-class Edwardian London families, published by Maud Pember Reeves and the Fabian Society's Women's Group in 1913.

I have to extend some thanks to the Italian island-palace of Isola Bella, whose garden terraces, sea grotto, peacocks, and golden pheasants I shamelessly stole for the Cheetham estate's landscaping project. And speaking of which: mild apologies to the locale of Cheetham, which I ennobled and dragged from Manchester to Essex.

My publishing teams have made the process of producing my first trilogy a voyage of delights despite all the stress. Thank you times a million to Diana and Ruoxi for making my books better, and for your patience when the pandemic killed my productivity for months and this book was produced in a wild rush towards the deadline. Thanks to the rest of my agenting team (Ari, Isabel, David, and Betty Anne), the Tor team in the US (Oliver, Sanaa, Irene, Devi, Caro, Jocelyn, Michael, Renata, Becky Y., Sam F., Yvonne, Jess, Megan, Steven, Sam D., and Lauren) and the Tor UK team (Bella, Georgia, Becky L., Grace, and Lydia). Rock stars all. And a special shout-out to Christine Foltzer for this beautiful cover and Heather Saunders for the sneaky and brilliant internal design.

This is a book about family, and I've been lucky enough to both love the one I got and to have built my own around it.

Sara and Magali: having two inboxes into which I can shoot scenes and chapters as they're written has become such an integral part of my writing process, I don't know what I'd do without you. Thank you for your unstinting belief in me and my characters. Parisians do it best, bien sûr.

Macey, without whom this book's magic system would be even more of a mess. Thanks for telling me what my series was about. All the trees are your fault.

Leife and Sam: thanks for coming down the coast with me during the time of maximum panic and generally being absolute stalwart friends.

Tegan and Stuart, my other stalwarts: you're simply the best.

Mei-ing Nieuwland, thank you for the gorgeous art and incredible eye for detail. You may claim sole credit for the on-page existence of Arthur Manning.

Iona Datt Sharma: thanks for your thoughtful sensitivity read and feedback in regards to Adelaide Morrissey. This read and the research mentioned above have hopefully allowed me to engage with the real and often fraught history of the setting in a meaningful way. Any remaining errors are my own.

To the early readers whose enthusiasm kept my spirits up, I can't thank you enough for being part of my community. Special thanks to Alix E. Harrow, Grace D. Li, Alyshondra Meacham, and Lex Croucher.

Thanks to my parents and siblings, for everything.

Enormous thanks once again to all of the booksellers, bloggers, librarians, reviewers, fan artists, and fan writers who've helped to spread the word of the Last Binding trilogy. I'm still a fandomer at heart, and seeing a fandom grow up around my own works has been *unspeakably* cool.

And thanks, beyond measure, to the readers who've found me and stuck with me through the journey so far. It's because of you that there'll be, I hope, so many more worlds and adventures to come.

Turn the page for a sneak peek at
a cozy, scorching enemies-to-lovers romance
where, yes, the swords do cross.

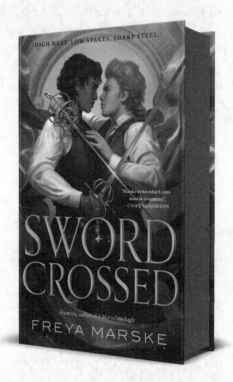

High heat. Low stakes. Sharp steel.

THE HARDCOVER EDITION FEATURES
GORGEOUS RICH ROSE SPRAYED EDGES!

Available Fall 2024 from Bramble

Matti laid his fingers on the polished edge of the bar's wooden surface and forced himself to stop counting sheep. And yards of twill. And looms in need of repair, and outstanding debts.

Instead, he counted today's collection of ink smudges, bruise-black on the brown skin of his hands: six. He counted the number of blue dyes that would have been used in the fabric of the bartender's layered skirt: four, possibly five if the palest shade was true dimflower and not just the result of fading.

The tense throb of pain like a fist clenched in his hair eased, grudgingly, to a quiet ache. Bearable. Normal.

It was busy in the drinking house, the post-dinner hour that usually found Matti heading back to his study to finish the paperwork that a member of his family had tugged him away from in order to eat. Matti counted the number of flavoured jenever bottles on the shelf behind the bar—fifteen—in the time it took Audry to finish serving her current customer and sweep her sky-coloured skirts to stand in front of Matti.

"And here's a face we haven't seen in a while! Something tells me you're here for a celebration, Mr. Jay."

Matti hoped the smile he'd pulled onto his face wasn't the wrong size, or the wrong shade of abashed. "News travels fast."

"Mattinesh Jay and Sofia Cooper. A match surprising exactly no one."

Matti kept the smile going. There was a silence in which Audry politely didn't say, *Pity she's in love with someone else,* and so Matti didn't have to say, *Yes, isn't it?*

Audry said, "Wait here a moment. I've got something in the back that I think will do nicely."

Matti cast a glance over the room as Audry disappeared. His cousin Roland made an extravagant sighing motion and pretended to check his watch when Matti's eyes landed on their table. A burst of laughter came from a dark-skinned woman nearby; she was wearing a dress that rode high at the knee to reveal a fall of lace like frothing water, a northern style of garment that Matti's own northerner mother seldom wore these days.

At the closest table the Mason Guildmaster, Lysbette Martens, was deep in conversation with a senior member of the Guild of Engineers. Martens met Matti's gaze with her own and nodded brief acknowledgement. He was sure she was weighing his presence as consciously as he was weighing hers. This was a place to be seen, after all.

"Here you are. Red wine for young lovers."

Matti turned around again. Audry named the price for the bottle as she uncorked it and set it on the bar. Matti paid her, ignoring the lurch like a fishhook in his stomach at the amount on the credit notes he was so casually handing over. Mattinesh Jay, firstborn of his distinguished House, had no reason not to indulge in one of the finest bottles of wine that money could buy.

No reason that anyone here would know about, anyway.

Matti took the bottle in one hand and hooked three glasses with the other. Making his way over to the table, his mind circled back to dwell on the wrong sort of numbers. The money in Matti's purse was painstakingly calculated: enough for the first round of engagement drinks, and enough for him to hire a top-of-the-range duellist who would step forward in the awkwardly likely event of someone challenging for Sofia's hand at the wedding itself.

Matti's skin prickled cold at the very thought of what might happen if Adrean Vane challenged against Matti's marriage to Sofia and *won*. His family's last hope would be gone. Matti would

have failed them in this, the most useful thing he could do for
them.

He was so caught up in this uneasy imagining as he wove
through the room that he collided, hard, with another person's
shoulder. Matti was both tall and broad, not easily unbalanced;
the unfortunate other member of the collision made a grab for
Matti's coat, couldn't get a good grip, and tripped to the ground
with a caught-back "*Fu—*"

Matti tried to step backwards. They were crammed into a small
space between tables and there were people moving around them.
His first panicked instinct had been to keep the wine bottle upright and the glasses safe, so he didn't have a hand free to steady
himself on a chair.

He wasn't quite sure what happened next, except that he ended
up wobbling and stepping forward instead, and he felt his boot
come down on something that was not the floorboards. A small,
pathetic, grinding mechanical sound crawled up Matti's nerves,
heel to head, and reached his ears even amidst the noise of the
busy room.

"Sorry!" he said at once. "I'm sorry. Was that— Oh, Huna's
teeth."

The man on the floor jerked his head up, staring at Matti, and
Matti stared back.

For a moment all that Matti could see was the wide, straight
line of the man's mouth, set beneath an equally straight nose,
and the frame that set off the whole: the dark, luminous copper-
red hair that seemed to be trying to grow in about ten different
directions.

The man's tongue darted out in a nervous mannerism, wetting
his lower lip. Something in Matti's own mouth tried to happen in
a yearning echo.

"Would you please *lift*," the man said precisely, "your gods-
damned *foot*?"

Heat flooded Matti's face. He snatched his foot backwards with enough force that his heel collided with a chair leg.

The redheaded man stood, his fingers closed convulsively tight around a small velvet bag. His brown coat was shabby and made of a coarsely woven fabric, though his shirt was good and his trousers had probably been equally so before they'd been overwashed into a patchy shine.

"Fuck fuck shitting—*fuck*," the man said in tones of despair, with a lilt to his accent that placed him at least one city-state farther east: Cienne, or possibly Sanoy. He shook the contents of the bag into his palm and ventured into new realms of inappropriate language as he did so.

Enough people had witnessed their collision, or had their heads turned by the stream of expletives, that there were a fair few necks craning to see what was in the man's hand. Matti, at whom the shaking fingers of this hand were pointed most directly, couldn't help seeing for himself the ragged, glinting pile of cogs and jewels and glass. Only the intact cover—monogrammed in a swirling, engraved *H*—spoke of this pile's previous existence as a pocket watch. A very expensive pocket watch, by the look of it.

The man's breath hissed out through his teeth. "Guildmaster Havelot is going to use my arm bones as a fucking *lathe*. He only had it made to order, and he only trusted me to pick it up, didn't he? Two hundred gold. Fucking fuck."

"I'm so sorry," Matti said again. He recognised the name: Havelot was the Woodworker Guildmaster in Cienne. "Truly. I can—" He stopped. The abrupt lack of his words created a silence that seemed to suck noise into itself, as conversations died to murmurs and the onlookers sensed something interesting.

The man looked straight at Matti with a stubborn lift of his chin. His brows, the same absurd colour as the rest of his hair, had sprung up into the beginnings of hope; as Matti's silence grew longer, they lowered again. And then lowered farther. He swept a look down and then slowly up Matti's own outfit, and now pride warred with scorn in the way those maddening lips pressed together.

Matti felt sick. His own coat was made of the finest wool, a midnight blue cut perfectly to his figure, and the rest of his clothes were of the same quality. He was holding a bottle of extremely good wine. Anybody looking at him would make immediate assumptions about the amount of ready money that Matti might have, and the ease with which he would be able to reimburse a poor clerk, if he'd just ruined a pricey piece of artificer's skill that the man's employer had trusted him to travel all the way to Glassport to collect.

Of course they would make these assumptions. That was the *point*.

Matti swallowed and felt the burning heaviness of his purse redouble. He'd be left with enough to a hire a duellist, yes, but not one of the highest skill. It wouldn't buy himself and his family the absolute security they needed.

His friends were looking at him. It seemed like every pair of eyes in the drinking house was looking, and in another moment the murmurs of curiosity would turn to murmurs of disapprobation. *I thought Matti Jay had more honour than that,* they would say. *What's two hundred gold to someone like him?*

Besides, the plain fact of the matter was that Matti had broken the watch. And he couldn't pretend that he and this man with his proud mouth and poor coat, patched at one elbow, were on an equal footing. Even if he were left without a bronze, Matti would still have influence, connections, the weight of his family's name. That was still worth something. For now.

So that was that.

"I—I really am sorry." Matti set the wine and glasses down on the corner of the nearest table and pulled his purse from inside his coat. He kept his gaze on the man's face, on a pair of eyes that were either grey or brown—impossible to tell from this angle—and urgently willed them not to look away. To a degree that seemed irrational, he wanted to banish the judgemental expression from the man's face. "Of course I'll cover the cost. Two hundred gold. Who did the work?"

The man glanced down at the metal scraps in his hand, as though the answer might be hidden in the pile. "Speck," he said at last. "Frans Speck, in Amber Lane."

"He's a fair man. Tell him what happened and he'll rush through the repair job," Matti said. He held out the century notes.

The man tipped the wreckage of the watch back into the bag and closed his hand around the money, slow and wary. His fingertips had rough patches that scraped against Matti's own, sending a tingle up Matti's arm.

"I appreciate it," the man said. He looked less cold now, though still nowhere near warm. "You've saved my life. Really."

Matti forced himself to smile. Forced himself to say, "It's nothing," as though it really were nothing.

The man nodded awkwardly at Matti and tucked both money and bag into a pocket. Then he turned and was gone, headed for the door.

Matti somehow made his way to his table and sat down. His heart was pounding so loudly that he could barely hear anything else, and he wanted to shout at his own blood to be quiet and let him *think*. He needed to be alone in his study. He needed to contemplate his options, and make lists, and pore over the accounts for the thousandth time, in case they transmuted themselves into a picture of prosperity instead of the ugly, desperate reality that nobody outside of Matti's immediate family knew about.

"Two hundred gold," he said, before he could stop himself. "*Two hundred.*"

"We saw. Hard luck," his cousin Roland said, making a face.

Perhaps it was stretching the term to call Roland and Wynn his friends, but they were the closest thing Matti had to members of that category, and the only people he'd been able to think of to form his wedding party. At least the three of them never found it too hard to pick up their acquaintanceship again, even if it had been months since their last conversation.

Wynn turned the bottle of wine to inspect the yellow butterfly on the label. "How appropriate that we're drinking wine from your betrothed's own winery."

"Audry's idea of a joke, I think," Matti said. The word *betrothed* had landed in his ears like a piece of music played in an unfamiliar key; his mind was still turning it over, trying to decide how it felt about the melody. His hand was shaking as he poured the first glass, sending the stream of dark wine shivering and slipping. He'd steadied it by the time he poured the second.

"Huna smile," he said, opening the toasts by lifting his own glass. "Thanks for agreeing to stand up with me, you two."

"Drown your sorrows in this one, and by the time we hit the next bottle you'll remember that you're here to celebrate. And that once you're married to Sofia Cooper," Roland went on, lowering his voice sympathetically, "Jay House will be rolling in enough money to replace a hundred watches."

Except that Matti had to get himself successfully married in the first place. And he'd just lost his best guarantee of doing so.

He let the old, gorgeous wine flood down his throat until a good third of his glass had vanished. He felt lightheaded; it had to be panic, because the wine couldn't be working that fast. Panic and a sense of becoming unmoored. And the image of the man's face, pale and sharply beautiful, gazing up from where he was kneeling at Matti's feet.

"A fair effort," Wynn said, when Matti put the glass down. "But I'll show you children of Huna how it's done." He raised his own glass. "Agar fill your plates and cups."

Matti smiled and drank again, accepting the toast. Maybe the wine was working after all. He could still feel his panic, the wound-up watch of his worry, but he shoved it away into a recess of his mind: its own small, dark velvet bag. It would be safe enough there. It would last until tomorrow. Matti's ability to worry was shatterproof.

For now, he was going to drink.

———————————

The sun was making a personal project of finding Matti's eyes as he walked through the Glassport streets the next morning. Every gap between eaves and chimneys was a new opportunity for glaring rays to assault his eyelids. His head felt like one of the snow-baubles you could buy in the winter markets, flurried and shaken into a confusion of water and oil and small flecks of metal, and fragile. Prone to cracking. The sunlight was one source of cracks; the rumble of carts and carriages, raised voices, the rattle of machinery— the everyday racket of city life, which Matti could easily ignore on a normal day—was another.

Matti was not a drinker, as a rule. His family brought out the occasional decanter of good spirits if a deal was being struck or they had particular reason to please someone. On those occasions Matti had learned to spin out a glass across hours, to honour the work of Maha's children by rolling each sip over his tongue, and to forget that alcohol had any ability to muddle the thoughts.

He'd also managed to forget that the state of existence known as Maha's Revenge awaited anyone who had, for example, spent the previous night sharing two bottles of wine among three people and chasing all of that with glasses of rosemary jenever. Not that Matti could remember the jenever portion of the evening. He'd made an educated guess at that upon waking, based on the smell of his wrinkled shirt.

Matti had escaped his house relatively unmocked for his delicate state. His family knew where he'd been and what he'd been celebrating. The slight change in the set of his father's shoulders, the new and terrible light of relief in the communication-dense glances his parents exchanged . . . those were a form of celebration too. A piece of lowered horizon glimpsed after a long, long uphill trek, whispering at the possibility that soon their feet might find the road sloping downwards.

Matti had awoken to the twins hurling themselves onto the lump of him in his sheets, delighted to find their older brother abed at a time of day when he'd usually have been awake for hours. Joselyne had chased them away and brought peppermint tea, which had helped the uneasy roil of Matti's stomach but hadn't done much for the head-bauble.

As much as Matti would have liked to stay in bed, or even to sit in his study with a plate of greasy spiced potato dumplings at his elbow, there was something he had to do this morning.

Matti ducked his head to avoid another piercing sunbeam and rounded the corner into the street that held his destination. The city's only agency of swords-for-hire had its office tucked incongruously above an apothecary's shop front, with a narrow flight of stairs leading up from street level. Matti passed through a doorway with the symbol of Pata, patron god of soldiers, guards, and duellists, set as a plaque above the doorframe. The room it led into was small, with a single window looking out onto the street, and it was dominated by a pair of wooden cabinets set on the opposite wall. A man with thinning blond hair sat behind a desk in front of the cabinets, and he was climbing to his feet even as Matti walked in.

"Mr. Jay," he said. "What can I do for you, sir?"

The man's face was vaguely familiar, but even Matti's trained memory couldn't attach a name to it. "I'm afraid you've got the advantage of me."

"Tolliver." He extended a hand and Matti shook it. "Hardy Tolliver. I stood swordguard for your sister's naming ceremony, several years back. This was my father's agency. Now it's mine."

"I need to hire a best man."

"Of course. Is there reason to expect a challenge?" Hardy Tolliver's voice was polite, his face impeccably blank. Matti didn't have the energy to try to work out if Tolliver was being deliberately obtuse, or just displaying professional courtesy. If he knew who Matti was, he might well know more than that, and it wasn't as though Adrean Vane made any secret of either his feelings for Sofia or his enthusiasm for the blade. He'd even set those feelings to music. There'd been a time last year when you could barely walk down a street in the city without hearing someone whistling "Wildflowers Under Glass"; it was the kind of tune that nestled merrily in the ear for days on end.

"Yes, there is," Matti said.

"I can think of a few people on our books who would do nicely." Tolliver waved Matti into a chair, and turned to open one of the cabinets. He began to flick through folders.

"I should probably tell you," Matti said, "I can pay four hundred gold, and not a bronze more."

Tolliver turned back to him, surprise splashed across his face. "We aren't, ah, in the habit of bargaining—the Guild allows for rates to be set—"

"I'm not trying to bargain with you."

Tolliver still looked bewildered. Matti steeled himself and gathered his most businesslike voice. It was the voice of a man who'd grown up in a townhouse in the Rose Quarter, who could count back eight generations of his House's current trade, and whose father was currently in his second three-year term as elected Guildmaster.

It was Matti's voice, even if these days Matti himself rattled around in its cadences like a slim foot in a shoe of overstretched leather.

"Jay House is having a rough quarter. I would appreciate it," he said, "if this fact were not to become public knowledge." He could only hope that wielding this little power would be enough to suppress the Glassport instinct for gossip; if not, *a rough quarter* was more forgivable than the truth.

"Four hundred gold?"

"Four hundred."

"That does rule out a lot of our most talented people."

"I thought that might be the case." The memory of century notes leaving his hands bounced queasily inside Matti's rib cage. "I'd appreciate anything you can offer me within that budget."

Tolliver sat. He opened a leather folder and flicked through some loose pages, moving each one neatly from one side to the other. Then he looked up.

"There's someone. He's new to town. No prior duels to his name in Glassport and I only put him on the books two days ago, so I can't give you a full reference, I'm afraid, but I tried him out. He's not bad; he's certainly better than what he's charging. Probably the best value you'll get for that price."

It took Matti a moment to recognise the second layer of generosity there, no matter the truth of the "value" that Tolliver was offering. Someone new to town and unfamiliar with Glassport society might not recognise Matti as anyone significant. They might not bat an eye at the fact that Matti was paying midrange rates for a best man. It was another way to contain the gossip. It wasn't an outright guarantee of Tolliver's own silence, but it was a gesture. A statement of faith that one day Matti would be in a position to return the favour.

Matti nodded, trying to convey both understanding and appreciation. "Could I meet him before deciding?"

"Absolutely." Now Tolliver smiled the relaxed smile of someone close to a sale. "Right now, if you'd like. He's renting the attic from my wife and me, while he waits for a room that's coming free in a boardinghouse at the end of the week. We're just a few doors down. Wouldn't be a moment to fetch him."

Matti could see no reason to object, and Tolliver's feet were fading on the stairs within a minute. In the sudden lull of thought and speech, Matti's head began to remind him again about the jenever. He stood up and paced in the small space, taking deep breaths that smelled of dust and leather and, faintly, acrid herbal scents seeping up from the apothecary. He felt clearer by the time he heard Tolliver's feet on the stairs again, this time accompanied by a second pair.

"Mr. Mattinesh Jay," Tolliver said in tones of announcement as he entered. "And this is Luca Piere."

Matti's first thought was one of irrational despair: that Huna had decided to twist her knife, because far from assuming Matti to be a man of modest means, the man was now going to think him even *more* cheap.

Then reality elbowed him in the brain, and he felt his expression freeze onto his face.

Luca Piere was no longer wearing his brown coat with the patched elbow. He *was* wearing his good shirt and his thin trousers. And along with those, as he stood frozen behind Tolliver's shoulder, he was wearing an expression of guilt so naked and obvious that Matti remembered, abruptly, that the man worked for Havelot. That he was visiting the city to pick up a watch.

Except that he clearly was not.

Matti's heart leapt into his throat and then slammed back down again. He brimmed with a feeling of foolishness rapidly bubbling into fury. It was a con as old as the very idea of marketplaces: "break" something already broken, and demand compensation. And Matti had fallen for it simply because this man had had the gall to try it on a scale of two hundred gold, with a full audience of Glassport's finest looking on.

Matti opened his mouth to say something—what exactly, he wasn't sure—but before he could, that guilty expression widened into panic, and Piere took a smart few steps forward.

"You've told Mr. Jay he'd be taking a chance on me, Hardy," Piere said. "How about you let us into the practice room and I'll give him a bout, so he can see to his own satisfaction what he's paying for?"

Matti stared at him. Piere's head tilted towards the other door in the room, a mute and desperate invitation. His lips were pressed together hard enough that the already pale skin around them was bone-white. Matti, feeling the power in the room shift palpably in his own direction, found it easier to breathe and to think.

Tolliver looked dubious. "Have you done any duelling, Mr. Jay?"

Matti had never lifted a finger in a violent pastime in his life. But right now, experiencing the unusual palm-tingling urge to get his hands around another person's throat and *squeeze,* he quite fancied the idea of picking up a weapon. Even if he hadn't the faintest clue what to do with it. And he could feel his own sheer curiosity rising like a vine from the rich mud of his rage.

"I'll give him a try," he said shortly.

He followed Piere into a long, narrow room that stretched back away from the street, with light coming from a single street-end window and a series of skylights. The floor was heavily scuffed, and bolted along one wall was a rack of swords.

Luca Piere had stopped in the middle of this room. As soon as the door closed behind Matti, he turned, as though the click had triggered some small mechanism within him. In the daylight, his hair was a riot: a true, bright copper. It looked as though he'd sat in front of a mirror with a curling iron and painstakingly coaxed small pieces of it to curl in different directions. Or else he'd crawled out from a pile of pillows and not bothered to run a comb through it, and gravity had been so amused at the sight that it hadn't interfered.

Matti's hands, which were still tingling to be placed against the vulnerability of Piere's pale throat, now began to take on an edge of interest in the hair instead. About how it might feel for them to be buried in it. About how ideal that length was for *pulling*.

Matti closed them both into fists, and ignored them.

"All right," Matti said. "Now start talking."

ABOUT THE AUTHOR

FREYA MARSKE is the author of *A Power Unbound*, *A Restless Truth*, and *A Marvellous Light*, which was an international bestseller and won the Fantasy Romantic Novel Award; her Last Binding trilogy was also a Hugo Award finalist for Best Series. Her work has appeared in *Analog Science Fiction & Fact* and has been short-listed for five Aurealis Awards. She is also a Hugo Award–nominated podcaster, and won the Ditmar Award for Best New Talent. She lives in Australia.